"Are you always so proper, Elsbeth Carew . . . ?"

She looked up at him, her gray eyes making him want to just watch her for an hour or two.

He discovered he liked teasing her. He didn't move away, but deliberately got closer. It would be so easy to kiss her right now. That wouldn't be at all proper, would it?

He stepped back, thinking that he should apologize. But he'd only thought it. He hadn't actually kissed her. Should he apologize for thinking it?

"Can we warm up somewhere first?" he asked. "Before we go and see this castle?"

Her smile was enough to heat him from the inside out. And damn near made him kiss her.

Romances by Karen Ranney

KAREN RANNEY

The Texan Duke

AVONBOOKS

An Imprint of HarperCollinsPublishers

THE TEXAN DUKE. Copyright © 2017 by Karen Ranney LLC. All rights reserved. Printed in the United States of America. No part of this book may be used or reproduced in any manner whatsoever without written permission except in the case of brief quotations embodied in critical articles and reviews. For information, address HarperCollins Publishers, 195 Broadway, New York, NY 10007.

First Avon Books mass market printing: November 2017
First Avon Books hardcover printing: October 2017

Print Edition ISBN: 978-0-06-246693-8
Digital Edition ISBN: 978-0-06-246694-5

Cover illustration by Patrick Kang
Cover images: © Getty Images (background); © Shutterstock (details)

Avon, Avon & logo, and Avon Books & logo are registered trademarks of HarperCollins Publishers in the United States of America and other countries.

HarperCollins is a registered trademark of HarperCollins Publishers in the United States of America and other countries.

FIRST EDITION

17 18 19 20 21   QGM   10 9 8 7 6 5 4 3 2 1

The Texan Duke

Chapter 1

Scottish Highlands
January, 1869

Connor McCraight was half tempted to stop the carriage, release one of the horses, and ride bareback to Bealadair.

He'd rather be on horseback for twelve hours than just sitting here doing nothing. He refused to allow himself to consult his father's watch tucked into the inner pocket of his vest. He didn't want to know how many hours he'd wasted so far today.

At home, the setting sun—an explosion of orange and red in the direction of the Western Division—was accompanied by a feeling that he'd accomplished something. Either he'd ridden the fences, met with some of his foremen, inspected the newest outbuildings, or even sat himself down at his desk and forced himself to handle the never-ending paperwork.

Here? The end of the day didn't mean a damn thing other than that he couldn't see any more snow.

It snowed in Texas. It snowed a lot in certain parts of Texas, but there was something about a winter day in Scotland that buffaloed him. It was a colder kind of cold, seeping past his coat and into his bones. If he hadn't been trapped in this carriage, he could have moved around and pushed past the discomfort.

He was used to being out in near-blizzard conditions, the ice freezing his eyebrows and lashes, his cheeks feeling so stiff they'd never thaw. But this Scottish wind came out of the north like a newly stropped razor. The Scottish snow was glaringly white and almost angry looking as it clung to vertical shapes and scraggly trees.

Why did one place have to have so damn many hills? They weren't called hills, either. They called them Ben something or other, each name more unpronounceable. They weren't like the mountains in West Texas. They didn't soar majestically into the sky, making a man think of the Creator and other weighty subjects. No, they stuck out of the ground like fat black thorns with jagged edges now covered in ice and snow.

"It's flat," his father had often said, staring out over their land. "You can almost see from one side to another."

That wouldn't have been possible, but he now understood why there'd been a sense of wonder in Graham McCraight's voice. Here you couldn't see past the next snowflake for some damn hill or deep gorge.

He hoped this Bealadair place had enough fireplaces to heat him through. By the time they reached their destination—he'd been promised it would be soon, that word bandied about a little too often lately—he would probably be frozen from his boots to his hat.

When he'd said something about the weather to Augustine Glassey, the solicitor had only given Connor that thin-lipped smile of his. He didn't know if the man was just naturally bilious or so damn cautious that each word was weighed and measured and weighed again before he uttered it.

Most of the time Glassey sat in the corner of a room like a crow, watching the proceedings with beady eyes.

At least he wasn't in the carriage now.

Sam, wedged into the corner on the opposite side of the vehicle, opened one eye, closed it, and finally spoke in a tired voice.

"We're almost there. Might as well hold on for a little longer."

"I've been holding on for a damn sight too long," Connor said. "I feel like I'm in a coffin." A cold coffin. The heater down by his feet might keep the side of one booted foot warm, but that was about it.

"It's better than the train," Sam said, keeping his eyes shut.

He didn't have any argument with that. The journey from London had been an orchestrated disaster. They'd had to change trains twice, moving all their possessions from one railroad company to another. What genius had decided to make different gauge tracks in the same country?

Glassey had made a point of telling him that they'd be traveling first class from London. He hadn't been impressed then and he wasn't now. The windows in the back of the car hadn't closed all the way. But at least the cold of the snow had been offset by the warm soot from the engine.

They'd finally made it to the north of Scotland which didn't mean that things got easier. They'd had to stop more than once, connect with another line, lose cars, pick up cars, and generally make the distance in a pace slower than he could have on a good horse.

But he probably would have frozen to death.

At least, at the last station, Glassey had done something right. The solicitor had prepared ahead and they'd had two carriages and drivers waiting for them. To his relief, the solicitor had chosen to ride in the vehicle behind them. It was the first time in weeks that Connor had been spared the Scotsman's company. He wouldn't have to listen to Glassey's opinions, of which the man had many, uttered in an accent that was beginning to grate on him.

The man didn't talk right.

Every word sounded like it had an edge and was sharp like glass. He didn't just state his opinion—something Sam did often enough—Glassey pontificated. The man reminded Connor of their cook back home. Cookie had a point to make about a dozen things every day. It wasn't enough that he had to salt you with his thoughts. He wanted to convince you that he was right and have you come out and say it.

The solicitor wouldn't like being compared to a cook. He'd probably get that pursed-up look, the one that made Connor think the man smelled a dead cow.

Glassey had a long face, one that looked as if someone had grabbed his chin at birth and pulled it toward his feet. Age had given him lines that traveled the length of his cheeks, from the corners of his eyes to the corners of his mouth. He dressed in somber black like the undertaker in Austin. The worst thing about his appearance was that Glassey favored a bowler hat. It rounded off the top of his head and looked wrong with the rest of his angular appearance.

The only thing the man did that was a relief was melt into the background when Connor gave him a look. It was the McCraight glance, the one that said he'd just about had enough of this nonsense and wanted it to stop immediately.

His mother told him that he'd had it since birth. As the youngest of six children, the previous five having been girls, he'd been the spitting image of his father, down to imitating his mannerisms before he could walk.

"You just don't sound like your papa," his mother said. "Not that anyone could."

Nope. He was a Texan. His father had sounded like a Scot. There were times when Connor couldn't understand him, especially when he started talking Gaelic.

Connor countered by talking Mexican, which made Graham give him the McCraight glance.

He missed his father. He'd missed his father in one way or another since he'd come home that day two years ago, tired of war. At the tearful reunion with his family, he'd been given the news that his father had unexpectedly died in a line shack after a day of inspecting the fence line. The cause? He'd been cleaning his gun.

That hadn't made sense then and it didn't now.

Until Glassey showed up on his doorstep a few weeks ago, Connor had no idea that there was a family in Scotland. He hadn't known about his aunt and three cousins—all girls—or that he had an uncle who'd died. He sure as hell hadn't known about any estate or that he was the heir.

He had no business freezing in a strange country. He should be home where he was needed.

"Your father would have wanted you to go."

Those words, uttered in a soft voice by his mother, had been the reason he'd agreed to accompany Glassey back to Scotland.

Now he wished he could have refused his mother. However, in the history of the XIV Ranch he doubted anyone had been able to say no to Linda McCraight.

She stared at you with those big brown eyes of hers—eyes that were replicated in all her children—standing there tall and proud, her hands folded in front of her. She was a statue of stillness, her bright red hair tucked into a braid coiled into a pattern his sisters called by a French name.

"It's your obligation as a McCraight," she continued. "The last male McCraight."

"Yes, ma'am," he'd said, despite the fact he was no longer in his boyhood and had been running XIV for the past two years on his own. All he could do was nod his head, bite back every objection that came instantly to mind, and make arrangements to have Joe Pike, his soon-to-be brother-in-law and one of his division managers, take over in his absence.

He couldn't disrespect his mother, but damn, he

wished he'd been able to say something, anything, to keep from being here in Scotland, of all places.

Sam unfolded himself from his scrunched position in the corner, grabbed his hat from his chest and planted it on his head, shivered, made a face, then shook his booted feet one by one.

Sam didn't say much, but his expression left you with no doubt about what he was thinking. Right now it looked like he was wondering why the hell he'd agreed to accompany Connor to Scotland.

Sam Kirby had been his father's friend. Tall, rangy, with a bald head and face that bearded up despite how often he shaved, he reminded Connor of a picture of a Jesuit priest he'd once seen. The man wasn't a monk, however. Tales of Sam's conquests had been legendary throughout the XIV Ranch.

Sam and Graham had been friends ever since Graham McCraight had come to Texas. Connor didn't know how it had been done, but somehow his father and Sam had not only funded the syndicate that had built the state capitol, but they'd overseen the architecture and the construction. In return, the legislature had awarded them the land to begin the ranch.

Sam wasn't an entrepreneur. He wasn't even much of a rancher. Graham had called him a mental tumbleweed. If something interested Sam, he got involved in it, whether it was gold mining or some business venture with a man from back east who wanted to build a series of stores. But he always came back to the XIV Ranch as if it were home. Because of that, Connor considered Sam almost like an uncle. Not like the stranger whose death was the reason he was here now.

Before they left Texas, he'd asked Sam about the man.

"Did my father ever talk to you about his brother?"

"Once in a while," Sam said. "When we were drinking."

"I can't remember him ever mentioning him to me."

He should have asked his mother before he left Texas, but he tried not to mention his father any more than necessary. Every time he did, or when one of his sisters said something, his mother would get that look in her eyes. The one that made it seem like she held all the world's sorrow in her heart.

She still cried every night.

He'd even broken down and asked Glassey, just before they boarded their ship. The solicitor had no idea why Graham had spent the past forty years in Texas.

Except for that, there wasn't much about his father that had been secret. Graham was an open, boister-ous, giant of a man who had a sense of wonder about everything, from the birth of a calf to the expanse of stars over their heads. He was given to philosophical discussions at strange times, often over a campfire or after bathing in the river.

When Connor came home from college, his father had tested his knowledge about a great many things. He'd found himself defending his beliefs, being forced to think long and deep about a subject before responding. Up until then he'd never considered his father an educated man, not like his professors. He soon realized that it was his own knowledge that was lacking and that Graham McCraight was the equal of any learned man he knew.

What would his father think about this journey, done so reluctantly? Graham was all for a man doing what he thought was right in his own mind. He'd instilled that thought in Connor along with another one: he had to accept the consequences of his actions. He couldn't blame anyone else for the choices he made if he'd done so freely.

The problem was he hadn't in this case.

Nor was he prepared to be the 14th Duke of Lothian and Laird of Clan McCraight.

Chapter 2

What were they going to do? Something had to be done, that was certain. Ruin faced them. The new duke was about to arrive any minute according to one of the stableboys who'd been positioned at the entrance to the road. Five of them, tucked into heavy coats and woolen hats, had been dispersed to various places around Bealadair in order to report on the first sighting of the new duke from America.

No one in the parlor looked remotely upset. Perhaps they were following Her Grace's often-expressed adage: anxiety does nothing but bring wrinkles. The Duchess of Lothian looked at least a decade younger than the age she was reputed to be.

Yet didn't the circumstances call for a little panic? Elsbeth certainly felt it. How could you not?

The room was filled with people yet none of them were talking.

Lara sat on the sofa with her husband, Felix. Anise sat on a nearby chair looking bored. Muira, Elsbeth's favorite of the three sisters, was delicately nibbling on one of cook's tarts. Rhona, the Duchess of Lothian, was sitting in a chair in front of the fire, pretending that it was just another evening at Bealadair.

Muira took another tart.

In any other situation, Rhona would have chastised her daughter for marring the perfection of the tray of delicacies already set out for the new duke. Maybe she wasn't looking. Or maybe she was a little anxious after all.

There was plenty of food in the kitchen. They'd been baking for a good ten days, preparing for this moment. Ever since word had come that the new duke was in London and making his way north.

Two hours ago, Her Grace had given orders for several of the best bottles of wine to be brought up from the cellar. All the decanters were filled with McCraight whiskey. No one was imbibing because of strict orders from the duchess.

Meanwhile, Muira stole another tart.

"It's time," Rhona said, suddenly standing and facing them all.

A chorus of moans greeted her words.

"It's snowing," Elsbeth said, her comment earning her a sharp look from Rhona.

"It doesn't matter," the duchess said. "It's tradition. It's something the McCraights have always done." Implicit in her tone was the rebuke: *You wouldn't understand. You're not one of us.*

Even if she wasn't technically a McCraight, she was still expected to appear in front of Bealadair to welcome the new duke.

They stood and followed the duchess to the front of the house, the staff following like starched ducklings behind them.

Surely tradition allowed them to don coats and cloaks before venturing outside? Or were their frozen bodies supposed to show some measure of respect? The snow was coming down so thick that she wondered if the stableboy had actually seen an approaching carriage or simply wished it to appear. They formed a long line in front of Bealadair, the weather keeping all of them silent. If they made the mistake of speaking, no doubt the frigid temperature would freeze their lips to their teeth.

Elsbeth couldn't help but wonder if everyone was as cold as she was. According to the duchess, they were to stand there without coats or cloaks or hats or scarves, guaranteeing to the new duke that they posed no harm or risk. Nothing was concealed in their garments. No claymores, dirks, or shields.

She could only assume that this idiotic tradition had begun before there was any civilization in the Highlands.

She couldn't help but think that the McCraight ancestors were laughing uproariously at the sight of all their descendants shivering in the snow and nearly turning blue, like the early Picts. Perhaps they didn't paint themselves blue. Maybe the color came from experiencing a Highland winter.

If the 13th duke had been alive, Gavin wouldn't have agreed to such a foolhardy gesture. A foolish thought, since if he had been alive they wouldn't be standing out here praying that the carriage reached Bealadair quickly.

Night was almost upon them and in welcome or maybe to offer the frozen McCraights a touch of warmth, torches had been lit behind them, illuminating the curved approach to Bealadair.

The home of the clan had begun as a medieval

keep in the fifteenth century on lands that had been acquired by the McCraights a hundred years earlier. The original castle with its stone walls still perched on a steep hill overlooking Dornoch Firth and was used in several McCraight celebrations including the Welcoming of the Laird. Thankfully, Rhona had decided to break with tradition in this instance. Otherwise, they would have had to trudge all that way in the freezing cold. The blizzard that had arrived this afternoon, lowering the sky until it felt like it pressed down on them, would have made the trek to the old castle suicidal.

Instead, they assembled on the east side of Bealadair below the Hammond Tower, named for the architect who'd designed the renovations of Bealadair in the past century. The house may not have been built for protection, but there were hints of fortifications in the elaborate surrounds of the roof, the oversized turrets, and the statues of clan members carved in stone, standing ready on the parapet to defend the laird and his family. In better weather the new duke would have been able to see the pennants flying, the McCraight colors of red and black distinctive against the backdrop of the white stone of Bealadair.

The newer section of the house was an immense quadrangular structure of five stories with towers on all four corners. The older portion of Bealadair was to the rear and connected by a four-story building.

The entire complex, consisting of one hundred and eighty-nine rooms, had been swept, dusted, polished, and refreshed with new potpourri in the past several days. The chandeliers had been lowered, each crystal immersed in a bucket of vinegar and water, then polished to a sparkle before being replaced. The tapestries had been gently brushed, even the ones that were four hundred years old. The runners had been removed from all the corridors, taken outside and beaten by a laughing team of maids and footmen.

Everything was being readied for the man in the carriage approaching the long drive.

Would he care? Would he even notice?

The blowing snow obscured everything but the yellow glow of the carriage lanterns.

None of it belonged to them anymore. It was all owned by the man who would soon emerge from the carriage, the same man who could so easily wave his hand and banish them.

She shivered, wishing she had been able to wear her cloak. And a scarf around her throat. And a hat pulled over her hair. She couldn't feel her lips or her fingertips.

People were stamping their feet against the packed snow of the drive and wrapping their arms around themselves. She could see plumes of their breath against the night sky.

Didn't Rhona notice that everyone was about to freeze to death?

Sometimes, she thought that Rhona forgot that the people who staffed Bealadair were human beings. A great many of her dictates didn't make sense. Yesterday she'd given an order that the laundress was to starch all the maids' aprons and today no one was to sit or otherwise crease their uniforms until the duke arrived. You could either do the job you were supposed to do or you could walk around acting like a marionette.

Rhona made decisions like that, making changes that weren't the least practical. A few months ago she'd given an order that all of the maids were to have their hair arranged in the same fashion, in an overly intricate braided bun. It took so long for the girls to arrange their hair that way that Elsbeth had countermanded Rhona's orders, more than willing to go to battle for the staff. Fortunately, the duchess hadn't noticed.

Rhona liked to issue decrees. She made pronouncements, waved her hand in the air like a queen, and demanded certain behaviors. Just as quickly, however, she forgot what she'd ordered.

Elsbeth had the feeling that Rhona really didn't care. The duchess just liked being obeyed, even if it was only momentarily. Elsbeth took great pains to ensure that Rhona got that impression, even if it wasn't exactly correct.

In the past year she'd taken on the duty of housekeeper. Mrs. Ferguson had increasingly incapacitating arthritis. It was easier for the poor woman to remain in her quarters than it was to traverse the many staircases of Bealadair.

None of the family had any objections to Elsbeth assuming the role. They wanted their meals on time, their suites kept clean and sparkling, and their lives not disrupted by petty things such as laundry, staffing expectations, and inconsequential details like leaky roofs.

As for Elsbeth, she enjoyed having something to do every day. Each evening she met with Mrs.

Ferguson, consulting the woman over the tasks that needed to be done. The housekeeper had been at Bealadair for over twenty years and knew the house as well as—if not more so—the McCraights. The woman was an organizational genius, acquiring details about the many collections housed at the estate from armaments to historical documents.

No doubt the new duke would want to know the extent of his inheritance. Thanks to Mrs. Ferguson, she could provide him with an exact inventory.

The carriage was turning into the drive. A stableboy ran out to steady the horses. A footman strode forward to open the carriage door.

Rhona stepped up, accompanied by her oldest daughter, Lara, and Lara's husband, Felix.

Elsbeth was too far away to hear the duchess's words, but they were probably those of welcome. Maybe the duchess said something in Gaelic, evoking Scottish sentiment. After all, the new duke was an American who needed to be educated on his Scottish heritage. At least that's what she'd been told.

No one had ever spoken of this unknown nephew. Until Mr. Glassey had sent back word from America, they had expected that the 14th Duke of Lothian and the Laird of Clan McCraight would be Gavin's brother.

This man who stepped down from the carriage was a complete mystery.

She saw his boots first, well-worn with a pointed toe and quite unlike the polished black leather favored by the previous duke and his son-in-law.

He was wearing what looked to be a black wool suit but his coat was unlike anything she'd ever seen.

Of brown leather, it hung nearly to his ankles and seemed to be lined with thick white fleece. A hat was pulled down over his head, but she didn't recognize the style of it, either. How odd that she'd never considered that the new duke would be dressed unlike anyone she'd ever seen.

He glanced behind him, said something to a tall thin man dressed in a similar fashion, who followed him out of the carriage. Then he went to speak to the driver. The man nodded, responded, and whatever he said seemed to satisfy the duke because he returned to stand in front of Rhona, removed his hat, and nodded to her.

His hair was dark brown, soon dusted with snow, but he didn't look as if the weather concerned him at all. His companion was not so impervious, having turned up his collar before glaring up at the sky.

Nor did Mr. Glassey, having exited the second coach, appear fond of the weather. He greeted the duchess, said something to both of the Americans before turning and offering Rhona his arm, evidently intent on entering Bealadair.

The new duke, along with his companion, followed, then the rest of them. Elsbeth fell back, gave instructions to the maids she'd separated out for the task, telling them to begin serving the heated refreshments. No one had known what time the carriage would arrive or even if the duke and his party would make it through the storm. But she'd planned for either a dinner repast, a midnight supper, or a breakfast.

Would more people be arriving? That, too, had been a mystery. She would have to pull Mr. Glassey aside and ask him. Was the duke married? Did he have a family?

It would be so much better for them if he didn't have a wife or children. He wouldn't be in such a hurry to banish Rhona and her daughters.

As for her, Elsbeth knew her time at Bealadair was nearly over.

The previous duke had been such a gentle soul, the first genuinely kind person Elsbeth met after her parents' deaths. The day she arrived at Bealadair, he'd tried to reassure her that she'd always have a home there. He and her father had been best of friends, he'd said.

"This house is full of daughters," he'd added. "You'll just be one more. Besides, your father would have done the same for my girls if the situation were reversed."

Had Gavin given any thought to what would happen when he died? Or had he, like so many people, considered that he might live forever?

Had her own parents felt that way?

They'd been in her mind often recently and she couldn't help but wonder if it was because of the uncertainty she felt about her future. On their deaths they'd left her a small bequest, which the 13th Duke had supplemented. She'd never be a pauper. If she wished, she could buy a small cottage somewhere and live a demure, if lackluster, life.

The duke had gifted the rest of his family with bequests as well, but she doubted if they would ever live as magnificently anywhere else as they did at Bealadair.

Their way of life might only be days away from

ending. None of the family, however, considered that they might be sent packing. The one and only time she'd brought up the subject, the duchess had excoriated her with a few words.

"You don't know what you're talking about. Graham is my dear husband's brother. Of course he won't turn us out. Don't be foolish."

But it wasn't Graham who was to be the new duke. As Elsbeth made her way to the Laird's Hall, she couldn't help but wonder if the duchess was reconsidering her comment about familial feelings.

Graham's son had been born in America. He had no ties to Scotland. She doubted if he spoke Gaelic. What did he know of Bealadair? Or of the family, for that matter? What would keep him from pitching them from the estate? Or dismissing all of the servants and installing his own staff? Would he bring Americans here to serve him? Were there more people to follow?

A dozen questions crowded into her mind as she slowly pushed open the doors.

Chapter 3

It was night by the time they got to their destination. Their safe arrival was due only to the skill of the carriage driver and the fact that there were no inns between their last train station and Bealadair. If there had been, Connor would have made the decision to stop, rest the horses, and get warm.

When the carriage slowed, he peered out the window, but all he could see was white. Snow pelted the window, slid down to pile in mini drifts on the frame.

A few minutes later they lurched to a stop. The carriage rocked a moment. Connor opened the door to be greeted by a faceful of snow blown at him by an angry wind.

A voice sang out. "Welcome to Bealadair, Your Grace."

The woman who greeted him was attired in a dark green dress festooned with snow. She wore no coat or cloak, had nothing to protect her from the elements. Her smile was fixed—he suspected it was frozen—and her eyes, a deep brown, were narrowed against the wind.

A torch behind her sputtered and he suspected

the warmth from it was the only thing keeping her from freezing where she stood.

He left the carriage, the words forming on his lips to urge her inside when he saw the rest of the coterie to welcome him. At least he thought that was the reason why about fifty people were standing in the snow.

"I'm the Duchess of Lothian," she said, her voice beginning to tremble. "Welcome to Bealadair," she repeated.

"Madam, may we go inside?"

He was willing to concede that the Scots were hardier than he was. He already knew they were dumber. Who stood outside in this weather without a coat or hat?

He wanted a warm room, a roof over his head, and something hot to drink. First, though, he thanked the driver and urged him to find shelter as soon as possible.

Glassey emerged from the second carriage, greeted the duchess, and escorted her up the steps to iron-studded double doors. He and Sam followed her like motherless calves.

He didn't suppose that the Duchess of Lothian would appreciate being compared to a Longhorn. But she had a commanding presence and she gave him a look like several of his cows did. As if she were measuring him, considering what he might do in a certain situation.

He probably should have said something conciliatory. Or maybe she was waiting for him to congratulate her for the stupidity she'd just demonstrated. Granted the receiving line lit by torches was impressive, but didn't they have the sense God gave a goat? Why in hell would they stand out in the cold like a turkey in the rain?

The duchess glanced at him several times as they passed through a foyer that was probably bigger than the front parlor at home. However, she didn't speak and neither did he. He was getting the feeling that he needed to treat her like a new cow in an established herd.

Longhorns that had been reared around humans were friendly and malleable. They didn't give you any trouble and they were docile to a degree. But if you were unlucky enough to get one that had been left alone and without much human interaction, they got it in their minds that they were boss.

He wanted to make sure that the duchess knew who, exactly, he was.

Thank God for Sam. The man had an uncanny knack for smelling trouble, even before it made an appearance. It was like he could tell who was going to start throwing fists first.

The duchess turned left, nodding to a footman standing beside double doors.

"The Laird's Hall, Your Grace."

The doors opened as Sam stepped forward, did a pretty little bow in front of the duchess and reached for her hand, holding the tips of her fingers like he was some sort of Spanish grandee.

"Your Grace," he said, his voice strangely unaccented, "I am Sam Kirby. Thank you for welcoming me to your home."

Sam could—and had—sounded like a New Yorker,

someone from Alabama, and a native Texan. It all depended on what suited him at the moment.

Evidently, it suited him to sound like he was from nowhere now.

Sam had lived in Washington DC once upon a time, which is probably where he'd learned to handle people. He didn't talk about those days any more than Connor talked about the Civil War.

"Are you a relative, Mr. Kirby?"

The duchess, like the other Scots he'd met, sounded odd, as if the words she was speaking were all crunched together or slid off into nothingness. He could only understand about half of what she was saying. Maybe Sam was faring better.

Connor hadn't thought he'd need an interpreter in Scotland.

He took the opportunity of Sam's glad-handing to look around.

In Texas he was used to open spaces, grand prairies that stretched as far as the eye could see. Their houses were modest, places to rest and recuperate from a day of good work.

It seemed to him that the Scots had it backward. They were all for trapping the outside in. A good-sized herd could winter here in the room the duchess called the Laird's Hall. He guessed this was the place where the leader of the clan called together all the able-bodied men, where elections were held and disputes adjudicated.

He'd learned clan behavior from his father. He just wished Graham had told him about Bealadair.

From what he'd seen of the exterior, it was more

than just a castle and definitely more than any other private house he'd ever seen.

The XIV had four major divisions, the ranch split up into manageable areas. Each division had a center of operations with a bunkhouse, various buildings and stables, and a main house for the division manager. All of those houses, plus the one where his mother lived, as well as his own, could be put into Bealadair and probably have plenty of room left over.

Glassey had told him that there were only the five of them. Why would they live in such a huge house? It seemed to him that it would be a waste of effort trying to find somebody or even getting from the bedroom to the kitchen. And all the staff? He'd already seen dozens of women dressed in black dresses with white aprons and caps and men all gussied up in uniforms that looked like they were going to a parade.

"The duke was one of the wealthiest men in Scotland, Your Grace," Mr. Glassey had said. "Of course, that might not be an important consideration for you, given the size of the XIV Ranch."

He hadn't responded to the solicitor's almost question. He had no intention of telling the man anything about the financial health of the ranch. Nor was he about to mention that the size of his inheritance from his uncle made the future of the ranch more certain.

At least he wouldn't have to worry about cattle prices. Or buying new stock. He could invest in the railcars he'd thought about, plus other advances throughout all four divisions. He could hire more men, buy more horses, and afford to send his sisters and mother to New York for shopping if that's what they really wanted.

From his inspection of the Laird's Hall, he was beginning to think that Glassey hadn't exaggerated. The brass and crystal fixtures looked fancy enough to have come from France.

The walls were covered in crimson fabric, the same material as the floor-to-ceiling curtains covering the dozens of windows. All the females in his family would have loved the room and been impressed with the furniture groupings, settees, couches, chairs, and tables that looked as if they'd also been made in France. He could always tell from that kind of swooping leg that looked too delicate to support a man's weight.

He liked leather. Give him a comfortable chair, something he didn't have to worry about ruining. A chair built to handle a little abuse. It didn't have to have horns like the last chair his father had had made in Austin, a big, wide, comfortable chair adorned with about ten horns from their cattle mounted on the back. His mother had categorically refused to have it in the main parlor, so Graham had taken it to the house Sam had built on the property.

This Laird's Hall could do with a few leather chairs and less fancy furniture.

It seemed to suit the duchess and his other relatives just fine, however. They all took their places either on the sofas or the chairs, looking at him expectantly. What was he supposed to do now?

Sam was still doing his diplomat thing, explaining about the train journey from London. The duchess—his aunt, although he had difficulty thinking of the woman in that way—smiled and began introducing him to his cousins.

"Lady Lara Gillespie, Your Grace," she said. "My oldest daughter."

He wondered if he should stop her now. He was tired of Glassey calling him *Your Grace*. Why did he have to have a relative do the same thing? And what was this *Lady* nonsense? These people sure liked titles.

Was the rest of Scotland like this? Or was it only his heretofore unknown family? Were they truly as odd as they appeared to be? After all, they'd been out in a blizzard—without coats—to welcome him, and other than standing in front of the fire for a few minutes, none of them looked the worse for wear.

He was still bone-deep cold. They'd gotten here by the skin of their teeth before the blizzard got them. Scotland was damned determined to freeze him to death. He removed his hat, because that was just polite, but he kept his coat on as he met his cousins.

Lady Lara was tall, with brown hair and brown eyes, similar to the other two cousins. She had a mole at the corner of her eye and the fastest smile he'd ever seen. If he'd blinked he would have missed it.

Her brown hair, the mass that wasn't fixed in a bun at the back of her head, was curly, tendrils coming down on either side of her face. Her nose was prominent and her mouth wide. He had a feeling that if she allowed herself, she would have a boisterous laugh.

From the look in her eyes, however, he doubted she found anything all that funny.

He'd seen that same look on a ranch hand's face

when he was tired of staring out at the horizon. A man could get weary of seeing nothing but grass, occasional mesquite trees, and clumps of cactus. He yearned for hills and valleys and rivers wider than the streams they could cross on foot.

He couldn't help but wonder what Lady Lara Gillespie yearned for. Or what she was tired of seeing.

Felix Gillespie was slightly shorter, with a goatee-like beard, a mustache that was impeccably trimmed, and hair Connor considered too long.

Felix stood with his legs slightly apart as if he was ready to take on the world. His lips curved, but the smile didn't reach his eyes.

If Felix had applied for a job on the XIV Ranch, Connor wouldn't have hired him because of the feeling he got—one that indicated that it might be a good idea to keep that man in his sights for a while, at least until he proved to be either friend or foe.

Felix and his wife still lived at Bealadair, which surprised him. At home, his youngest sister was getting ready to marry in a few months, the other four having already found husbands. Eustace and Joe would occupy one of the houses in the Western Division, at least until they could build their own home there.

Although he was the heir to the XIV Ranch, Connor had been more than willing to share the wealth. Joe Pike, the man Eustace was going to marry, had proven himself a dozen times over. He had no qualms about deeding them a few thousand acres, enough to give the couple a start.

Lady Anise, the next in line to be introduced, had a softer face, with a less prominent nose and a mouth that wasn't as wide. She wasn't smiling at him. Nor did she deign to do so when her mother announced her name. She did, however, incline her head, almost regally.

Lady Muira, however, was a change from her two older sisters. She surprised him by smiling brightly.

"Would you like to go stand in front of the fire?" she asked. "I can't imagine that the journey here was a warm one. But I'm so glad you arrived before the snow got worse."

Muira's eyes were smaller, her eyebrows surprisingly bushy. Her cheeks were like two pink biscuits on her face and her mouth was as large as Lara's. He had the feeling that people didn't care about Muira's appearance. All he knew was that for the first time since he'd walked through the door he felt welcomed. Maybe part of that feeling was the fact that she reminded him of Eustace.

"You mean the snow can get worse?" he asked, smiling at her.

"Oh my, yes. It looks as if we're to have one of our spectacular Highland blizzards. We might be snowed in for weeks."

He sincerely hoped that wasn't true. He wanted to conduct his business, get it out of the way, and be home again in a matter of weeks.

"We're preparing for the Welcoming of the Laird, Your Grace. It will be held in ten days."

He turned to face his aunt. "What's the Welcoming of the Laird?"

Glassey, who had disappeared after they'd entered Bealadair, hadn't mentioned it.

"It's typical for all the members of the clan to

greet a new laird, Your Grace. Once, it was a very formal affair, begun at Castle McCraight and completed in this very room. But in the last hundred years it's been in the form of a ball. Less formal, but a great deal more entertaining."

He doubted it. The idea of a ball didn't sound fun at all.

"Of course, in normal circumstances we wouldn't be entertaining at all, because of our dear Gavin's death, but introducing you to the clan is a special event. People from as far away as London have indicated they would like to attend."

He knew a bit about distances and how long it took to travel. If the future guests for this ball had to endure what he and Sam did traveling from London, he wondered if the occasion was worth it.

There was a light of zeal in the duchess's eyes, however. He'd seen that look in his sister Barbara's eyes when given the opportunity to attend some kind of party and she needed an escort because her husband was out of town. A sure and certain indication that he was doomed to attend whatever kind of soirée the duchess and his cousins had devised.

He sent a look toward Sam, but Sam had taken a seat near the duchess and was still staring rapturously at her.

His aunt struck him as one of those snobby people who thought they were better than someone else just because they were born into a certain family. It was luck and that was it. Otherwise, they could easily have been the daughter of a ranch cook or a blacksmith.

That's why titles didn't mean much to him, a fact that Mr. Glassey had yet to understand.

Pride came from a job well-done. He liked what he could accomplish from dawn till dusk. That's what mattered.

When he was invited to sit, he remained standing. He didn't want to sit. He'd been doing enough of that for the past twelve hours. Nor did he want to make small talk. He didn't want to discuss the weather. It was still snowing and looked like it was going to keep snowing for a while. What was there to say? Nor did he want to talk about his father. Not right now. Especially not when he felt a little off-kilter.

This place, this huge house, was where his father had grown up, where Graham had spent twenty years of his life. A place he'd never mentioned.

He didn't feel his father here, not in this fancy room with its chandeliers and crimson velvet. But there was every chance that there were nooks and crannies throughout the house that would suddenly remind him of Graham. He wasn't entirely certain he was ready for that and it was a strange and unsettling thought. Maybe that's why he hadn't wanted to come to Scotland, for fear that he would be face-to-face with his father again. Instead of ghosts there would be memories. Not his, but his father's and the family he didn't know. Nor was he entirely certain he wanted to.

He walked from the middle of the room to one of the long windows. As he reached it, feeling the cold from the outside, he couldn't help but wonder why they hadn't closed the curtains against the weather. The view was pretty, though, with the torches illuminating the falling snow.

He found it odd to be witnessing a blizzard and

not having to be concerned about his men or his cattle.

Another reason why he shouldn't be here. Winter was a treacherous season on the ranch. Still, he had a team of reliable and dedicated managers. He had to trust in them, just as his father had trusted him.

I'm not going to be here one day, Connor. I believe in you. I know you'll do the right thing. You always have.

But had coming to Scotland been the right thing? According to his mother, yes. Even his sisters had been in agreement. Now, however, standing here and feeling the echo of the past push against his back, he wondered if he'd made a mistake.

He didn't want to be here. He had to converse with people he didn't know, over topics he didn't care about, in a setting he didn't like.

"Don't you think so, Connor?" Sam said.

He knew, without turning, that Sam's glance would be filled with admonition. He was being chided and he probably deserved it. He hadn't been polite. In fact, he'd been borderline rude.

Or, as his sister Alison often said, "Connor, you can be unbearably terse sometimes."

He didn't think she used the word correctly, but he understood her meaning well enough. He needed to be more social, more outgoing, spend time acting inane and saying idiotic things.

Turning, he forced a half smile to his face.

The door opened and any thought of mouthing pleasantries flew from his mind when he saw *her.*

Chapter 4

As Elsbeth slid open the door to the Laird's Hall, the new duke turned to look at her.

No one had told her that he was a man in his prime. Why had Mr. Glassey failed to mention that he was so tall, or that he could command a room, even one so large and impressive as the Laird's Hall?

She felt her breath catch, which was ridiculous. She had never once lost her composure around a handsome man. Nor was she about to now, especially around a man who could have such a deleterious effect on her future.

She stepped aside as a parade of maids entered the room, carrying trays of heated refreshments that they placed on various tables. The hour was late, past the normal time for dinner, but they had provided the food in case the duke and his companion were hungry.

The new duke looked as if he wished to say something, an impression that lasted just a second before he turned his glance away from her and toward the duchess.

He hadn't removed his coat. The majordomo was

ill, but surely one of the footmen could have performed that most elementary of tasks?

Elsbeth walked to his side, extended her hands, and said, "Your Grace, if you'll permit me, may I take your coat?"

He glanced at her.

Was he remarking on her gown? Unlike those dresses the McCraight sisters were wearing, there wasn't a swath of tartan on it. Instead, her dress was a simple black silk that didn't show wear or stains. Did he consider it too plain?

No, she was not going to be that foolish. What did she care what he thought of her dress?

Her feet were cold. Her shoes had not fared well in the snow. She wanted, like Felix, to go and stand in front of the fire. Or like Muira, serve herself to hot chocolate. Instead, she stood there like an upper servant waiting to take his coat in a simple gesture of hospitality.

"Thank you," he said. He shrugged off his coat, folded it lengthwise, and handed it to her.

It was surprisingly heavy, more than she'd anticipated.

She glanced away to encounter Rhona's look.

Evidently she'd done something wrong again, but she was too busy at the moment to worry about it. She'd given up trying to win the duchess's approval years ago.

"It's because you're so much prettier than all of us," Muira had once said.

She'd only stared at her friend.

"Don't be silly. Of course I'm not."

"Oh, you are," Muira had continued in an unconcerned voice. "Everyone sees it. You're a beauty while we're just acceptable." Muira's smile had the effect of transforming her face, making her brown eyes sparkle and her plump cheeks turn a flattering shade of pink. "I don't mind. I wouldn't want to be so pretty that everyone stares at me. I don't think Lara minds, either. Anise might be the only one who cares, but everyone knows she's vain."

She'd discounted Muira's words. She hadn't chosen her gray eyes or black hair. But the McCraight girls were just as pretty, especially Anise.

If the duchess disliked her because she wasn't ugly, there was absolutely nothing she could do about that. She suspected, however, that the true reason she and the duchess didn't get along lay in the relationship Elsbeth had had with the duke. Over the years they'd become fast friends, with Elsbeth taking tea in the library every day with Gavin. She'd gotten into the habit of discussing anything with him from the repair of the roof tiles to poetry. He, in turn, had confided in her about his difficulties in finishing his volumes on the McCraight history and fussed at her about working too hard.

Those hours were special to her because they made her feel as if she belonged at Bealadair, the few times she did. Not surprisingly, she hadn't felt the same way since Gavin's death.

Before she left the room she gave Maisie, one of the senior maids, instructions to stand by the door in case anyone needed anything.

"Monitor the trays, Maisie," she added. "If you

see that we need anything else replenished, go to the kitchen." Heaven knows they had enough food.

She gave the duke's coat to one of the maids with instructions to have it carefully dried. The two of them shared a look as they examined it. It was lined with fleece, so soft and thick that it was surely the warmest coat she'd ever seen. The leather on the outside was sueded, water beading on it.

"It's American, then," the maid said.

"I suppose so," Elsbeth replied.

Why hadn't Mr. Glassey informed them that the new duke would be attired in such a startling manner? For that matter, where was the solicitor?

She found Mr. Glassey supervising the distribution of the baggage from the two carriages.

"You shouldn't have to do that," she said, explaining that their majordomo would have helped if he'd been well. "Mr. Barton is suffering from a case of the gout," she said. "The poor man has been laid up for nearly a week."

"It's no trouble, Miss Carew."

Just then one of the footmen stumbled in, struggling under the weight of the strangest saddle she'd ever seen. It didn't look anything like the one she used in shape or adornment. The tooling was ornate and complex, covering most of the leather.

When she gave instructions for the saddle to be taken to the stable, Mr. Glassey interrupted her.

"I'm sorry, Miss Carew, but His Grace would want that in his room, at least until he was certain the stable was acceptable."

"Acceptable?"

"We have carried that saddle in coaches, aboard ship, and on various trains, Miss Carew. I've never seen anyone as possessive of an object as His Grace is about that saddle."

How very odd.

"Are you very certain, Mr. Glassey?"

"I am more certain of that than of anything, Miss Carew, including the fact that I'm currently drawing breath. The man has not let it out of his sight."

"Very well," she said, countermanding her own order. The saddle would go into the duke's suite.

She couldn't help but wonder what else the new duke had brought from America.

"I'll direct the footmen to put the rest of the trunks in the proper rooms," she said. "Why don't you join the others in the Laird's Hall?"

The man certainly knew the way. It was where Gavin's will had been read, instead of the library where he'd spent most of his days. He had, in the way of the preceding Lairds of Clan McCraight, requested the presence of the members of his clan. Nowadays, they numbered a little over two hundred. On that day they'd filed into the Hall and listened as their laird bequeathed each of them a sum. The amount wasn't large, but it would go to making their lives easier. When there were tears shed, it was not only in appreciation for the laird's generosity, but also in genuine grief for the duke they'd lost.

Would the new duke understand his obligation to the clan? Only time would tell.

"I'd much rather do this if you don't mind, Miss Carew. His Grace and I have been having a difference of opinion these past few days."

Normally, she could curtail her curiosity, but not tonight.

"Does he have a difficult nature?" she asked.

Mr. Glassey glanced at her and then away.

She thought he wasn't going to answer, but he finally sighed before turning to her again.

"It's his way of thinking that takes some adjustment, Miss Carew."

She remained silent, waiting for him to elaborate on his answer.

"His Grace didn't want to come to Scotland. He even asked me if there was a way he could turn down the title."

"He couldn't have been serious, Mr. Glassey," she said, surprised.

"I'm afraid he was, Miss Carew. Each day of our journey, he regaled me with tasks that he needed to perform at home. He is not pleased to be here."

She had the distinct impression that Mr. Glassey had not enjoyed either his visit to America or the journey home. When she said as much in as tactful a manner as possible, the solicitor shook his head rapidly.

"It isn't America, Miss Carew. It's Texas, a fact that I was reminded of almost hourly. The 14th Duke of Lothian is a Texan."

"What's a Texan?"

He shook his head again. "I have no doubt that he will inform you soon enough."

The solicitor said nothing further, but he also refused to budge from the door. When all the trunks had been distributed and sent to the various rooms, Mr. Glassey looked longingly up at the staircase.

"I don't suppose you could tell everyone that I've taken ill and retired to my room?"

The solicitor rarely socialized with the family. He didn't even eat dinner with them when he was at Bealadair, choosing instead to take a tray in his room. She'd always wondered if it was because he didn't like the McCraights personally or if he considered himself staff more than their social equals. It wasn't a question she could come out and ask.

"Do you really wish me to?"

He sighed again. "No, I don't suppose so. Such behavior would be rude and Her Grace might have questions for me."

Mr. Glassey offered his arm and she placed her hand on it, the two of them heading back to the Laird's Hall. *Bearding the dragon*, Gavin would've said.

A Texas dragon, at that.

WHERE HAD THE woman gone? She'd entered the Laird's Hall, taken his coat, and then disappeared. Connor stopped himself from following her only because Sam was glaring at him.

With some difficulty, he applied himself to his manners. As the only brother to five sisters, he'd often been put into the position of being a dummy cow. When a bull didn't seem interested in mounting a particular female, they sometimes brought in a ringer, another cow that might just get him interested in the act. He was the dummy cow for his sisters whenever they needed an escort, accompanying them to cotillions and parties, getting years of practice in hiding his impatience and learning to charm the matrons who'd assumed the task of watching them all with a critical eye.

He sat next to Muira, helping himself to some of the fried pies on the tray in front of him. To his surprise they weren't sweet but savory. Three pies later he was decided he was going to take the recipe home for his mother.

Anise hadn't said anything directly to him. Lara was involved in conversation with her husband. Connor might not have been in the room for all the attention she paid him. Muira was the only one he talked to, their conversation about food.

He was fine with being ignored.

All the women were dressed in dark colors with large swaths of plaid material draped from shoulder to waist. His mother still wore black, but by the time he'd gotten home, his sisters had come out of mourning.

The door opened again and there she was with Glassey in tow.

Her hair was black, her eyes gray, which should have rendered them cold and disinterested. Instead, when she looked at him, he had the distinct impression of heat. He wondered if she wanted to say something, offer some words of welcome, something soft and sweet. Something to warm him down to the bones that still felt cold and brittle from the journey.

A foolish reaction to a woman and one he'd never before experienced. No doubt he was simply tired.

His aunt glanced at her. "Elsbeth, would you please arrange to have the shutters closed? I'm afraid it looks like an intemperate night."

Elsbeth nodded, turned and left the room again. This time, her absence wasn't as extended. She returned with a half dozen footmen as the duchess was expounding on the wonders of a Highland winter.

Sam was his usual diplomatic self, not mentioning that they'd both shivered for hours during the last leg of their journey and had spent considerable time lambasting the snow and the cold. You would think, from listening to him, that he was overjoyed to have been nearly frozen.

Elsbeth gave orders with the ease of someone long accustomed to doing so. When the shutters were closed and the curtains drawn against the night, she dismissed the footmen. Instead of leaving, she came and sat next to Muira, reaching for a cup and pouring herself some tea.

He hadn't the slightest idea who she was. Not his cousin, evidently. Someone that felt at ease with the family, however, or she wouldn't have come and sat among them. Or smiled at Glassey, who had taken one of the chairs close to the fire.

"Elsbeth?" Connor said. "An interesting name."

"It means 'God is my oath,'" she said. She didn't smile, but there was a twinkle in her eyes as if she were teasing him.

"Muira means 'from the moor,'" Muira said. "A great deal less profound, but I like that it's poetic, in its way. Of course, Father picked it, so it would have been. I think he was mostly a poet. More than he ever wanted to be a laird. Was your father the same?"

"We have plenty of time to learn about your uncle," the duchess said. "Don't badger His Grace with questions, Muira."

A sound reminding him of a cannon shot kept him from responding. The noise started at the top of the house and rumbled across the roof. They all looked upward, but only Elsbeth ran to the window, opened the curtains and the newly closed shutters to stare out at the snow.

"What is it?" he said, standing and moving to her side.

"I don't know," she said. "But I need to find out."

She was gone again, leaving the Laird's Hall without a word to anyone.

He turned and glanced at Sam. The other man knew him well enough to interpret the look. *Make my excuses. Be polite for me. Offer an explanation, if you can.*

How many occasions had he depended on Sam? Dozens, especially after his mother had gotten it into her head to begin introducing him to eligible women throughout Texas. Whenever he had to escort his mother somewhere, he found himself waylaid.

He had five older sisters and a mother determined to get him married off. Consequently, he'd spent the past two years feeling as if he was avoiding bear traps.

He left the Laird's Hall, retraced his steps, and found himself in the foyer. A footman was stationed at the door.

"Have you seen Elsbeth?" he asked.

The footman nodded. "Miss Carew has gone outside, Your Grace."

He pushed aside the irritation at being called *Your Grace* for another, more important point.

"Miss Carew? She isn't a McCraight?"

The footman looked uncomfortable at being addressed. Nor had his aunt and cousins spoken directly to any of the maids. Was it a Scottish rule not to talk to the servants? They were just going to have to get used to him because he was damned if he was going to ignore people around him.

"No, Your Grace, she's the ward of the 13th duke."

Interesting. Then why hadn't the duchess introduced her? He tucked that question away with the rest of them.

"Do you know where they put my coat and hat?"

The footman bowed slightly and said, "I do, Your Grace. Shall I fetch them for you?"

He nodded, determined to address the *Your Grace* matter in the morning. The footman reappeared a few moments later with his garments.

He put his hat on, then his coat, and would have opened one of the double doors if the footman hadn't gotten there before him. He thanked the man, left the house, and was immediately nearly pushed off the steps by the force of the wind.

Since they'd arrived at Bealadair, the blizzard had gotten worse. They'd been lucky to get here before the roads were impassable.

Half of the torches had been blown out by the wind, but a few of them were still lit, giving him enough light to see his way. He grabbed the banister with one hand and his hat with the other, making his way down the slippery steps. He squinted into wind that had a razor's edge. The air was thick with snow, making it difficult to breathe.

He'd faced a blizzard in the panhandle, but this

one seemed like it had a personality. Perhaps it was a raw and angry Scot, enraged that a stranger had invaded its land.

To his relief, he saw Elsbeth right away. She was dressed in a dark red cloak, the hood covering her hair. She and a man dressed in a Bealadair uniform were bent over, digging in a snowdrift. As he approached, she glanced up.

"It's a soldier," she said, her words just this side of a shout. "One of the guardians on the roof. The snow must have built up and pushed him off."

"I don't think it's entirely safe for you to be standing there if that's the case," he said.

He glanced up but couldn't see the roof for the snow.

"You're probably right," she said, grabbing the statue by the arm and pulling it free.

The stone soldier was attired in a kilt with a length of tartan across his bare shoulders. He clutched a dirk in one hand and a small shield in the other. To his surprise, the statue hadn't shattered into pieces, only cracked across the middle.

She looked up at him and smiled, the first true smile he'd received since arriving at Bealadair. He wanted to thank her for that.

"Elsbeth! Your Grace!"

They both turned to see the duchess peering out the front door.

"Please, come inside this instant!"

Elsbeth turned to the footman. "Jim, if you'll take the statue inside, we'll see if we can repair the damage tomorrow."

Without another word, she brushed past Connor and headed toward the front door, leaving him to follow.

Evidently, one obeyed the duchess. Or at least Elsbeth did.

INSTEAD OF RETURNING to the Laird's Hall, Elsbeth headed for the kitchen.

She'd forgotten to ask the duke about his saddle. A saddle, of all things. She wanted to know why he'd transported a saddle all the way to Scotland. Did he think they didn't ride in Scotland? Or that they rode bareback?

There was also the matter of what he wanted to eat. Despite going to a few people in the village, she was still ignorant about what Americans liked.

"I've heard that they don't like blood sausage at all," Mrs. Condrey had offered. "Or puddings."

"I think they like fried eggs," Mrs. McGuffin said. "And rashers."

She really should have asked him what he wanted for breakfast. But she'd taken one look at him and every cogent thought had flown from her mind.

She would check in with the staff and see if they needed anything, give orders about the statue, and then wait in the kitchen until the duke retired in case he needed anything.

In the morning, she'd ensure he was served a good Scottish breakfast. Perhaps they would have an opportunity to speak.

There was absolutely no reason to feel warm at the possibility of having a conversation with a man she didn't know. None whatsoever.

Chapter 5

Connor hadn't slept well, waking in the suite that had housed several generations of McCraights and feeling uncomfortable and out of place.

In the war he'd learned to sleep anywhere. More than once he'd simply leaned against a wall or a tree and dozed sitting up. But in the luxurious set of rooms with its velvet-and-gilt-covered furniture, he found himself waking every hour.

At dawn, he dressed and made his way down the stairs, declining the assistance of a sleepy-eyed footman who was stationed outside the double doors of his suite.

Finding his coat this time required the assistance of two footmen, one of whom finally returned to the base of the stairs holding the garment. Connor thanked the man, which evidently surprised him if the wide-eyed look was any indication, and made his way to the front door.

"It looks to be a good morning, Your Grace," the footman said as he opened the door.

Connor peered outside at the mounds of snow. "Does it always snow so much here?"

"No, Your Grace. It's been a difficult winter."

Glassey could have told him that, too, along with information about Bealadair. Details he'd never divulged, like how damn big the house was.

Connor nodded, put his hat on, and walked outside.

At least the wind had subsided a little and it wasn't currently snowing. The sky, with its cover of clouds, wasn't all that promising, however.

His boots crunched on the snow as he made his way to the circular approach. He hadn't been able to see much last night and maybe that was a good thing. Turning, he looked at Bealadair for the first time.

The white stone of the house looked almost yellow against the pristine snow. He counted four floors, but he wasn't sure if the line of windows along the roofline meant there was another floor up there. A row of dark gray statues, each of them different—at least from what he could see from here—stretched along the parapet. One of them was missing and its absence stuck out like a missing tooth.

The main part of the house stretched for a considerable distance and was buttressed on either side by two more wings.

How expensive was it to maintain this place? How many servants did it require to run it? Questions he needed to have answered before he made a decision.

He stuffed his gloved hands into his pockets, turned and began to walk.

Snowdrifts covered the scenery. He couldn't tell a hedge from a hill. Tree branches were dripping with icicles. The land undulated, giving him the impression that something beneath the earth was pressing up, trying to push out, to be free. Some distance away, the ground sloped, descending to a fairly wide river that curved through what was probably his property.

His. This didn't feel like his. Not like the ranch did when he rode out to inspect fences or meet with one of his division managers.

This world was alien to him. This land was strange and old and unlike the raw newness of Texas. In Texas, the land seemed to go on forever; everything as far as he could see belonged to the XIV Ranch. He missed the sound of cattle moving over the earth, the dust rising from their hooves. He missed his cattle dog, Serephus.

Why hadn't his father ever mentioned this place? Had he ever felt a longing for it, like Connor felt a need to be home?

He wanted to find something about Scotland that was familiar, but the longer he stood there, the stranger it felt. His father's family—his ancestors— had made their mark here, had claimed this land, had been born and had died here.

Yet that knowledge didn't make him feel more connected.

He continued to walk down the road, keeping Bealadair to his left. Ahead of him in the distance was the purplish hue of mountains. Not anything like those in West Texas, but respectable peaks. He wondered what those were called. No doubt something else he couldn't pronounce.

When he came to the end of one wing, he left the road and followed a path thick with snow. In a short time he found himself at the back of Bealadair where various lanes led to outbuildings and, farther away, to the stable.

He took a smaller path to the left and walked around a copse of trees. The small hill he was on gave him a view of the landscape to the back of the house. Here the river appeared again, this time the water covered by ice and snow.

His stomach rumbled and he suddenly wanted breakfast. And coffee. He needed to find his way to the kitchen and officially start his day. He needed to meet with the steward and the housekeeper, the majordomo—a position he'd never heard of before, but which, according to Glassey, held some responsibility.

She came to mind.

He'd get to see her again. She'd disappeared last night. After he'd come inside she'd simply vanished. Nor had his cousins been forthcoming with any explanation. It was as if she'd been invisible, but he'd seen her well enough.

He turned back to the house, feeling the first threads of optimism since he'd arrived.

ELSBETH HAD ALWAYS awakened at dawn, preferring the early morning hours the best, before all the servants were at their duties and hours before the rest of the family rose. Often, the sun hadn't made an appearance by the time she was dressed and downstairs.

She and Gavin would often take tea together in the library, before he began his work for the day. Sometimes, he'd have questions for her, a concern that had occurred to him the night before. He wanted to know about the roof tiles or the frames for the portraiture on the third floor.

When he'd asked why she wanted to take on Mrs. Ferguson's duties, she tried to explain how she felt.

"To give me something of consequence to do," she'd said. "And I think Bealadair needs an ombudsman. Someone to speak for it. It's like this giant creature that shelters us all, but someone should polish its teeth and make sure its fur is combed."

The duke had laughed at that, but it hadn't been in ridicule as much as fondness. He had been like a second father to her, offering her his wisdom and his affection in equal measure.

Somehow, he'd known that his time was limited. At first, when he'd wanted to discuss it she'd demurred, attempting to change the subject. Once, she even left the room. He got his way, though, as he did most of the time. She listened as he talked about his own mortality and didn't try to hide her tears.

"What shall you do when I'm gone, Elsbeth?" he'd asked in their last conversation.

She hadn't hidden her grief from him, but reached over and laid her hand on his.

"I don't know," she said. "I guess it's all up to the next duke."

"I think you'll find my brother to be a generous man."

She wanted to know how he could be so certain of that, not having seen Graham for forty years, but she didn't ask.

"I shall miss you," he said. "Perhaps I'll be an angel," he added. "I'll be perched on a cloud and be able to watch everything that goes on here."

"Do you think you'll still be able to give me advice?" she asked, grateful for feeling amusement when she wanted to cry.

"I can't see why not. Of course, I may be overruled, being an inhabitant of Heaven."

For a moment she could almost see him fixed with wings, a halo above his head, and an ethereal light dancing on his face, illuminating his mischievous smile.

"I'll miss you, too," she said softly.

She'd probably shocked him then, by throwing her arms around his shoulders and hugging him in his bed. But Gavin didn't say anything, only held her tight.

When she pulled back, his eyes were moist.

"You've been the very best gift I've ever been given," he said. "It's been a pleasure watching you grow up, my dear Elsbeth. I know your parents would have been as proud of you as I am."

Those were the last words he'd ever said to her.

Now as she left her room, heading for the kitchen, she glanced down the corridor to the duke's suite. Had the newest duke, the most surprising duke, spent a restful night? Was he settling into his role easily?

She took the servants' stairs to the back of the house. When she entered the kitchen, it was to find that Addy, their cook, and Betty, her helper, were staring out the window above the sink. At first she thought they were marveling at the amount of snow that had fallen the night before. Their conversation, however, indicated that they weren't concentrating on the weather or the landscaping, but they were certainly admiring the scenery.

"Ach, he's a finely built man," Addy said. "He puts me in mind of my own Jock gone these ten years or more."

Betty only sighed.

Elsbeth didn't say anything as she came and stood behind the two women, peering over their shoulders.

The duke evidently liked to rise at dawn as well. It was barely light outside and the lowering clouds promised more snow. But there he stood on a snow-bank, his booted feet planted wide apart, his arms crossed in front of him, his strange hat solidly on his head and the thick coat bundling him against the cold.

She wanted to know what he thought as he stood there surveying the snow-covered hills. Everything he could see belonged to him. Did he feel the press of responsibility? Or was he only experiencing acquisitive glee?

"Is he married?" Betty asked.

"I don't think he is," Addy said. "Wouldn't he have brought his wife with him? Do you think he's a widower? He's old enough to have married and begun a family. Do you think he's been disappointed in love?"

She really should quash their questions right now. Gossip was not encouraged among the staff. The fact was, however, that she had been as curious as the other two women.

Addy turned her head and smiled, indicating that she'd known full well when Elsbeth had entered the kitchen.

She was never hungry first thing in the morning and always delayed eating until nearly noon. The smell of raisin scones, honey icing, and oatmeal perfumed the air, reminding her, however, that she hadn't eaten last night.

She poured a little cream into her black tea and sat at the long rectangular table. The other two women remained staring out the window.

The room was so warm from the oven that the snow had melted on the other side of the glass, granting them an unobscured view of the man surveying his domain.

After a few days, their fascination with the new duke would certainly ease. But she could understand how they might be taken with him. He was exotic and fascinating in his Texas hat and coat. He was large and solid and taller than their most gangly footman.

He had an air about him, one of . . . Her thoughts faltered for a moment until she found the right word. *Certainty*, that was it. She had a feeling that he knew exactly who he was and how he fit into life. Qualities that had been present before he'd ever known he was the 14th Duke of Lothian.

What had given him that quality? He'd evidently been raised to believe in himself, to have a certain confidence. The duchess had that same attitude. Anise had it as well. Rhona was the Duchess of Lothian and Anise was beautiful. One had position and the other appearance.

Had Connor McCraight been told from an early age that he might one day be duke? Or had he simply been feted from birth? Was he an only child? Did his parents dote on him?

More questions. Each time she thought about the man she only ended up with more questions and none of them appropriate. She didn't need to know anything about him beyond what he wished for his meals and if he liked starch in his shirts.

Suddenly, both women dispersed, Betty darting across the kitchen as if she had fire on her heels. Addy went to the oven and removed another pan of scones.

The kitchen door abruptly opened and the duke stood there. He stopped on the threshold, stomped on the mat to rid his boots of snow, and removed his hat, threading his fingers through his thick mane of brown hair.

Elsbeth stood. "Good morning, Your Grace," she said, grateful that her voice sounded calm and resolute. He wouldn't know that her heart was beating wildly or that she was having thoughts that had nothing to do with acting as Bealadair's housekeeper.

The cold had made his cheeks ruddy and his brown eyes sparkle. He was entirely too handsome a man to have remained single. Perhaps he'd just left his wife in Texas.

She must do something about this curiosity of hers.

"Will you allow me to show you the family dining room?"

To her absolute horror, he shook his head.

"No," he said. "And it's Connor. Not this *Your Grace* business."

As she stared at him, he approached her, and then took a chair next to her at the long rectangular table.

Addy turned to look at him and Betty peered around the corner.

"You can't sit here, Your Grace," she said, startled.

"Why not?"

"It's the kitchen."

He looked around him before his gaze returned to her. "You're right," he said. "It is the kitchen."

Addy was frozen in front of the stove. Betty smiled, evidently delighted to be able to tell the rest of the staff what happened this morning at dawn.

"You can't sit here, Your Grace," Elsbeth repeated.

"This is Bealadair, is it not?"

She nodded.

"According to Mr. Glassey, I'm the owner of Bealadair, am I not?"

She nodded once more.

"Then I can sit anywhere I wish, including the kitchen."

"It's never been done, Your Grace."

He ignored her, turned and smiled at Addy and said, "Those smell wonderful. May I have one?"

Addy nodded, finding her voice a moment later. "Of course, Your Grace. They're my raisin scones with honey icing."

She served him a plate of three scones and added a cup of tea.

"Have you any coffee?" he asked, staring down into the cup.

"Of course, Your Grace," Addy said, picking up the cup and replacing it a moment later with coffee.

The duke sent the same disgusted look at the coffee. Had they done something wrong?

He frowned, took a sip of coffee, then placed the cup back on the saucer.

The duchess was not going to be happy. Rhona was a stickler when it came to etiquette, and there was nothing in the rules that said a duke could take breakfast with the staff.

She would have to take the brunt of the blame in order to spare Addy and Betty. Of course, the three of them could always remain silent about the occasion. If they could hurry the duke out of the kitchen before members of the staff wandered in.

Everyone began their duties with a briefing and a cup of tea. She, herself, had begun the habit when she'd taken over Mrs. Ferguson's duties. The staff's hours were staggered, the better to ensure that the family's requirements were met at any time.

The footmen who were on duty at night would not report again for work until the late afternoon. The kitchen staff under Addy was always up at dawn, but they didn't work past supper. The maids assigned to clean the public rooms began their tasks earlier than those designated to service the family's quarters.

How could she get the duke out of the kitchen before more of the staff arrived?

He seemed to be savoring his scones and said so in more than one comment to Addy. The cook preened, her cheeks deepening in color.

Some people thought that the mark of a good cook was someone who sampled their own wares excessively. If that were true, then Addy was not a good advertisement for her own skills. She was stork thin with a narrow face and long neck. Although she was taller than most of the females on staff, her shoulders were continually slumped, giving her a shorter appearance.

"You disappeared last night," the duke said, glancing at her.

Elsbeth looked at him, startled. He'd actually noted her absence. What did she say to that?

"You were my uncle's ward?"

She nodded.

"No one introduced us."

No, they hadn't.

"I'm Elsbeth Carew, Your Grace."

He startled her by extending his hand. "I'm Connor McCraight, Miss Carew."

She didn't know what to do so she took his hand, finding it large and warm. They shook hands, the first time she'd ever done so. She removed her hand, placed it on her lap, and stared down at her tea.

He really needed to leave the kitchen.

Chapter 6

What do you think of Bealadair, Your Grace?" she asked.

"I'm used to more room," he said.

"You don't think the Duke's Suite is spacious enough?" she asked, slightly offended.

The suite was a beautiful set of rooms. She had helped the girls tidy it up herself. In addition to a sitting room with a view of the river, there was a magnificent bedroom with en suite attached. The 13th duke had even, in his later years, transformed one of the adjoining bedrooms into a small library for his use on days when he didn't feel like going downstairs.

Were four rooms not enough for this American duke?

"Your home in America must be monstrous," she said.

He glanced over at her. "I think you could probably put my house in a quarter of Bealadair," he said.

"Yet you don't think it's spacious enough."

He frowned at her for a moment before he sat back and chuckled.

"I wasn't talking about the house, Elsbeth," he

said. "But the land. I'm not used to the hills and the trees. Or even the river."

The land? "You don't have hills and trees and rivers in America?"

"We've got all of that and more," he said, still smiling at her. "It's just that they're not all crammed together like they are here."

Was he intimating that Scotland was so much smaller than his country? Of course, that was undeniably true, but must he be so arrogant about the fact?

"Have I offended you, Elsbeth?"

He really shouldn't continue calling her Elsbeth. Still, at the same time, she didn't feel that it would be entirely proper for her to correct a duke, even one so contemptuous of his dukedom.

She glanced at Addy who was making another batch of coffee. Betty wandered in from the scullery, looking as if she were engrossed in the pots and pans she carried. Elsbeth knew they were both listening intently to her conversation with the duke.

Even worse, the kitchen would soon be filled with other members of the staff.

She really did need to insist that he retire to the family dining room. When she whispered as much to him, he responded with another smile.

"Only if you'll accompany me, Elsbeth," he said. "After all, you're family, aren't you? Aren't you considered that, being a ward of my uncle?"

She abruptly stood, glanced at Addy, and said, "We'll finish our breakfast there, Addy. Thank you."

She glanced at the duke. "Would you come with me, Your Grace?"

Frankly, she didn't know what she was going to do if he said no, but to her relief he followed her through the labyrinth of corridors. She stopped beside the door to the family dining room.

The family didn't actually rise until midmorning, at least. Later, if the night's entertainments had been lengthy.

"It's quite a ways from the kitchen, isn't it?" he said. "Is that entirely practical?"

No, it wasn't, but she was surprised that he had deduced that. It had been her experience that most men did not pay any attention to domestic affairs.

She shook her head, gestured with her hand that he was to precede her. He didn't. Instead, he folded his arms, shook his head and pointed his chin inside the room.

How odd, to have a battle about who would enter the room first. Of course, she should if their ranks were equal. But he was the Duke of Lothian and she was along the lines of a poor relation.

"Your Grace," she said inclining her head.

"Elsbeth," he responded. "I am more than willing to stand here all day, if that's what you wish."

She had a feeling he would, too. What on earth would Rhona say to see them staring at each other across an open doorway?

After a last glance at him, she entered the room. She didn't wait for him to pull out a chair, but sat herself, smiling as he frowned at her. Truly, she didn't want to battle the man, but it wouldn't do to allow him to win without some token show of resistance.

"You mustn't call me Elsbeth," she said, daring to

correct him. "It's so much more proper to address me as Miss Carew."

"While you call me Your Grace, is that it?"

She nodded.

"I think I'm going to continue to call you Elsbeth. And I insist that you call me Connor."

She folded her arms and allowed herself to reveal a little of her irritation. "Your Grace, I'm afraid that wouldn't be acceptable. We may be in the Highlands, true, but you are the Duke of Lothian. The title has always garnered respect. You are expected to be the epitome of all that's right and proper about Scottish heritage."

"I'm an American," he said. "Even more important, I'm a Texan. If I'm the epitome of anything, Elsbeth, it's the XIV Ranch and Longhorn cattle."

She sat back and stared at him, more than a little concerned.

"But this is Scotland. You need to learn more about the country. And adapt to your new role."

She felt a little strange telling him what he should do. However, he didn't appear irritated by her words. If anything, they seemed to amuse him.

"I have no intention of adapting, Elsbeth. Scotland isn't my country. Besides, I won't be here long enough for that."

She had the most peculiar feeling right then. She didn't know whether she was disappointed or elated. On one hand, she truly didn't wish to see him leave. Not so soon. He was an anomaly and inspired her curiosity. However, if he did leave, that meant everything might return to normal or as normal as they could be without the duke in residence.

"You want to go home," she said.

"I do."

At that moment, one of the serving maids entered, bearing a tray filled with scones and the duke's coffee.

"Is there anything you wish prepared for your breakfast in the future?" Elsbeth asked. "Or any other meal? Is there anything you would like to ensure isn't on the menu?"

He looked at her strangely, as if the question she'd just asked was very odd.

"Do you like fish? We have a wonderful selection of salmon available to us. And venison if you like that as well."

"I'm partial to chili," he said. "But I don't suppose you have that here."

"I don't even know what it is," she admitted.

"Maybe I'll make some for you," he said. "I brought some peppers along, just in case."

She didn't have the slightest idea what to say to that. Saddles and peppers—what else had the man brought from Texas?

"So you're responsible for statues that fall from the roof. And my meals. What else are you responsible for? Do you do laundry, too?"

She shook her head. "No, Your Grace. We have a laundress and a full staff to do that. Is there something you would like washed?"

Please, don't let him mention his small clothes. She didn't know what she'd do if he talked about his unmentionables. Did they discuss that sort of thing in mixed company in America?

"What are your responsibilities?"

She had the sudden thought that she'd offended

him somehow. He was going to punish her by taking her job away. What had she done? As she looked at him, her mind traced back to that moment he'd walked into the kitchen. Had she stared at him too long? Had she allowed him to see that he fascinated her? Had she been too transparent?

"What are my responsibilities?"

"What do you do here, Elsbeth?"

Please don't let him take her job away. It gave her great pleasure to make things work correctly. She liked order. She craved organization. She liked soothing ruffled feathers and keeping everything working just as it should from the hinges on the front door to the number of chickens in the roosts.

"I've taken on the duties of the housekeeper," she said. "No one has objected until now, Your Grace."

"Are you paid for your work?" he asked.

She really wished he wouldn't frown so. He was quite stern looking when he frowned. You could forget how handsome he was when he looked at you with such a direct stare.

"Am I paid?"

"Yes, Elsbeth, are you paid?"

"Not in the way that you mean, no. I inherited some funds from my parents, plus there was a bequest from the duke. But I don't receive an annual salary, no."

"Who the hell decided on that?"

She didn't know what was more offensive, the fact that he had sworn in front of her or his anger. Why was he angry?

There were certain jobs that people took on, that

they did for the sheer joy of it. She didn't require a salary. What she did she did for Bealadair, the duke, and to assist Mrs. Ferguson.

She didn't get a chance to explain any of that to him. He reached into his vest pocket and pulled out a notebook and pencil and began to write. He didn't say anything for a moment, but when he was finished, he frowned at her once more.

"We're going to change that, Elsbeth. If you insist on acting as the housekeeper, you'll be paid a salary."

"That's not necessary, Your Grace," she said.

"Then I'll have to hire a new housekeeper. Someone who will be paid."

"We already have a housekeeper."

The minute the words were out of her mouth, she regretted them. He would, no doubt, fire the poor woman, and then what would happen?

"Mrs. Ferguson's been poorly for a while," she said. "She has terrible arthritis, and this winter has been very difficult on her. But I beg you, Your Grace, please do not dismiss her. She's been with Bealadair for two decades. It would be like tossing her into a snowdrift. You can't do it."

"Connor," he said with not a single bit of amusement on his face.

"What?"

"I won't toss her into a snowdrift, Elsbeth, if you'll dispense with *Your Grace* and call me Connor."

She blinked at him, not one word coming to her rescue.

For years and years upon years she'd been lectured on proper behavior by the duchess, as if the woman was afraid that Elsbeth might shame the family somehow by saying the wrong thing at the wrong moment or by not being conversant with the rules of polite behavior. She'd done her utmost to learn.

Not one person in the whole of Scotland could ever say that she'd done anything to bring an iota of shame to the McCraights. From the moment she rose at dawn until she went to bed, she considered every single action, every word. Now, just like that, the new Duke of Lothian was demanding—commanding— that she break the habits of a lifetime.

"I couldn't possibly," she said, wishing he would understand. What he asked for was impossible.

"I take it Mrs. Ferguson lives here at Bealadair?"

She frowned at him. "What you are suggesting is improper," she said.

"Why? It's my name."

She could just imagine what Rhona would do the first time she heard Elsbeth calling the duke by his first name.

"It's not done, Your Grace."

"Where do you think I can acquire a new house-keeper?"

"That's extortion, Your Grace."

The ghost of a smile appeared on his lips.

"Are you always so proper, Elsbeth?"

"Yes."

"Why?" he asked.

"What do you mean, why?"

She stared at him. The fact that her heart was beating too fast was only one warning sign. She wanted, strangely, to smile at him, to prop her chin in her hand and stare at him for an hour or two, admiring everything about him.

No, she really should leave. Now. Before she made even more of a fool of herself. Proper? She wasn't feeling the least bit proper right now.

Chapter 7

She was frowning at him again. Good. He had the feeling that keeping Elsbeth Carew a little off-kilter would be a good thing. He was tired of being called Your Grace all the time. Maybe if he ignored her for a while she would come to realize that his name was Connor and he preferred that to all the bowing and scraping.

He couldn't help who his father had been. Who he was—not what he had accomplished or achieved on his own—had led him to Scotland, nothing else. He didn't want to be treated differently. Yet when he'd made that remark to Sam, the older man had laughed at him.

"You're not just yourself," Sam had said. "You're Connor McCraight of XIV Ranch. You're the owner. You might be judged by what you do, but you'll first be judged by who you are."

What had he said in response? He couldn't remember, only that Sam hadn't stopped smiling.

"I understand how you feel," the older man had said. "I can be anyone I want because people don't know who I am. If you really want to be anonymous, then move to another country."

Well, he was in another country, but he was far from anonymous. He was the 14th Duke of Lothian and Laird of a clan he was about to meet in a few days.

And it looked like he was going to wear that label as long as he remained here.

She sat back in the chair, folded her hands, and stared at him as if he had grown two heads.

He'd seen a two-headed goat once and almost told her about it but then decided it probably wasn't the subject for breakfast conversation. He didn't want to scare her off or send her fleeing from the family dining room.

Thankfully, there was a roaring fire warming the space. The wallpaper was an emerald green and the upholstery on the chairs around the rectangular table was plaid, the same pattern his aunt and cousins had worn the night before. For some reason, he couldn't quite see the family dining here. The room needed to be larger, almost a baronial setting, with lots and lots of gilt and paintings on the ceiling.

Too bad he hadn't brought his dress uniform, the one he'd only worn twice. The first time he'd been marching off to war. The second time he'd been coming back from it. It was a little worse for wear but had shiny epaulets and silver buttons and he looked mighty fine in it. Of course, he couldn't wear his hat or boots so that diminished it a bit. And there was some blood on the right leg. He didn't even want to remember how that had happened.

"Will your wife be joining you, Your Grace?"

"I'm not married."

She glanced at him. "I'm sorry."

"Nor am I a widower."

She looked as if she wanted to ask another question, that it trembled on her lips. He bit back his smile and asked his own.

"And you, Elsbeth?"

"Am I married?" She looked startled by the question. "No, Your Grace, I'm not."

"No suitor in the wings? No beau waiting to take you away from Bealadair?"

"No."

"Why is that?"

She only blinked at him in response.

A moment later, he asked another question, one less troubling to her. "How many rooms are there at Bealadair?" he asked.

"One hundred eighty-nine," she said.

"That's a great many rooms," he said, startled. "I've never heard of a house having that many rooms. I certainly never considered that I would own one."

"Well, if you didn't, your father certainly did."

He looked at her. She didn't glance away.

"What do you mean?"

"The name of your ranch. XIV. Isn't that fourteen in Roman numerals? You're the fourteenth duke."

"That's just a coincidence," he said, even though he'd wondered more than once if it was, ever since Glassey had shown up. "It does mean fourteen, but that's not the reason it was named that. My father and Sam tried to find a brand that couldn't be altered, something that would foil any cattle rustlers."

"What's a cattle rustler?"

"A thief," he said. "Somebody who wants something of mine."

"There's an old Scottish expression," she said. "'They wha begin stealing pins and needles go on to steal cattle.' Although I can't imagine anyone trying to steal our cattle. Poachers, now, that's a different story. Our deer population is smaller than it has ever been, so we try to protect them. How do you catch a rustler?"

"By not making it possible for them to steal from me," he said. "If they're foolish enough to try, we follow their trail."

"What do you do when you find them?"

Perhaps it would be better if he didn't go into that aspect of XIV Ranch justice. He might shock her further and that was the last thing he wanted to do.

He was grateful for all those cotillion lessons his mother had insisted upon, and all the times he'd been forced to escort one sister or another somewhere. He could be a gentleman when he needed to be.

He considered his sisters pretty and he supposed his cousins were, too. He had met his share of beautiful women and most of them, in his estimation, had a very good idea of how attractive they were.

Elsbeth Carew, however, was different from all of them.

He had the feeling that if he leaned over and said, "Elsbeth, you're one of the most beautiful women I have ever seen," she would be surprised, first. Then, no doubt, she would demur, claim that she was no such thing, that he was mistaken or that fatigue had caused him to make such a comment. Or perhaps his eyesight was failing. Then she would ask him what he wanted for his dinner.

Her gray eyes reminded him of a Texas sky in winter. Or the fog around San Antonio. There was a black circle around the iris as if to further enhance the distinctive color. Her feathery lashes were so long that they brushed her cheeks when she blinked. He found himself caught up by the sight.

Her hair was black, but not just any black. It reminded him of midnight, when the world was silent and he was awake and staring at the canopy of stars above him.

He studied her face for a moment, wondering what it was that made her so beautiful. It wasn't just the color of her eyes. Her nose was neither too large nor too pointed. Her mouth was the perfect shape, even at rest. When she smiled, the expression lit up her face. Her chin wasn't too squared. Her forehead wasn't too broad nor too short. Everything about her was separately perfect and together they created a memorable face.

Yet there was something else about her, something that intrigued him. Perhaps it was the determination he'd bumped up against accidentally.

She was a head shorter than he, but he had the impression that the difference in size didn't matter to her. If it came to a war of wills, Elsbeth Carew would give as good as she got.

He found himself smiling, and when she frowned at him, his smile only got bigger.

Her hands attracted him as well, and he couldn't ever remember being fascinated by the shape of a woman's hands or how she used them. Her fingers were long, the nails short, and he found himself watching her gestures.

Perhaps he was fatigued from the journey after all. Not thinking straight was what Sam would call it.

"I would appreciate it if you would call me Connor," he said. "Glassey has already treated me to chapter and verse of why I must be addressed as Your Grace. I know I won't be able to change everyone's mind, Elsbeth, but it would be nice if there was one person in Scotland who could be a friend."

"Perhaps you could convince your cousins," she said. "After all, they're your relatives." Still, there was a look in her eyes, the same compassionate expression as when she'd been discussing Bealadair's housekeeper. He had a feeling that she was on the cusp of committing etiquette treason.

"Please," he said, realizing that he wasn't fighting fair. His sisters had always told him that a pleading man was nearly impossible to refuse.

"Perhaps not in public," she said.

He was gracious in her capitulation.

"Not in public, then," he said. "Only in private."

For a moment she looked as if she wished to take back her agreement. Or maybe she was simply determined never to be alone with him like they were now.

"Do you always wake at dawn?" he asked.

She nodded. "There's a great deal to be done," she said. "I like to get a good start on the day. Plus, I find it nice to be awake when others are asleep."

He felt the same.

"Do you like to dance?"

Her eyes widened and he wondered if he had broken another Scottish rule.

"I'm afraid I was the bane of our dancing instructor," she said. "Your cousins are all quite accomplished dancers. I am not."

He had the feeling that she'd be good at the Texas two-step and was determined to dance it with her, at least once. "Do you ride?"

"I'm afraid I don't have a great many talents," she said. "Your cousins, on the other hand, are very accomplished in a great many ways."

He didn't give a flying flip what his cousins could do.

He forced himself to drink some of his coffee. This batch was as bad as the first. He liked his coffee strong and this was like weak tea. He wasn't fond of tea.

"Why did you bring your saddle?" she suddenly asked.

She sat with her hands together at the edge of the table, reminding him of a student awaiting the answer to an important quiz.

"I can tell you've never been to Texas," he said. "A man's saddle is one of his most important possessions."

"We have saddles here at Bealadair. Did you think we wouldn't?"

"I don't care if you have saddles here or not," he said. "I prefer my own."

"I'm surprised you didn't bring your own horse."

He grinned at that, amused by the look in her eyes—a combination of surprise and annoyance. She was very protective of Bealadair.

"I wanted to," he confessed. "Glassey assured me

that I would have some suitable mounts here. Plus, I didn't think it would be fair to subject my horse to an ocean voyage. He's used to riding among Long-horns, not waves."

She looked away at that, concentrating on the scone on the plate before her. She didn't seem to be hungry, but he polished off the other two scones he'd been given.

As long as it wasn't oatmeal, he was fine. Oatmeal harkened him back to the days of his childhood sitting around the family table being bedeviled by his older sisters. He could never put enough cream or enough sugar in it to make it palatable. It still tasted like paste to him.

Elsbeth wasn't talkative, a difference from most women he knew. Yet while he found it restful, he also discovered that the silence was niggling at him. He had a great many questions about her, but other than asking about his wife and his saddle she didn't seem to want to know any more about him.

The lack of anyone's curiosity about Texas or America—or even how he felt about becoming the 14th Duke of Lothian—was irritating. It was as though no one thought he had a life before coming to Scotland. Or maybe they thought that everything that had transpired until the moment he became duke was inconsequential.

Neither his aunt nor his cousins had asked about his family, the XIV Ranch, his past, or his hopes for the future. What would they think if he told them that a title didn't mean anything to him? It was like the chilled air that had nearly frozen his face this morning.

Something he noted, but that was gone the moment he came inside.

She took a sip of her tea, set the cup back in the saucer, and regarded him for a moment.

"What's a Longhorn?" she asked.

Finally, another question.

"The type of cattle we raise on the XIV Ranch. They're big and they've got horns that can easily stretch six feet or more."

He pulled out his notebook, turned to a clean page, and sketched a picture of one for her.

She glanced at the notebook, then up at him before returning to the sketch again.

"You're very talented," she said.

He shook his head. "No. My mother's the one with the real talent. I just amuse myself with it."

She shook her head. "I would disagree," she said, her finger reaching out to trace the horns he'd drawn. "Are you certain you haven't exaggerated?"

He smiled. "I'm certain." He glanced down at the sketch. "They're not all that fearsome up close. Most of them aren't. Those that have been around cowboys are pretty easily handled. The others? It takes a while."

"We raise Highland cattle," she said. "Have you ever seen one?"

He shook his head. "I've never even heard of one."

"I'll have to show you one of our herds. They winter outdoors. They're very hardy that way."

He never once considered sitting with a beautiful woman and talking cattle. Perhaps that was his fault. He didn't often go into Austin, and when he did it was mainly because of his sisters, not any personal inclination.

A man had needs, of course, but he found if he kept himself busy—and that hadn't been difficult in the past two years—he was often too tired to worry about any libidinous desires.

Until now, that is. The room was quiet. In the distance he could hear the sound of voices and occasionally laughter. He thought he could also pick up the sound of the winter wind soughing against the stone of Bealadair.

"You weren't wearing any plaid last night."

"Plaid?"

"On your dress."

"Oh, the McCraight tartan," she said. "No, I wasn't. I'm not a McCraight."

"You're not allowed to wear it—is that what you mean?"

She seemed to consider the matter for a moment. "I guess I could wear it if I wished. I don't think anyone would have any objections. It's just that I've never asked."

He was getting a picture of Elsbeth's life at Bealadair and it wasn't sitting well with him. He had a feeling she was little more than an unpaid servant for the family. They certainly hadn't expressed any appreciation for her actions last night. Plus, she'd gone out in a blizzard to check on a statue and none of them had seemed surprised.

He suspected that she would disagree with his assessment and perhaps he'd been too quick to judge. Maybe he should watch and learn for a little bit longer. Sometimes his first inclination was to think that coyotes got into the henhouse when it was only the family dog.

Twice, she glanced toward the door, then wiggled a little in her chair as if she were uncomfortable.

"Are you concerned because we're alone?" he asked. "Granted, we're not related, but doesn't being the 14th Duke of Lothian give me some kind of latitude?"

She startled him by shaking her head.

"No, it doesn't. If anything, it forces you into even more rectitude. You mustn't be caught in a compromising situation. People could say things about you."

Amused, he sipped at his coffee. "I can almost guarantee you, Elsbeth, that people are going to say things about me regardless of what I do. However," he added, "you can be proper for both of us."

She glanced at him again, her gray eyes wide with surprise.

"Gavin used to say the same thing," she said.

"You called my uncle Gavin?"

She didn't meet his eyes.

"You didn't call him Your Grace?" he asked.

She sighed. "I called him Gavin. But not in public. The duchess would have thought it improper."

"Were you given to chiding him, too?"

Her smile was lovely, making him wonder what memories he'd summoned.

"No, but he thought I was very proper for my age. Too much so, perhaps."

No doubt because of his aunt, a comment he didn't make.

"Since you're acting as the housekeeper for Bealadair, would it be possible for you to show me the rest of the house?"

"I believe the duchess has planned on the family

doing that, Your Grace." She sent him a look, then sighed again. "Very well, Connor."

He would much prefer to have Elsbeth show him around the house, but he knew this was a battle he was probably not going to win. He would take his victories where they came. Being alone with Elsbeth Carew counted as a victory—a large one—but one that didn't last long. Less than a minute later, she excused herself, citing her responsibilities, and left him sitting there staring after her.

Chapter 8

Elsbeth had a great deal to do and spending time with the duke at breakfast hadn't helped her schedule.

She needed to check on the roof above the housekeeper's room. The last time it had rained, Mrs. Ferguson's ceiling had showed a sign of leakage. Had the recent snow caused any further damage? If it warmed up just a little this afternoon, she would visit the roof to check on the statues. She'd already noticed signs of predation around the chimney stacks. She also had to discipline a maid for tardiness and talk to one of the footmen about his penchant for swearing.

She kept a notebook just like His Grace—Connor. Otherwise, she'd forget all the details that were now swirling around in her mind. She pulled it from her pocket and read her notes. The parquet floor in the ballroom needed to be polished. The chandeliers were in the process of being cleaned. The heavy velvet curtains had already been removed, brushed and beaten thoroughly and were being replaced, window by window.

Everything had to be perfect for the Welcoming of

the Laird celebration. Even if the Laird didn't seem to want to be the laird. Or the duke.

She wished she could follow the members of the family through their tour of Bealadair. What would they say to Connor about the various rooms? Would they bring up the history of the Laird's Hall and the room it had replaced after the great fire of 1605? Would they relate the history of the conservatory wing?

Would Connor realize that he would need weeks in order to study all the various plants that had been brought back from South America, China, and Japan? Even in the most bitterly cold weather, they ensured that the conservatory was warm enough so that the plants didn't suffer.

No doubt the McCraight daughters would concentrate on the most attractive of Bealadair's features, not those with more historical significance. The house was a treasure known throughout Scotland and England.

Would Connor, as an American, realize the depth of his good fortune? Would he acknowledge the responsibility of being a steward to the great house? It was for him to protect his heritage for the next generation.

Why hadn't he married? Another question that hadn't been answered to her satisfaction. How very odd that he hadn't. He was at the age where a man would've had a wife and several children by now. Why hadn't he?

He didn't consider Scotland his home. Perhaps he would after he had the opportunity to get to know his heritage. Would anyone show him the portrait gallery?

It was really none of her concern. She wasn't a McCraight. She simply occupied a strange and novel place at Bealadair. Neither fish nor fowl, but something in between. She wasn't a servant, exactly, but neither was she a member of the family.

Nor did she have any right to be curious about the 14th duke for all that he hated being called that.

ACCORDING TO ELSBETH, the rest of the family didn't rise until midmorning, or until half the day was done as far as he was concerned. He could accomplish a hell of a lot by noon, but evidently accomplishment wasn't a goal for his relatives.

What did they need to do? Everything had already been done. They had land. They had possessions. They had a standing in the community. They had a house to live in, one that amazed him with its very size.

He left the family dining room and found himself at the base of the staircase.

The foyer was paved in stone squares that looked as if they'd been polished for a few hundred years. It was so shiny that he could see the reflection of the soaring ceiling in it.

Snow had accumulated on the glass of the cupola. He bet on a fair day that sunlight blazed through the glass, illuminating the area and the double staircase with its mahogany trim.

He'd seen stairs like that only once, on a plantation in Georgia. He'd thought, then, that the architect had to have been touched with whimsy to create such a marvel. Other than the landings, this staircase didn't look as if it was anchored to anything, either.

The plantation had burned to the ground, but Bealadair had lasted hundreds of years. In fact, the house had an air of permanence about it, as if it had sunk its foundations deep into the soil, becoming part of the landscape.

You can't burn me out, the house seemed to say.

He nodded to the footman standing at the door, almost like a sentry at his post. The young man was tall, equipped in the Bealadair uniform of dark blue, and standing at attention, his gaze on a spot far away.

"Do you stand there all day?" he asked.

The man blinked and focused on him. "Yes, Your Grace."

Something had to be done about that title.

"Why?"

"In case anyone needs help at the door, Your Grace."

Connor glanced outside. "I doubt anyone is going to be visiting today, don't you?"

The young man looked confused.

"Who says you're to stand at the door all day?"

Now the footman looked scared, as if the answer to that question would deliver a hammer blow to his head.

"Mr. Barton, Your Grace. The majordomo."

"Where is Mr. Barton now?"

"He's got a touch of the gout, Your Grace."

Were all the senior staff ill? No doubt Elsbeth took up the slack with Barton's duties as well.

Connor took pity on the footman. "Do you know where Mr. Glassey's room is?"

"He's in the guest wing, Your Grace. In the Turquoise Room."

"You're going to need to be a little more specific than that," Connor said. "Since I don't know where the guest wing is."

The young man gave him directions. As Connor turned toward the stairs, the footman spoke again.

"But I saw Mr. Glassey go into the library a few minutes ago, Your Grace. It's down the main hall, second door on your right."

Connor thanked him and headed in that direction. As long as he stayed in Scotland, perhaps he could find something more important for the young man to be doing than to be guarding the door.

He found Glassey rightly enough. The solicitor was sitting at a large desk in front of what looked to be a wall of windows, the view nothing but white with a few touches of dark green to mark where trees were standing.

The room was unlike anything he'd ever seen or, for that matter, imagined in a private home. He could envision this library in a place like his alma mater, Rutgers, or even in the Austin capitol. Not in the Highlands of Scotland.

The ceiling looked to stretch to the top of Bealadair, the room nearly as wide as it was tall. Two spiral staircases, one leading to the first floor, the other to the second, sat on either side of the room. Ladders on rollers rested in front of twelve-foot-high mahogany bookcases.

Each bookshelf looked to be labeled in block lettering. Animal husbandry, adventure, art—he caught those titles before his attention was once more drawn to the ceiling. Here, magnificent mahogany arches framed a stained glass roof patterned in a mosaic of jewel-like colors.

The glare from the snow merged with the yellowish light from gas lamps burning throughout the room. Coupled with the oversized fireplace on the far wall, blazing merrily, the result was a room that was cheerful and bright, not to mention comfortably warm.

"It is amazing, isn't it?" Glassey said. "It was your uncle's favorite room. And mine, for that matter."

When Connor still didn't say anything, Glassey continued. "It's due to the dedication of your various ancestors that the room is what it is."

"I wouldn't exactly call this just a room," Connor said, directing his attention to the solicitor. "How many books are here?"

"I don't know. Perhaps your uncle did, but I haven't found any records that indicate the number of volumes. I imagine it numbers in the thousands. Perhaps Miss Carew would know. She's very conversant about Bealadair."

"My uncle's ward," Connor said.

Glassey nodded, stacked his papers, and stood.

"What, exactly, is a ward?"

The solicitor smiled. "A dependent. In Miss Carew's case, her father and His Grace were good friends. When he and his wife perished in a train accident, His Grace took in Miss Carew. She had barely escaped death herself."

"So she's not a relative of any sort."

"No," Mr. Glassey said, frowning at him as he moved from the desk. "However, she is to be accorded all the care and politeness you would show your cousins, Your Grace."

The solicitor's instant assumption that he was going to treat Elsbeth rudely irritated him.

"She isn't drawing a salary."

"No, I don't believe she is."

"That stops today. I want her paid. Figure out what would be a fair amount for a highly skilled housekeeper, Glassey, and pay her that."

"I will, sir," the solicitor said, although he looked surprised at the request.

"You don't have to move," Connor said when he realized that's exactly what Glassey was doing.

"Of course I do, Your Grace. It's your desk. Your room."

He wasn't going to call it his. Nothing about Bealadair was his. He hadn't earned it. He hadn't built it. But he knew, even without starting the conversation, that Glassey wouldn't understand.

Instead of moving to the desk, he stood where he was.

"If you hadn't found me, what would you have done?"

The solicitor looked confused. "I would have continued to look for you, Your Grace."

Connor shook his head. "If I hadn't been born, if my father hadn't had any male heirs, who would own all this?" His hands stretched out to encompass the library and beyond, to the whole of Bealadair. "My cousins?"

"No, Your Grace. The title is reserved for male heirs by letters patent."

He wasn't an attorney. Nor was he conversant in

English law. He had to depend on Glassey to tell him what was what, but it seemed as if the solicitor was willfully not understanding him.

"So they couldn't inherit?"

"No, Your Grace."

"And if there wasn't a male heir?"

"Then I imagine the title would be placed in abeyance. But, Your Grace, you are here. You are the heir."

He nodded. "And this is mine to do with what I wish?"

Glassey only stared back at him.

He'd gotten used to the man's beady-eyed look after traveling half a world with him.

Connor made his way to the window, surveying the white world before him. The rolling landscape beyond the lawn looked to be covered in cotton, hinting at hills and hedges. To his left, the earth formed a V shape leading down to the river. Woods to his right had a fairy-tale appearance with ice creating a curtain of stalactites from the branches.

This was not his home. This wasn't his land, for all that it was his father's birthplace.

He'd been born on the XIV Ranch with his father and a grizzled ranch hand in attendance. As he'd been told, Matt Thompson had a lot of experience with pulling calves, and it looked like he was going to have to use it in helping to birth the last of the McCraight brood.

His mother, as stubborn a woman as he'd ever met, had decided that she didn't need anyone other than one of the maids with her. He'd been born ten hours later, the largest of the six McCraight children and—as his father would attest—the loudest.

Something squeezed around his chest. What would Graham have thought to see him here? Would he have apologized for never mentioning Bealadair in all those years? Would he have said anything about why he'd named their home the XIV Ranch?

He'd gotten a blow to the chest when Glassey had first told him he was the 14th duke. What if Elsbeth was right and the name of the ranch was some sort of reference to Scotland, to the possibility that he might be the next in line?

He'd never know, just as he'd never know what Graham would think.

"Is it mine to sell?" he asked.

"Your Grace?"

He turned and looked at the solicitor. "Is the house mine to sell?"

"Yes, Your Grace. But . . ." Glassey's voice halted.

Connor had known, ever since learning that he was his uncle's heir, that he wasn't going to remain in Scotland. Instead, he was going to divest himself of the property and use the proceeds to benefit the ranch.

If Glassey had been paying attention all this time, he would've figured that out. Connor had been uncomfortable ever since learning he had a title. Some of the ranch hands had snickered and he could just imagine what they were saying behind his back. A man who put on airs wasn't welcome in Texas.

"You can't do such a thing, Your Grace."

He didn't take kindly to people telling him what he could or couldn't do. Not unless that person was either his father or his colonel. Since Glassey was neither of those people, he ignored the man.

"The property is entailed," Glassey said. "For the 15th duke. It can't be sold."

"Then you just lied."

He folded his arms and waited for Glassey to explain his way out of that.

The other man looked to his left, then his right, then back to his left. Connor had once questioned a ranch hand accused of theft by another man. He'd had the same kind of shifty eyes, while his accuser had met Connor's gaze and hadn't looked away.

"No, Your Grace," Glassey finally said, "I didn't lie. Castle McCraight is the only part of your inheritance that's entailed. Everything else can be sold."

"Bealadair and the land?"

The solicitor nodded, although he looked pained to have to admit it.

"But Your Grace . . ."

"I want to sell it, then."

Glassey was looking a little pale.

"If you can't arrange that, I'll find someone who can."

"I'll make inquiries, Your Grace."

Connor interrupted him. "My name is Connor," he said. "From now on, if you want me to pay any attention to you, you'll call me by my name. I'm nobody's grace."

He didn't look at the solicitor as he left the room.

Chapter 9

Elsbeth walked into one of the downstairs parlors, the one favored by the McCraight sisters. The patterned yellow silk on the walls had been made in France. Perhaps at one time it was a darker color, but over the years it had faded to a pale yellowish white. Rather than remove the wall covering, they had simply compensated by changing the furniture.

Two years ago, the specially made settees and chairs had been delivered. The upholstery fabric very nearly matched the French silk. Emerald green accent pillows added a punch of color to the room.

The duchess loved to decorate, or modernize, as she called it. She was forever changing either one of the public rooms or one of those occupied by a member of the family. Last year she'd decided that Elsbeth should move from her suite so that it, too, could be altered. Elsbeth had pleaded with Gavin. There was nothing she needed or wanted changed in the rooms she'd lived in ever since coming to Bealadair. Gavin and Rhona had a rousing fight on the subject, but Gavin had emerged victorious. The duchess hadn't been happy about the outcome, however, and had frowned at her for weeks.

Rhona wasn't in the Yellow Parlor, thank heavens, but the sisters were. Anise was holding court, marching back and forth in front of the roaring fire.

"It isn't fair," she was saying. "I don't know as much about the older wing as you do, Lara. You should take it, and I'll show him the family wing."

Elsbeth knew what they were talking about immediately. Rhona had decided that her three daughters were to give the tour of Bealadair to His Grace—Connor.

Perhaps she should have taken tea somewhere else, but she'd wanted to visit with Muira. Her friend turned and smiled at her, making her feel somewhat welcome. The other two girls had always been a little standoffish, even when she was a child, but they were that way with everyone. It wasn't as if they had singled Elsbeth out for rudeness.

She nodded to one of the maids, and the girl left the room. In moments she would be back with another cup and perhaps even another tray, one filled to the brim with treats they'd prepared over the last few weeks.

"I'm not going to trade with you," Lara said. "It's bad enough that I have to traipse around the house with the man in his outlandish clothing. Why hadn't Mr. Glassey outfitted him better in London? Hopefully, no one saw him. Can you just imagine what people would say?"

Elsbeth couldn't allow Lara's comment to remain as it stood.

"He's from Texas," she said. "Of course they don't dress the same as Scotland."

"What do you know about it?" Lara said. "You

don't have an eye for fashion. You don't care what you wear. How do you know what they wear in Texas?"

"Both His Grace and his friend were wearing boots," she said. "They were both wearing the same kind of hat. And the same kind of coat. Perhaps if it was just His Grace, you could make the assumption that he's iconoclastic in his dress. But two men? You can only assume that it's a Texas style he's wearing. Shall we ask Mr. Glassey? He'll know."

Lara looked away, the same as dismissing her. Elsbeth was used to it. Lara had always been that way, behavior that wasn't isolated to Elsbeth. She treated everyone the same, as if they were beneath her.

When she was thirteen, on the anniversary of her mother's death, Lara told her half sisters that she considered them upstarts.

"I'm the only child of our father's true wife," she'd said.

Ever since that announcement, there had been a separation between the sisters. Lara didn't seem to care. The only person she treated well was Felix. She was devoted to her husband.

Elsbeth didn't like the man. It was difficult to be fond of someone who always looked at you as if he smelled something bad.

"I wouldn't give any thought to his opinion of you, my dear," Gavin had said. "Felix is one of those people who doesn't approve of anyone unless they have a title or significant riches to their name. He is, I'm afraid, a hanger-on."

His words had surprised her. So, too, the fact that he'd agreed to Lara marrying the man. But, then, Lara always had her own mind. As a child, she would threaten to hold her breath until she got her way. When she had a tantrum, Gavin had always given her a sideways look, shrugged, and walked away.

Felix was absent from the parlor. With no occupation of his own, Felix was often to be found underfoot. He, like his wife, spent a great deal of time in criticism. Yet they never did anything to correct what they disliked. They simply liked to talk about it.

No doubt Felix was occupied in his only interest: his guns. He was quite a good shot, but there was no reason he shouldn't be, having endless hours in which to practice. When he wasn't taking one of the footmen away from his duties—in order for the man to toss glass balls as targets for him—he was cleaning one of his rifles.

Even Gavin had commented on the number of guns in his collection.

"I do trust my son-in-law is devoid of a bloodthirsty nature. Otherwise, I fear for our safety. He has enough weapons to arm a rebellion."

She hadn't responded. There were times when Gavin spoke only to hear himself talk. She had the feeling, occasionally, that he would have said the same words had she not been in the room.

She did miss him. Did his daughters? In the past few months she'd never heard them mention him, which was a shame. It seemed to her that a person never truly died if you remembered him and shared those memories with others.

"I'll take His Grace on a tour of the older wing if you wish, Anise," Elsbeth said.

For a moment she didn't think the woman was

going to answer, merely point her nose up toward the ceiling and sigh heavily as if she were annoyed to have to speak to Elsbeth.

Anise stopped pacing to look at her. "Why would you do that?"

"You evidently don't wish to. I don't mind."

Anise studied her for a moment, long enough that she was growing uncomfortable.

Did they know, could they tell, how fascinated she was by the new duke? How she wished to speak with him further? She might have a chance at breakfast again, especially if he rose as early as she. But to be able to show him Bealadair would be a treat rather than a duty to be dreaded.

She kept silent, knowing that if she said anything further, it would just incite their curiosity.

When the maid arrived with her tea, she occupied herself by taking the cup and then selecting a piece of jewel cake.

"Mother will not be happy," Anise finally said.

Elsbeth couldn't dispute that.

"As long as the tour is done, what does it matter?" Lara said. "Why can't he simply roam around Bealadair and find his own way?"

"Mother wants to ensure that the American gets to know all of us," Anise said. "Make sure he knows we're family."

"How are we supposed to do that?" Lara asked. "Keep reminding him that we're cousins?" She shook her head. "I'll ensure I'm charming at dinner. I don't have to wander all over the house." She smiled at Elsbeth. "You can do my part. I'll tell Mother I was feeling ill."

Lara had been looking a little pale lately. It had been a difficult winter and for the most part, the family had remained inside the house. Of course, Bealadair was so large that it wasn't a hardship to do so.

Elsbeth didn't say anything. She merely nodded her agreement and sipped at her tea.

"I have the towers to show him," Muira said. "Mother is all for me going up and down the steps. She says I need the exercise. That I'm getting as plump as a partridge. If you want to do my part, I wouldn't object, Elsbeth."

"And as long as you are doing everyone else's duty, you might as well show him the old wing," Anise said. "All those weapons and tattered flags." She shuddered dramatically.

In for a penny, in for a pound. The duchess was going to be annoyed at her anyway—why not show Connor the whole of Bealadair? When she said as much, the three women nodded. They were well aware that Elsbeth was held to a different standard. Sometimes, even when she was doing the right thing, the duchess found a reason to be irritated.

"Who will show him the outbuildings? And the public rooms?"

"I'm sure mother has the public rooms picked out to do herself," Anise said.

What about the old castle ruins? Someone would need to explain the history of the clan to Connor. Unless, of course, his father had already imparted that knowledge.

The duchess would say that she was expressing an errant curiosity, that she was being improper.

Elsbeth suspected that if Gavin had known her thoughts he would have smiled fondly at her, patted her on the back of the hand, and said something wise and trenchant. "Of course, my dear, you're curious about him because he's unlike anyone you've ever met. Why shouldn't we be curious about other people and other places?"

She should search the shelves in the library, scan the thousands of books there to see if there were any volumes about America. Or Texas, perhaps. Or even about Longhorn cattle.

She frankly doubted the latter and wasn't excessively hopeful about the former, but perhaps she could find something.

Would Connor be as amenable to learning about Scotland? She would just have to wait and see, wouldn't she?

"Very well," she said. "I'll show him around Bealadair."

She took a last sip of her tea and stood.

The thought of the duchess, however, kept her from smiling brightly at all of them as she left the room.

Chapter 10

Connor was all for telling his aunt that he didn't need or want a tour of the house. He could wander around on his own just fine. If he got lost, he could ask directions from one of the servants.

Except, of course, all of his objections flew out the window when it turned out that Elsbeth was going to accompany him.

There she stood at the doorway to his suite, hands folded in front of her, her plain black dress making her complexion seem even more delicately pale. He wondered if she knew how beautiful she was or if she was one of those women who couldn't quite believe it, no matter what anybody said.

From the interaction he'd witnessed the night before she wasn't highly valued in the family. Instead, she acted like a hybrid, kind of a like a calf born of a Longhorn cow and a Hereford bull.

"Have I amused you?" she asked, tilting her head slightly.

He decided not to tell her why he was grinning. Instead, he grabbed his hat and coat and was ready to follow her.

"We aren't going outside, Your Grace."

He looked at her.

She sighed and said, "Connor. We aren't going outside, Connor. You won't need your coat."

He reluctantly hung it back up, along with his hat.

"I have to admit, Elsbeth, that I've been cold ever since I arrived in Scotland. I hope every fireplace in this house is blazing away."

Her eyes widened as if she were surprised. Was she unused to honesty? Or did the Scots not mind the weather? Did they have ice in their veins?

"It is certainly within your purview to order that, Connor." Her voice only hesitated a little at his name. There, progress. These Scots sure liked their titles.

He wasn't interested in seeing Bealadair. He was, however, interested in seeing more of Elsbeth. She intrigued him although he couldn't say exactly why. Maybe it was because he'd been around beautiful women before, but none so self-deprecating. He wanted to know what made her that way. Was she simply modest, was it a pretense, or did she need a little more confidence?

"We'll begin in the older wing, if you don't mind."

"As long as it's warm," he said.

She looked a bit worried at that. He had a feeling he was going to be cold and stay that way.

For some reason she looked uncomfortable with him walking beside her. He wondered if he was supposed to precede her—which would be ridiculous because he didn't know where they were going. Or would it be more proper for him to follow her? That didn't seem right, either.

She was just going to have to get used to him matching his gait to hers.

She was taller than his cousins, but she was still a head shorter than he was. She parted her hair perfectly in the middle and had arranged it in an artful bun at the nape of her neck. Because it was braided, he guessed that it was longer than it looked. For a second, and just long enough to warm him from the inside out, he imagined himself unbraiding her hair, slipping his fingers through the length of it.

Would his fingers meet if he put his hands around her waist? That was another thought he shouldn't have, but he really couldn't help himself.

His sisters would say that she was a little top-heavy—a comment he'd heard them make numerous times—but that was okay by him. He liked the way she filled out the bodice of her crow's dress.

She smelled of lemons, of all things, and something else that reminded him of Bessie from home. Bessie liked to polish the parlor furniture with a combination of beeswax and lemon. He should ask Elsbeth what the scent was, rather than have all those thoughts about her shape.

She didn't wear any jewelry, which made him wonder why. Was it out of respect for his uncle? For that matter, why was she still wearing mourning like the duchess when his cousins weren't? Was it because she didn't have any other clothing? That thought warmed him, too, but with irritation, not incipient lust.

"I'd prefer your amusement," she said, startling him. "You have quite a fierce frown."

He glanced down at her.

"Begging your pardon, Elsbeth. My thoughts ran away with me."

"Have I done something?"

"Do you always take someone's moods on yourself?" he asked.

"I don't know what you mean."

"If I'm happy or I'm sad, it's not necessarily because of anything you did, Elsbeth. It might be me, just me. I own my emotions. You own yours."

"You don't think people can influence other people's moods?" she asked.

"You can't make me happy or sad," he said.

She stopped in the middle of the corridor and regarded him solemnly.

"Very well, perhaps I can't influence your moods. But surely someone can. Don't you feel grief for your father? Does no one in Texas make your heart beat faster?"

He didn't want to discuss his father. Not now.

She might look delicate, but he had a feeling she had a temper on her. That was okay with him. He was used to fiery women. There were six McCraight women back at home who weren't wallflowers. They came out and said what they felt, and if you didn't understand, they kept talking until you did. Being the only male in a house full of women these past two years had taught him a great deal. Granted, four of his sisters were married, but they still came home a lot.

None of them, however, had given him any insight into a Scottish lass with distinctive gray eyes and a mulish set to her lips. She didn't look like she was going anywhere until he said something placating.

"My father was the finest man I've ever known,"

he said, giving her the truth and a little more emotion than he felt comfortable revealing. "I didn't know he was dead until I came home. When I found out, it was like the world stopped for a little while. I couldn't imagine anything being the same without him. And it wasn't."

There, would that be enough to get her started again?

"Where were you?"

"What?"

"You said you came home. Where were you?"

"I was at war, Elsbeth."

She didn't say anything for a moment. Finally, she spoke. "Would you like to see a portrait of your father?" she asked softly.

The question startled him.

Until now, it had been difficult to imagine that Graham had grown up in this house, that he hadn't left until he was twenty. Graham had barely been mentioned.

Granted, Connor had only arrived last night, but surely someone—Glassey, his aunt, an older servant—should have said something that called Graham to mind. Something like: *Your father liked this view best of all*, when standing before a window. Or: *There is the tree your father used to climb.*

Yet here was Elsbeth asking a simple question that flummoxed him. *Would you like to see a portrait of your father?*

He could only nod in response.

He walked with her down the corridor to the main stairs, that same sweeping staircase that reminded him of the South. She took hold of the banister with her right hand, the left holding her voluminous skirt and ascended the steps with him following.

"The portraits of the family are on the third floor," she said. "The ducal portraits are next to them." She glanced over her shoulder at him. "You'll have to sit for your portrait, of course."

He had no intention of doing any such thing, but decided not to tell her that right now. He only nodded again. Silence was the best recourse when you didn't want to explain yourself or argue. It had taken him years—and a few brawls—to learn that lesson.

Connor hesitated just before the landing, taking in the view from the stairs. Looking down he could see the four corridors that branched off the foyer, all leading to different wings of the house. Above him the snow was still obscuring the glass of the ceiling, but the windows on the back wall revealed a frozen, white world.

Elsbeth had hesitated on the landing, waiting for him. She, too, had learned the value of silence because she didn't say anything as she watched him.

Oddly enough, he felt as if Bealadair was waiting for something, that the great house was this massive Scottish monster he'd climbed inside, and that it was ready to devour him unless he said the secret word. Perhaps he should have promised allegiance, or cut himself to bleed on the carpet. Maybe the house needed proof that he was a descendent, that he was the rightful duke.

He smiled at himself, wondering where those thoughts had come from. He was probably tired from weeks of travel. Or perhaps he was feeling something despite his earlier words. Did Bealadair have the ability to pull emotion from him?

He nodded to Elsbeth and she turned, ascending the steps once more. As he followed her, he tried to marshal his thoughts. He was not given to whimsy. Nor did he believe in ghosts. The moment seemed to portend one, however. If nothing else, the shade of his father as a boy racing down the steps in violation of his tutor's rules. Or the young man standing at the door, looking upward in a final view of Bealadair before he left forever.

Did his father know in that moment that he would never return? Had he set it as a goal? Had he ever wanted to come back?

What had sent him away from Scotland?

Once, the two of them were riding a fence line and his father had stopped, his gaze on the expanse before him. Some would say that area of the XIV Ranch was nothing but desert and prairie dogs, but they didn't know where to look. Connor knew the undulations of the land itself, the unexpected green spots where a creek bubbled to the surface, the signs of deer, the hints of earlier habitation.

They'd talked about a man's destiny that day. Whether what he became was laid out by the Almighty or was strictly a man's choice.

"A man will make of himself what he wants," Graham had said. "What he believes he can be."

He looked up, realizing they'd reached the third-floor landing. Elsbeth didn't question his hesitation, simply turned and walked down the corridor, stopping in front of a set of double doors like those that led to his suite.

She opened one door and stepped aside, a set expression on her face that warned him they were about to have another battle of the doorway. He bit back his smile and stepped inside, only to be confronted with a portrait gallery of his ancestors.

The dark mahogany floorboards were so polished that he could see the reflections of the gilt frames. His boots sounded loud as he walked to the middle of the room, almost as if this was a hallowed spot, a temple of memory.

No hint of laughter reached this room. No conversation. Nothing but the ponderous passing of time, one second ticking off after another.

Solitude wasn't unknown to him. Many times he'd taken off, alone, to ride the ranch or to visit the other divisions on the ranch. He was comfortable in his own skin and didn't need diversions or company. Now, however, in this gallery, oddly lit by the gray skies visible through the high-placed windows, he was glad of Elsbeth's presence. Glad, too, that she didn't seem to feel the sudden ominous press of Bealadair or its history.

Chapter 11

Connor began at the end, at the very first Duke of Lothian and slowly walked the portraits, seeing the change in artist style, dress, and expressions of his ancestors. By the time he made it to the tenth duke they'd begun to smile, as if certain of their place in life, certain that the dukedom wasn't a plum to be snatched from their grasp if they showed any signs of levity.

The space occupied by each duke was greater, too, as wives and children were featured. His steps lagged as he walked, reluctance making it feel as if he was tromping through Guadalupe River mud.

He hesitated at the 12th Duke of Lothian.

This man was his grandfather. The woman to his left must be his grandmother. Had his father ever mentioned either of them? He couldn't remember. His mother's parents lived in Austin and visited a few times a year. Surely, as a boy, he'd questioned his father about his parents? Yet the answer, if it had been given to him, eluded him now.

This grandfather bore a vague resemblance to his father with his squared chin, thin line of lips and broad nose. The eyes were the same, brown and piercing, as if wanting to see the depths of a man's soul. His hair was silver at the temples and he'd been portrayed standing in the library Connor had seen earlier. In this painting he saw the view that had been obscured by snow: an undulating valley down to a wide and sparkling river. He paused for a moment to appreciate the scene, then glanced to his right and froze.

Here the children of his grandfather were portrayed, both sons sitting together, side by side.

"They were twins?"

"Yes," Elsbeth said, coming to stand beside him. "You didn't know?"

He shook his head, his gaze never leaving the portraits of the twin boys. They'd been pictured sitting on matching chairs, smiling at a long-haired puppy sitting on the floor between them. The dog's back was to the artist, his pose one that made Connor think the dog had been real and had alternated between looking at one boy then the other.

"I understand Gavin was born only a few minutes before your father," Elsbeth said.

He didn't want to look to his right, but his mind had already furnished what he knew he was going to see. The image of his father stared back at him from Gavin's portrait.

"When was this painted?" he asked, grateful that his voice sounded steady and without a hint of the emotion surging through him.

"About five years ago," she said.

If his voice gave nothing away, hers was the opposite. He heard the compassion in it. Or was it pity? Perhaps another time he would have refuted that emotion, but not right now. He felt unsteady and unprepared for the sight of his father's twin brother.

The man in the portrait looked exactly like his father down to the small smile playing around his lips. Graham often wore that look, especially when witnessing his five daughters. Sometimes, he and Connor would glance at each other across the room as if to say, *What are you going to do with them? They're loud. They're boisterous, and we probably don't understand everything they're saying, but we love them anyway.*

Elsbeth turned slightly and smiled at the portrait. Maybe at another time he wouldn't have understood so quickly, but he did now.

"You loved him, didn't you?"

"Yes," she said softly. "He was my best friend in the whole world. I could tell him anything and I did."

Her smile was tinged with sadness, but he was glad for it all the same. Her love for Gavin and his for Graham linked them, the knowledge of that connection right for this moment and this place.

"I'm glad you were the one to show me," he said, realizing it was the truth.

He wouldn't have been able to hide his shock from his aunt or his cousins. Now he realized he didn't have to. Yet revealing himself to her didn't disturb him as much as it probably should have.

She was Elsbeth, and that simple statement explained it all, even though he'd known her for less than a day.

"Did he ever talk about my father?" he asked.

"Yes," she said, startling him. "He often did."

She was still looking at the portrait, and when he glanced at her, she turned and smiled.

"He told me that he wrote to Graham years ago, but never received an answer. He said that he knew Graham was still alive. He would have felt it, otherwise."

If his father had ever received a letter from his brother, Graham had never said.

"Why did he leave?" he found himself asking.

Had Gavin told her? Had there been a rift between the brothers? Had his father been disappointed that his twin became the duke? He couldn't reconcile that idea with the man he'd known. His father had accomplished what few other men had in building the XIV Ranch.

Elsbeth didn't say anything for a moment and for the first time since he'd met her, the silence wasn't comfortable. He wanted to draw back the question or reframe it. Or simply turn and walk away. He would go and visit with Glassey once again, do what he could to expedite finding a buyer for Bealadair and the land.

He didn't need to know the reason why Graham had created his own dynasty in America.

But the war had taught him the true meaning of courage: to stand your ground even when everything in you was fighting to flee.

He didn't move and he didn't speak.

She took a few steps to the right, looking at a small portrait he hadn't seen. This one was half the size of Gavin's and positioned slightly lower than his.

The woman bore a slight resemblance to Elsbeth,

but he couldn't say why he thought that. They didn't look like each other. The woman had brown hair instead of black and her eyes were a soft shade of blue.

Perhaps it was something about her pose, seated and facing the artist, her hands folded calmly on her lap, her smile causing the corners of her eyes to crinkle. Perhaps it was her air of studied calm or something more, a sense of peace he got when looking at her.

"This is Marie. She was Gavin's first wife and Lara's mother."

He didn't say anything, waiting.

"She died in childbirth."

She glanced over at him and he returned her look.

"A story as old as time itself, Gavin said. Two men in love with one woman. In the end, she chose Gavin. He said your father left Scotland shortly before they were married. The last time he heard from him was when he let Graham know that Marie had died."

He found himself nodding again.

"You were going to show me the oldest wing," he said, determined to get back on an even keel.

The reason why his father had left Scotland forty years ago didn't matter in the end. The lingering sadness of Elsbeth's words shouldn't affect him. Nor should he feel this discordance, trying to equate the young man he imagined with the strong, able father of his memory.

Elsbeth nodded, turning and leading him back to the stairs. He followed, wondering if Graham had felt any emptiness in his life. Had he ever thought of Marie? Had he felt envious of his brother, the duke?

Not because of his title, but because Gavin had married the woman he loved.

He would never know and maybe that was the source of his discomfort.

THE DISCOVERY THAT his father had been Gavin's twin had evidently shocked Connor. How odd that he'd never known. Would it be helpful to tell him how many times Gavin wished that their estrangement had ended? Especially toward the last, when he'd grown weaker and weaker. He'd talked about Marie, then, and how much he'd loved her.

"She had a voice like bells," he said one day. "I used to sit and ask her to speak, simply because I loved the sound of her voice so much." He'd smiled, then. "She laughed at me, but I didn't mind. I can hear the sound of her laughter even now."

He had brought her to tears more than once with his words.

She wanted to know about Graham's life in America. Why had he decided to go to Texas? Had he been happy? Had he loved Connor's mother or was she only a replacement for Marie?

None of those questions would be proper, however.

"I like that you're not a chatterbox," he suddenly said.

"You say the strangest things, Your Grace. Connor."

"I've been told that I'm too direct. Do you think so?"

Rather than answer that question, she asked one of her own.

"Who said that to you?"

"One of my sisters," he admitted.

"You have five, Mr. Glassey said."

He nodded. "Alison, Barbara, Constance, Dorothy, and Eustace."

"They have alphabetical names," she said, smiling. "Why doesn't your name begin with an *F*? Or with an *A* as the only boy?"

"My father put his foot down," he said. "I understand Connor is a McCraight name."

"It is. Two of the previous dukes were named Connor."

By the time they reached the old wing, Elsbeth was wishing she hadn't taken him to the portrait gallery. Connor McCraight had changed from a charming, fascinating man to a truculent one. He didn't speak. He only nodded when she showed him the armament the McCraights had carried into battle hundreds of years ago. The colorful rendition of the clan badge, mounted over the massive fireplace, didn't seem to interest him. Nor did the various artifacts lovingly and carefully restored over hundreds of years.

Gavin had been most proud of the display case he'd had made for the Bible belonging to the third Duchess of Lothian. A devout and religious woman, it was rumored that she was responsible for the clan motto: God guides our endeavors.

He didn't say anything to that, either.

"Do you know anything about the McCraight clan?"

At that, he turned and faced her directly. She was an inch from apologizing for the presumptuous nature of her question and its curiosity. Who was she to want to know such things?

"No," he said, his gaze direct and unflinching. "I thought I knew something about the clan history in Scotland, but I realize I don't know anything about my own heritage. At least not that from Scotland. In Texas, you don't have to ask a man about his past. If he wants to tell you, he will. If he doesn't, you just simply forget about it."

She tried to reconcile the image of Graham with his brother. Had the younger twin simply walked away from Scotland, erasing everything about his heritage? It sounded like it.

"The laird is responsible for the clan's well-being. In turn, the clan is responsible for supporting the laird, granting him fealty and loyalty. One doesn't exist without the other."

"That really doesn't have anything to do with me," he said. "I'm an American. I was born there. Even more important, I'm a Texan. My father might have grown up here, but I didn't."

Nor would he feel any kind of kinship to the family who was waiting, almost breathlessly, for him to indicate by word or deed what their future might be.

It wasn't, after all, her task to educate him. Yet she could almost hear Gavin whispering in her ear. She turned and walked to a bench located some distance away. She heard Connor's boots on the stone floor behind her.

This particular section of Bealadair was a long rectangular structure constructed of stone two stories high. The rest of Bealadair had been added on to this original part of the house. Although it was cool and pleasant in the summer months it was difficult to keep warm in winter. The windows always seemed to have a draft no matter how many times the glaziers worked to seal them. Here, the air was chilled, the fireplace not normally lit. Few people ventured to the old wing in the depths of winter.

A house was only a structure unless the people within warmed it with emotion, laughter, and conversation—the daily business of living. No one warmed this place.

He came and sat beside her. For five minutes, perhaps more, they sat together silently. Finally, Connor leaned forward, his elbows on his knees, his hands clasped together, looking out at the display cases and framed artifacts.

"Mr. Glassey said you came here as an orphan."

"When I was eight," she said.

"What happened?"

With anyone else she would probably have demurred or changed the subject. She strangely wanted to tell him her story.

"My parents and I were traveling somewhere. I don't know where and I can't remember why. Only that I was excited to be on a train again."

She shook her head, not telling him how many times she had tried to unearth the memory. Or how many times she had buried it on purpose.

"The train was on a bridge and the bridge collapsed. All I can remember after that is darkness and screaming. I felt this sense of separation." She stared off into the distance. "I've never been able to explain that to anybody, but it's as if I knew that my parents had died, that they'd left me alone." She shook her head. "The next thing I knew I was on a cot along with hundreds of other people. I was freezing and shaking. I couldn't stop shaking. Someone kept asking me my name and I kept telling them. I wanted my mother and father, but that's the one thing they couldn't give me."

She took a deep breath. When he remained silent, she kept talking.

"I don't remember how many days passed, but all of a sudden there were people there, then a man. Everyone seemed very impressed by him. But all I can remember is that he told me he was my father's friend."

She could remember that moment like it was yesterday. Gavin had bent down and looked directly in her face.

"'I know you are hurting, my dear child, and I understand. William was my friend and I will miss him as well.' He told me that he had agreed that if anything happened to my parents, he would be responsible for me. I don't remember having any say in the matter, but the next thing I knew, I was here at Bealadair."

In the past minute, he'd turned and was looking at her. She glanced in his direction and then away.

"I'd gone from not having anyone to having a family and a home." She glanced at him again. "It's the same for you. I understand if you feel like you don't belong. But that's not true. The family needs you. The clan needs you."

"I'm not a Scot," he said. "This isn't my country. This isn't my land."

He looked around him, his gaze finally returning to her.

"You aren't staying, are you?" she asked.

He didn't fit here. Nor did he seem to want to. This was his ancestral home, but he rejected it with every step, every breath, every glance.

She knew they were in peril, the three girls she had considered almost sisters and Gavin's wife. She felt as if she owed it to Gavin, if no one else, to try to protect them. Not for their sake, but for his, because of all the kindnesses he had extended to her.

"As soon as I can sell Bealadair, I'm leaving. Maybe my uncle wouldn't understand, but my father would. A man needs to create his own destiny, not depend on those who came before him."

She had a feeling that rugged individualism had probably marked the very first Duke of Lothian. He, too, had carved his destiny, but in Scotland not Texas.

"Thanks for the tour," he said, standing. "I won't take up any more of your time. There's no need."

She watched as he crossed the floor, the sound of his boots on the stones sounding like heartbeats.

She gripped the material of her skirt, realized what she was doing and released it, smoothing the wrinkles out with her fingers. She forced herself to remain seated until she calmed, until her pulse was once more normal, and she could breathe easily.

The family was not destitute. Gavin had gifted them each with enough funds to live a modest life. But when had the McCraights ever lived modestly?

Money had never been an object at Bealadair. It wasn't that anyone ever talked about it. Such things were considered crass. Jewelry was commissioned from the finest London firms. Felix had gunsmiths at his beck and call. Anise loved shoes and had standing orders for the newest fashions to be sent to her. Muira loved confections and received monthly orders from Edinburgh.

The only time there was an attempt at economy was once a quarter when the duchess was forced to look over the household expenditures. Those times passed quickly. All too often everyone was back to buying what they wanted.

Now the future was there before them, written out for all of them to see. There would be no more jewelry, shoes, chocolates, or guns. Anise would not have another season and Muira would not have her first. As for the duchess? She would not be able to rule like a queen. And, if Connor was serious about selling Bealadair, Rhona wouldn't even be able to live at the Dower House.

Connor had brought disaster with him, just as she had feared. Someone needed to tell the duchess, and she fervently prayed it would be Mr. Glassey.

She wasn't brave enough for that task.

Chapter 12

Connor hadn't seen Sam since the night before. Sam wasn't known for getting up with the dawn, but he should have been up and about by now. Connor knocked on the door of the room Sam was occupying, only for his knock to go unanswered.

"Begging your pardon, Your Grace," a voice said.

He turned to find a short maid with curly red hair bobbing a curtsy at him. That's another thing he didn't think he would ever get accustomed to, people bowing and scraping in front of him.

"I believe Mr. Kirby is taking lunch, Your Grace. He went down with the rest of the family a few minutes ago."

He nodded and thanked her.

"Would you like me to show you the way, Your Grace?"

"Thank you, no."

He wasn't in the mood for the rest of his new-found family. He was out of sorts and irritated and he knew why, but the knowledge didn't matter. It didn't make him any less angry or confused.

He didn't want to be here. He didn't want to be here more than at any time since he left Texas. He felt sick to his stomach, the kind of sickness that has nothing to do with physical symptoms and everything to do with one idea colliding against another.

In the last months of the war he'd come to grips with the realization that he didn't want to be where he was. It had nothing to do with cowardice or courage and everything to do with the fact that he didn't believe in the cause for which he was fighting. He'd fought for the South because Texas was part of the Confederacy. Yet everything in him believed in keeping the Union together.

He was feeling the same conflict right now.

He couldn't imagine walking away from his home and never seeing family or friends again. Or having a twin yet turning his back on the man for forty years. He couldn't understand why Graham had never mentioned the home his ancestors had built. Or why he'd never commented on the history or the heritage about which they'd evidently felt great pride.

The man he'd always respected was fading, to be replaced by a cipher, a shadowy figure he realized he might never have truly known.

He thought about changing his mind and going down to the dining room again, but the idea of being around his aunt and his cousins kept him from following through with that thought. He didn't feel like being companionable at the moment.

Instead, he made his way to the duke's suite again, walking into the sitting room with its blue-and-gray upholstery, then to the small library with its oversized desk. The desk sat out in the middle of the room so that anyone sitting at it would have his back to the window. It struck Connor as a deliberate act, one he didn't understand.

If he'd designed this room, he would have turned the desk around, faced the view and Bealadair land.

Graham had taught him pride and stewardship of his heritage. Even though Sam had been his partner, over the years, he'd sold his half—in parcels—back to Graham. The purchase had made the McCraights land rich but cash poor.

His inheritance from his uncle, plus selling Bealadair, would provide for the future of the XIV Ranch and the American McCraights.

Of course, the only person who knew that was Sam. He hadn't even confided that information to Glassey. The less the solicitor knew the better. Otherwise he had a feeling that everything he told the man would go straight to the duchess.

He sat on the chair behind the desk, then turned it so he could put his boots up on the windowsill and survey the view. He had to admit that the scenery of the hills and rolling grass was pretty even buried under snow. But it didn't matter if it was the most beautiful place on earth. In a contest between Bealadair and the ranch, the ranch would always win. His father was buried there. His mother was there and not far away his five sisters, four of them married with their own families.

He'd wanted to go home ever since he left Texas, a fact that he didn't try to hide from Sam, who occasionally teased him about it.

"Somebody would think that you've never been outside of Texas," Sam said.

He'd gone to college and had gone to war. The

former had been a hell of a lot easier than the latter. Yet he'd been one of the lucky ones. He'd come home with all his limbs as well as his mind. He wasn't like those poor souls he'd met who cringed at any loud sounds. He'd seen one man who sat in the corner of the medical tent rocking back and forth with his arms over his head, his eyes closed tight as if he were hiding in a small dark place in his soul. He wasn't like that man, but he understood the need to go away for a little while, to escape.

Maybe that's why he'd come to Scotland, to give himself a change of scenery. Or maybe it had simply been curiosity that brought him here, wanting to know about the young man his father had been. Only to be given a story that was the antithesis of the man he'd come to know.

In the past decade, he'd been away from his family more than with them, but he missed them all now. The way his mother could take one look at his face and decipher what he was feeling. How his sisters would arrive, one by one, to check on him and offer some older sister advice even if he didn't solicit it. Especially if he didn't solicit it.

What would they think of Scotland? Or of the Scottish McCraights? Dorothy, the most blunt spoken of his sisters, would have planted her fists on her hips, tilted her head a little, and announced her opinion of the duchess: *She's a priss, isn't she, Connor?*

Alison, the oldest, would have made a face and whispered that she mustn't say things like that. Eustace, the sister closest in age to him, would have simply smiled and shaken her head. Barbara would have reported Dorothy to their mother as if they

weren't all grown women, mothers of his six nieces
and nephews. Constance, heavy with child and due
to give birth any day now, would have ignored all of
them, waddled to a chair, and demanded to know
when he was going to get married.

What would she have thought of Elsbeth? She
might have admired her industriousness, the fact
that she had seen a need and fulfilled it. He suspected
that Bealadair ran smoothly all because of her.

His mother would have wanted to know about
Elsbeth's family. Her real family, not the group of
people with whom she lived. It disturbed him that
his cousins and aunts weren't kinder. Perhaps he
misjudged them. Were they simply more formal in
his presence because he was a stranger? Or did they
treat Elsbeth like a servant?

He needed to meet with the real housekeeper.
Was Mrs. Ferguson genuinely unable to work? Or
was she just taking advantage of Elsbeth's kindness?

If he was going to leave as quickly as he'd come,
he had a great deal to accomplish in a very little
time. He'd set himself the goal of going home in
a month. That would give Glassey time enough to
find a buyer for the house. Perhaps even one of the
wealthy New Yorkers he and Sam had met on
the ship would be interested. They could brag that
they'd purchased a duke's home in Scotland.

Today he would have to speak to his aunt. What
he'd seen of her made him suspect that she was one
of those people who only saw things from the outside of a person. What they wore, how they spoke,
how much prosperity their appearance revealed. She
would probably overlook someone she considered

beneath her, never figuring out that the outside can always be changed, but it was the inside that truly mattered.

Were his cousins from the same cloth? Only Muira had struck him as the type of person he'd like to get to know.

And Elsbeth, of course. The beautiful housekeeper whose smile lit something up inside him.

Of all the people at Bealadair, he wanted to get to know her the best.

ELSBETH HAD CARED for Mr. Glassey like any guest who arrived at Bealadair. She had seen to his dietary restrictions, ensured that the laundress had instructions as to his clothing, had made notice of his tastes in wine and food, including his dislike of any kind of fish. She always made sure that the same room was kept ready for him when he visited them from Inverness.

Mr. Glassey, in turn, had always greeted her by name. Their relationship was, if she had to define it for anyone, that of cordial strangers.

This afternoon, however, she was going against the rules. She waited until lunch was finished and Mr. Glassey made his appearance outside the dining room. Since it wouldn't be proper to knock on his door, she was going to waylay him, take him into the anteroom set aside for the servants, and ask him if what she'd been told was the truth.

Everything went according to her plan. The surprised man allowed her to grip his elbow and guide him into the small space.

"I apologize, Mr. Glassey," she said to the solicitor. "But His Grace has just told me something disturbing. Is it true that he plans to sell Bealadair?"

Before the solicitor could speak, she added, "He cannot sell Bealadair, can he? It's entailed, isn't it? It must pass to the next heir."

"I wasn't aware that His Grace had made his plans known," Mr. Glassey said, his voice icy. "I wish he'd informed me first."

"The duchess doesn't know yet," she said. "I haven't told her, Mr. Glassey, and I don't think the duke has, either."

Mr. Glassey nodded, his expression easing.

"I'm relieved, Miss Carew. That will give me time to prepare Her Grace."

"Then he can do it," she said, feeling her stomach drop.

Was this what fainting felt like? She was not going to do something so out of character now, but she did wish there was a chair nearby.

Mr. Glassey nodded. "Technically, the only entailed property is the old castle," he said. "And a few acres surrounding it. His Grace, however, was ever mindful of his brother and their estrangement. He saw fit to give Bealadair and the land to him. No one knew, of course, that Graham had already died by the time His Grace passed."

"Has the new duke always planned to sell Bealadair? From the very beginning?"

The solicitor shook his head. "I have no idea, Miss Carew. The duke does not confide in me. I can tell you this. He was none too happy to learn about his ascension to the title. That surprised me originally, but it shouldn't have. As I have come to know His Grace, he has no love for what he calls *airs*. He honestly believes that becoming the 14th Duke of Lothian is an impediment rather than an honor."

From what she'd learned of Connor, she couldn't help but agree.

What a fool she was for feeling anything like disappointment. She hadn't known Connor McCraight a few days earlier. His absence wouldn't affect her life. He would simply be a fascinating man she'd once met, a Texan who'd carried his saddle halfway around the world, but that was all. Nothing more.

"Will you be telling her soon?" she asked.

It wouldn't do for someone else to tell the duchess of Connor's plans.

"I am thinking that it should be very soon," Mr. Glassey said.

They shared a glance. She knew exactly what the reluctance in his gaze meant and commiserated with the man. He didn't want to have to tell the Duchess of Lothian that she and her family were about to be evicted from Bealadair.

"THAT AUNT OF yours, she's something," Sam said, entering the small library. He hadn't knocked, but Connor wasn't surprised. Sam sometimes treated him as if he were the youngest puppy in a litter and he were the older, wiser dog.

"She gets you with that way of hers."

"What way is that?" Connor asked, leaning back in his chair.

Sam shook his head. "Could be her smile. She's

got the prettiest mouth. Or her eyes. Beautiful brown eyes, all big and warm."

Connor studied the other man. Sam had a knack of singling out a female wherever he was. You could almost see him throw a rope over her head and cull her from the herd.

"She doesn't seem your type," Connor said.

Sam arranged himself on the corner of the desk, folded his arms, and stared out the window behind Connor.

"I wasn't aware that I had a type," Sam said.

That was different. Whenever he'd commented on one of Sam's women in the past, he'd been met with amusement, not a tight-lipped response.

Was it because his aunt was a duchess? He never thought that Sam would give a flying flip for a title.

"She just doesn't seem like someone who would tolerate a backward American," Connor said.

"Who are you calling backward, boy?" Sam asked with a smile. "I can wine and dine with the best of them. I have lots of charm when I need to use it."

"Did you know?" he asked, turning the conversation away from Sam's attraction to his aunt. "About my father being a twin?"

Sam's gaze moved from the view to Connor's face.

"He might have mentioned it once or twice."

"Why didn't he mention it to me?"

"Don't think it was important to him."

"Or the reason he left Scotland? Did he tell you that?"

"By the time I met your father he'd already been in America a few years. I wasn't interested in his past. Neither was he. Why are you?"

"The past is reaching out and biting me, Sam, and has been since I set foot in this place. I'd think you'd be smart enough to figure that out."

Sam didn't say anything else, but then Connor didn't expect him to. Sam was one of those men who didn't care what other people thought of him. If they liked him, he was fine with that. If they despised him, he was fine with that, too. He rarely explained himself—the only occasion Connor could remember was when Sam and his father had been late getting home from Austin and had to face his mother's anxiety and ultimate irritation. The fact that his father stood by his horse for several minutes, his head resting on the saddle, was a dead giveaway. Graham McCraight was, on the only occasion Connor could remember, stinking drunk.

"We just got a little carried away, Linda," Sam had said. "He's fine."

"And why did you get a little carried away, Sam Kirby?"

Connor had recognized that tone in his mother's voice and wanted to warn Sam that he was in deep trouble. Sam evidently knew it, too, because he bowed his head, staring at his hat in his hands and uttered the closest Connor had ever heard to an apology from the man.

"My fault, Linda. All my fault."

His mother had eventually forgiven Sam, especially since the man had done everything he could to ease her burden after Graham died.

"I think what you want to know is if he regretted his decisions," Sam said. "Did he want to redo any of it?"

Connor didn't answer, but maybe Sam was right.

"He didn't," Sam said. "He was damn happy with his life, with Linda, with you and the girls. He was proud that he was giving you something that would live on." He looked around the room. "Maybe like this place."

"Then why'd he kill himself, Sam?"

Sam didn't say anything, maybe to give himself time for the shock to wear off. He looked away, focusing on the view once more, probably visually trailing the footprints of the fox Connor had seen earlier.

"Did you think I couldn't figure it out?" Connor asked. "My father taught me everything he knew about guns, Sam, and that was plenty. I knew from the story you told that it couldn't have been an accident. It had to have been deliberate."

"You weren't there. You were off playing soldier."

He didn't say a word, merely continued to look at Sam.

According to the story he'd learned on coming home, the two men had spent the night in one of the line shacks along the northern property. The night had been a cold one, the small building erected for times like that. Why they'd been riding the line, he didn't know.

Graham had been sitting at the table, cleaning his pistol, an action that wouldn't have been necessary unless he'd shot it during the day. Sam had gone outside to use the necessary, heard the gunshot, and returned to find Graham dead.

The facts hadn't added up.

"Why didn't you say something before now?" Sam said.

"I don't know. Maybe I wanted to believe that it was an accident. Maybe I didn't want to accept the truth."

"I don't know what happened for sure," Sam said, leaving the desk to go and stand in front of the window. "What I told you was the truth." A moment later, he added, "I had my suspicions, but that's all they were. I didn't think it would help your mother or your sisters any to tell them what I thought."

Connor let the silence stretch between them.

"Why?" he finally asked. "There must have been a reason."

"All I know is that one day he visited his doctor in Austin," Sam said. "He got some bad news." Sam turned his head, his gaze meeting Connor's. "If I took a guess I'd say he chose his own death. He didn't want to be a burden to your mother."

"That wasn't his choice."

"Hell it wasn't. He made his own way through life, Connor, and so do you. The two of you create your own path. God help anyone who stands between you and what you want."

"I'll take that as a compliment."

Sam turned back to the window. "Your father was also difficult to get to know. He didn't let many people get close to him."

That wasn't, as Connor saw it, a bad trait to have.

"You don't think he would have wanted me to come to Scotland, do you?" he asked.

"Hell, yes, he would have wanted you to come," Sam said, coming back to the desk. "I think he would have wanted to know what you thought of the place."

Connor smiled. "I think he'd have been more interested in what you thought of my aunt."

Sam's answer was a grin.

"Does my mother know?"

Sam turned his head slowly and looked at him. He got the impression that the older man was stalling for time again.

"About what?" Sam finally asked.

"About the reason he left Scotland. And don't tell me you weren't interested in his past. That tale might satisfy some people, but I know you, Sam."

The man could be damned nosy. Sam had been adopted by the American McCraights and acted the part of doting uncle. He'd interrogated Connor's younger sisters about the suitors who'd arrived to call on them, gave marital advice to the older girls and, when he was at the ranch, inserted himself into any problems arising between the men.

Sam didn't say anything for a minute. He perched himself on the corner of the desk again and stared out at the view.

"She does," he said. "But it never mattered to her. Any more than her first love mattered to your father."

That was a surprise.

Sam glanced at him and smiled. "Most people think that everyone's life begins when they're born. They never look back or around them. Your mother had a sweetheart before she met your father, but the man died of influenza before they could be married. When Linda met Graham, it was like the two of them found each other. They were friends who fell in love, Connor. If they thought of the past it was with kindness, not longing."

Connor nodded, grateful that he only had to keep one secret from his mother. Or perhaps she already knew the truth about his father's death. He wouldn't be surprised. Linda McCraight was one of the smartest women he knew.

"Better get a move on," Sam said, standing and moving toward the door. "You'll be late for dinner."

He left the library, no doubt in a hurry to see the duchess again.

That was a development Connor hadn't anticipated. He couldn't help but wonder what his mother would have thought about Rhona. He had a feeling she would have had no time for Rhona, but would probably like Elsbeth.

The thought of seeing Elsbeth again propelled him out of his chair to prepare for dinner.

Chapter 13

Elsbeth was late for dinner, but it couldn't be helped. There had been a near disaster in the laundry, and she'd assisted the head laundress in repairing the lace on the duchess's favorite blouse.

Normally, her maid would have overseen Rhona's wardrobe, but Adelaide had been suffering from a vile cold in the past week. Rhona disliked illness of any sort and had banished the woman to her room on the third floor until she was well. At least Adelaide was able to rest and the family was spared Her Grace's complaints about servants who were inconsiderate enough to be sick around her.

Thankfully, Mr. Barton had recovered from his gout and was able to carry on his duties.

Unfortunately, however, Adelaide's temporary replacement was a girl who had no training as a lady's maid. Consequently, Elsbeth was called in almost daily to soothe the girl's fears and tears.

While the family dining room was small, almost intimate, the same could not be said for the Black Dining Room, named for its most distinctive feature: a black-and-gold silk wall covering that made the room feel like a black box to Elsbeth.

It was, indeed, a striking chamber, but one so over-powering that she always took a deep breath before entering. Giant gold emblems she suspected were of French design were stamped on the black silk every few feet or so. The floor-to-ceiling curtains were also black, blending in so well that you didn't even see the windows at the far end of the rectangular room.

Bealadair's public rooms were oversized, almost as if they had been designed for the entire clan and this room was no exception. The dining room was probably twice the size it needed to be and sufficiently far away from the kitchen that the servants nearly had to race through the corridors in order to deliver the food before it got cold.

A dark mahogany-and-brass inlaid neoclassical table stretched the length of the room and was surrounded by twenty-four thickly padded chairs upholstered in black and gold. The three brass chandeliers were lit but couldn't offset the effect of all that black. The light seemed to be swallowed up and to disappear.

Tonight, in honor of the duke's first official dinner at Bealadair, the duchess had requested a number of dishes that were not normally served. At least a dozen brass chafing dishes sat on one of the sideboards, the smells emerging from them making her stomach growl. Curry, that was one of the odors. Venison as well.

The rest of the family was already seated, and her late arrival earned her a frown from the duchess and a smile from Connor. He was seated in the position of honor, Gavin's place at the head of the table.

How odd to see someone there when it had been

kept vacant for months. Felix had sat there once, but the glance the duchess had given him had been enough to singe his ears. He'd never made that mistake again.

Elsbeth slid into her usual place, a chair near the end of the table. When the footman came to stand at her left, she nodded and he ladled soup into the bowl on her plate.

Connor had stopped eating his soup before half of it was done. Didn't he like the chowder Addy had made?

The footman gathered up his bowl, and Connor thanked him, something he wasn't supposed to do. How many lectures had she endured from Rhona? The servants were never to be thanked. One didn't notice the servants.

Nor did he seem very impressed with the sweet-breads and she couldn't blame him. But he had smiled when haggis was served, adding a comment that his father had told him about it. At least he'd eaten some of that.

That was the last thing he'd said. He'd been content to remain silent for most of the meal, only answering questions in monosyllables. She just wished Felix, who had a penchant for talking about himself, would emulate Connor's behavior.

What a pity Felix had no friends at Bealadair. The only person he was remotely polite to was his wife. Lara looked at Felix as if he were the most wonderful man on earth, not noticing that few people could tolerate her husband.

Did the duchess know that Elsbeth had given Connor an abbreviated tour of the house? A quick shake of Muira's head indicated that the subject hadn't been addressed.

As if the duchess had heard her thoughts, Rhona smiled brightly at Connor and said, "What did you think of Bealadair?"

"I've seen the elephant."

The duchess looked slightly taken aback. Elsbeth wondered if it was because of Connor's comment or the fact that he hadn't appended a *Your Grace* to his answer. Rhona was a stickler for formality.

She wouldn't have been at all surprised if Connor called the duchess *Aunt*. She could just imagine what would happen, then. Rhona would draw herself up, her face stiff, and address Connor with ice in her voice.

No one had a frozen tone like the Duchess of Lothian.

"What a pity the weather is so bad," Rhona said, her equanimity evidently restored again. "We could have shown you just a portion of the acreage that belongs to Bealadair."

"Two hundred eighty thousand acres, to be precise," Felix said, sounding as officious as if he, himself, had made a gift of the land to Connor.

"Our family is one of the largest landholders in Scotland," Lara said, her tone mimicking her husband's. As if it was their bequest to Connor.

"It's not a bad size," he said.

"I beg your pardon?" Felix said.

"It's not a bad size," Connor repeated. "It's not as big as the XIV Ranch, but it's a good size."

"I suppose this ranch of yours is so much bigger," Felix said, derision coating every syllable.

Connor didn't comment, merely put down his wineglass, sat back in his chair, and regarded Felix almost as if he were a child misbehaving at the dinner table.

"The XIV Ranch is one of the largest in Texas," Mr. Kirby said before Connor could speak. "If not the world. It's over two million acres."

No one said anything for such a long time that Elsbeth knew she would forever recall this occasion when the McCraights were struck dumb with disbelief.

The duchess turned to Mr. Kirby, her face blank of any expression.

"Certainly you're mistaken," she said. "Two million acres? How is that possible?"

"A little over two million acres," Connor said. "More than two hundred miles. It takes a number of days to ride from one side of the ranch to the other."

Elsbeth sat back in her chair. Of course nothing at Bealadair had impressed him. She couldn't even conceive of two million acres.

What could Scotland possibly offer him? His ancestry, the history of his forbearers, except that hadn't seemed to impress him, either. What would cause him to be glad he'd come to Scotland? Would anything?

"I've heard that you Texans are given to exaggeration," Felix said.

Felix had just made a grave error. Surely everyone at the dinner table could figure that out just by looking at Connor's face. His expression had smoothed, but there was fire in his eyes.

Didn't Felix have any concept of self-defense?

Didn't he realize that Connor's expression was, if not murderous, then certainly threatening?

"I'm certain Felix did not mean to make that sound like an insult," Elsbeth said.

Not one person took up the refrain.

She looked across the table and met Mr. Kirby's eyes. He seemed strangely amused. Perhaps he had never seen anyone challenge Connor quite like Felix was doing at the moment.

She didn't know anything about Texas. Was it an unruly place where a man needed to protect himself?

Dear heavens, did he have a gun?

To her horror, Felix evidently had the same thought.

"I suppose you can hit a bull's-eye while balancing your rifle over your shoulder and not even looking at it. Is that correct?"

One of Connor's eyebrows inched upward, but he still didn't say anything.

Mr. Kirby, however, spoke into the silence. "Connor is an excellent shot, Mr. Gillespie."

Only that. No challenge, no taunting of the other man. Felix must've heard something in Mr. Kirby's words that no one else did.

Felix glanced from the older man back to Connor.

"Would you care to have a match, Your Grace?"

The worst thing about that question was not that he was actually challenging Connor to a shooting contest. No, Felix had to inject derision into the way he said *Your Grace*. As if he knew how much Connor disliked being addressed in that fashion. It was almost as if he were saying, *You don't deserve the title, you ignorant American.*

She sent a quick look to Mr. Kirby, but he wasn't looking at her. His attention was on Felix.

"I didn't bring my guns with me," Connor said.

Guns?

"I'd be happy to lend you one of my rifles," Felix was saying.

Elsbeth glanced toward Lara, but she wasn't looking at her husband. Instead, she was smiling down at her plate.

Did she think that Felix shaming the new duke would end well? There was no question that Felix was the better shot. The man practiced hours every day. Crates of ammunition arrived at Bealadair every week. When he wasn't telling someone what a good shot he was, he was out proving it. She couldn't walk along the edge of the forest without seeing a tree riddled with Felix's bullets.

"There's no need for His Grace to prove his marksmanship, Felix," she said.

Connor turned his head slowly until his attention was directed solely on her. For a moment, she thought there was something in his eyes that surely wasn't there: a warmth, an understanding of her fear. In an instant it was gone, leaving her to wonder if it had only been her imagination.

"It's all right, Elsbeth," he said. "If Mr. Gillespie feels the need to display his ability, I've no objection to giving him a chance. If he wants to make a fool of himself, that's on him."

She bit back her moan with some difficulty, certain that she was witnessing the beginning of a terrible tragedy. And that was before anyone knew Connor was selling Bealadair.

RATHER THAN FOLLOW the family into the parlor, Elsbeth murmured some excuse about having to talk to Addy and escaped from the dining room.

Instead of heading toward the kitchen, however, she made her way to the fourth floor, knocking on Mrs. Ferguson's door as she did every evening. When she heard the housekeeper's voice, she pushed open the door, the odor of camphor reaching out to surround her.

She wasn't surprised to see Molly there, the upstairs maid tucking in a few heated bricks around Mrs. Ferguson's hips as she sat in her rocking chair.

The older woman had always been like a surrogate mother to the girls under her charge. Molly, like several of the maids, had chosen to go into service rather than take a factory job. Since the staff numbered over a hundred people and the house was so large, Bealadair was like its own village.

All in all, she thought the staff was happy here. What would happen to them when Bealadair was sold?

Elsbeth greeted Molly before crossing the room to close the curtains. She held out her hand, testing the seal around the window, pleased when she didn't feel any drafts. The room was, she was grateful to see, warm and comfortable despite the frigid night. The air was clear and crisp, stars blinking at her from a midnight sky.

She closed the curtains and took a chair beside the fire, all three of them chatting before Molly left.

Once they were alone, Mrs. Ferguson extended her hands toward the fire. The winter months had been difficult for her, and it seemed as if Elsbeth could see the nodules grow larger on the other woman's fingers every day.

Mrs. Ferguson's face was moon shaped, her cheeks plump and her lips full. Her body, however, didn't seem to match. She was tall and thin, with bony shoulders and sharp elbows. Her brown eyes were expressive and could go from approval to censure in an instant, as easily as they could from irritation to amusement.

She was a favorite of the staff and when they could, almost every one of them took time during the week to come and visit her. Even the major-domo, Mr. Barton, unbent enough to call from time to time.

Elsbeth hadn't expected the duke to visit, however. When the housekeeper announced that he had come to her suite, she simply stared at the older woman.

"He came to see me, he said, to make sure there was nothing I needed." Mrs. Ferguson smiled. "A very handsome man, is he not?"

Elsbeth nodded.

"He is very . . ." Mrs. Ferguson's voice trailed off, then resumed a few seconds later. "Not overpowering, exactly, but there's something about him. You would never miss that he came into a room."

"No," Elsbeth said. "You would not."

"How do you find him?"

She'd never lied to Mrs. Ferguson. Next to Gavin, she was probably more honest with the housekeeper than with anyone else at Bealadair. As much as she liked Muira, Elsbeth was hesitant to be too frank with her. Muira often used information as a weapon or a way to protect herself from her sisters' caustic words.

"Intriguing," she said.

Mrs. Ferguson sighed. "I found him the same. He certainly reminds a woman that she's female."

The comment so surprised Elsbeth that she studied the housekeeper. The woman's cheeks were pink and her eyes sparkling. She hadn't looked so well in weeks.

The duke had evidently made a friend.

"Did he say anything else?" Elsbeth asked. Had Connor told Mrs. Ferguson of his plans to sell Bealadair?

"He asked about my health and told me that they used something in Texas on their horses that might prove to be beneficial to my arthritis."

The housekeeper's brown eyes were alight with amusement.

"Can you imagine? But he's going to try to find the ingredients to—as he said—stir up a batch to see if it would work."

"That's very kind of him."

And exceedingly strange. However, Elsbeth had the feeling that she would be thinking that often, or as long as the duke remained in Scotland.

They sat in silence for a moment, Elsbeth remembering the look on Connor's face as he gazed at the portraits.

"The duke didn't know that Gavin and Graham were twins," she said. "Evidently, his father never told him."

Mrs. Ferguson stuck her gloved hands beneath the blanket on her lap. Her hands pained her the worst in the winter months.

"Has he any siblings?"

Elsbeth nodded. "Five sisters," she said, wishing she could remember their names.

"The McCraights always have produced more girls than boys. Has he any children of his own?"

"He isn't married," Elsbeth said. "Nor did he mention planning on marrying."

She told the housekeeper about the Texas saddle, Connor's comments about his cattle, and his insistence that she call him by his first name.

"What does Her Grace say?" Mrs. Ferguson asked, her eyes twinkling.

They both knew that the duchess was a stickler for propriety, forever lecturing Elsbeth on one thing or another. It was as if the woman, having agreed to take Elsbeth in when she was eight, thought she was a foundling, someone who'd never been reared with any kind of rules or proper manners.

Over the years Elsbeth had developed a way of half listening to Rhona at the same time she appeared to be intent on the duchess's criticism. It was the only way she could tolerate the other woman's constant efforts to change her. Nothing she ever did was proper enough. That was made abundantly clear only a few years after moving to Bealadair.

Thank heavens for Gavin. If she never felt a mother's love from the duchess, at least she had a father figure.

From what Connor said, he had the same respect for his father.

Would she feel betrayed if she discovered Gavin had hid information from her? Perhaps she would have. Or would she have just been curious as to the reason why?

"She doesn't know, even though she did look a little surprised when His Grace referred to me by my first name." She'd been waiting for the duchess to ask her about that, which was just one of the reasons she had escaped to Mrs. Ferguson's room.

She proceeded to tell the other woman what she'd learned at dinner. The housekeeper looked as stunned as she'd felt about the size of the XIV Ranch. When she came to Felix's challenge, Mrs. Ferguson shook her head.

"He thinks he's big, but a wee coat fits him," the housekeeper said.

Elsbeth nodded.

"Surely they won't go through with it?"

"I can almost guarantee you that the contest will take place," Elsbeth said.

There'd been a look in Connor's eyes, one that warned her he didn't take well to being challenged by Felix. Not because he was the Duke of Lothian, but because he was Connor McCraight. Or maybe even because he was an American. Or a Texan.

"Felix is quite a good shot," the housekeeper said.

"He has little to do but improve his marksmanship."

"Perhaps it would be foolish to wish that he'd let His Grace win."

Felix had nothing else to brag about; his prowess with weapons was evidently important to him.

Was it as important to Connor?

"He's selling the house," she said. "The new duke. He's selling Bealadair."

She truly wished she hadn't been the source of that quick look of fear on the older woman's face. But if she didn't tell the housekeeper she would be doing the woman a disservice.

Bad news delayed didn't mean bad news erased.

"Oh, dear, is he really?"

She nodded.

"Are you certain?"

Elsbeth nodded again. "Yes. It's definite."

Mrs. Ferguson, probably more than anyone, needed to make arrangements for her future. Gavin had made very generous bequests to the servants and hadn't forgotten the housekeeper. Thanks to him, Mrs. Ferguson had enough funds to care for herself for the rest of her life. She had a widowed sister who lived near Glasgow. She'd often spoken of how they had planned to live together in their older years.

The housekeeper nodded several times as Elsbeth told her about the tour of the house and the duke's revelations.

"Well, it's what we feared, isn't it? At least we no longer need to worry."

That was true enough.

"The rest of the family won't feel that sanguine about it," Elsbeth said.

"No, they won't, will they?"

They exchanged a glance. The next few weeks were bound to be tumultuous ones.

She really should tamp out that fluttering feeling at the thought of seeing Connor tomorrow. He would be returning to America soon, but not before disrupting all their lives, hers included.

A good reason not to be fascinated with the man.

Chapter 14

Elsbeth knew the exact minute Mr. Glassey had a conversation with the duchess the next morning. She knew, because she could hear Rhona shouting her name.

Despite Rhona's penchant for propriety, she was not above raising her voice to make a point.

Before she could reach the duchess's sitting room, Elsbeth heard her name again. More than one maid sent her a commiserating glance as she moved from the kitchen, through the hall, and up the grand staircase.

She would not take the servants' stairs. Refusing to do so now was a small, secret act of rebellion.

The duchess was not in her sitting room as she expected.

The third time she heard her name being called, Elsbeth sighed, turned, and walked to the end of the corridor.

One of the previous dukes had a bit of whimsy about him. He'd taken perfectly ordinary rooms and made them odd. The Ship Room was one of those. The first time she'd entered, she immediately had the impression of angles and walls jutting toward her. Only after a moment had she realized that by taking a series of small steps to the right, then turning to the left, she would enter what looked like the bow of a ship. From there, she could look down on the rest of the room. The windows mounted high in the wall became the horizon. Perhaps you could imagine yourself the captain of this imaginary ship.

When she'd asked Gavin if he and Graham had played there, his smile had been so sad that she wished she hadn't been curious.

"Yes," he'd said. "We loved that room. We were pirates or buccaneers. Graham was always besting me with a sword."

"A sword?"

"We borrowed them from the old wing," he said, his chuckle banishing the sadness for a bit. "Our mother was furious with us, of course, but we didn't stop. We loved that place. And the Bubble Room."

She opened the door to the Bubble Room, so called because of the odd window glass that took up most of the far wall. The glass bulged outward, making it feel as if you were in the middle of a bubble. The view of the eastern section of Bealadair was slightly blurred around the edges, but in the center it was spectacular, especially on this bright morning with the sun glinting on the snow.

The room was filled with greenery and lush growing things, smelling of spring. The fireplace was small and to the left, barely warming the room. The duchess had compensated for the chill by wearing a thick-wool half jacket over her black dress.

Mr. Glassey sat in the second of the two chairs in the small room, not looking as warm or as comfortable. At her entrance, the solicitor stood, but the duchess waved him back into place.

"Is it true?" Rhona asked.

"Is what true, Your Grace?"

Rhona frowned at her.

"Mr. Glassey said that His Grace told you he was selling Bealadair. Is this true?"

Elsbeth's gaze went to the solicitor. She wished the man had kept their conversation private.

She stood near the door, her gaze leaving the duchess and focusing on the white, frozen landscape beyond. From here, she could see the river undulating through the glen.

"Well?"

Elsbeth glanced at the duchess. "Yes," she said. "He told me."

"Leave us, Mr. Glassey," the duchess said, her gaze never leaving Elsbeth.

The very last thing Elsbeth wanted was to be left alone with the duchess while she was in this mood. Mr. Glassey, however, looked relieved to be able to escape the room.

"Of course, Your Grace," he said. "I am at your disposal."

When he closed the door behind him, Rhona still didn't speak. Her eyes however, were more than capable of expressing her emotions. Elsbeth had never seen them as cold and flat as they were right now.

"You knew his plans," the duchess said. "Yet you didn't come to me. Anyone else would have. How very odd that you did nothing, Elsbeth."

Elsbeth clasped her hands tightly together.

"Did you want us taken unawares?"

"Why would I want that, Your Grace?"

"By not coming to me immediately, you've proven to be disloyal."

"No," Elsbeth said. "I haven't. It wasn't my place to tell you, Your Grace. He might change his mind."

"He has no intention of changing his mind, Elsbeth. He's already announced himself to Mr. Glassey."

Then why was she being criticized for not saying something when the solicitor already knew?

For nearly two years she'd done her very best to ensure that Bealadair ran smoothly. She had taken on duties no one wished to do. She'd never refused to perform a task with the excuse that it wasn't her place. Nor had she ever whined or complained.

Not once had anyone thanked her, and as time passed, she realized it was foolish to want some measure of gratitude.

The McCraights simply didn't notice what was below their noses. As long as their food was delicious and hot, they didn't care how it was made. As long as their laundry was done, their apartments clean, they were content. It never occurred to them to care how it was done or to thank the lowly servants who worked around them.

Muira was the only one who had ever said something nice to a maid, but one person's voice hardly made up for the actions of an entire family.

Elsbeth had made that comment, or something similar, to Mrs. Ferguson only once, and the woman's pitying glance had been a lesson of sorts.

"Servants are invisible to them, my dear girl. They're our betters and we simply don't matter. The key is to accept that and move on. We have our own life, our own friends among the staff. You mustn't think that they will ever change. They won't."

In Mrs. Ferguson's words she'd heard another message, one she'd finally understood. She might be the duke's ward, but she had never truly been one of the family.

Her position was similar to the one Miss Smythe had occupied in the five years she'd been on staff. Strange, Elsbeth could barely remember the woman, yet she'd eagerly absorbed all the lessons the governess had taught.

Did the duchess expect her to apologize? No doubt she did, as well as grovel a little. That was hardly fair, especially since she didn't think she'd done anything wrong.

"You may go, Elsbeth," the duchess said, waving her hand toward the closed door. "I don't want to hear anything else from you. What a blessing Gavin never had to witness your betrayal."

That was too much.

"Your Grace, I wasn't certain if Connor meant what he said. I didn't even know if he could sell Bealadair."

One of Rhona's delicate arched eyebrows moved upward.

"Connor, is it?"

Elsbeth could feel her cheeks warm.

"He doesn't like being called Your Grace. I think it's because he's an American."

"He called you Elsbeth last night. Did you give him leave to do so?"

Elsbeth smoothed her hands down her skirt,

wishing a few magical words would come to mind to explain. Nothing she said would make a difference. When the duchess decided to be angry, no one—not even Gavin—could alter her mood.

She opened the door, glancing back once at the duchess, seeing in that proud, immobile figure a woman she'd never understood. Elsbeth wanted to ask what it was about her that seemed to summon the woman's antipathy. Had it been that Rhona was forced to take an eight-year-old child she hadn't wanted into her home? Or was it the fact that she and Gavin had a bond that hadn't existed between Gavin and his daughters?

She didn't know, but for the first time she was glad she was going to have to find another place to live. A place that would be home, as Bealadair hadn't been ever since Gavin's death.

"IS IT TRUE?"

Felix appeared in the corridor as if by magic. It wasn't magic; it was just that Bealadair was so big and Sam hadn't gotten the lay of the land yet.

"Is what true?" he asked.

"That the fool is going to sell Bealadair."

Sam bit back his first retort—that the only fool he saw was Felix—and said, "I take it you're referring to Connor?"

Felix nodded.

He disliked being waylaid in a corridor, let alone by Felix. He'd formed an impression of the young man the night before at dinner that wasn't flattering. Felix was a blowhard, a man who evidently disliked who he really was and therefore assumed talents he didn't have.

Most of the time he could ignore men like Felix. Unfortunately, Felix was now making that impossible.

"I think it would be best if you ask Connor his plans," he said.

"I'm asking you."

He tried to be on his way, but Felix moved to stand in front of him. Short of bodily removing the man—and if Felix remained obtrusive he just might have to—he was forced to listen to him.

"He can't sell Bealadair. Or the land."

He really didn't want to have to talk for Connor. The man was more than capable of explaining himself, but it looked like he was going to have to have this conversation whether he wanted to or not.

"I believe he can," Sam said.

"So it's true? What about the family? What does he expect us to do? Bealadair is the only thing the McCraights have in their favor."

"That's hardly the way to talk about your wife's family." And, if he had it right, the people who'd supported Felix since his marriage. "It's my understanding that the previous duke was very generous in his bequests."

"If he'd only given me an inkling of what he was planning, I would have been able to talk him out of it."

"Talk him out of dying?" Sam said. "Now that's a trick."

"Out of signing away everything to a stranger from Texas."

Words were powerful weapons, a fact Felix had

evidently learned. Sam's expression didn't change, but he was beginning to actively dislike the younger man. He liked the man even less when he said *Texas* in that jeering way.

"The bequest is a pittance," Felix said, "if we have to move away from Bealadair. We can't subside in London on such an amount, not for more than a few years. Having to buy a property would deplete us of a large sum. The least the duke could have done was to turn over the London house to Lara."

"Perhaps you can apply to Connor for relief," Sam said, his words laced with sarcasm. Felix, however, didn't pick up on that. The man was not only a braggart and a popinjay, but he was regrettably stupid.

He sidestepped Felix, more than willing to bodily remove the other man if he tried to waylay him again.

There wasn't as much money in Connor's inheritance as Felix evidently thought. Sam hadn't lied. From what he knew, Gavin had been remarkably generous to his family.

That wasn't enough for Felix, which meant that he possessed another trait: greed.

A greedy man, especially one who was as stupid as Felix, could be dangerous. A thought Sam tucked into the back of his mind.

Chapter 15

*A*fter dinner, Elsbeth disappeared again.

Instead of engaging in desultory conversation in the parlor or complimenting the McCraight sisters on their pianoforte skills, Connor opted to return to his room and try to sleep. Sam didn't notice, trailing after the duchess like a bird dog on a scent.

The second night at Bealadair was more restful than the first. At least Connor had been able to sleep for a few hours. He awoke at dawn, his first thought that he would get to see Elsbeth again.

He liked how she behaved when she wasn't around the family, a thought that irritated him somehow. At dinner she'd hardly said a word, and when she had, no one seemed to pay her any attention.

She wasn't in the family dining room. Nor was she in the kitchen. According to the cook, whose name was Addy, and who giggled a great deal when he spoke to her, she was checking the cattle.

"She's all for looking out after the poor, dear things," Addy said. "Especially with all the snow we've been having."

"Don't you have a foreman to do that?"

Her brow wrinkled in confusion. "A foreman,

Your Grace? Do you mean like Mr. Condrey? He's the steward and does all the bills and orders the supplies, but he doesn't actually go out and check on the cattle. Now, the ghillie, that's Hamish Robertson, he makes sure there's always game, and it's looked after by him and his boys, but he always meets with Miss Elsbeth, too."

Evidently, Glassey's briefing had left out some details about the estate, namely that Elsbeth seemed to be managing it.

"How does she check on the cattle?"

"Why, she rides out to see them, Your Grace."

"With all this snow?" he asked.

"Oh, her and that mare of hers, Your Grace, they go everywhere together, no matter what the weather. Why, it's a common sight to see Miss Elsbeth and Marie racing over the hills."

He'd gotten the impression from Elsbeth that she didn't ride.

He thanked the cook and left the room without his breakfast or the faintly colored water they called coffee. Later, he was going to brew some on his own. No doubt he'd shock the servants. From what he was able to determine, being a duke meant sitting in the library all day and nothing more.

He grabbed his coat and hat, heading toward the stables. The building was as ornate and fancy as the rest of Bealadair and built of white stone like the main house.

He was all for treating his horses well. After all, a horse was a lifeline in Texas. He couldn't go anywhere without one. But the stalls at Bealadair were adorned with plaster decorations, what looked like cupids riding horses and nameplates for horses that were long gone. He'd only stepped a few feet inside the building when a man introduced himself as Douglas McCraight, the stablemaster, no doubt another cousin somewhat removed.

He was about to introduce himself, but the man called him Your Grace, which was a dead giveaway that he knew who Connor was. Another man who was going to *Your Grace* him to death.

"We have your saddle, Your Grace, I put it in the tack room. It's a beautiful example of Spanish workmanship."

"Mexican," Connor said, correcting him. "It was done by Pedro Florian, one of the finest saddle makers in Texas."

The other man nodded. "A beautiful piece of work, Your Grace. I can see why you brought it with you."

"Have you got a suitable mount?"

He must have just accidentally insulted the man, because Douglas got a prune face. "Of course we do, Your Grace. Bealadair's stables are some of the finest in Scotland. I might even say the entire empire."

He hadn't considered that the stablemaster might be as pompous as his cousin's husband, but maybe it was just pride that made the man look all puffed up.

It was most definitely pride, he decided, as he was led from one stall to another. He had the distinct impression that the stablemaster was introducing him to each of the horses and not the other way around.

He had to admit, though, that they were some of the most beautiful mounts he'd ever seen. But he doubted they could outmaneuver a good quarter horse or be as valuable as a horse that had learned to be around cattle, especially Longhorns.

He kept his opinions to himself, however, asking a few questions about bloodlines and breeding stock, enough that he didn't look like an idiot to Douglas. The fact was, he didn't care all that much for Bealadair's stable. Unless, of course, the future owner wanted to keep everything intact. If not, Connor didn't have an objection to selling the horses to the highest bidder. With the money he could buy some additional quarter horses, hopefully bred out of Shiloh, one of the great horses that helped define the breed.

A working horse was better than a show horse any day.

The stablemaster hadn't lied. His saddle was mounted on a wooden block in the middle of the large tack room. The smell of leather thickened the air and vied with the odor of horse for dominance.

"Which of the horses would you like to ride, Your Grace? I'd recommend Samson, since he doesn't have a problem with snow. Sir Guilliuame is a little less skilled, but I'd also recommend Nancy."

He chose Samson, and when the stablemaster said that he'd have the horse saddled, Connor evidently shocked the man by insisting that he'd do it himself.

He picked up his saddle and walked back to Samson's stall. Instead of entering right away, he stood at the door making sure the horse was acclimated to his smell.

Horses were a great deal smarter than most people gave them credit for. All you had to do was watch a cow pony work a herd of Longhorns and you figured that out pretty fast. They learned quickly, too. Plus, they had a sixth sense about people. Maybe they could smell fear or incompetence. They weren't just dumb beasts of burden.

He knew the stablemaster was right behind him holding the tack and blanket. He was probably giving the man a tale to tell around the dinner table tonight, but he didn't care.

He introduced himself to Samson again, told the horse a little about himself.

"I've been riding since I was about three," he said. "At least that's what I was told. My first horse was Charlie and he wasn't anywhere near your size. I don't think I've ever ridden anyone quite as magnificent as you, either."

That wasn't a lie. The stallion was black with a mane of hair so thick and rippling that it looked like a woman's hair. The eyes that stared back at him were intelligent and measuring, almost as if Samson was saying, *I'm not sure I trust you, but keep talking pretty to me.*

He opened the stall door, approached the stallion, and stopped.

"How do you feel about a ride? There's snow on the ground, but the sky is clear. It's on the cold side, but we'll soon get warm. What do you say?"

Samson turned his head, then gave a little shake. An agreement if he'd ever seen one.

Once he was mounted, he left the stable. An army of servants was already about, clearing the road at the rear of the house. Two were guiding plow horses along the lane, each dragging a set of boards behind them to smooth out the snow. He nodded to each man, was surprised and pleased when each of them met his eyes.

"They're a rebellious bunch, the Scots," his father had once said. "They'll work for you for a decent wage, but never think they owe you loyalty or allegiance. That's not for sale and can only be earned."

Graham had earned the ranch hands' loyalty and trust. A ranch the size of theirs needed a great number of loyal people to run it. Connor had known that all his life, and it was a lesson doubly reinforced after his father's death.

They had a number of rules, some of which didn't suit every man. There was no drinking alcohol unless it was an official celebration. No gambling was allowed at any time, including playing cards.

Yet for all the rules, men wanted to work at the XIV Ranch. The wages were good and the work, though hard, was equally shared. Every man worked as hard as the newest hired hand.

He couldn't help but wonder how Joe was handling the problems that were sure to come up in his absence. His future brother-in-law was a competent manager and the experience would be good for him. Still, Connor wanted to be home more than he wanted to be here.

Samson was prancing along on the snow, sure-footed, his head tossing—a sign that he was enthused to be out and about. Connor felt the same; he'd rather be on horseback, even on an unfamiliar horse, than anywhere else.

He followed the directions the stablemaster had given him, wishing he'd felt comfortable enough to ask the man a few questions. He'd learned not to reveal himself too quickly to a stranger, even here at Bealadair. Perhaps especially here at Bealadair.

Except for Elsbeth. He'd never felt the same reserve with her that he experienced around other people. He'd told her things he'd never mentioned to anyone else, even Sam. He'd let her see how he felt, unable to hold back his emotions on first viewing the picture of Graham and Gavin.

She'd been as free with him, talking about his uncle with sadness in her eyes.

The air was crisp and clean, the sky a brilliant blue with not one cloud overhead. Evidently they were done with the snow for a while, a fact he welcomed.

The road he took, little wider than a lane, was lined on either side by trees boasting dripping icicles. The snow hadn't been smoothed away from the lane here, and for a moment, he wondered about the advisability of going any farther. The tracks convinced him, and he followed a horse's hoofprints, wondering if they were from the horse Elsbeth was riding.

He must've gone a mile, maybe a mile and a half before he saw the herd. Connor stopped the stallion, his gloved hands on his thighs, staring. He would have to write his mother and sisters about this. Elsbeth hadn't told him everything.

Highland cattle were the funniest looking things he'd ever seen.

They had broad triangular faces, short legs, and stocky bodies. Their bodies, including the tails hanging to the ground, were covered in long tan or brown hair. The hair dripped down over their eyes and almost to the end of their snouts. Their horns stuck out straight from either side of their heads, above their hairy ears. Although not as impressive as a Longhorn's, the horns ended in a wicked-looking point.

He hadn't considered that they would be so hairy, but of course they would need to be to winter outside.

There was Elsbeth in the middle of them, her horse tied to a tree branch as she traipsed through the snow.

He didn't fool himself that he was out exploring Bealadair. He'd come looking for her and now he'd found her, hatless, her bright red cloak a spot of color next to the cattle.

He sat where he was, feeling oddly content, and watched her.

Chapter 16

$\mathcal{A}$ few minutes later, Connor dismounted and tied his reins to a tree branch not far from a pretty little roan mare that regarded him with intelligent eyes. After a moment of inspection, she nodded just once, as if finding him acceptable before turning her attention to his horse.

He grinned at the stallion's toss of his hair and thought that whoever had named him Samson had chosen well.

Instead of the simple pasture he'd expected, the area had been augmented by a long wooden structure. About five feet high, it stretched from the base of a modest hill down to a creek bed. It took him a moment to realize that it was a windbreak serving a dual purpose: it cut off the worst of the Highland winds, plus it was a bedding-down area where the cattle slept. Grass was mounded and contoured to provide cushioning on the cold ground and probably to aid in drainage.

Two troughs about six feet long sat perpendicular to the windbreak. He guessed one held water and the other food.

He leaned back against an oak that looked as

if it had been there a couple hundred years and watched Elsbeth. She was walking among the herd, and it looked as if she was talking to the cattle. Occasionally, she would slap her gloved hand against a flank, stop, and look appraisingly at the animal's condition. From time to time, she would push one of them out of her way, and sometimes the cow would butt her back.

Her laugh traveled over the space between them, the sound of it making him smile.

She surprised him by looking comfortable, even in the middle of the herd. Highland cattle were, no doubt, more docile than Longhorns, but he bet they could still be dangerous, especially with those horns. She was agile in avoiding those, however, and twice used a horn as a kind of handle to move one of the cows.

She turned her head, caught sight of him, and hesitated for a moment before raising her hand in a wave. He waved back, but she didn't move to join him. Instead, she continued with her inspection.

How had she learned about Highland cattle? Was it something his uncle had taught her? Or had she simply decided one day that someone had to do the job and learned what she needed to know?

He wouldn't put it past her. He'd known her for one and a half days exactly, yet he already had an idea of her character. He both respected and liked her, the thought catching him off guard. He also wanted to know more about her.

Perhaps he'd felt that way about another woman in his past, but it was so long ago that he couldn't remember.

When she finally started to head in his direction she did so with her head down, her eyes on the snowy ground.

"Where did you learn about cattle?" he asked when she was close enough to hear him.

She raised her head and met his gaze.

"Some from our previous steward," she said. "Some from our ghillie, although he would much rather not work with cattle. Some from Gavin. And some from wonderful books on the subject."

"Don't you have anyone to help you?" he asked.

"Of course," she said. "But they don't deliver the feed and the water until I give them the order."

"Water?"

She smiled. "You'll laugh. You'll think our cattle are coddled too much."

When he didn't say anything, she continued. "We heat the water on the coldest days. They can eat snow, but it lowers their body temperature and they can get too chilled. It's easier to keep their weight on than to replenish it."

"And that's why you come here every day?" he asked, his amazement growing.

"Not every day," she said. "Only on the coldest ones. I need to make sure the cattle are healthy, that none of them is lame, that their hair hasn't become wet or matted. It doesn't protect them, you see, if it does.

"They'll eat almost anything. It's why we have to keep the branches around the lower pastures trimmed. Otherwise, they'd eat all the leaves. They'll eat weeds and vines and anything that remotely looks like food."

She was warming to the topic, and he wasn't about to stop her, fascinated by her smile and the light in her eyes.

"In winter we feed them hay," she said. "This year we were lucky. We had only an A herd."

"An A herd?"

She nodded. "I grade the herd in autumn. If a cow is too thin, it's a B. If it's too fat, it's a C. They get separated into different sections depending on their condition. That way the thin ones are fed more and the fat ones less."

"So an A cow is one that's just right?" he asked.

She nodded.

"And you do this grading yourself?"

"With the help of our steward," she said. "He doesn't like the task much," she added, smiling. She glanced over her shoulder. "I think he's afraid of them."

"It's a good-sized herd," he said, having estimated the number to be about one hundred fifty. Nothing like the thousands of head of Longhorn on the XIV Ranch, but acceptable for a small pasture.

"This is just one of them," she said. "There are six more pastures."

"And you oversee all of them?" he asked, amazed.

She shook her head. "Not all of them. Some are too far to easily reach. We have crofters who look after the cows and ensure they're well fed."

She came and stood beside him, looking out over the pasture.

"They're normally very healthy, even in the winter. And they calve small babies so they rarely need any help."

One of the cows raised its head and stared at her.

At least he thought it stared. It was difficult to tell with all that hair.

"The whole herd seems to protect them," she said. "They seem to shield the little ones, forming a barrier between the calves and the outside world."

"You didn't tell me they were so hairy," he said.

"Oh, that's one of their best traits. Of course, in the summer their hair isn't as long, but it still protects them from flies. Summers are harder for them than our wet, cold winters. In summer we move them to the western pasture. It's shadier in the afternoon, and they stay cooler."

A tendril had come loose from her bun. He wanted to push it back into place, but he kept his hands in his pockets.

"I've been listing all the cattle in a book," she said. "A registry, of sorts, for Bealadair's herds." She glanced up at him. "Did you know that they were written about as early as the thirteenth century? The crofters used to bring them into their homes to sleep in the winter."

"I guess that kept them from being rustled," he said.

"And they kept the owner warm," she added. "They're good milk cows and good oxen. They're a very hardy breed."

She looked around her. "This afternoon, we'll send some men here and to the upper pasture to plow some of the snow." She glanced at him. "I hope that when you sell Bealadair you find someone who'll treat them well, Connor."

"Perhaps you should stay on at Bealadair," he said. "I doubt anyone would be as conscientious as you."

She turned and stared out at the pasture and beyond, to the windbreak. "No, it's time for me to leave."

The words irritated him for some reason. If all went well, Bealadair would sell quickly. Perhaps the servants would remain, but that was all. His aunt and cousins would have to find other living arrangements.

He was land rich but cash poor. He needed an infusion of money to ensure that the ranch lived on, just as his father had intended.

Still, it annoyed him to think of Elsbeth leaving.

"Your Highland cattle sound a lot like a Longhorn," he said, deciding that cattle were a safer subject. "They can live on the open range and eat things most other animals ignore."

"They're actually *your* Highland cattle," she said with a gentle smile. "Perhaps you could take a few back to Texas with you."

That was an idea. He tucked it away to think about later.

"The duchess knows that you're going to sell Bealadair," she said, glancing up at him.

"Did you tell her?" he asked, surprised.

She'd spared him a difficult meeting, but he didn't like the idea of hiding behind a woman's skirts.

She shook her head. "I'm afraid that was Mr. Glassey's doing."

"I should have known he'd do that. He has more loyalty to the duchess than to me." He shrugged. "It's to be expected, I guess."

She glanced at him, then away. He wanted to ask her what she was thinking. Normally, he just waited until a person spoke, but with Elsbeth he was impatient.

"You really don't want to be duke, do you?"

"I don't. Seems like a lot of foolishness. I can't help the family I was born into. Maybe my great-great-great-great-grandfather did something that attracted the attention of some royal person. Maybe he got an award for it. Why should I be singled out as being special because of that?"

"You have to admit that the rest of the world doesn't feel that way," she said. "Most people would very much like to be a duke. They'd like all that respect."

"But it isn't, you see. It's not real respect. A man earns real respect because of what he does." He pulled his gloved hands out of his pockets and looked down at them. "What he makes with his hands. What he imagines with his mind." He glanced at her. "Maybe even how he treats other people, especially those who can't do anything for him. That's real respect. That other stuff? That bowing and calling me Your Grace? That's just either habit or something you're taught to do. It doesn't mean anything. It's just a waste of time and speech."

She studied him for what felt like a long time, not saying anything. He wanted to ask her if she thought he'd just spouted a bunch of nonsense. He was at that point when she nodded.

"You're a unique man, Connor McCraight. I think your uncle would have liked you very much."

He wasn't sure how he felt about that comment. He didn't know his uncle from Adam's off ox, but Gavin was Graham's twin so he owed the man some respect.

"Are you going to go through with that idiotic contest with Felix?"

She kept unsettling him with her questions or comments.

"It seems to me the man wants to show me what a great shot he is. Who am I not to allow him that opportunity?"

"You could just walk away. Tell him you have better things to do."

He didn't bother hiding his smile. "That wouldn't accomplish anything. Men like Felix don't stop badgering. They get something stuck in their craw and they won't let it loose until you do what they want."

She shook her head. "He won't let you forget it," she said. "When he wins."

"He might win," he agreed. "Then, again, he might not."

"Are you a very good shot, Connor?"

"I didn't bring my rifle," he said, "but I'm passable. I do have my revolver from the war, though."

Her face changed a little. It wasn't all that noticeable, and if he hadn't been watching her closely he probably would have missed it. There was a look in her eyes that resembled the expression his mother wore sometimes, a sadness that couldn't be talked away.

He wanted to tell her that he didn't need her to be sad on account of him, but something stopped him. Maybe he liked it a little, a woman as beautiful as Elsbeth Carew feeling something for him. Or maybe he was just feeling a little sad for himself, and it eased him to share it with someone else, someone he liked.

"What else do you have to do today?" she asked. "Would you like to see the old castle?"

"I'm going to have to, sooner or later, aren't I? It's part of being a duke, right?"

She nodded.

"Well, hell, we might as well see it, then."

"You're supposed to beg my pardon when you swear in my company," she said.

"Who came up with that stupid rule?"

"It's just being proper."

He bent down until he was just a few inches away from her face.

"Are you always so proper, Elsbeth Carew?"

She looked up at him, her gray eyes making him want to just watch her for an hour or two.

He discovered he liked teasing her. He didn't move away, but deliberately got closer. It would be so easy to kiss her right now. That wouldn't be at all proper, would it?

He stepped back, thinking that he should apologize. But he'd only thought it. He hadn't actually kissed her. Should he apologize for thinking it?

"Can we warm up somewhere first?" he asked. "Before we go and see this castle?"

Her smile was enough to heat him from the inside out. And damn near made him kiss her.

Chapter 17

At the side of her mare, Connor cupped his hands and bent slightly. She hesitated for a moment, then placed her left boot in his palms, thanking him as he helped her mount. Below the red cloak she wasn't wearing a riding habit, but something that reminded him of the garment his sisters wore when they rode astride. The skirt was divided, making it look like extra-wide pantaloons. She didn't, he was happy to see, use a sidesaddle. In this weather and on the snowy roads, it couldn't be safe. Instead, her saddle was what he'd come to think of as the English style.

He wondered how she would've mounted without his assistance. He didn't doubt that Elsbeth would've found a way. Perhaps she was expert enough to simply put her foot in the stirrup and bound over the mare's back.

She was one of the most interesting women he'd ever met. Even more important, he wanted to know more about her, and that curiosity was a surprising twist for him.

He'd been around women all his life. He was accustomed to their conversations, to his sister Alison's somewhat hysterical rantings, to Constance's hyperbole. He liked the way Dorothy's mind worked and had asked her a few questions about the way women thought.

"We don't think all that differently from men," she'd said.

He'd disagreed. "You think about things I would never consider."

"Like what?"

"Whether something looks good with something else. If something is comfortable. Habitable. You're wallpaper and furniture. Men are mostly brick and mortar."

Dorothy had only looked at him, but she hadn't countered his argument.

If she were here, what would she say about Elsbeth? What would her opinion be of this fascinating Scottish woman?

Instead of leading him back toward Bealadair, Elsbeth continued on the road, traveling upward and around the side of the hill to a tidy little cottage tucked between an outcropping of shale and the beginning of a valley. A glen, that's what the Scots called it.

When she stopped, she swung her leg over the mare's back, was off her horse and tying the reins to a post beside the cottage steps before he could offer to help her.

He dismounted as well, mimicking her actions in tying the reins, grinning as Samson edged closer to the mare. She ignored him, which only made his horse more determined to capture her attention.

He was probably acting a little like the stallion.

As Elsbeth knocked on the door, she glanced at

him and said, "Mr. Stuyvesant lives here. He's from Germany, but he's been living in Scotland for so long that he has the most curious accent."

She didn't get a chance to say more before the door opened.

Mr. Stuyvesant was a gnome of a man, at least a foot shorter than Elsbeth, bent over from age, and fiercely gripping a cane that looked as if it had been carved from a tree root.

His hair was white, as were his eyebrows. The blue eyes beneath them were alight with humor. His mouth, surprisingly prim, broke into a smile that immediately removed twenty years from his weathered face.

"Elsbeth, my little one!" he said, opening the door wide and stepping back. "I didn't think to see you until next week. Come, come inside."

"We came to warm up, Hans," she said, smiling. She stepped inside, but not before reaching back and gripping Connor's sleeve and pulling him with her.

"This is the Duke of Lothian, Hans. His Grace feels the same about Scottish winters as you do."

She made the introductions so quickly that he didn't have an opportunity to protest the *His Grace* part of it. Stuyvesant did a quick nod of his head, which was, thankfully, the only acknowledgment of his new rank. The man proceeded to ignore him, his attention on Elsbeth. He pointed to a chair with his strange knotted cane.

"Sit, sit. I'll get you some tea, shall I?"

The inside of the cottage was surprisingly cozy. Connor had expected something like one of their line shacks at home, a sparsely furnished building consisting of a chair or two, a table, one or two cots, and maybe a few bowls and pots.

Here, though, Stuyvesant had surrounded himself with things of beauty. A tapestry hung on a far wall, the scene one of a princess and a white unicorn kneeling at her side. Blue-and-white plates were aligned in a breakfront on another wall. Before it, sat a table with two chairs, with an assortment of dried flowers in a vase atop the table. A selection of pipes with elongated bowls or stems sat on a mantel above a large fireplace with a roaring fire.

A closed door in the opposite wall probably led to a sleeping alcove. All in all, it was a snug little home.

Two chairs sat in front of the fire, but Connor stood beside the mantel, refusing to sit when a man old enough to be his grandfather would be forced to stand.

Elsbeth removed her cloak and hung it on a peg near the door. He merely opened his coat but kept it on. He was still bone-deep cold. He did remove his hat, though, and held it with one hand.

The old man busied himself taking a kettle from the fire and pouring boiling water into a brown ceramic teapot.

Something hot to drink sounded good, but he wasn't sure he was ready for what the Scots called tea. It was either as weak as water or strong enough to etch his teeth.

There were only two cups, and he was more than willing to decline, but Stuyvesant was adamant.

"Sit, sit," he said to Connor, handing him a cup.

Elsbeth sent him a look, one of those that said, *What are you going to do?*

He took the cup and sat, thanking the man.

"You get cold, too?" Stuyvesant asked.

Connor nodded.

"I almost left the first five winters. If it hadn't been for my Moira, I would have. But she loved her country and didn't want to go back to Germany. So I stayed and told myself I would get used to it. I never did. But I never left, either."

Stuyvesant sat on the brick hearth, propping his cane on his left side.

"Hans takes care of the cattle on the western side of Ben Ecshe," Elsbeth said, sipping delicately from her cup. "He also has an uncanny knack for predicting the weather."

"My left knee," Stuyvesant said. "It hurts when snow is coming. My right elbow when it's going to rain. It's clearing, little one. No more snow for a week or so."

"That's good to know, Hans. I'm growing a little tired of it."

They talked a while of weather and cattle stores. The windbreak in one section needed to be repaired. Elsbeth nodded, put down her teacup on the table between the chairs, and took out a notebook from her pocket to make a notation.

"Do you need anything, Hans?" she asked, her pencil poised above the page.

"A little flour," he said. "Some honey if you have it. And some bacon."

He added a few more items and Elsbeth wrote them down. He grinned at her, his eyes twinkling. "And if Addy has any more scones, you might pass them along as well. My baking is not as good."

The tea was surprising, not as strong as what Connor had had before, but a good flavor. When he said as much to Stuyvesant, the man beamed.

"My Moira taught me how to make tea," he said. "I think of her every morning. I add a little cinnamon to the tea. Not much, just enough to add to the flavor." He glanced at Elsbeth. "If you could add cinnamon to your list, little one."

She nodded.

He wanted to ask about Stuyvesant's wife, but was reluctant to do so. He had a feeling that Moira might have been gone for some years, but Stuyvesant kept her alive in small daily ways, like the way he made his tea and the tidiness of the cottage.

At home, he'd done the same in his father's office. He never entered the room without thinking of Graham. Every Monday, after he had gone through all of the bills and made the payments and instructions to his bank, he straightened the blotter, returned the pen to the place that Graham had always left it, making everything look the same as it had been the day he returned home.

Maybe in that way he kept his father alive.

He felt a curious affinity to the old man sitting on the hearth. Did he spend the winters alone, except for sporadic visits from Elsbeth and caring for the cattle? Was it a happy life or did he simply mark the hours until it was time for him to join his beloved Moira?

He sat silent as Elsbeth and Stuyvesant talked. Elsbeth asked the older man a dozen questions about the cattle, the weather, the upkeep of the cottage. As they conversed, he realized that she probably knew most of the answers or didn't really need the information. But she was drawing the old man out, taking the time to listen to him. The simple kindness of her conversation made Connor like her even more.

He was sometimes impatient to be about his tasks, maybe more than he needed to be. Whatever he needed to accomplish could wait a few minutes, long enough for him to spare time to listen to others.

Would Elsbeth know that she'd served as an example and a lesson?

Finally, their tea was done, he was warmed, and the visit was over. He thanked Stuyvesant, stood aside while Elsbeth made her farewells. Once again, he helped her mount, but this time he asked, "You can do this on your own, can't you?"

"I've never had anyone help me," she said. "But it's a nice change. I'm sure I look ungainly otherwise."

"I doubt that," he said.

She looked surprised at his comment, but didn't say anything further.

As they rode away from the cottage, he glanced at her. "How long has his Moira been gone?"

"Ten years," she said, confirming his earlier guess. "She's buried in the chapel grounds at Bealadair."

For several minutes they didn't speak. To his surprise, they retraced their path, but at a fork in the road, she stopped and turned to him.

"Hans is only one of the crofters we have at Bealadair. He's not one of the clan, exactly, but he's considered part of the family. When you sell, is there a way to ensure that he's protected? I think it would be terrible if he had to move at this stage of his life, don't you?"

He nodded, wishing he could guarantee what she wanted. Perhaps there was a way that he could make provisions with the new owner to leave things as they were. Perhaps he could also ensure that Elsbeth always had a home at Bealadair.

Elsbeth's future, he told himself, was none of his concern. How odd that it didn't feel that way. Not at all.

Chapter 18

She really should limit her time with Connor. The American—the Texan—was proving to be entirely too charming.

When she'd turned to find him standing at the edge of the pasture watching, her stomach had leaped to her throat. He was such a sight with his hat and his strange coat. She'd nodded, continuing on with her inspection, but she'd paid as much attention to him as she did the cattle.

She'd seen handsome men before. More than a few of them had visited Bealadair over the years. None of them, however, had ever impressed her as much as Connor McCraight with his way of planting his feet in the earth, an almost-defiant stance. He wasn't going to budge, she knew, in his determination to sell Bealadair. Just as she knew that the whole situation was rife with tragedy and angst.

She had to make him see that people depended on Bealadair for not only their sustenance but their reason for waking in the morning. The great house was more than a structure; it contained history and the story of a clan, tales of valor and heartbreak, as well as the dreams of so many more people than simply the Duke of Lothian.

Gavin had taught her that. He'd been so determined that his stewardship of Bealadair would be a wise one, that he'd leave a thriving estate for those who followed. In this case, Connor, who wanted nothing to do with it.

How did she change his mind?

She didn't know. Perhaps if she just showed him how she felt, it might impact him in some way. She'd begin by taking him on her route.

If she hadn't had to meet with the duchess she would have been farther along in her morning routine. She began at the stable. Mr. Condrey, the steward, would much rather occupy himself with the paperwork concerning the estate than deal with its people. Mr. Barton, the majordomo, considered it beneath him to have to deal with the stablemaster and his staff. The ghillie would much rather concern himself with the game on Bealadair land. He knew little about horses, but everything there was to know about a den of kits. That left her to ensure that Douglas had everything he needed.

After she left the stable, she began her Y-shaped path, visiting three pastures as she went. She veered to the right to visit Hans, who was located at the very top of the Y then back down and to the left side of the Y, where she normally visited two other crofters. Today she would do the same and introduce Connor to the people of Bealadair. It might be a good time to also take him to see Castle McCraight.

The fortress had been built, Gavin told her, in the seventh century. Overlooking Dornoch Firth, it commanded a perfect defensive position. No one had ever been able to conquer Castle McCraight.

The clan had given up the castle in the fourteenth century. The winds and the humidity along with age had reduced it to a few roofless walls and chunks of fallen stone. She often thought it had been allowed to erode because no one was left to care for it.

No doubt Bealadair would be the same if the new owner didn't love it as much as all of the previous Dukes of Lothian.

Her heart felt heavy, almost as if she were filled with unshed tears. Everything Connor was doing, everything he planned, seemed like a betrayal of the man she'd come to think of as her second father. Gavin, however, would no doubt have been sanguine about the future. He had a pragmatic way of looking at the world. She could imagine his advice: Bealadair will survive and if it doesn't, perhaps it was not meant to.

The sun's warmth was beginning to melt the icicles hanging from the branches above them. From time to time a droplet would splash down on her, making her wish she'd taken the time to pull the hood over her head.

The day was not as cold as it had been the past week. If it continued to warm, the roads would be difficult in the next few days.

"Bealadair is a working estate," she told Connor. "We cut from the forests on even-numbered years. In addition to the Highland cattle herds, we also have sheep. Plus acres and acres of farmland, most of it managed by crofters. We have grouse moors and herds of deer, but the ghillie handles those."

"And, I would assume," he said, "that you manage most everything."

She smiled at him. "I don't, actually. I do things when the steward doesn't want to do them. Or when the ghillie refuses to do them. I am, if you like, an intermediary among all the factions at Bealadair—the house and the rest of the estate."

"I told Glassey to give you a salary," he said. "Now I'm thinking I need to double it."

"You didn't need to do that."

"'The workman is worthy of his hire.'"

"Gavin often quoted scripture to me," she said. "I never expected you to do the same."

He only smiled at her.

Connor was a comfortable companion. She thought he might ask more questions but he was content to ride in silence.

She liked the way he handled Samson, with a nonchalance that spoke of his ease around horses. He was a good rider, neither allowing the stallion too much head or sawing his mouth with the bit.

You could tell a great deal about a person from how he treated the animals in his care. She knew that only too well.

She'd given orders that Felix, for example, wasn't allowed access to certain horses in the stable. If at all possible, the stablemaster was also to ensure that Felix was accompanied on his rides by a stableboy who could make note of his actions.

No one, so far, had countermanded her orders. Perhaps they knew that Felix was a cruel person at heart. Or maybe they simply didn't want to visit the issue. Too, there was also the possibility that they didn't want to irritate her, for fear that she would give up the duties that she performed around the house.

That was probably the least likely scenario.

Gavin had always treated people with honor, dignity, and respect. That was his initial attitude toward anyone he met. If they subsequently did something that caused him to lose trust in them, then he behaved accordingly.

Connor seemed similar to his uncle in that respect. When he met Tom and Mary McCraight, he was gracious and kind. Especially to Mary, who offered him a raisin scone. Elsbeth truly wanted to warn him, but there was no way to do so. Yet Connor managed to bite through the scone, then said something complimentary to his hostess. She doubted that anyone besides her saw him tuck the rest of the scone into his oversized pocket. He was as kind to Tom, a tall thin man who looked as if he were on the verge of starving. Given that his wife was such a terrible cook, that might be more truth than jest.

Their two little girls stood in the doorway to the kitchen staring at the new duke with wonder on their faces. It was very possible that they'd never seen such a large man in their three-room cottage. Or perhaps it was the fact that Connor was so different, dressed in his coat, hat, and boots that proclaimed him as a stranger to Scotland. Or it might've even been his voice, and the accent that was so unlike how the rest of them spoke.

When they left, she finally allowed her smile to burst free.

"I am sorry about that," she said. "The birds might like that scone."

He grinned at her. "I've had hardtack that was softer," he admitted.

"Perhaps one of her daughters will end up being a better cook. I should check with their teacher to see if they have any inclination."

He glanced at her, a question in his eyes.

"We provide school for all the children in the clan," she said. "Even the girls. If they show an affinity for something early, then we concentrate on that. We've had several of our students go on to pursue an even broader education. It was one of Gavin's projects."

"What was he like?"

The wind was picking up and it seemed to have a bite to it, almost as if Gavin's shade dared her to tell the truth.

"Determined," she said. "I think he annoyed other people because he had a penchant for asking how things were done and why. Of all the things I remember about him, his curiosity was his greatest trait."

Connor didn't say anything in response.

"He loved this land." Was there a way to explain that to Connor? "He felt tied to the land, to the history of it. That's what he was working on when he died—an entire history of the McCraight Clan."

When he didn't speak, she said, "What about your father? What was he like?"

"You've just described him," he said. "Except for the history of the clan. I should have considered that they would be alike in temperament."

"They were twins, after all."

He nodded.

She decided to change the subject.

"The next crofter we're going to visit is Daniel McCraight. He, too, is a widower."

"Is everyone named McCraight?"

"They're members of your clan," she said. "Around here, it's not unusual to bear the name."

At least he didn't argue with her about it being his clan.

She had a surprise for him at Daniel's cottage. Fiona, Daniel's Scottish collie, had had a litter of puppies a few weeks earlier.

The cottage was one of the larger structures at Bealadair, Gavin having given Daniel permission to build onto the house. Altogether there were five rooms, four for humans and one for the dogs and their puppies when they came.

She always enjoyed her visits with Daniel and purposely made this the last stop of her circuit so she could spend more time with him and with Fiona.

A few times, she'd joined them on the slopes of the glen, watching as he demonstrated the dogs' talent at interpreting his whistles and unspoken commands. With each new litter, Daniel kept a few puppies for up to a year, training them as well.

Connor dismounted first, came to her side, and reached up to help her. She didn't tell him she was more than capable of dismounting herself. When he gripped her waist, it seemed as if his hands lingered.

She'd never before wondered what a man's hands would feel like on her bare skin. Oh, she'd imagined a wedding night, but the husband she'd envisioned hadn't been real, just a filmy, indistinguishable, hazy figure. Not once had she paired her imagination with reality. Especially someone as *real* as Connor McCraight.

She thanked him just as the dogs began to bark. Not a welcome greeting as much as a warning one.

"Daniel has Scottish collies," she said. "They don't bark when they work," she told Connor as they took the path to the door. "They don't make a sound around sheep or cattle. Only an occasional yip when Daniel gives them the command. At home it's different, however."

"Scottish collies?" he asked.

She nodded. "McCraight collies," she said. "Prized for their bloodline, intelligence, and their herding abilities. Daniel's dogs are renowned throughout the Highlands and are very much in demand."

The door opened suddenly and Daniel stood there, a tall, overpowering figure of a man. She'd always thought that he was the tallest person she knew, but to her surprise Connor topped him by an inch or two.

Connor was clean shaven; Daniel had a bushy beard hanging nearly to his chest, but in all other ways the two men were alike: tall, broad shouldered, with an air of command about them.

"I'm guessing you'll be wanting to come in," Daniel said, stepping back. "I'll not be heating the outdoors for you."

Connor grinned at him and she understood immediately why he was so pleased. Daniel wasn't going to be obsequious. Nor did he seem overly impressed when she introduced Connor as the 14th Duke of Lothian. Daniel didn't care. Daniel hadn't even cared when Gavin came to visit him. He was a man who knew his own worth and wasn't about to bow and scrape before anyone. Nor was he about to *Your Grace* Connor a hundred times.

The two men shook hands, seeming to take the measure of each other before they separately nodded.

She occupied herself by bending and picking up one of the puppies that had come rushing to the door. He was a fluffy ball of gray, brown, and white fur, all paws and nose, little triangle-shaped ears peeking up from his round furry face.

She held him against her cheek, smiling when the puppy licked her cheek.

"I'll be keeping him, Miss Carew," Daniel said. "He's a smart one, he is."

"Have you named him yet?" she asked.

Connor bent and scooped up another puppy. For such a large man he was incredibly gentle.

For the first time since she'd known him, Daniel looked decidedly uncomfortable.

"I have, Elsbeth," he said. "But I expect that you won't approve."

She had an inkling of what Daniel was going to say before he admitted it.

"You named him Gavin," she said.

He looked shocked. "No, Elsbeth. I would never do that. But he does look like a duke to me."

Connor chuckled. "I agree. What have you named this one?" he asked, holding the puppy up at eye level.

"He needs a name," Daniel said. "Nothing has occurred to me. He's got all the instincts of a good herder."

"We use the dogs mostly with our sheep," Elsbeth said. "Although there are some people who use them to herd cattle."

Daniel nodded, then turned and led the way into the main room of the cottage. Unlike Mr. Stuyvesant's sparsely furnished home, this cottage was difficult to navigate because it was filled with Daniel's treasures. He hadn't thrown anything out since his wife had died and Diane had collected everything from pitchers to dresser scarves to thistles she'd dried and made into potpourri.

Since Diane's death two years ago the dogs had claimed pride of place. In addition to the two puppies she and Connor held, there were three more, plus their mother and father. Once they'd given the alert to Daniel, they'd stopped barking, but Fiona was whining a little. Elsbeth knew what that meant. She sat, the puppy on her lap, and motioned the dog closer.

"I've missed you, Fiona," she said, scratching in front of the collie's ears. "I'm not taking your baby away, I promise." Fiona nosed her puppy, then looked up at Elsbeth.

She dug down into her cloak pocket and pulled out the two bones she'd gotten for the dogs earlier, looking at Daniel for approval.

"From Addy?" he asked.

She nodded. At his okay, she gave one to Fiona and the other to Hamish. Once she placed Duke on the floor, he trailed after his mother, hoping for a taste of the bone.

"Have you ever trained your dogs to herd any other kinds of cattle?"

Daniel frowned at Connor, sat in the chair on the opposite side of the room and took up his pipe, nodding toward the settee nearest him.

Connor sat, opened his coat and the puppy made a home in the folds of the sheepskin lining.

"A cow is a cow," Daniel said. "There's not much difference between them."

"Ever hear of a Longhorn?" he asked, his hand gently stroking the puppy, who promptly curled up into a ball and fell asleep.

"That I haven't," Daniel said.

Connor described the animal and talked about the cattle dogs he had now.

"I've given some thought to getting a Scottish collie or two and seeing if they would work."

"Oh," Daniel said, drawing on his pipe, "they would work. The dogs always do what they're trained to do. The cows might have a different mind for a little while, but they would eventually catch on. Are you asking me if I'm willing to part with a few of my dogs?"

Connor seemed to study the other man for a moment, and then he nodded, just once. "I am. Two of them."

"Well, it would take a few instructions with you," Daniel said.

"With me?"

"Aye. Like I said, the dogs always do what they're trying to do. It's the human that's often the problem. You would have to learn how to give them instructions." He drew on his pipe then said, "You think on that for a while and if you agree, we can come to some kind of arrangement."

Perhaps she should have warned Connor that Daniel charged a great deal for his dogs. They were worth it, but they didn't come cheap. Of course, Connor was beyond wealthy now, wasn't he? He would never have to worry about money again, especially if he went through with his idea to sell Bealadair.

That was such a sad thought that she bent and began to play with a puppy tugging on her shoe-laces.

Chapter 19

*D*aniel invited them to stay for tea, but Elsbeth wanted to get to Castle McCraight before it turned dark. In the winter the days were short. Plus, the weather could turn bad again. Mr. Stuyvesant's knee notwithstanding, it could begin snowing at any time.

"You liked Daniel, didn't you?" she asked, once they were back on their horses. "I suspect it's because he didn't call you Your Grace once."

"You're right about that."

"Did you mean what you said?" she asked. "Are you really interested in taking the dogs back to Texas?"

"I am. We have cattle dogs, but my father used to talk about Scottish collies. Maybe they could learn to work Longhorns."

It was a comforting thought that a little bit of Scotland would return to Texas. Before she could tell him that, he spoke again.

"My father never spoke about Bealadair. I think, now, that it's because he wanted to avoid thinking about Scotland. I'm surprised that he spoke Gaelic."

"Or it could have been because he couldn't bear

it," she said softly. "Sometimes, those things we miss the most are the least spoken of."

He looked at her. "Is there something you miss, Elsbeth?"

She considered the question. "Perhaps my parents, but my memories of them have faded over the years. I miss Gavin." She missed the security his presence had given her, a fact she'd never considered until his death.

She had the feeling that if she had told Connor what she felt, he would have understood. She really needed to find something terrible about him, some flaw in his character that would shock or repulse her. Some trait he possessed that would make him irredeemable in her eyes.

He loved dogs—that had been plain to see. He was patient—look how kind he'd been to Mr. Stuyvesant. He was intelligent. He'd obviously loved his father, and there was a fond look in his eyes when he spoke about his mother and sisters. He'd even seemed interested in her tasks and wanted to ensure she drew a salary. Not once had he acted like Felix, who occasionally ridiculed what she did but never stepped up to do it.

No, the man was dangerously intriguing. Not to mention attractive, a fact that made her feel silly and too young to be alone with him. What nonsense. She was Elsbeth Carew and she'd been schooled in propriety, had she not?

At least she should stop looking at him so often. Granted, his profile was strong, perhaps almost perfect. He had the McCraight nose, but it fit his face. His jawline was firm.

At first his hat had seemed odd to her, but now she was more accustomed to it. It looked right, just like the coat turned up at the collar.

He smiled, an expression she'd seen a thousand times on many different faces. Why, then, did it stop her heart? She looked away quickly, feeling her cheeks warm.

It wasn't her fault that he was so handsome. Or that he fascinated her. Any woman would be stirred. Mrs. Ferguson had blushed when speaking of him. Look how Mary McCraight had behaved around him, all fluttery and girlie.

"You must miss your family," she said.

"Yes."

Just that one word and nothing more. No information about a sweetheart or an impending marriage.

"I've often wondered what it would be like to have a family," she said. "A real family. Not a borrowed one."

"Do you have no one else?" he asked.

"A great-aunt," she said. "I understand she's up in years, though." She'd never met the woman. If her great-aunt had ever inquired about her, Elsbeth didn't know about it.

"I might have other relatives, but Gavin was never able to find them. My father was an only child. As to my mother, I don't know."

"I wouldn't have asked if I'd known it would bring such a look to your face," he said.

Startled, she glanced at him. "Then I should apologize," she said. "You said nothing wrong."

"Where are you going to go, Elsbeth? When Bealadair is sold, what will you do?"

"Find a cottage," she said. "Maybe in Glasgow. Mrs. Ferguson has a sister there and it would be nice to have a friend nearby. Or maybe just in Inverness. Or Edinburgh. I've never seen the castle or the other sights of the city. I should like to, very much."

She smiled brightly at him. "You mustn't worry about me, Connor. I'm quite fortunate, all in all. Now let's talk about less dour things, shall we? Let me tell you about Castle McCraight."

She began to slow, wanting to tell Connor the story of the castle before he actually saw it.

"They say that the original McCraight came from Ireland, although Gavin did everything in his power to research and debunk that rumor. Wherever they came from, the very first of your ancestors decided to settle here, on a bluff overlooking Dornoch Firth. It leads out to the North Sea, which is why Gavin thought the first McCraights were Norse."

He didn't say anything, and when she glanced over at him, he seemed to be studying her intently.

She stopped her mare and returned his look. Right at the moment, she could very easily believe that his ancestors were Vikings. With a strong square face and impressive physique, she could almost imagine him wearing a metal breastplate and carrying a double-headed ax. A berserker, but one with judgment and fairness. He wouldn't be afraid of a fight.

Of course he would face Felix. How foolish she'd been to suggest that it might not be a good idea. Connor would never run away from a challenge.

She pulled her thoughts away from him and slowly edged the mare forward, glancing at Connor to see the reaction to his first sight of Castle Mc-Craight.

CONNOR HAD NEVER visited the Parthenon, although he'd seen etchings of it. What had struck him on first viewing the structure was the shout that had seemed to come from the building. A declaration and a warning that stated: *Here I am as of today, but once I was a mighty place filled with warriors and statesmen. People with dreams once occupied me. They have died but the dreams remain, sheltered by my ruins.*

He had the same thought about the castle he stared at now.

Snow was still mounded high against the roofless walls. Arches, like eyes, stared out at the sea. Nothing grew there. Neither ivy nor weeds filled in the cracks of masonry.

Castle McCraight gave off a proud loneliness.

The war he'd fought in had been filled with both patriotic and sad songs. As he slowly walked Samson forward, a ballad came to Connor's mind. The tale of a woman waiting at home for a man who would never return, a soldier lost in the war. Castle McCraight seemed to embody the hopelessness of that eternal vigil.

This was the cradle that had guarded the seed from which his family tree had sprung. Men had lived and died here, had built this place in defiance of their enemies. When war and battles no longer raged, they'd moved their home farther inland, away from the cliff fortress whipped by a freezing, briny wind.

It wasn't Bealadair he would remember when he

thought of Scotland, but this place. This was the true anchor, the place where his heritage began.

The forest encircled them on three sides. Ahead was the sea, stretching across the horizon.

It was, perhaps, fitting that his father's ghost should join him here, that he could feel Graham walking beside him as he advanced a few more feet.

Had his father played here as a boy or had it been forbidden him? He had the idea that the twin boys had defied the rules and come here as often as they could. Had they played scenes from Scotland's history? Had one of them been English and the other a Highlander?

He could almost feel Graham smiling beside him. He had the sudden notion that his father would be pleased to see him here.

Pulling out his notebook, he began to sketch the castle, knowing that he'd like to show the place to his mother and sisters.

Elsbeth sat quietly beside him. He glanced at her more than once, wanting to thank her for not only bringing him here but for the look in her beautiful eyes. As if she understood the emotion of this moment.

She'd featured in his important discoveries at Bealadair. Standing off to the side, almost as if she were waiting for him to turn to her for comfort or peace or understanding.

"'Keen blaws the wind o'er the braes o' Gleniffer, The auld castle's turrets are cover'd wi' snaw.'"

"What is that?" he asked. "A McCraight poem? Was my uncle given to writing verse?"

She smiled and shook her head. "It's a poem by Robert Tannahill called 'The Braes o' Gleniffer.' I've always thought it matched Castle McCraight."

His sketch done, he put away his notebook and slowly dismounted, tying Samson's reins to a branch before approaching the castle.

All of the walls looked as if the masonry had broken off at an angle. Only one whole wall remained, standing as a bulwark against the elements.

The brick and stone was gray with black patches, while the snow mounted on the arches and against the walls was pristine white. A monochrome picture that reminded him, oddly enough, of the morning of the Battle of Chickamauga with its deep fog. He pushed those memories aside.

"Do you sketch everything you see?" Elsbeth asked.

He glanced over at her, surprised that he hadn't heard her approach. He hadn't helped her dismount and apologized.

She brushed away his words with a smile. "You drew the cattle, too," she said.

"I had to draw them. No one back home would believe me if I told them about your hairy cattle."

Her laughter echoed in this lonely place. Elsbeth was exactly what Castle McCraight needed. Someone filled with life and purpose and determination.

"I didn't sketch the war," he said, his memories of Chickamauga coming back with a vengeance. As a member of the cavalry corps under General Wheeler, he'd seen too much combat. War wasn't romantic. It wasn't noble. Let people put up bunting. Let them wave their flags. The soldiers knew what the truth was, and they kept it to themselves in an effort to spare the civilians.

She came closer, standing so near he could have embraced her easily.

He wanted to. Because of that sudden wish, he should have moved away. He didn't.

"Would you show me your drawing?"

With anyone else he probably would have declined, but this was Elsbeth. A thought that startled him. He hadn't known her last week.

He pulled out his notebook and showed her the page.

She leaned closer. "You really are an artist," she said. "You've captured it perfectly."

He smiled at her. "I'm a rancher."

"Would you rather be an artist?"

The question surprised him. No one had ever asked him something like that.

"You didn't exactly have a choice in what you would do, did you?" she said, before he could answer.

"Does anyone? I didn't have a choice about becoming the Duke of Lothian, either."

She smiled, and he was struck again by how beautiful she was. Her red cloak was the perfect color to flatter her coloring, her gray eyes as warm as smoke as she looked at him.

"I love my life," he said. "I love everything about it, even the things that are annoying. I like riding out in the morning and knowing that everything I see for that entire day belongs to my family. I like knowing that the ranch provides a living for hundreds of men and their families. I like seeing the herds and the horses, trying new things, new ways of doing things. I like my freedom."

"And you don't think you have freedom here, is that it?"

She had placed her hand on his arm and he could swear that he felt her touch through her glove and his sleeve. There was something magical about Elsbeth, something that caught at him whenever he looked at her.

The whole of the fortress was shadowed as if nature was beginning to pull a blanket over the day.

He pocketed his notebook again and walked into the ruins. Once inside the structure, he looked up to where the roof would have been a century or two earlier. The wind created an eerie moaning sound almost as if Castle McCraight was grieving about its fate.

When he said as much to Elsbeth, she didn't disappoint.

"It's the spirit of winter," she said. "The sea has a winter spirit and a summer one. The winter one is angrier."

He decided he wasn't going to comment on that, either.

"Did my uncle tutor you?" he asked, genuinely curious. She seemed to know a lot about many subjects.

She smiled. "No, but he did quiz me on the lessons my governess taught me. I learned to pay attention so I wouldn't disappoint him."

Their gazes locked and her smile faded. He reached out and placed his cold hand against her face. She didn't flinch. Nor did she move away.

He should have issued a caution to her, explained that he was feeling somewhat odd at the moment. Perhaps it was Castle McCraight pulling emotions from his past. He hadn't had a sweetheart before he went off to war, but if he had he would have wanted her to be like Elsbeth. She had a core of deep loyalty and a sense of duty that equaled his.

Regardless of how people treated her, she fulfilled her obligations. It didn't matter what the weather or the obstacles, Elsbeth forged on. He suspected that she didn't care if she ever received praise for her actions. Yet he couldn't help but wonder if anyone ever thought to thank her.

Not only did he like her, but he admired her. Plus, there was another feeling, one thrumming beneath the surface. True, he thought she was beautiful, but this was something more.

He looked away, toward the open side of the ruins.

"What is it?"

"I thought I heard something," he said. "Twigs breaking."

"It could be the Urisk," she said. "He sits on lonely spots and watches intruders. Especially those who would invade his solitude."

"Urisk? A ghost?"

She shook her head. "A solitary being, a result of the union between a mortal and a fairy."

"And you believe this?" he asked, unable to keep the incredulity out of his voice.

She shook her head again, her look chiding. "It's

not important what I believe, Connor. It's lore. It's history. People who have lived here for millennia believe it. This land is built on the bones and the souls of those who've gone before."

"We have our own past in Texas, Elsbeth. We're also a damn sight warmer."

He wasn't going to ridicule Scottish beliefs. Whatever they chose to accept was fine with him; just don't make him think the same thing.

She smiled at him and he couldn't help himself. Slowly he leaned in, giving her time to say something, to issue a caution of her own.

She didn't. Instead, she was motionless, her beautiful eyes wide as he lowered his mouth to hers, feeling her breath warm against his lips.

He'd anticipated a kiss; he hadn't expected the surge of feeling. He wanted to love her, gently, sweetly—at the same time he wanted to protect her. He wanted to push her away and lecture her on the dangers of giving herself so easily to him—at the same moment he drew her closer, wrapping his arms around her.

He forgot that they were standing in the middle of a Scottish ruin, that the fierce cold was seeping into his bones.

Instead, there was only Elsbeth, only the feel of her in his arms, the soft sound she made as the kiss deepened.

Another sound brought him back to the present. Maybe the memories of Chickamauga had somehow alerted him. In those years he'd always been vigilant.

It was a small noise, nothing more. It could have

been a falling rock, an icicle dropping from a branch to the ground.

Or something else.

He broke off the kiss, looked up, alert to something else, a click and rasp, followed by another click that abruptly ricocheted him into the past.

Pushing Elsbeth to the ground, he followed her, covering her with his body. She gasped in surprise or pain or perhaps even outrage. The sound of the shot silenced her.

"Someone's shooting at us," he said, stating the obvious. "And it's not your Urisk."

He heard a second shot, an echo accompanying it. A rifle, then, the sound too powerful to be a pistol.

Where was the shooter standing? He rose up, enough to peer through the arched window. Another shot rang out and the question faded beneath instantaneous pain.

Damn it, he'd been hit.

He stayed on his knees, dragging Elsbeth by the hand as he made it to the shelter of the tallest wall. From his calculations, the shooter was on the west side of Castle McCraight, probably hiding near the tree edge.

The pain in his shoulder angered him. He'd been shot before and didn't have any desire to repeat the experience, especially not in the same spot.

"Why is someone shooting at us?"

"It's your country, Elsbeth. Damned if I know."

He hadn't done anything to anyone. He wasn't at war.

He held his good arm around Elsbeth, waiting. A few minutes passed. Removing his hat, he raised it a little. Nothing. He tossed it into the air, but nothing happened. Either the shooter wasn't taking the bait or he'd left.

After a few more minutes passed, Connor pointed to the trees on the east side of the ruins, opposite from where he thought the shooter was.

"It's not great cover," he said, "but it beats the hell out of sitting here waiting to be shot."

He probably should have apologized for swearing again, but he had cause right at the moment. She didn't lecture him on etiquette, either, for which he was grateful.

Keeping hold of her hand, he got to his feet and pulled Elsbeth with him, both of them ducking beneath the ruined walls to the edge of the woods.

He would bet that no human had been in this area of the forest in years. The undergrowth was so thick his boots sank to his ankles. He thought he saw the sharp nose of a fox, but it disappeared so quickly he could have been mistaken.

"You've lost your hat," she said, her voice sounding breathless and thin.

"I don't do everything with my hat on. My boots, now that's something entirely different."

She didn't smile. Instead, her eyes widened as she stretched out her hand and touched his right shoulder.

"You've been shot!"

He pulled her behind a massive oak, bent his head back, and looked up through the archway of branches to a darkening sky.

At least it wasn't snowing.

The sound of tearing fabric startled him. He

glanced over to find that she had lifted the corner of her cloak and was ripping the hem of her riding garment.

"What are you doing?"

"You're bleeding," she said. "I need something to staunch the wound."

Her voice was remarkably calm. He'd known nurses in the Civil War who hadn't sounded as serene as Elsbeth did at the moment.

"I do wish I'd brought some extra handkerchiefs," she said. "But I didn't know you were going to go and get shot."

"It's not exactly my fault," he said, grateful for the amusement he felt. It took his mind off the pain.

He glanced to his right and bit back an oath.

"I've only had this coat six months. The hole can't be patched and I doubt the blood can be cleaned. And, damn it, I've already been shot there before."

She hesitated in the act of pulling his coat off his shoulders and stared at him as if she'd never before seen a wounded man. Maybe she hadn't. Maybe he ought to apologize for that, too.

"He could very easily have killed you," she said. "And you're worried about your coat."

He started to nod, thought better of the gesture, and said, "I think that was the objective."

She was frowning at him as she pulled back his jacket and shirt.

"Why?"

He had a couple of reasons ready, but he didn't think he had to tell her. Elsbeth had struck him as perceptive from the beginning.

Either someone didn't like the fact that he was

the Duke of Lothian, and in that he couldn't blame them. Or someone was angry about his decision to sell Bealadair. Either way, he had a target on his back.

"It's not in the same place," she said. "Nearly so, but your other scar is a few inches to the right."

He closed his eyes, but only for a moment as she pressed against the wound. This one hurt more and he couldn't help but wonder if the bullet had hit his collarbone.

"We're near Ainell Village," she said. "There's a physician there. I could go get him."

He opened his eyes. "I have no intention of remaining here while you're off getting reinforcements. No, Elsbeth."

Just no. He was more than willing to tie her to him if necessary. Maybe his look gave his feelings away, because she frowned at him again.

This was the woman he'd lost his mind kissing just a moment ago. Now she looked like she wanted to smack him.

Chapter 20

Could a hunter have shot Connor? Granted, this was McCraight land, but poachers had been known to come onto their acreage. Yet they hadn't had a problem for years, ever since Gavin had made sure that all the crofters had a subsistent income. They would never starve and consequently didn't need to hunt illegally.

But there were plenty of people in Ainell Village who might have been poaching. Anyone could've taken a shot at Connor, especially since his leather coat made him look like a large elk.

When Elsbeth said as much to him, he gave her a look like she was slightly demented. Or weak in the mind.

"It's possible," she said, annoyed.

"Not very probable," he countered. "I think whoever took a shot at me knew exactly what he was doing."

She sat back on her heels and considered that someone had tried to kill him.

What a ghastly thought. No, worse than that.

Her stomach churned.

If he hadn't pushed her to the ground, he would probably have been struck directly in the chest. She would be sobbing over his lifeless body, instead of trying to tend to his wound.

"I won't leave you," she said. "I'll protect you."

He closed his eyes and laid his head back against the tree trunk. "God help me."

"What, exactly, does that mean?"

"That if I am so infirm and unable to protect myself to the degree that a delicate woman has to do so, I must be more badly wounded than I thought."

"I am not delicate," she said.

He opened his eyes at that comment and studied her.

"Even in that voluminous red cloak of yours, Elsbeth Carew, you're very delicate. You walk with a certain grace, I think. I've yet to figure out what it is. Perhaps I should just ask you to parade in front of me for an hour or two until I can work it out."

"You're delirious," she said. "We need to get you help and quickly."

"I'm not," he said. "Although I'll admit it smarts a bit. I think our shooter has left."

She was afraid he was losing too much blood. What was she going to do? She looked at him, still large and impressive sitting at the base of the tree, and then at Samson.

He was right, though; no shots had come for quite a few minutes. Did that mean that the shooter had given up and gone away? Or was it simply that he was waiting them out, hoping they would emerge from the woods?

"Here," she said, raising his left hand and placing it against the wound. "Hold that tight until I come back. Don't let it go."

"I'm cold," he said. "You strip me practically naked and it's damn cold out here."

She frowned at him again. "You're very argumentative when you're not feeling well. Did you know that?"

"I will apologize later," he said, reaching for his coat and pulling it over his wound. "Where do you think you're going?" he asked as she began to cautiously move away.

She glanced back at him and made a motion with her hand. He didn't seem to understand that it meant be silent because he said, "Elsbeth, where the hell are you going?"

Now was not the time to give the Duke of Lothian lessons in etiquette. A severe frown would have to do.

At the edge of the forest she stood, scanning the castle, the cliff area, and the far trees. She couldn't see anything.

Slowly, she emerged from the trees, heading to where Samson stood beside her mare.

Nothing happened.

Nobody shot at her when she grabbed Samson's reins and made her way to a fallen stone near the edge of the forest. She was going to have Connor stand on it so he could mount the horse.

Was the duchess going to get a tearful visit from one of the villagers tomorrow along with a confession? The more time elapsed, the more she wanted to think that it had been a horrible mistake. Of course no one had deliberately tried to harm Connor.

Except that she thought that might be a naive assumption. After all, he was going to change everything by selling Bealadair.

She made her way back to Connor's side. His hand had slipped away from the wound and it was bleeding profusely.

"You have to stand up," she said. "I can help you get to your horse, but I can't make you stand up. Please, Connor."

His eyes fluttered open.

"Kiss me again, Elsbeth."

"I beg your pardon?"

"That kiss was not long enough."

"You're feverish," she said.

"I'm not."

"You've been wounded."

"I have at that. That's why you should kiss me again."

"Your Grace."

"Even that doesn't sound as terrible uttered by those luscious lips of yours."

"Connor!"

"Kiss me, Elsbeth."

"If you'll stand up," she said in desperation, "I'll kiss you."

"You promise?"

She nodded.

"Do you ever break your promises?"

"Never," she said.

"Never?"

"Why do you ask me questions if you don't want to hear my answers? Or don't believe them?"

"You're very fiery. Are all Scottish women fiery? You remind me of a Texan."

He was not moving to stand and if he didn't do

so quickly, she was very much afraid he would be too weak.

She moved to his left side, grabbed his arm, and began to pull.

"You have to stand, Connor. If you want that kiss, you have to make it to your horse."

Blood was seeping over his shirt down to the waistband of his trousers. He wasn't cooperating, and her fear gave her a strength she didn't know she had. She nearly pulled him upright all by herself.

He leaned on her heavily as they made their way to Samson.

"My hat," he said.

She almost said a swear word, something she'd heard from the stableboys. Or the 14th Duke of Lothian.

"Once I get you on Samson," she said, "I'll go back and get your hat."

If she couldn't get it now, she'd come back for it. Him and his hat. She led him to where Samson patiently stood.

To her surprise, he leaned down and kissed her before she knew what he was going to do. At least that's what she told herself. Nor did she push him away because he'd been wounded. She didn't want to make his injury worse.

The man was dangerous. Even hurt, he kissed like a devil.

She lost herself for a few moments, and when she finally stepped back, he smiled down at her.

A few minutes later they reached the stone at Samson's side. Now, all she needed to do was to get him to climb on it and he could drape himself over the saddle. The stubborn man, the foolish man, the idiotic man, refused to do as she asked.

"Please, Connor," she said. "Just step up there and we can get you on Samson."

To her amazement, he gripped the reins, put his left foot in the stirrup and mounted the horse with accustomed ease. Only the look on his face betrayed the effort it had cost him. He was suddenly stark white, his lips thinned.

"Let's go."

She told herself she was an idiot as she went to retrieve his hat.

"Good afternoon, Duchess."

Rhona halted in the corridor and slowly turned to find herself being addressed by Mr. Kirby.

He walked toward her, holding his oddly shaped hat in his hands.

"A lovely afternoon, isn't it?"

"You'll have to forgive me, Mr. Kirby, but I don't have any idea whether it's a lovely afternoon or not. I've been involved with a great many tasks."

"Then would you care to take a walk with me?" he asked, having the effrontery to offer her his arm.

"I beg your pardon?"

"Take a stroll with me, Duchess. You can show me the sights around Bealadair."

She wasn't the type to show someone "the sights" as he called it. Only one thing kept her from informing him of that fact in as terse a manner as possible, and it so surprised her that she could only stare at the man.

His eyes were lit with admiration.

Was he one of those Americans who were fascinated with titles? Was he simply impressed that she was a duchess?

"I'm afraid I don't have time," she said.

"What is so pressing that you can't take a moment out of your day?"

He was presuming a great deal, but then he was an American. They had a way of speaking bluntly.

"Mr. Kirby, I have the duties of my station."

"Wouldn't one of those be showing a guest around your house?"

He stretched out his hand, leaving it in the air between them. She didn't know what else to do so she placed hers atop it. He bent and kissed the air above her knuckles, just like the French and German dignitaries she'd met. When the kiss was done, he squeezed her fingers as if he were loath to relinquish her hand.

"Mr. Kirby," she began, only to be startled by his smile. He had a way of looking at you as if there was not another human being in existence.

"Even if that guest is in awe of your beauty?"

He really did have a way of flummoxing her with his questions. She didn't think anyone had ever said anything like that to her in years. She really should dismiss the man immediately.

Yet there was the possibility that Mr. Kirby might have some influence with His Grace. Perhaps the man might even be able to convince him to change his mind and remain in Scotland. Or allow the family to continue to reside at Bealadair. Surely he didn't need to sell the house and the land.

She fingered the cameo at her neck. It was the

only spot of color she wore. Black was expected. Black was proper. Black, however, washed out her complexion and made her hazel eyes seem more brown than green.

Yet in his glance she wasn't a widow. Nor was she the mother of two grown daughters and the step-mother of another. She felt—impossibly—young again, her wardrobe designed to augment her beauty.

"Do you have a rose garden?"

"A rose garden? Yes, we do. Of course, it's dormant now since it's winter."

"Would you show it to me?" he asked.

"I do not know if you've noticed, Mr. Kirby, but there is at least two feet of snow on the ground. The roses have been bagged and mulched. There is nothing to see. Besides, it's almost dark."

"Then perhaps you can show me some of your glorious home."

He really was the most persistent man. But there was something about the look in his eyes, and the undiluted admiration that she hadn't seen for a very long time. Her youth, in fact, when she had, as the daughter of the Earl of Debish, been courted and feted for her beauty and vibrancy.

She had married Gavin, believing his words and his implicit promise. Believing, too, in a future that had never materialized. He had not continued to love her. Instead, he had put his books and his histories above her and his children.

"What would you like to see, Mr. Kirby?" she asked, surprising herself with the question. She told herself that it would be foolish to overlook an opportunity to influence His Grace.

"Anything you would like to show me, Duchess. But, please, couldn't we be a little less formal? Call me Sam."

He squeezed her fingers again. His grip was warm as his smile.

How absurd. But this American with his engaging grin wouldn't be at Bealadair for long. What was the harm?

"My name is Rhona," she heard herself saying. "I have to inspect the larder, Sam. Perhaps you would like to accompany me?"

He folded her hand around his arm.

"Shall we go, then?" he asked.

She nodded and led the way.

Chapter 21

*E*lsbeth was nearly weeping by the time they made it back to Bealadair. Twice, Connor almost fell from the saddle. Finally, she rode so close to him that her mare was bumping Samson, something he didn't like. He'd tossed his head more than once, threatening a tantrum. She found herself talking both to Connor and the stallion—encouraging the human and calming the horse.

Once back at the stables she sent one of the stableboys to fetch a cot and another to alert Mrs. Ferguson. The housekeeper had quite a bit of experience in nursing and could do what was necessary until the physician was summoned from the village.

After they carried Connor to his suite—while he was complaining the whole time—the housekeeper arrived.

"Perhaps it would be best if you left the room, Elsbeth," Mrs. Ferguson said. "It is the duke's bedchamber, after all."

Elsbeth only shook her head. She was not going to leave Connor's side until she was certain he was going to be all right. She didn't know how deep the wound was. She didn't know if it had nicked any bones or hit his lung. Besides, he had gripped her hand and refused to let it go, even as they tried to remove his coat.

"Connor, let go," she said, bending close to him. "If you don't, we'll have to cut your coat off you and it will be totally ruined."

He finally let go of her hand, and they were able to remove the garment.

In the last few minutes his color had gotten worse and he was shivering so hard his teeth were chattering.

"His body is reacting to the wound," Mrs. Ferguson said. "It's to be expected."

"Will he be all right?"

The housekeeper didn't answer her, merely took the scissors from one of the maids who had fetched her sewing kit from her room. With deft precision, she cut off Connor's bloody jacket and shirt, revealing the wound.

Elsbeth closed her eyes, surprised at the wave of dizziness. She had never before been affected by the sight of blood. But this was a different matter entirely. This was Connor.

Mrs. Ferguson bent close. "I think it would be best if you left, Elsbeth. Especially before the duchess gets here."

"I'm not leaving," she said. She was already in for a lecture. How much worse could it be if she remained a few minutes?

The room was growing crowded. She turned her head to see Lara and Felix standing in the doorway. Behind them were a few maids and footmen. She could also see Muira and Anise. Any moment now, the duchess would arrive and demand to know what had happened.

What would she say? Should she even mention her suspicions? Or merely announce that Connor had been shot by a poacher?

She had to figure out something before Rhona arrived.

Someone grabbed her shoulders and pushed her down on a chair that had been moved to the side of the bed. She grabbed Connor's hand again, clasping it between both of hers, wanting to warm it somehow.

Why hadn't she become more adept at treating wounds? She knew how to handle burns in the kitchen or minor cuts and scrapes. Where did she go for education on how to handle bullet wounds? And why did she think that she would have ever needed such knowledge?

Who'd done such a thing? That thought had vied with another all the way back to the house until it was a refrain: Was he going to be all right? Who had done such a thing? Was he going to be all right?

Now all she could do was sit and watch as Mrs. Ferguson cleaned the wound.

Connor didn't say a word. He didn't moan. He didn't gasp in pain. He only lay there, his eyes closed, his thinned lips the only indication that he felt what was being done to him.

She wanted to tell him that she would protect him and make sure that no one did anything that would bring him undue pain. Nothing more than was necessary to heal him. She wanted to reassure him somehow, but what words would she use?

It's all right, Connor. I'm here.

She didn't know many men, only the ones that visited Bealadair. Or Gavin, of course. She'd cited him as a model for others. But not even Gavin had been stoic and uncomplaining. He occasionally whined about his ailments, and she listened and commiserated when necessary.

Connor still hadn't said anything. When Mrs. Ferguson began to probe the wound he gripped Elsbeth's hand tighter.

She wanted to ask him if he would like some Scottish whiskey, something to dull the pain.

"The bullet is still lodged inside," Mrs. Ferguson said. "It will need to come out."

There was entirely too much blood. It was soaking into the sheets. Elsbeth averted her eyes, concentrated on Connor's hand.

"Can you do that?" she asked.

"I've never removed a bullet," Mrs. Ferguson said. "But if the physician doesn't arrive soon, I'm going to have to. The longer we delay the more blood he'll lose."

"Do it," a voice said from behind her.

Elsbeth glanced over her shoulder to see Mr. Kirby standing there, his expression somber, his gaze fixed on Connor's face.

"I can help you," he said. "I've had some experience with bullet wounds."

What kind of place was Texas?

As if he had heard her unspoken question, Mr. Kirby glanced at her.

"Men are occasionally hotheaded, Miss Carew."

Within moments, Mrs. Ferguson had arranged what she needed: extra toweling, hot water, two pairs of tweezers—one pair long and one short—embroidery scissors, and a needle and fine thread.

She would've moved away except that Connor wouldn't relinquish her hand.

"I'm in the way," she said to him, so softly that only he would hear.

"Don't go."

She looked up at Mr. Kirby. "He wants me to stay."

"Nonsense," the Duchess of Lothian said. "You shouldn't be here."

Of course she'd come into the room. Elsbeth didn't even turn. She wasn't going to argue, not now. This wasn't the time or the place.

The duchess, however, was not accustomed to being ignored. When Elsbeth didn't respond, she merely issued a command.

"You're not needed, Elsbeth. Be on your way."

Mrs. Ferguson glanced at her across Connor's body.

Elsbeth interpreted the look as a warning. Perhaps a year ago she would have acted differently, but what did she have to lose now? She knew she was going to leave Bealadair. It wasn't as if she needed to curry the duchess's favor anymore. It was only a matter of time until she made her departure.

She turned her head and looked beyond Mr. Kirby to where the duchess stood.

"The duke wishes me to stay," she said. There, let that sink in. His Grace wished her to remain. His wishes were more important than Rhona's.

"Texan."

She glanced at Connor to see that he'd opened his eyes and was looking at her.

"I beg your pardon?"

He closed his eyes again without answering her.

"He called you a Texan, Miss Carew."

She glanced over at Mr. Kirby. "Why would he do a thing like that?"

"I believe he meant it as a compliment," Mr. Kirby said, smiling down at her. "I sure would take it like that."

Mrs. Ferguson braced herself on the mattress with her left hand. In her gnarled fingers she held a long pair of tweezers. Elsbeth said a quick prayer that the housekeeper's arthritis wouldn't prevent her from doing what she needed to do and quickly.

"I'm ready to remove the bullet, but it's important that you hold him still. He mustn't move."

"I think Mr. Kirby would be better at this," she said.

The housekeeper made an impatient sound. "You've never been missish, Elsbeth. I heard the story of you helping a goat give birth. And what about the time you set Jed's arm?"

"Both of those were emergency situations and there wasn't anyone around to help. This is entirely different. Mr. Kirby would be stronger, don't you think, and able to hold Connor down if he moves."

"You're doing fine, Miss Carew." Mr. Kirby reached over and patted her on the shoulder. "He won't move as long as you're here."

"Don't flatter her too much, Sam," Connor said, his eyes still closed. "She was a harpy at the ruins."

She frowned at him. How dare he say such a thing about her, especially in front of all these people? She wasn't going to turn and look at Rhona. She could just imagine the duchess's expression.

She placed one hand on his wrist, the other on

his left shoulder. Did he have any inkling that, until this afternoon, she'd never touched a man's chest? Or that it was scandalous that she was looking at it now?

Mrs. Ferguson leaned over Connor, probed at the wound with the nasty-looking tweezers, and then sank them deep into his flesh.

Connor didn't move. His expression didn't change. Only the hiss of his breath indicated that he was in pain.

"He's being stalwart and brave because you're here," Mr. Kirby said, leaning down and whispering to her. "He doesn't want you to think he's a coward."

"I'm not a coward," Connor said, his voice faint. "If you're going to insult me, Sam, at least make it a halfway decent insult."

"I can assure you, Miss Carew," Mr. Kirby said, "I do not lie. It is the presence of a beautiful woman such as yourself that keeps my young friend from shouting all manner of obscenities."

She expected Connor to say something, but Mrs. Ferguson was digging into the wound. She felt Connor's arm tighten beneath her. Her hand moved from his wrist to his palm. Their fingers interlocked and he squeezed her hand just once, a wordless acknowledgment of her need to offer him comfort.

"I'm sorry if I was a harpy, earlier," she said softly. "I was just worried."

"I want another kiss."

It was evident from Mr. Kirby's chuckle that he had heard Connor's comment. Had the duchess? She was most definitely not going to look in Rhona's direction right now.

She really did need to deflect everyone's attention. Just for a few moments until her cheeks cooled.

Thankfully, Mr. Kirby came to her rescue.

"What happened, Miss Carew?"

She half expected Connor to answer, but he kept his eyes closed.

She glanced over her shoulder at Mr. Kirby. "Someone shot at us," she said.

"Did you see who it was?"

She shook her head. "Would you please ring for the majordomo? I need to send some men over to Castle McCraight to see if they can find any clues."

"I have some experience at tracking men, Miss Carew," he said. "If you'll allow me, I would be pleased to supervise the investigation."

She glanced at him and then away, certain that she'd never seen a man's face change so quickly. One moment he was affable, even teasing. The next, his eyes had flattened and turned hard.

She was very grateful he was Connor's friend and that he was demonstrating some loyalty. No one else was. Members of the staff looked more concerned than the family. Rhona hadn't gasped in horror. The three daughters didn't look distressed. Felix certainly hadn't stepped up and offered to help.

For the first time since she'd come to Bealadair she was ashamed of the McCraights.

"Thank you, Mr. Kirby," she said. "I would appreciate your help."

No doubt she was going to pay for those words, too.

The bullet wasn't easy to find.

A few minutes into the operation, Elsbeth closed

her eyes and practiced breathing very slowly. It didn't seem to quell her nausea, however. To keep herself from becoming sick at the smell of Connor's blood, she concentrated on the feel of their linked fingers.

Mrs. Ferguson was pressing Mr. Kirby into service. Were the two of them probing the wound? She wasn't going to look. She couldn't. Instead, she bent her head, almost as if she were praying, and rested her cheek against the back of Connor's hand, willing this ordeal to be over for him.

"Tell me about Texas," she said. "However do you manage two million acres?"

"Not all at once," he said. To her amazement his tone sounded almost amused. Pained, but holding a dose of humor.

With her eyes closed, and so close to him, she could almost pretend they were alone. If somehow she could ignore Mrs. Ferguson talking about the bullet slipping from her grasp and Mr. Kirby marveling at the amount of blood.

"Do you have a great many cattle?"

"About a hundred seventy thousand head," he said, the words spoken from between clenched lips.

Was he delirious? She couldn't even conceive of that many cattle.

She felt him stiffen just as Mrs. Ferguson made a triumphant sound.

"Got it!" she said.

Elsbeth opened her eyes to see the housekeeper's blood-drenched hands triumphantly holding the bullet. She was truly afraid she was going to get sick. If she was with anyone else, she might have succumbed, but she didn't want Connor to see her that way.

She must be his equal in courage. She focused on his face, now too pale.

"Was the war terrible?" she asked. She'd never known anyone who'd fought in an actual war. Would he consider the question naive or silly?

He opened his eyes again, looking as if he were trying to focus on the ceiling before he turned his head slightly.

He had the McCraight brown eyes, but his seemed different somehow, deeper, the color more intense. They seemed to have a sparkle, as if God had, just prior to his birth, dropped gold dust in them.

How foolish she was becoming.

She didn't know how long their gazes locked. It felt like a very long time. She wanted to ease his pain, both the physical pain he was enduring now and what she saw in his eyes.

"Yes."

It took her a second to realize that he was answering her. Yes, the war was terrible.

Her hand squeezed his.

She heard her name being called and reluctantly glanced toward the duchess.

"I do believe Mrs. Ferguson has the situation well in hand," Rhona said. "Besides, the doctor is here."

In other words, she should release Connor's hand, stand, and exit the room, to be subjected, no doubt, to the duchess's scrutiny and interrogation.

She didn't want to leave.

She didn't want to leave *him*.

"Elsbeth."

It wasn't a request but a command.

Mr. Kirby placed his hand on her shoulder. "I'll be here, Miss Carew."

She nodded, gently released Connor's hand, her fingers stroking softly along his palm. Resolutely, she stood, looked down at him, and forced herself to smile.

Be well. Words that never made it past her lips to be heard by the others in the room.

Chapter 22

I don't see why we have to move," Anise said.

Muira put down her fork and stared at her sister. "Because we don't belong here. Not anymore."

"But that's silly. Someone can't just come along and tell us to move and we have to obey them."

Elsbeth stood in the doorway regarding the sisters. Barely two hours had passed since she'd brought Connor home, and yet they were acting as if nothing had happened. Had they always been as selfish and she was just now noticing it?

Maybe she was being too harsh. They'd been given a shock by Connor's decision and that was at the forefront of their minds. But couldn't they spare a moment or two for thoughts of him?

Lara was reclining in one of the wing chairs by the fire. She didn't look at all well. A cup of tea was sitting beside her on the table, but she wasn't drinking it. Instead, she was staring at the fire as if to see the future in the flames. Her feet were on a footstool, one that bore the McCraight clan crest in needlepoint.

Muira was helping herself to another piece of

chocolate cake, one of Addy's brilliant pastry confections.

Anise was walking in front of the windows, turning and retracing her steps. Pacing wouldn't make the situation any better than it was. All it would do was annoy the people who had to watch her relentless marathon.

At least Felix was nowhere in sight. Normally he was to be found wherever Lara was, as if he was afraid his wife might forget about him.

What kind of man had no occupation? He simply had moved in after their marriage, obviously content to live off Gavin's generosity and his wife's allowance. He purchased what he wanted when he wanted it, offering no excuses or apologies to anyone for being a spendthrift.

"He can't sell the house," Anise said.

"I'm afraid he can," Elsbeth said. "Bealadair belongs to him, after all."

Anise stopped and glared at her. "Well it's not fair. It's certainly not right or proper. He's just a rude American."

"Texan," Elsbeth said. "He prefers to be called a Texan."

"I haven't the slightest interest in what he prefers to be called. Evidently, you do. I saw how solicitous you were at his bedside. You were nearly in tears. It was barely a scratch."

Anise was given to announcing her opinion with authority, as if it had the weight of truth. In actuality, she was rarely challenged and was therefore allowed to get away with the most idiotic pronouncements.

This was one of those occasions.

It was simply not worth Elsbeth's time or effort to try to convince Anise otherwise. Mrs. Ferguson said that the bullet had been a good two inches deep and had required some effort to remove. Consequently, Connor had lost a great deal of blood.

For the next few hours he'd be fed one of Addy's restorative hot tonics. A mixture of ground-up herbs and vegetables, it was supposed to work wonders when you were ill. All she knew was that it smelled horrid and tasted the same.

"You were quite friendly with him," Muira said. "Surprisingly so, Elsbeth."

Lara only turned her head slowly and looked at her. She didn't say anything, but there was condemnation in her gaze.

Why? Because she liked the man?

"I merely showed him around Bealadair," she said. "I got to know him a little."

They didn't need to know about the kisses.

Elsbeth moved to the grouping near the fireplace, sat on the end of the settee and arranged her skirts.

The Ladies Parlor was a place they normally congregated in the evening. Elsbeth rarely joined the McCraight women, visiting Mrs. Ferguson instead. If the housekeeper was not up for a visit, Elsbeth would take tea with Addy in the kitchen.

However, the duchess had sent word that she wished to speak with her. Better to face her now and get all the unpleasantness out of the way.

She'd behaved in an improper manner and she was certain the duchess would enumerate all the instances. She'd been alone with Connor as she'd performed her errands this morning. She'd spoken of topics other than the weather. She'd sat next to his bed and held his hand.

She'd kissed him. More than once.

Surely the duchess didn't know that. Dear heavens, hopefully the duchess hadn't heard that part of their exchange. If she had, Elsbeth could anticipate a long lecture as to her morals, what was expected of her, and her great good fortune in being practically adopted by such a renowned and famous family. How dare she act like a doxy?

If the duchess was feeling exceptionally cruel, she'd say something like, *I'm so glad Gavin hasn't lived to see your perfidy.* A remark similar to what she'd said this morning.

No doubt there were a few more rules she'd broken, a few more dictates, all selfishly done, of course. She'd had no consideration for the family—that accusation had been made numerous times in the past few years. She was ungrateful, never mind that she worked on their behalf each day and sometimes well into the night.

She knew better, however, than to make that comment or anything similar to it. No, the best option was to simply sit there and allow the words to wash over her like water.

Tonight, Rhona would fuss and she would apologize and in the end it wouldn't matter. Elsbeth knew all the rules she'd broken, but she hadn't cared and that was the truth of it. Being with Connor had been worth any type of penance she'd have to pay, even another of Rhona's innumerable lectures.

On another night, she might have marshaled her

arguments, deciding how best to convince Rhona that she wasn't an ungrateful foundling. Now it didn't matter. There were other considerations much more important.

Who had shot Connor?

The only person who had seemed remotely interested in that question was Mr. Kirby. Would he find anything at Castle McCraight? Would he tell her?

Why hadn't anyone in the family expressed their outrage? Why hadn't one person acted the least disturbed? That fact was telling, wasn't it?

She had the horrible thought that someone in the family was responsible. If Connor died, they'd have to find a new duke, wouldn't they? But Bealadair wasn't entailed, according to Mr. Glassey. It wouldn't pass to the next duke, but to Connor's heirs.

Did the family know that Connor's death wouldn't solve anything?

At last the duchess sailed into the room, her color high. Elsbeth bit back a sigh, arranged her face in an expression of what she hoped would be perceived as humility, and stared down at her folded hands.

"Elsbeth, thank you for coming."

That was new and somewhat surprising. She glanced up at the duchess.

They would adjourn to another room if this lecture followed the pattern of previous ones. Perhaps the cold conservatory. Or the Ladies Study that was a library but not one as fulsomely furnished as Gavin's.

However, the duchess surprised her again. She waved at her daughters and said, "We'll use this room, I think. It's warm and I have no intention of being uncomfortable."

Another surprise—the three girls didn't offer a word of protest to their mother, but left the room quickly. Had this been preordained? Had the duchess already spoken to her daughters and told them that she planned to excoriate Elsbeth? If so, that might account for the look of sympathy on Muira's face.

A third surprise—the duchess came and sat on the same settee, folded her hands, and stared into the fire for a moment.

Elsbeth had the most horrible feeling that this was going to be a lecture like none other.

Better to get her apologies out of the way.

"I know, Your Grace," she said. "I haven't behaved as well as I should have."

"You kissed him."

Before she could offer up any kind of explanation, the duchess continued.

"Mr. Kirby says the duke is quite taken with you."

Rhona turned her head and stared at Elsbeth, but instead of condemnation, there was only curiosity in her gaze.

"Why would Mr. Kirby think that?" Elsbeth asked.

"I've seen it myself. Last night at dinner, for example. The man couldn't keep his eyes off you."

"Really?" She hadn't noticed. She had been trying hard not to look at him.

"We have a problem, Elsbeth."

Now came the lecture.

"We must do something to try to change his mind,"

the duchess said. "He wants to sell Bealadair because he has no wish to remain in Scotland."

Anyone around Connor for more than a few minutes knew that.

"The right person, I believe, could get him to see the error of his ways. The right person might even convince him to remain in Scotland."

She held herself still.

Rhona's hand reached out, cupped her chin, and turned her head to the left and then to the right.

"You are a remarkably beautiful young woman," she said.

Elsbeth blinked at her.

"I've always thought so," she added, dropping her hand.

If so, the duchess had never before said anything. Her appearance had been the one thing Rhona had never mentioned.

"Beautiful women can accomplish a great deal, Elsbeth. Beautiful women have changed the course of history. Why shouldn't you change the course of the McCraights' history?"

She didn't know what to say first. Or perhaps it would just be wiser to remain mute and let the duchess infer anything she wished.

Her cheeks were warming even though her hands were cold. Even her toes felt cold. It wasn't being in the Highlands in winter. It wasn't even the occasional draftiness of Bealadair that was making her feel frozen. No, Rhona's words were accomplishing that.

"You want me to try to convince the duke not to sell Bealadair?"

The duchess smiled. "Yes, I do. I believe that it's within your power to do so."

"How?" she asked.

"A little seduction would go a long way to accomplishing that task."

Elsbeth's eyes widened.

"Come now, Elsbeth, if you've already kissed the man you evidently feel something for him. Would it be all that difficult to seduce him?"

How many times had she been lectured on propriety? On how many occasions had her behavior been held up as a lesson of how not to act or what not to do?

And now the Duchess of Lothian was urging her to seduce Connor?

"You would have me ruin myself to protect the family. Is that it?"

How very odd that her voice was so level and even. She wasn't shrieking. She didn't even sound angry.

Perhaps she was coming down with something. Or perhaps, somewhere deep inside, she wasn't surprised at Rhona's words.

If Gavin had suggested such a thing, she would have been distraught. She would've felt betrayed. But the duchess?

"Don't be dramatic, Elsbeth. What is going to happen to you otherwise? You'll probably go off and live by yourself somewhere in the country. Something good might come from an alliance with my nephew."

What about a child, if that should happen? What about people finding out she'd been a light skirt and shunning her for her loose morals?

"Just what kind of good do you think might come from my seducing Connor?"

"There, you see, right there," Rhona said, pointing her finger at Elsbeth. "You called him Connor. None of us do. I suspect there is a closer relationship there than you want to admit, Elsbeth. Why, that scene at his bedside was positively romantic."

"Your Grace," she began, a little annoyed that she suddenly felt so close to tears. "There is no relationship there. Perhaps friendship, but nothing more." The woman did not need to know that she found Connor fascinating or that she knew she'd never forget kissing him.

"I think you're being too modest, Elsbeth, and while there is always a place for modesty in a young woman's deportment, it's wasted in this situation. Let us be honest with one another, shall we? We have always been able to do that, haven't we?"

When she remained silent, the duchess smiled again.

"A man is often dictated to by his needs, Elsbeth. A beautiful woman can make him think of those needs."

Really, she had had enough of this.

"Your Grace, even if I followed your advice and seduced the Duke of Lothian, it wouldn't stop him from selling Bealadair."

"Of course it would. Especially if you asked him not to. Especially if you shed a few tears, perhaps. But most definitely if you surrendered your innocence to him."

This was a man who'd gone to war. This was a man who was still a warrior in a great many ways.

Didn't Rhona see that? He wouldn't be swayed by a woman's tears. Or even a woman's virginity.

Was the duchess daft?

"I don't know anything about seduction, Your Grace."

"You don't have to know, Elsbeth. Nature will guide you. It's all instinct."

Elsbeth had had enough. She stood, forcing a smile to her face. "I'll think about what you said."

When had she become so adept at lying?

"I hope you do, my dear child. The future of the family is at stake. You are probably the only one who could alter that for the better."

Elsbeth didn't know what to say to that. She opted for a nod and made her way from the parlor.

Chapter 23

*I*t's about time you woke up."

Connor struggled to push up from the sea of sleep, but it was tempting to float back down into the abyss.

Sam, however, was having none of it.

He clamped his hand on Connor's good shoulder and shook him a little.

"That hurts, dammit."

"Now you sound like one of your sisters," Sam said.

Connor slit open one eye and looked at the older man.

Sam looked a little the worse for wear, which was surprising, because he always prided himself on being the Beau Brummell of the Texas set. He purchased his clothes from a tailor in Dallas, ordered bay rum aftershave from a store in Houston. He might wear boots, but they were the finest money could buy.

Right now, however, his jacket looked as if Sam had rolled around in a bunch of leaves. He even had pieces of leaves in his white eyebrows. His cheeks were bright red and Connor wondered if it was from embarrassment or cold.

"Where have you been?" he asked.

"Looking for who shot you, you fool."

After they'd excavated in his shoulder, the physician had given him something to drink. He suspected it had laudanum in it. He felt exactly like he had when he'd gone to the barber and had a molar extracted. More than a little woozy.

Of course in the war, there hadn't been any pain medication. They'd been damn grateful for a few sips of bourbon to take the edge off.

"Did you find anything?"

"Not a damn thing," Sam said. "But I did get to be around that cousin-in-law of yours. Is that what he is? A cousin-in-law?"

"Hell if I know."

Connor used his left arm to prop himself up, wishing his shoulder wasn't throbbing. Wishing, too, that it wasn't such a familiar feeling. He would just have to get used to the idea that he was going to heal again, just like he had once. With any luck he wouldn't be shot again. Or not in that one spot.

"Whatever he is, the man is as irritating as a horsefly. When he wasn't lecturing me on what was normal in Scottish society, he was telling me that you couldn't possibly sell Bealadair."

"I wouldn't expect anything else from Felix," Connor said.

"He's a little too interested in your shooting ability. Wanted to know if you have a favorite weapon, what kind of shot you use, that sort of thing."

Connor raised one eyebrow. "Maybe he just wants to know about his competition."

Sam shook his head. "That's another thing. He

still wants to shoot targets with you. That's the stupidest thing I've ever heard."

"Why?"

"You've got a hole in you, Connor, or haven't you noticed?"

Sam's bushy white eyebrows were drawn together. The patches of color on his cheeks deepened in hue. His answer, then: it wasn't embarrassment or cold, but anger. And it was directed at him, for being so stupid as to get himself shot.

"At least I'm not being sent back into battle after this wound," Connor said. "I don't mind meeting Felix in a contest," he added. "You can tell him that for me."

"Why would you want to do a fool thing like that?"

"Maybe he's a good shot. A very good shot. It would have taken someone with skill to have made that shot through the window."

He didn't reduce Sam to speechlessness often, but it always pleased him when he did.

"You think he shot you?"

"He's the only one around here who's been bragging about what a great marksman he is."

"Why would he shoot you?"

Connor swung his legs over the side of the bed, gripping the edge of the mattress with both hands. The room tilted a little, and he was suddenly violently nauseated. That's why he didn't like to take pain medication. The stuff was vile. He didn't like going around with his shoulder on fire, either. Wasn't there some kind of happy medium?

He glanced down at himself. "What the hell am I wearing?"

Sam's laughter was irritating.

"A nightshirt."

"A nightshirt?" The garment was white with long sleeves that ended in buttoned cuffs. From what he could tell it was long enough to fall to his ankles and had a row of buttons from his neck to his waist.

"It looks like a woman's nightgown," he said.

"It's what all the proper dukes are wearing."

"Who the hell undressed me?" He turned and looked at Sam, who was grinning at him.

"Relax, Connor, your virtue is safe. The doctor and I did the honors."

It was going to play hell on his arm to get the damn thing off. Maybe he could just rip it at the shoulders.

"But you didn't answer me. Why do you think Felix shot you?"

"I haven't the slightest idea why, Sam, other than it was some fool idea that killing me would make everything better. I wouldn't sell the house. They could live here just like they always have."

"Maybe it's time to tell them you've already made a will, Connor. That your mother and sisters are your beneficiaries."

He nodded. "I don't expect Mom or my sisters would evict them, though. They'd probably let them stay on." He glanced over at Sam. "If anything happens to me, I want you to insist that they sell Bealadair. Don't dicker about the price. They need the money more than they need a place in Scotland. Besides, I can't see any of them—except for Dorothy—wanting to leave Texas. Dorothy might like living here."

He could even see Dorothy being Elsbeth's friend. The two of them would probably get on well. He could almost hear their laughter now. A thought that shouldn't have put him in a bad mood.

"Where are my clothes?" he asked, only to hear Sam laugh again.

"You have your days and nights mixed up, Connor. It's not time to get up. It's midnight. Now tuck yourself back into bed."

"I'm hungry." Despite his earlier nausea he was suddenly feeling starved.

Sam laughed at him again. "If you're a good little boy and get back in bed I'll call for dinner. Maybe gruel and one of those jellies they're always talking about."

"Make it salmon or beef."

At home, he wouldn't be eating this late, but at home he wouldn't have been shot, either. Or if he had, there would've been at least thirty ranch hands out to find the man who'd done it.

"Did you find anything at the castle?"

He glanced over at Sam, who was standing at the end of his bed with his arms folded and a grin still on his face.

Sam reached out and made a twirling motion with his finger. Connor knew what that meant. Get back in bed like a good little boy and he would answer. He debated for a moment—just a moment—making a break for it, finding his clothes, and then doing something constructive for an hour or two. When he stood, however, the room tilted again and it took him a moment until he got his equilibrium back.

That was the effect of the laudanum. Or the gunshot wound.

"What do you think you're doing?"

"I'm not bedridden," he said, and made his way—staggering a little—to the bathing chamber. When he returned, having splashed some water on his face, Sam was opening the sitting room door.

"That was fast," he said.

"I ordered you shepherd's pie. Good for invalids and oldsters."

He shot Sam a look but the older man wasn't paying him any attention.

To his surprise, Sam sat at the table and began to eat.

"Are you eating my dinner?"

"I took the precaution of ordering two servings."

"You're not an invalid. So you're calling yourself an oldster?"

That didn't sound like Sam. He prided himself on the fact that he could keep up with the youngest ranch hand as far as stamina throughout the day. He was damn good at keeping up with them at night, too. Sam had a collection of women in Austin, Dallas, and Houston, and from the stories he heard, they were all happy to entertain him at a moment's notice.

No, Sam wouldn't call himself an oldster even if he was. He'd have to be dragged, kicking and screaming, to his grave. Sam was having too damn much fun living.

"I'm a friend to an invalid and therefore will eat what he eats," Sam said.

"I'm not an invalid."

"Tonight you are," he said, waving his fork in the direction of Connor's nightshirt.

He shook his head, but decided not to argue with the man.

Sam was also one of the most stubborn cusses he'd ever met. His father had thought the same. As much as he liked Sam, Graham could be heard shouting at him often enough. Connor felt like doing a little of that himself, but not here at Bealadair, where there were maids around every corner and footmen just standing there with nothing to do but listen.

"So you didn't find anything?" he asked. He took a bite of his dinner, nodded, and concentrated on his meal for a while.

"It was dark by the time we got there, but we had some torches. We didn't see anything but footprints. Damn hard to track anything when it's snowing."

He didn't know where Sam had gotten his skill at tracking, but he was good. If he hadn't found anything, there was nothing to be found.

"No trace of a horse?"

"Nope, but they could have come through the trees. We wouldn't have been able to see anything in the dark. I'll go back in the daytime."

Sam poured himself a glass of wine. Connor noticed that there wasn't a second glass.

"Don't I get any wine? Or whiskey?"

"It doesn't mix," Sam said. "Not with the medicine you had. Doctor's orders, Connor."

"You're enjoying this, aren't you." He sat back in his chair.

"You getting shot? Hell, no. You in a nightgown?

Hell, yes. I even enjoyed how you acted around Miss Carew. You were like one big puppy dog."

He didn't know what part of that he should counter first. He opted to eat his vegetables.

"If you're determined to meet Felix, can you at least wait a few weeks?"

"It's not a duel, Sam. It's just a shooting contest."

"I don't cotton to the man," Sam said.

"Me neither."

Sam sipped from his wine and watched him, his gaze intent over the rim of the glass.

"A few days, then. Until you can walk upright without looking like you're going to fall down any moment."

He nodded, then occupied himself by uncovering the rest of the dishes to see what was for dessert. Better that than see Sam's grin. Or consider his words about Elsbeth.

A big puppy dog, huh?

He didn't have a damn thing to say to that.

ELSBETH REALLY WANTED to go see how Connor was feeling, but there was no way to call on him without raising eyebrows. Of course, if she did and word got out about it, the duchess would be pleased, thinking that Elsbeth was going ahead with her suggestion.

Was Rhona daft?

The woman had just proposed the most outlandish idea and she'd been serious. No, worse than serious, she'd been intent. Determined. Elsbeth had been on the receiving end of the duchess's determination in the past and she knew that Rhona, once she had an idea, didn't relinquish it easily.

What was she going to do?

The easiest thing, perhaps the best thing, would be to make arrangements to take one of the carriages to Inverness and begin making inquiries about properties for sale. She should do that as quickly as possible. She needed to find a home, somewhere where she was not subject to the will of other people.

Before retiring, she visited Mrs. Ferguson, thanking the woman again for her skill in extracting the bullet from Connor's wound.

"Where did you learn how to do that?" she asked.

Mrs. Ferguson was massaging balm into her distended, enlarged knuckles, holding her hands close to the fire.

"Once you've supervised a staff as large as Bealadair, you become familiar with almost any type of injury. I even helped deliver a baby once. Poor girl, one of the upstairs maids, managed to hide it until the very last."

"What happened to her?" Elsbeth asked. She hadn't heard that story.

"Not a sad tale, I'm happy to say. The girl married and went on to have five more children. She's a matron now at Ainell Village. I used to see her from time to time and we would reminisce. I've removed an iron spike from a footman's leg, various metal objects from stableboys—besides treating them for injuries they got from being around horses." She smiled into the fire. "No doubt you will develop your own expertise, Elsbeth."

"Do you resent me for taking on your duties?"

Mrs. Ferguson looked surprised. "Resent you? Why on earth would I do that? If anything, you've saved my job for me. Someone had to ensure that all those tasks were done, Elsbeth. Who better than someone who knows the family as well as you? But was I wrong to think it was something you wanted to do?"

Elsbeth shook her head. "I very much wanted to help. Doing something makes me feel . . ." Her words trailed off. "Perhaps important. Or maybe needed."

"That you are, Elsbeth."

Part of her wanted to tell the housekeeper what the duchess had suggested, only because she'd often gone to Mrs. Ferguson for counsel or support. Many times since Gavin's death she'd confided in the woman. Together, they'd come up with strategies to either avoid Rhona or handle her newest demand.

But how to mention that the duchess wanted her to seduce Connor? Even the thought of it brought a blush to her face. Or was that because she wished there was a reason for her to seriously contemplate such an idea?

Life happened around you. Gavin often said that. People did things you didn't expect, like the valued servant stealing the silverware or a footman walking away from his duty. Lovers met and loved without benefit of clergy and in violation of every societal rule.

It simply happened.

It wasn't planned.

It certainly wasn't suggested in such a way it was almost a command.

The duchess had always insisted that Elsbeth's comportment be perfect. The duchess had lectured her endlessly about how to act in certain situations, how to address various personages, how not to shame the McCraights. After all, they had been generous in taking her into their home.

Yet the woman had just said something so outlandish, so foreign that it made Elsbeth's toes curl to even contemplate it.

"What is it, Elsbeth? You have the strangest look on your face."

She blinked several times, brought back to the moment by Mrs. Ferguson's comment. She couldn't possibly tell the woman what the duchess had said. No, that burden was going to have to remain hers alone.

"I'm sorry," she said. "I was woolgathering, I'm afraid."

"Oh, my dear Elsbeth, of course you were. Have you decided what you're going to do?"

It took a second for Elsbeth to realize that Mrs. Ferguson wasn't talking about the duchess's command, but of her plans for the future.

"I've been thinking of getting a cottage," she said. "Or perhaps a property in Inverness. I could hire a companion or at least a servant or two."

Mrs. Ferguson sat back in her chair, the balm forgotten, her eyes wide as she regarded Elsbeth.

"You would set up your own establishment? What a daring thing to do."

Hardly daring when it was the only option left to her. She only smiled in response.

"I do wish he'd chosen a better season than winter," Mrs. Ferguson said.

"I think he's just in a hurry to return home," Elsbeth said. "He must miss Texas very much, and after the events of today, I can't blame him."

The housekeeper began massaging her hands once more. "Could it not have been the ghillie? He or one of his men could have mistaken the duke for a deer. He does have a distinctive coat."

She stared into the fire, considering the housekeeper's words. It was possible that someone had thought Connor might be an animal, especially if they had only seen glimpses of him through the ruined arches and windows of Castle McCraight.

Hamish Robertson, the ghillie, and his sons were responsible for the game and fish on the vast acreage of the estate. They didn't live in close proximity to Castle McCraight. The ghillie himself lived in a two-story cottage on the other side of the glen. He wouldn't have known about the shooting unless someone had sent a servant to inform him. Had anyone done so? Would Mr. Kirby have thought of such a thing?

"I'll send word to Hamish tomorrow," she told Mrs. Ferguson.

The elder woman nodded. "It might be wise," she said. "What is thought to be a malicious act often turns out to be a simple mistake."

She couldn't say why she thought the shooting was more than a mistake, but she put those thoughts away to consider later and spoke about less consequential things with the housekeeper. The price of flour had gone up again. Linette, one of the maids they'd recently hired, was homesick. Perhaps a conversation with Mrs. Ferguson would be in order.

Most of the younger girls felt better after speaking with the older woman. She took on the role of being a second mother to many of the maids.

Elsbeth said good-night, and went down to her own rooms, the same ones she'd occupied since she was eight. More than once, the duke had offered to have them refurbished for her or suggested she might want a larger suite, one of those in the northern wing with the rest of the family. She'd always thanked him, but told him no, she was fine where she was. That hadn't been a falsehood. Her sitting room, bedroom, and bathing chamber had become home over the years, a refuge, a place to go and close the door against the world.

She did so now, wishing she could wall off all the emotions she was feeling as easily.

Chapter 24

Sam knew, quite well, that Connor wasn't the only one trailing after a woman like a puppy, but he couldn't help himself. Rhona McCraight wasn't the most beautiful creature he'd ever met, but there was something about the woman that called to him. Maybe it was the loneliness he sensed, an emotion she would probably deny if he brought it up.

He had thought this visit to Scotland would be boring and it probably would have been if not for Rhona. He found himself wanting to spend every hour with her, even if it meant her telling him all the rules of etiquette she was sure he didn't know and, if truth be told, didn't care about. But he liked listening to her speak and he liked the way her eyes lit up when she was amused.

If he'd had something else to do, he probably would have put it aside in order to visit with Rhona or follow her around Bealadair.

"I have to hand it to you Scots," he said now as they entered the ballroom. "You sure know how to build houses. You trap a lot of the outside in, while we Texans leave the outside out."

She glanced up at him.

"You have the oddest way of saying things, Sam."

He smiled at her use of his name. That was a battle he'd already won. Nor was he offended by her comment. She said it with a twinkle in her eyes, which meant that she was teasing him.

Another milestone.

He saw Elsbeth on the other side of the room, talking with one of the carpenters. According to Rhona, they were enlarging the stage for the musicians arriving from Inverness.

This ball was important, since it was the main topic of Rhona's conversation. The Welcoming of the Laird was a tradition, and evidently tradition was very important to the Scots.

There'd been nothing traditional about his life. No history he wanted to repeat. Born in New Orleans as the only child of a woman who made her living in ways that didn't bear mentioning in polite society, he'd never known the identity of his father. He'd wanted more for himself, and his mother's greatest gift to him had been her optimism that he could achieve it.

Orphaned at sixteen, he survived by gambling, small games on the street at first before graduating to higher and higher stakes card games. Along the way he began to observe the men with whom he played. They talked different. They dressed different. They were as foreign to him as someone from New York.

He was determined to remake himself in their image. It might have taken him a decade or so, but he'd managed it. He'd also acquired a bit of polish himself and something else—a fortune.

As a gambler, he'd learned two lessons about

life: you never won anything if you didn't play, and losing wasn't permanent unless you never played again.

Graham had known about his past, one of the few men who had. Sam had thought he'd known everything about Graham, but he'd been as surprised as Connor when the McCraight solicitor had showed up at XIV Ranch, claiming that Connor was the 14th Duke of Lothian and Laird of Clan McCraight.

Now he could only bless the circumstances that led him to this place. Unlike Connor, he was enjoying almost everything about the experience.

Of course, he hadn't been shot, either.

As if Rhona heard his thoughts, she asked, "How is His Grace today?"

He smiled at her, amused at her insistence in calling Connor *His Grace* despite the fact he was her nephew. Rhona was dead set on being proper.

"He's determined to be up and about today. He'll do it, too. I've never known anyone as stubborn as Connor."

She nodded, but he could tell she wasn't paying any attention to his words. Instead, she was looking toward Elsbeth, who, instead of walking in their direction, was leaving the ballroom by the other door.

"Is there a problem between the two of you?" he asked.

He half expected Rhona to announce, in that frosty tone she could adopt, that it was none of his concern.

To his surprise, she glanced at him and smiled faintly.

"Do you think there's any possibility that His Grace

will change his mind?" She placed her hand on his arm. "Is there anything that can make him reconsider?"

"You mean about selling Bealadair?"

She nodded.

"No, Rhona. He's pretty set on getting rid of the place. But you must have known that something like this could happen."

Had the McCraights just assumed the new duke would take residence and allow them to live cheek and jowl next to his family? What if Connor had been married with a family of his own?

"I wish I could tell you different," he said, placing his hand over hers. Warmth filled him at the look in her eyes. He'd been around women enough to know that the Duchess of Lothian was not immune to his charm, such as it was. "But I can only tell you the truth. Connor only came to Scotland as a favor to his mother and to honor his father's memory. He doesn't want to live here."

"Are you very sure? Can nothing change his mind?"

He patted her hand again, then gave her fingers a gentle squeeze. If they hadn't been in full view of at least a half dozen people in the ballroom, he would have leaned over and given her a kiss. She might slap him, but it would be worth it.

As far as Connor, he would do as he wanted. Sam knew that well enough. Connor had been different ever since coming back from the war, but that was to be expected. He'd been working all hours of the day, filling Graham's place, introducing new ways of doing things, and being the head of the family. He'd been too busy to have any fun. If nothing else, this visit to Scotland might provide some of that.

He'd seen the look on Connor's face when he watched Elsbeth and Elsbeth's furtive glances in return. There was something brewing there. Was it enough to keep Connor in Scotland? He didn't know.

Nor was he sure that it was altogether safe for Connor to remain here. He had been assured, by Rhona, Glassey, Mr. Barton, and a variety of footmen and stableboys, that the shooting had to have been a simple accident. Some fool with a rifle had thought Connor was dinner.

No one had come forward to own up to their stupidity. Nor had he been able to find any clues at the old castle. Still, he didn't like this feeling he was getting. He didn't think it was an accident any more than Connor did. The only question was whether it was Felix or someone else responsible for nearly killing the new duke.

"YOU AREN'T SUPPOSED to be up," Elsbeth said, stopping abruptly in the doorway of the kitchen.

There was Connor, sitting at the scarred oak table in the middle of the kitchen with Addy and Betty, all of them smiling and looking as if they had been friends for years.

Connor didn't even have the sense to wear the sling they'd arranged for him. No, his right arm was braced on the top of the table and he was sipping his coffee with his left.

"Oh, Miss Elsbeth," Addy said, "His Grace has made the best coffee. It's better than my own, I have to say."

Elsbeth headed toward the table. Connor would have stood, but she waved him back down.

"You made the coffee?"

"I like mine a bit strong," he said.

"Texas style?"

He grinned at her and she couldn't help but smile back.

"That it is."

She sat opposite him. "How are you feeling?"

His eyes were clear and his cheeks weren't flushed. He had no indication of fever. She wanted to reach over and place her palm against his forehead, but doubted the other two women would understand.

She wasn't certain she did, either. She had no right to feel irritated when Addy and Betty looked at him with smiles on their faces and stars in their eyes.

The truth, and it came as a shock, was that she had considered him hers, and wasn't that idiotic? From the first moment in front of Bealadair with the fallen statue, she'd felt as if she protected him, supported him even when the family had ridiculed him. She'd tried to explain him, defend him, and none of that was necessary.

"I'm as good as can be, what with another hole in me."

He grinned at her again, and this time she didn't smile back. Really, he had no right to be so charming so early in the day.

Had he slept well? Was that a question she could ask him? She didn't, only because Addy and Betty were looking at her with great interest.

"Would you like to try some of His Grace's coffee?" Addy asked.

"No, thank you. Tea, please," she said.

"What are you going to do today?" Connor asked.

"What am I going to do today?"

No one had ever questioned her about her duties. Not even Gavin. She'd met with him in the morning, and then gone about her business, knowing they would meet again at dinner.

"I'm going to give the maids instructions on waxing the ballroom floor," she said, beginning to explain her schedule. "I have to interview a footman with the majordomo, look over the household expenses for the past month, and inspect the repairs to the barn roof. After that I have a meeting with the steward to tell him what I've found."

"All that?" he asked, still smiling.

"All that," she said.

"So you'll be staying at Bealadair? No riding out to far pastures?"

"Not today."

He only nodded in response.

How very odd to feel as self-conscious as she did at the moment. Did he think she wasn't busy enough? Was he going to criticize how she used her time?

"Why are you asking?"

"Curiosity," he said. "Do you never take a day for yourself?"

She thanked Betty for her tea and took a sip before forming her answer.

"No. I don't think you do, either. If you were the indolent type, Your Grace, you'd still be in bed."

"When I was injured in the war," he said, "I was expected to be up and about the next day. Maybe it's just a habit I learned."

She took another sip of her tea, conscious that Addy and Betty were listening intently.

"You'll have to spare some time in a few days to attend our shooting match."

She put down her cup and stared at him. "Shooting match? You and Felix?"

He nodded again.

"Are you daft? You can't possibly consider something like that so soon. You were just wounded yesterday."

Both Addy and Betty gasped, making her realize she'd just insulted the Duke of Lothian. He only smiled at her, took a sip of his coffee, and let the moment stretch thin.

She really should apologize for her quick and unthinking response. However, she wasn't going to take back her words. He'd lost a great deal of blood. He should be weak. In fact, he should be in bed, taking toast and tea for breakfast instead of looking hale and hearty and too attractive for her peace of mind.

She could see the bandage beneath the fine lawn of the shirt he wore. Did he think himself more than human?

He put his coffee cup down, trailed his finger around the saucer, still not speaking.

She couldn't stand the silence one second more.

"Please, don't do this. Felix only wants to embarrass you." Conscious of the other women's glances, she added, "Your Grace."

"I'm well aware of that," he said, smiling once more.

She sat back in her chair, wondering how she

could reach him. Could anyone? He had a mischievous grin on his face and his eyes were alight with humor.

Addy stood, retrieved the coffeepot from the stove and poured him some more coffee, while Betty filled a plate with raisin scones and put them in front of him. She'd never seen the two women so solicitous, but then the Duke of Lothian had never shared their breakfast table, either.

"You know he wants to embarrass you?"

She should have, perhaps, waited until they were alone before questioning him further. She didn't even bother asking him to join her in the family dining room. He looked too comfortable being waited on hand and foot. She was stuck either containing her curiosity or having an audience to it.

"Never trust a man who brags a lot," he said. "Words are no substitution for deeds."

"That sounds like something Gavin would say."

He shrugged, grimaced, then said, "I'm not surprised. It's a comment my father often made. I suspect they were more alike than different, even after so many years."

"You shouldn't have agreed to the match so soon." She almost forgot and added, "Your Grace," again. She had started to think of him as Connor. Connor McCraight, Texan, impossible man, fascinating male.

The title Duke of Lothian didn't quite fit him. Not that he didn't have an aristocratic look about him. He did. He also had a way of chilling you with his gaze. But she suspected that the peerage demanded that a person be pressed into a certain kind of mold, and Connor would always be his own man.

"I didn't," he said. "I was the one who suggested we meet."

That didn't make any sense. She frowned at him, but he met her expression with another grin.

"I've found that the first few days after being wounded are better than later. The muscles hurt more then."

What was she supposed to say to that? What was she going to say when he lost and Felix wouldn't shut up about besting the new Duke of Lothian? Lara would preen. The duchess might even be pleased that the same man who wanted to disrupt their lives so much had been soundly humiliated.

She really should stand, right this moment, announce something along the lines of, *Well, I certainly hope you're ready to be trounced*, and be about her duties.

But she didn't want to leave. Something about him, about being in his presence, was almost magical. As if she were like those metal filings Gavin had shown her once. Irresistibly drawn to a magnet, they had no power to resist.

Neither did she.

She suspected that losing to Felix wouldn't bother Connor one whit. He didn't value the man. He didn't think highly of him; that was obvious. Shouldn't you have some respect for your opponent? Connor would simply flick off the loss as if it were inconsequential. That would only outrage Felix, Lara, and the rest of the McCraights.

Nothing good could come of this, but how did she convey that to Connor?

One of the bells on the board near the door rang.

She glanced up to see that it was the duchess's room. Rhona was ringing for her breakfast early.

Was she going to summon Elsbeth to her room and demand to know what she'd decided? Would she banish her from Bealadair on the spot if she refused?

Betty stood and went to the side table, beginning to arrange the duchess's tray. Addy excused herself to go to the stove, retrieving the toast she'd made earlier.

"I'm supposed to seduce you," Elsbeth said, glancing at Connor.

She'd never seen anyone's face turn to stone quite the way Connor's did. One moment his eyes were filled with humor. The next they were flat and expressionless. His mouth assumed a straight line, his beautiful smile gone in an instant.

"What?"

She was as surprised as he. She hadn't meant to say anything to him, especially not with Addy and Betty so close. She lowered her voice further.

"The duchess wants me to seduce you," she said. "So you won't sell Bealadair. Evidently, I'm supposed to have such extraordinary feminine wiles that you'll immediately change your plans and give up any thought of moving away from Scotland, of selling Bealadair and displacing the family. All because you kissed me."

He was watching her with that intent gaze of his. She wished he wouldn't, but she could hardly say that, could she?

"Not that the family is truly being displaced. I mean, they knew once the new duke arrived that there was every possibility they would have to move. After all, even Gavin planned for that contingency or he wouldn't have been so generous in his bequests, don't you think?"

She finally took a breath when Addy moved back toward the table.

He still hadn't said anything, which made her feel even more foolish. No, she was acres past foolish. She'd been an idiot. Why had she said what she had?

"Have you ever heard of anything more ridiculous?"

After Betty left with the duchess's tray, Addy returned to the table, smiling as she sat.

Elsbeth was hoping he didn't say anything now, not with a witness.

She didn't get her wish.

"Not so ridiculous." His voice was calm as he reached for another scone. "My mother would love these," he said to Addy.

Elsbeth's face felt hot. Her heart was beating furiously. She stared down at her nearly empty cup. If she raised it now, they'd both see her shaking hands.

Why had she said anything?

Why?

What did he mean, *not so ridiculous*?

Chapter 25

$\mathcal{F}$or nearly a week, Elsbeth managed to avoid a great many people at Bealadair. First of all, the duchess. Her excuse for not meeting with the woman centered around the upcoming ball. She was simply too occupied with the details. She didn't have time to spare. That's the excuse she gave every maid and every footman Rhona sent looking for her.

Although it was more work for the staff, she took breakfast in her sitting room every morning. Nor did she return to Bealadair for lunch, instead taking some cheese and bread with her as she made her rounds. She would much rather sit in a stable stall and have a solitary lunch than be forced to face the duchess or the rest of the McCraight family.

She even stayed away from her suite until she was certain the duchess had retired for the night.

As far as Connor? She was avoiding His Grace at every possible occasion. The closest she'd come to seeing him was when she'd met with Mr. Kirby to tell him that neither Hamish nor his men had been near Castle McCraight on the day of the shooting.

"Do you believe him?" he'd asked.

"He's a very reputable man," she'd said. "Most of the people at Bealadair are."

"Someone isn't."

That comment lingered between them. He was right. Someone at Bealadair, or on Bealadair land, had tried to kill Connor.

She knew he'd gone into the village to make inquiries, but hadn't turned up any information. He had promised her to be as tactful as he could be and not antagonize the villagers.

"I'll be on my best behavior."

She'd slipped out of the housekeeper's office next to the kitchen only to almost encounter Connor. He was talking with Addy and had his back to her. She shook her head when Addy saw her, and dropped back into the scullery, leaving by the rear door.

One of these days she was going to have to face him. Hopefully, by that time, her embarrassment would have faded somewhat.

"Connor wants to know if you have the key for the desk in the library."

She turned to find Mr. Kirby standing there, smiling at her. He was certainly a genial man, and if she hadn't seen his expression at Connor's bedside, she would have never suspected that there were several layers to Mr. Kirby.

"The main library or the duke's library?" she asked, turning back to watch as they raised one of the chandeliers in the ballroom. It was a delicate operation, but the footmen assigned to the task had done it twice before and were as skilled as anyone at Bealadair.

The massive chandeliers were quite heavy and the

pulleys to raise and lower them were not operated more than once a year. This particular chandelier's pulley was slightly rusted, a minor detail, but one that concerned her. Why had it rusted? Was there a leak somewhere that she hadn't been able to detect?

Finally, they tied off the chain, replacing the panel in the wall that hid the mechanism from sight.

"I believe it's the one in the main library," he said.

She nodded and pulled out the ring of keys from her pocket. Selecting a small brass key, she pulled it free and handed it to Mr. Kirby, but he had already begun to walk away.

"Just see that Connor gets it, will you?" he said over his shoulder.

She would've gone after him except for the fact that the duchess was entering the ballroom. There were a few other exits and she headed to the nearest one, hoping that Rhona hadn't seen her. She wasn't fooling anyone. Everyone on the staff knew she was avoiding the duchess, and more than one footman and maid had actively assisted her.

She'd already spoken to Mr. Glassey and had gotten the name of an attorney who would help her find a place to live. She would meet with him in a few days, staying at the McCraight home while she made her inquiries. Until then, she was going to avoid as many people as she could.

She stared down at the key on her palm, deciding that she'd send a maid with it. She didn't need to see Connor. After all, she'd managed to go a week without being in his company.

True, it had felt as if he could become a friend, but that had just been foolishness on her part. He was the new Duke of Lothian, however much he may despise the title and the role. He was Gavin's heir.

Never mind that he'd kissed her.

This afternoon, he and Felix would have their match. Was he feeling up to it? How was his shoulder? She hadn't asked anyone about his health for fear she would be misunderstood. She didn't want anyone to think that her concern was personal. Of course it wasn't.

She motioned to one of the maids.

"Abigail, take this key to His Grace, if you will."

The maid nodded. "Where, Miss Elsbeth?"

She'd forgotten to ask. "I think he's in the main library," she said. "If he isn't there, come and get me. I'll be with Mrs. Ferguson."

Abigail nodded again and did a cute little bobbing motion that was an abbreviated curtsy. Nobody curtsied to Mrs. Ferguson, but then she was a genuine housekeeper and not half family, half foundling.

ACCORDING TO ADDY and Betty, with whom Connor spent breakfast every morning, Bealadair had its share of ghosts. The first was one of his ancestors, an angry ghost attired in a kilt and always heard with the skirl of bagpipes.

"You'll be able to hear them at the Welcoming of the Laird, Your Grace," Addy told him.

Both Addy and Betty refused to call him Connor and he'd stopped asking. In addition, it looked like the ball was going to happen despite his wishes. He was going to have to attend.

Would Elsbeth be there?

"The piper shows up when a McCraight . . ." Addy's words trailed off.

Betty interjected with the rest of the story. "When someone dies, Your Grace."

"Did you hear him when my uncle died?" he asked.

The two women had looked at each other.

"I'm sure he was heard, Your Grace," Addy finally said. "He's always heard."

A great many things about Scotland, he was discovering, were rooted in lore. It's because his ancestors, people he'd never before considered, had lived and breathed and dreamed in this house or Castle McCraight for five hundred years.

Texas, in comparison, was almost raw and new. Not much was older than a hundred years, unless you counted the missions dotting the land.

The second ghost was an older one, a haunt from the original Castle McCraight. This ghost, the White Lady, according to Addy, was sent to a McCraight as a warning of danger.

Elsbeth might be a ghost as well.

She'd disappeared after her startling announcement that one morning and he hadn't seen her since.

Every morning he'd come to the kitchen, expecting her to be there. She wasn't. Addy had apologized to him, stating that Elsbeth had wanted a tray in her room. He hadn't said anything further, not that morning or the next, or for the past damn week.

She couldn't say something like that, and then vanish as if her words hadn't meant anything.

Seduce him? She was supposed to seduce him?

He'd almost gone to his aunt and demanded to know what was going on, but he'd stopped himself at the last moment. Of the two women, he trusted Elsbeth more than the duchess, a fact he didn't examine too deeply. He wouldn't have been surprised if Rhona had suggested the ploy to Elsbeth.

Have you ever heard anything more ridiculous?

He'd been so startled that he'd told her the truth: no, he didn't think it was ridiculous at all. It might well have worked, too. At least he hadn't said that.

Didn't she realize how beautiful she was? Or that he thought she was one of the most fascinating women he'd ever met? She played with puppies and inspected cattle, handled domestic crises and lectured him on history, all with the same grace.

He could see himself being with her, images that had warmed him ever since that morning.

Why was she avoiding him?

Had he misinterpreted her question? Had the idea of being with him appalled her? Was that why she'd been a living ghost of Bealadair?

He wasn't going to chase after a woman who evidently didn't want to be around him. If he visited Daniel to inquire after the Scottish collies, that's just because he wanted to go. If he'd gone to the stables at least twice a day, it wasn't to catch sight of her on her mare, but merely to ask a few questions of the stablemaster. Nor was he acquainting himself with the whole of Bealadair, sprawling as it was, to catch sight of her.

He'd drawn Elsbeth and he rarely drew portraits. When he sketched something, it was to explain it to another person who hadn't been able to see it, or to remind himself of something that needed to be done. Yet he found himself capturing her smile of delight, her annoyed frown, and the look on her face as she patted the flank of one of the cows.

He was an idiot. He had a hundred other things he could be doing rather than think about a woman who was so obviously avoiding him.

Elsbeth worked as hard as the most diligent servant. He heard her name constantly throughout the day, since she seemed to be the source of all knowledge about Bealadair from the old wing to the original castle.

He missed her, and that both annoyed and concerned him. He'd spent too much time thinking about a woman he barely knew. But she really couldn't mention seduction, and then disappear for days.

He didn't have all that much experience with women, but that didn't seem to stop his imagination. He was all for taking things he'd learned and practicing on Elsbeth, and if that wasn't the height of idiocy as far as thoughts went, what was?

"YOU'RE SPENDING ENTIRELY too much time with the American, Mother," Lara said.

Rhona looked over at the settee in front of the fire. Her stepdaughter half reclined there, as if she'd invited Lara into her sitting room. Lara and Felix had both gotten too lax in their courtesies and too bold in their demands.

When Connor sold Bealadair—and Rhona was almost certain that terrible event would indeed happen—she had no intention of taking Lara and her husband under her wing. Gavin had been extraordinarily generous to all his daughters. It was not her concern if Felix was doing his utmost to spend his wife's legacy instead of investing it for his future.

He was going to have to provide for Lara sometime. Rhona was not going to do it.

"I'm assuming you are speaking of Mr. Kirby," she said. "Although I don't know why you would think it any of your concern how much time I'm spending with the man."

"He's from Texas, Mother. He isn't your type at all."

Rhona drew herself up, frowning down at Lara, who was sprawled in the corner of the sofa. The girl looked as if she wasn't going to move, short of being shouted out of the room.

She finished fixing her bracelet and came and sat on the matching chair, facing the younger woman.

Lara was, unfortunately, not finished giving her opinions.

"He's coarse. He has no manners. He speaks in an odd way. He's entirely too familiar. He knows all of the staff by name and he addresses them that way."

She knew all about Sam and how he behaved. She knew, too, that the man was oddly charming in a way that had completely captivated her. Her daughter was not the only one who was surprised at her reaction to Sam Kirby. Rhona had already decided that she was being foolish, but no man had ever complimented her as fulsomely as Sam. And, if she looked in his eyes to gauge the sincerity of his remark, she could only assume that he was entirely serious.

He wasn't just from Texas. He'd spent a great deal of time in New Orleans, Chicago, San Francisco,

New York, Paris, and a few cities that she had aspired to visit, like Florence, but had not yet seen.

He was, if Lara but knew it, more well traveled than anyone she knew.

Certainly more than Felix.

Sam was amusing. He made her laugh in ways that she didn't think she'd ever laughed. Or if she had, it was years and years ago when she was more carefree and had fewer disappointments about her life.

Gavin McCraight had been a good man. He just hadn't been the right man. She'd known that he was still in love with his first wife when he married her. She'd suspected that the reason for their whirlwind courtship had been so he could find a mother for his child, the same one who now criticized her with such acidity in her voice.

"It isn't any of your concern at all, Lara," she said, not unkindly. "Not what I do or with whom I do it."

"You're a laughingstock. Even the servants are whispering about you."

"I don't doubt that," she said, standing and brushing her hands against her skirt.

Today the dress she was wearing was a slight departure from her usual mourning. The fabric was an emerald green silk, so dark as to appear black in a certain light, but when she turned, the color changed. It was like looking through a deep and dark pool of water. She'd fallen in love with the material the moment the seamstress had shown a sample to her.

Instead of criticizing her, Lara could've said something about the way she looked. She could have dredged up some kind words. Rhona knew, quite well, that she was appearing younger and younger lately, a fact that could be attributed to having a man pay attention to her after all these years.

"The servants will gossip about you regardless of what you do, Lara. We're characters in a play to them. We stride across the stage of Bealadair and the servants are our audience. Never forget that. Never forget, too, that you can look ridiculous doing absolutely nothing. Better that you should live your life the best way you can and let people say what they will."

Lara looked surprised at her words. As well she might; it was a newly adopted attitude, one that had its roots in a conversation with Sam. He had a great deal of common sense. She liked the man. Even more, she was charmed by him. If he'd tried to kiss her a time or two and she had allowed it, then it was no one's concern but hers. Certainly not Lara's.

She left the sitting room to meet the very man she'd just been warned about.

Chapter 26

To her great surprise, when Elsbeth went to ask Mrs. Ferguson about the rust on the chandelier chain, the older woman was bundling up in a sweater, a jacket, and a cloak over that.

"Is it very cold outside?" the other woman asked, reaching for her knitted gloves.

"No," Elsbeth said, watching as she donned a pair of leather gloves over the knitted ones. "The day is very fair. It's cold but it isn't a miserable cold. Where are you going?"

"To watch the match, of course," Mrs. Ferguson said. "Aren't you?"

"But it's outside."

Mrs. Ferguson never went outside, not in the winter. The cold made her arthritis so much worse. She rarely left her rooms, for that matter. One of the few times she had was to treat Connor.

"Of course it's outside." The housekeeper frowned at Elsbeth. "You are going, aren't you?"

She hadn't planned on it, but she couldn't think of an excuse, especially when she was being pinned by Mrs. Ferguson's gaze. She ended up nodding.

"I'll get my cloak and see you downstairs," she said.

She was nearly to the servants' stairs when she heard her name being called. Instead of turning, what she really wanted to do was run as far and as fast as she could.

She'd had a busy morning and her dress had suffered for it. She could feel tendrils around her face from where her hair had escaped its careful bun. Why did she have to see him looking like this?

Well, if nothing else it would prove that the duchess's plan was beyond foolish.

"Did the key fit?" she asked, keeping a smile on her face with some difficulty.

"I haven't tried it yet."

If anything, Connor had grown more attractive since she'd seen him last. He looked fit. No, that word hardly matched him, did it? She'd met other men who were tall, had broad shoulders, but they didn't have Connor's presence. You knew he was in a room. How could you possibly miss him?

Would she ever be able to forget his distinctive voice, low and deep, flavored with his strange accent? Even her name sounded different when he said it, as if he spoke the syllables slowly so as not to mispronounce them.

"You've been avoiding me," he said.

She didn't like to lie. Sometimes it was unavoidable, but not now. Yet it did take a certain amount of courage to stand there, look up into his face, and nod.

"Why?"

Because she'd made a fool of herself. Because she should never have told anyone what the duchess had suggested, let alone Connor.

Instead of answering, she turned and began to

walk toward the stairs again, intent on retrieving her cloak.

"Elsbeth?"

How could she possibly answer him? To do so would be to bring up that hideous morning again, and that was the last thing she wanted to do.

A thought occurred to her and she stopped. "I should have asked Mrs. Ferguson if she needed assistance getting down the stairs."

"It's why I'm here," he said, surprising her.

"You know she's all for watching the match between you and Felix, then?"

He nodded. "She's promised to be my biggest fan."

She glanced at his shoulder. "How is your wound?"

"Mabel says it's healing fine."

Mabel? He called Mrs. Ferguson by her first name? Did she reciprocate? Of course he would insist. Had Mrs. Ferguson examined his wound? She must have. How odd that the housekeeper hadn't mentioned it.

"Is your shoulder stiff?"

"About as much as I expected," he said.

Was he in pain? Had he taken the medicine the doctor had left for him? She shouldn't be curious, because none of those answers were any of her concern.

Mrs. Ferguson stepped out of her room. She smiled at Connor, then embraced him in a quick hug.

"Connor, you remembered. Thank you so much."

Of course Mrs. Ferguson and Connor could be friends. Why did she feel hurt? How foolish. There was no reason to feel as if both of them had gone behind her back. That was even more ridiculous.

"Thank you for that newest effusion," Mrs. Ferguson said. "I think it's worked better than the one before. I could feel my hands warming as I spread it on. Whatever is in it?"

"Peppers," he said, offering his arm for her. "I've brought some from Texas. I have a hankering for chili from time to time."

"So you came prepared," she said, smiling broadly.

Was Mrs. Ferguson flirting with Connor?

"Better to have something you don't use, Mabel, then to want something you don't have."

"A wise theory," she said, patting him on the arm.

Elsbeth followed them down the hall, feeling as useful as a single shoe. He used peppers in some sort of preparation for Mrs. Ferguson's arthritis? It must have been extremely helpful because the housekeeper was walking without evidence of pain.

At the front door, the footman offered Connor his hat and coat. Someone had evidently repaired his coat and it was a credible effort. The hole in the shoulder had been mended with an almost-invisible stitch, but it was still obvious that something had penetrated the soft leather. The bloodstains, however, had been mostly eradicated.

Elsbeth grabbed her cloak, annoyed and irritated because she couldn't figure out exactly why she was annoyed and irritated. Was it because she didn't know who'd gone to the effort of mending Connor's coat? Or was it because, until this moment, she'd not considered it? Or because Connor and Mrs. Ferguson had formed a friendship and she hadn't known about it? She'd done everything in her power to avoid Connor in the past week, and now she was out of sorts because he'd evidently not missed her.

She was behaving childishly, an awareness that didn't make her feel more adult.

She followed the two of them to the east lawn. It looked as if most of the staff was present, an observation Elsbeth made with some chagrin. Not one person had come to her and asked for permission to be here. Of course, she wasn't actually the housekeeper at Bealadair. It was just a role she played. She wouldn't have refused anyone, but perhaps it wasn't her decision to make. Connor may have gone around and told everyone about the match and invited them to attend. Who was she to counter the word of the Duke of Lothian?

None of the family members were in the crowd. It was entirely possible that they were viewing the match from one of the upstairs parlors. They would be warm and comfortable and spared having to mingle with the servants. She was not going to turn and look at the windows to verify her guess.

She hadn't considered that Connor would make friends so easily, and that was her foolishness. As he passed in front of the staff, quite a few of them waved to him and smiled. He waved back and nodded. Gavin had known everyone who worked at Bealadair, and it seemed as if Connor did, too.

What a surprising man he was. He wasn't like anyone she knew. She couldn't put him in a proper category. Was there a box labeled Independent Texan? Or Stubborn American?

What would she call it other than obstinacy that would make him, a week from being shot, engage in a match of skill? Anyone else would've begged off, would've offered his injury up as an excuse. Not Connor McCraight.

She had the odd thought that Connor was probably like his ancestors, a Highlander of old, the kind of man who had become the first Duke of Lothian: fiercely himself, dedicated to his own purpose, intensely focused.

This was the man Rhona wanted her to seduce? The idea was laughable. He would feel nothing more than pity for her, she was sure. No doubt he would try to spare her feelings as he bit back his laughter.

She wasn't unduly surprised to find that he had arranged a chair for Mrs. Ferguson along the periphery of onlookers.

Although the day was a normal cold winter day in the Highlands, there wasn't any wind. The sky was blue and the sun had melted the snowdrifts on either side of the lawn. Spikes of deep green could be seen through the snow, a faint and false hint of spring.

Several yards ahead, two tables had been erected. Felix was at one of them, readying his guns. A footman stood behind each table, no doubt to be pressed into service in some way. On either side of the lawn was a station where a stableboy waited with a pile of glass orbs to be used as targets. Felix bought them from a company in Inverness by the crate.

Would he be able to pursue his hobby once they were forced from Bealadair? She doubted it, unless his new property had sufficient space for shooting and he had enough income to purchase ammunition and targets.

All of them were going to have to change in one

way or another, and change was not something that came easily to the McCraights. No doubt it was because they lived in a home that was many centuries old and followed traditions that were equally as venerable. Change might not be anathema, but it was also not something they actively sought.

Had someone in the family shot him? It was not the first time in the past week she'd had that thought, but she always pushed away her suspicions because it was too difficult to consider. Today, looking at Felix, she couldn't help but wonder if it had been him.

Was Connor thinking the same?

She watched as he walked to the table on the left side of the lawn. He removed his coat, laying it across the table, then put his hat atop it. One by one he picked up the three rifles arranged there. She didn't know anything about guns, but it seemed to her that he examined them with some expertise, holding each one up to eye level and peering into various places, moving the lever that did something, and then placing each gun back on the table.

He nodded at Felix, who was hatless but still wore a coat, a long black garment that made him look like a starving crow. Connor picked up one of the guns and nodded again, which was evidently a signal to begin.

The stableboy to the left of Connor grabbed a target and threw it underhanded into the air between the two tables. Connor raised the rifle and shot it, shattering the glass ball into countless shards. It was only when he replaced the gun and picked up another that she realized he'd shot left-handed.

Felix had evidently made that discovery as well, because he was frowning at Connor.

She could hear murmuring behind her, equal parts amazement and admiration for their new duke.

When it was Felix's time to shoot, he hit the target, too.

It looked to her, over the next several rounds, as if Felix had met his match. That is, if you discounted the fact that Connor had been wounded and was using his left arm.

He was obviously more skilled, a fact that had evidently occurred to Felix as well, because he gave the command that his targets were to come in bursts of two at a time.

Connor did the same, and when he missed one, an audible moan traveled through the crowd behind her.

Felix was not beloved among the staff. The comments she'd overheard—people normally didn't speak freely around her—were that he considered himself better than those who served him. He looked down on Bealadair's servants, while they knew he was nothing more than the purchased husband of one of the McCraight daughters.

The new duke, on the other hand, had endeavored to learn their names. He made his own coffee, insisted on breakfasting with Addy and Betty, and—knowledge she'd just acquired—had made Mrs. Ferguson some type of balm to use for her arthritis.

When Connor missed another shot, Felix's smile grew broader.

There was no doubt of the disappointment in the

crowd behind her. She was annoyed on Connor's behalf. Didn't they realize he was shooting with his left arm? He'd been wounded. When it was over and the tally taken, Felix was the winner.

Only then did she glance behind her to see Lara standing at the windows clapping excitedly for her husband. If Elsbeth had been married to one of the men in the contest, she would've been on the front line of spectators. At the conclusion, she would've raced across the snowy lawn and hugged him. If nothing else, she would have helped him on with his coat.

Regardless of what anyone thought, she began to walk toward Connor.

He was thanking the stableboy who had thrown the targets as well as the footman who had rotated the guns.

She waited until he was finished, picked up his coat, and held it out for him.

"You don't want to compound your injury by getting pneumonia, too, Your Grace."

"What did you tell her?"

She knew, immediately, what he meant. Heat traveled through her, but it wasn't a sensation of embarrassment as much as acute awareness. She wondered if she should tell him the truth or simply attempt to change the subject and deflect his curiosity.

"I told her she was being ridiculous," she said, giving him the truth.

"Was she?"

The heat intensified.

He moved to put on his coat and made a face, a

small almost-infinitesimal grimace. His shoulder was paining him. Silly man.

She helped him ease his arm into the sleeve of his coat, then found herself patting the lapel, and, as if he were hers to protect, began buttoning the coat, getting to the second button before she realized what she was doing. She dropped her hands and stepped back, looking up at him.

"Was it worth it?" she asked, glancing at the tables and the dwindling crowd.

"Oh, yes, it was worth it," he said. "Now I know that Felix was capable of shooting me."

She glanced up at him, surprised. "Is that why you did it?"

"That, and to shut him up."

They smiled at each other.

"You used your left arm," she said.

He nodded. "After I was wounded in the war, I was put right back into combat. It was either learn to shoot with my left arm or be defenseless."

She reached up and patted his lapel again, needing to touch him.

"Was she being ridiculous, Elsbeth?"

"Does it matter?"

"More than you know."

She didn't say anything. Her mind would not work. She couldn't think of a thing to say to him. No quip, or rejoinder. Nothing witty came to mind.

"If there was no one here," he said, "I would kiss you again."

Now she most definitely couldn't think. But her imagination wouldn't cease. She would take a step forward, place her hands flat on his coated chest, and look up at him with her heart in her eyes. He would bend his head and gently place his mouth on hers.

She blinked, banishing that image with difficulty.

She forced herself to take a step away, heading back to Mrs. Ferguson so quickly that her departure might be categorized as an escape.

CONNOR WATCHED AS Felix gave instructions to the footmen, handed someone else the guns, and proceeded to bask in the glory of being the winner of their match.

The longer he was at Bealadair, the more Connor was certain he'd made the right decision. The sooner the house and the land were sold, the better.

He wasn't sure he wanted to have anything to do with the Scottish McCraights in the future. Ordinarily, he would've invited them back to Texas, proud to show this branch of the family the success Graham had achieved. However, he hadn't issued the invitation, and he wasn't certain he was going to.

"Good match. Sorry about beating you."

Connor turned to face Felix. "Never be sorry for winning," he said.

The man evidently took great pride in his victory because he couldn't hide his gloating smile.

He didn't give a flying fig that he had lost to Felix. Let the man boast. Let him brag about his accomplishments. It didn't matter.

"Surprised to see you shoot with your left arm, though," Felix said.

"It was a skill I learned in the war. Of course, I was shooting at live targets, then. Men, not glass balls."

There, that wiped the smile off the man's face.

"Did you shoot me, Felix?"

He hadn't given the man any hint of his question and he watched Felix's face closely. Surprise bloomed in the other man's eyes for a moment, and then was quickly gone.

"Of course I didn't shoot you."

"I warn you I'm not that easy to kill."

"Why would you think it was me?"

He ignored Felix's question for one of his own. "Do you think if I'm dead things will change? I've given instructions that the sale of Bealadair is to go through, regardless of what happens to me."

Felix didn't respond to that information.

Connor had never had the experience of being actively disliked simply because of who he was or the fact that he'd been born. No, not simply born. Born a McCraight.

He turned and, without another word to Felix, walked away.

Chapter 27

He's going to be unbearable," the duchess said, turning from the window. "I do wish His Grace had trounced him."

"Connor isn't into competition shooting much," Sam said, offering the duchess a plate of cookies.

He liked the way she took one delicately between thumb and forefinger. He liked most of the things she did, from her way of speaking in that Scottish brogue of hers to her quick smile.

He was smitten and well aware of it. Normally, his attraction to a woman took a little time in forming. He'd had some good relationships and some long relationships. He'd rarely had good, long relationships. Therefore, he was getting a little more cautious as he grew older, which made the situation with the duchess even more surprising.

The woman was a paradox. He recognized in her something he knew about himself. What people saw on the exterior was not truly how he felt inside. He knew, all too well, that he had a reputation for hard drinking, hard loving, and carousing from time to time. The people who willingly passed along such stories never saw him with a book, however, or at the opera, which he truly enjoyed.

Rhona worked hard at creating the perfect image of the Duchess of Lothian, of arranging her family around her almost like a protective wall. Her position was very important to her, as if it defined the woman she was. Inside, however, he suspected she was lonely and now terrified by Connor's decision. Everything she knew to be true, everything she had carefully erected for all these years, was about to crumble.

She was not unlike a hermit crab in the process of changing its house.

For all her flaws and faults, however, Rhona McCraight had a delightful sense of humor. She was, surprisingly, able to laugh at herself, although he doubted that she shared her wry observations with many people.

He suspected that her marriage with Gavin hadn't been all that pleasant, but she would probably deny it until her death. Evidently, aristocrats were not allowed to admit they were unhappy.

She got a look in her eyes from time to time, one that he thought of as farseeing. He imagined he had that look himself, staring out over the Texas prairie, wondering what the hell he was doing chasing cows with Graham when he would much rather have been in Austin or Dallas. Friendship exacted a toll on a person. It had never been more so than in his friendship with Graham. Graham was all work and little play, and it looked like Connor was following in his footsteps.

"The man will be unbearable," Rhona said again.

"He will do nothing but boast of today for weeks or months or however long we have here."

She sent a sideways glance in his direction, and he bit back his smile.

She kept hinting that he might be able to change Connor's mind. He never responded or gave her any inkling that he knew what she was doing. She wasn't the least bit subtle, but then he suspected Rhona had never had a reason to engage in subterfuge. After all, she was the Duchess of Lothian and her wishes were normally fulfilled the moment she uttered them. It must be galling to know that there was nothing she could do in this situation.

Connor wasn't going to change his mind. In that way, he was just like his father. Once Graham had set on a course of action, it would have taken an act of God to get him to change. It made him wonder if Gavin had been the same, a question he wouldn't ask his widow.

"A banty rooster," he said.

"I beg your pardon?"

He really did like how her eyebrows went up like that.

"Felix is like a banty rooster in a henhouse," he said, smiling at her. "Some men are like that. They feel the necessity to preen and strut."

"Do they?" she asked, nibbling at her cookie. "Are you like that, Sam?"

"Do you think so, Rhona?"

She tilted her head slightly and studied him. "I think, perhaps, that no one truly knows who you are, Sam Kirby. That you reveal only parts of yourself to one person and maybe different parts to the next."

That was so close to the mark he was surprised. Uncomfortable, he wasn't sure how to answer. Thankfully, she took command of the moment in a demonstration of her greatest talent: that of graciousness.

She moved back to where the McCraight daughters were sitting, took a place at the end of the settee and encouraged him to sit beside her with a welcoming smile.

He had the strangest feeling that his past was repeating itself. The moment reminded him of days spent with Graham's family. The difference was that Connor wasn't in the room. And he had never had more than a brotherly feeling for Linda, Connor's mother.

These women, for all their familial resemblance, were different from the Texas McCraights.

They had a reserve about them, which was probably due to being a duke's daughters, being Lady this or Lady that. Or it could have been Rhona's influence. She seemed a mite too fixated on propriety. He'd heard the word *proper* from her at least a dozen times in the past few days. It seemed to matter a great deal to her whether or not people were behaving correctly.

He'd met enough of those types of women in Dallas and Austin. They seemed to have their corsets tied a little too tight. They looked down at others, peering through their lorgnettes, raising their thin bridged noses as if trying to avoid an unpleasant smell.

But Rhona wasn't like that. There was a core of sweetness and softness to her, evident from the way she laughed at his foolish jests, or looked at him from time to time.

She'd let him kiss her, too, on more than one occasion.

He'd never attempted to be anything but the hoi polloi. He liked working around the ranch hands as much as he occasionally liked taking a cigar and a brandy with one of the state representatives.

Money was the great equalizer. It brought greedy people to your level, and it camouflaged you when you ascended to theirs. He could be as rude and as roughneck as any drover, but the minute people knew how rich he was, they forgave him all his assumed bad habits.

Being in Scotland was an unusual experience for him in that he didn't have to pretend to be anybody but who he was. He wasn't as uncouth as certain people thought him, or as polished as some believed him to be. He was simply Sam, a man from Texas. More than that, nobody seemed to want to know. And that was fine with him.

He sat and smiled at the girls.

He liked Muira because she had an open way about her. She smiled a lot and she said nice things about other people. Granted, she was a little too fond of sweets, but everybody had something they needed to work on.

The middle sister, Anise, seemed to think she was perfect. He'd caught her preening in front of a mirror twice now, as if she couldn't quite believe how pretty she was. He'd seen pretty women all his life. Time made them less pretty and so did their inner qualities. A grasping, cunning woman began to look like that after a few years. A pleasant disposition made a plain woman look prettier. But he doubted that

Anise would pay any attention to thoughts of beauty from an older man, especially one who wasn't fawning all over her.

He didn't really like the older sister. Lara was Rhona's stepdaughter, the product of Gavin's first marriage. Marie, that's what her name was. Graham had talked about her once, but only once, the moment fueled by good whiskey. He could still recall the tone of Graham's voice and the longing in it, even though he'd already been married to Linda for two years. Evidently, there were some loves that never left you.

Lara hadn't said more than two words to him the entire time they'd been there. Evidently, he wasn't of sufficient rank to attract her interest. Most of the time, she stared off into the distance as if the current company couldn't possibly meet her requirements for polite discourse.

The only person he'd ever seen her act remotely warm toward was Felix, and she doted on her husband.

He'd seen some strange pairings in his past: large women with tiny men, a handsome man with a plain woman, and the reverse—a nearly ugly man with a beautiful female. He would rank Felix and Lara up there among the strangest. She seemed to be personable enough, knowledge that came from overhearing her conversations with her husband. Felix, on the other hand, struck him as greedy and grasping.

He wasn't an unattractive fellow, but his voice was grating and his recitation of his accomplishments nearly laughable. As far as he could see, Felix had no occupation other than shooting. If he had other hobbies, he didn't brag of them. Nor did he do much in the way of adding to the conversation whenever they were together. Instead, he complained a lot.

They didn't have time for complaints in Texas. If a section of fence was down, no kudos went to the man who pointed it out. Why hadn't he fixed it?

Felix's complaints were primarily about other people and how they perceived him. The maid wasn't deferential enough. The footman smirked at him. On the whole, Sam preferred to ignore the couple when he could.

Rhona, now, was a different story.

He smiled at her and wondered when he could get her alone.

ELSBETH MADE HER way to the kitchen, hoping to get an early dinner and retire to her sitting room. She knew she was running out of time. She couldn't avoid the family any longer. She had to talk to Rhona. Hopefully, however, not until after her trip to Inverness tomorrow.

The weather was holding. The days were so cold that the air felt like you could snap it in two, but wrapped up in her cloak with an added scarf and her leather gloves, she was very comfortable on her rounds.

The cattle were doing well. So were the crofters she visited.

The McCraights were very proud. They didn't ask for handouts or help, normally. You had to be very cagey in how you asked if they needed assistance. She had always found that if she spoke about the children, the parents allowed as how maybe they could use a bit more flour or some help with cutting wood.

There was one family, so far away that she could only visit them every few weeks, where the husband had finally succumbed to a large growth on his throat. Patty was alone with their three children, and she worried about the woman enough to offer her a position at the house. Unlike other great houses, the children lived with their parents in small cottages on the edge of the estate. The children could go to the school they devised, half day while their mother was working. In such a way, Gavin had planned to educate all of Bealadair's staff, making it possible for them to go on to other positions if they wished. Some of the children were slated to go on to higher education, one of his longtime goals.

How much of that would remain once the house was sold?

If she genuinely believed that seduction would have any kind of impact on Connor's decision, she might've given it some thought and consideration.

Or perhaps she could hold herself out as a trade, of sorts. The good of the people of Bealadair for her virginity. She doubted she would marry. What good would a maidenhead do her when she could trade it for the benefit of so many other people?

She was not given to lying to herself. The sacrifice wouldn't be all that unpleasant. She wanted to kiss Connor again. Without thought of anyone's survival, but for her own sake.

Earlier, she'd patted his coat and she wanted to do more. She wanted to wrap her arms around his neck and pull his head down for a kiss and be lost in it for moments and moments.

What had the duchess said? Something about seduction being instinctive. Was she right? Was that
true? Did you simply get within touching range of
a male who attracted you and something took over?
You knew how to act and what went where and how?

She couldn't imagine something like that happening, especially around Connor. She would be inept
and silly. He was so overpoweringly male. More of a
man than anyone she'd ever met.

She'd never considered men in degrees of their
maleness before, but she found herself ranking them
as she made her way to the kitchen. She would definitely place Connor at the very top slot, and then,
perhaps in third or fourth position his friend, Mr.
Kirby. One or two of the crofters might be in the top
ten. Gavin, bless him, was a very studious man and
an enormously kind one, but she couldn't say that
he was exceptionally male. Had his brother been different?

Gavin had evidently felt his brother's absence
keenly, enough to remark on it more than once as he
grew more and more ill.

"You will like Graham," he said once. "He's always
had a better sense of humor than I. He's got this roaring laugh that used to embarrass Mother. She said
that he called attention to himself, and I suppose he
did, in a way."

She was curious about Graham. Had he been as
studious as Gavin? Or had he developed his own
character once away from Scotland? Perhaps she
could ask Connor.

No, it wouldn't be a good idea to be around him

any more than she absolutely had to. Although she had to see the family eventually, she was going to take precautions not to be alone with Connor.

She really did want to kiss the man again. Or even worse, test whether she was capable of seduction after all.

Chapter 28

For some reason, Connor thought Elsbeth would be at dinner. Especially since she'd come up to him at the shooting contest. Had she just felt sorry for him? Is that why she'd helped him on with his coat and been so sweet?

That thought was annoying, almost as irritating as her absence.

He was about to do something incredibly foolish. If pressed, he'd admit that he knew that his actions were also improper, but he needed to solve a mystery.

Exactly why was Elsbeth avoiding him?

Dinner had been the same as it had been for the past week, with the added fillip of Felix receiving kudos from the rest of the family while graciously admitting that Connor's injury might have had something to do with his loss.

He hadn't lied to Elsbeth; he didn't care about the contest. Nor had he told Felix a falsehood. When it had counted, when he'd needed to survive, he had shot well enough. He hadn't practiced on a bunch of glass balls.

But people like Felix—and unfortunately, Texas had a share of them, too—were all bluster and pomposity.

He and Sam exchanged a look across the table, one that was intercepted by the duchess. She only smiled, which made him wonder how well Sam's roping and culling was going.

After dinner he excused himself, heading for where he thought Elsbeth's suite was located, not with the rest of the family rooms, but in one of the older sections of the house.

The maid who'd given him that information had been a cheeky little thing with a saucy smile, twinkling eyes, and bright red hair. She reminded him, oddly enough, of his youngest sister and a surge of longing for his home nearly prevented him from thanking her.

The wing was connected to the main part of Bealadair by a bridge on the third floor. Arches made up both walls on either side. He wondered if, at one time, they'd been open to the elements. Now the arches were covered in a clear sparkling glass that brought the winter night close to him.

From conversations he'd had with the staff, Highland winters lasted for some time. He hoped to be gone from here by spring. He just didn't know when spring arrived.

He'd selected good men of character and determination to handle their assigned section of the ranch. They knew to report to Joe once a week. Joe would then forward on the reports to him. If anything needed to be done immediately, Joe and his lawyer together had legal authority to act in his stead.

He trusted the men he left behind, and that was the secret of being able to manage two million acres. No one man could oversee it all, but if you brought up men from trail riders to ranch hands to managers, you created a dependable and loyal crew.

That's what Elsbeth was doing, whether she knew it or not. By putting herself out there to the crofters, by ensuring that they knew she cared about them, she was creating loyalty. She was the face of Bealadair and perhaps its heart.

Had Gavin known that?

Why the hell hadn't his uncle written some kind of instructions or greeting? Why hadn't he communicated with his brother? Connor had been surprised when Glassey had shown up at the ranch one day, armed with legal papers but no personal correspondence from the Scottish McCraights.

If he'd been in Gavin's position, Connor would've written a letter to his heir, telling him what he hoped for in the future, what he had done to bring it about, and the people he considered of value. Not one word. Not one letter. Nothing at all.

In that, Gavin had been like his brother. His father hadn't left a message, either. Not one damn thing.

A flash of something white caught his eye.

He stopped, turning to the left, trying to figure out what he'd seen. From his calculations, this wing was perpendicular to where the duke's suite was located. Maybe he'd only seen a flash of something metallic or the glitter of the moonlight on snow.

No, it had been higher than that, almost on the roofline. There, there it was again.

He took a few steps to the left, braced his hands

against the brick, and wished the gas lamps installed every few feet weren't quite so bright.

What the hell had he seen?

"Connor? What are you doing here?"

He glanced to his right to see Elsbeth standing there. She'd begun to loosen her hair from its proper braid, and it was tumbling down over her shoulders. Her cheeks were pink, either from exertion or from the cold.

"I thought I saw something."

"What?"

"Someone on the roof," he said. "The parapet. A white figure."

Her smile startled him. If he studied her for a dozen years, he was certain that he'd never grow accustomed to her beauty. Now her startling gray eyes were alight with humor.

Her teeth were so white that her lips always looked pink in contrast. He wanted to watch the way she spoke, the way her mouth moved, even how she sometimes bit her bottom lip.

Or the way her smile faded into nothingness as it was doing right now.

"Connor," she said, and there was a note to her voice, something that hadn't been there before. A caution? A warning? Or maybe only a question.

He took a few steps toward her, but stopped when she held up her hand. She shook her head, then moved her gaze from him to the window.

"You saw the White Lady," she said.

"The ghost? I don't believe in ghosts, Elsbeth. I don't know what I saw, but it wasn't a ghost."

Her smile was back and it had a teasing edge to it. "You're in Scotland now," she said. "Every great house has a few ghosts. Bealadair is no exception. The White Lady is supposed to warn a McCraight."

"Addy has educated me on all Bealadair's ghosts. That still doesn't mean I believe in them."

He was close enough that he could smell her perfume, only she wasn't wearing anything flowery.

"You smell of bacon," he said.

"I was in the kitchen," she said. "It's not bacon. It's pork roast."

"Were you cooking? Do you do everything, Elsbeth?"

She shook her head. He took another step toward her.

He reached out his hands and, before she could stop him, placed them on either side of her waist. There, he was touching her. Finally.

"Is that where you went for dinner, the kitchen? I should issue an edict as the new duke that you are no longer allowed to eat in the kitchen with the rest of the staff or to hide in whatever room you choose."

He pulled her gently toward him and she didn't say a word. Not one protest. Nothing. But her eyes widened and it was enough for him to stop and step away.

"Why have you been avoiding me?" There, the question he needed answered. "You're not at dinner. You're not at the stables when I go. You're never in the kitchen. I think you're one of Bealadair's ghosts.

The Elusive Housekeeper. No one ever catches her, but you know she's always there."

"I didn't want to see you," she said.

It was the first time in his life that words ever had the power of a blow.

He took another step back. "Very well," he said. "Then I won't bother you."

He was turning to leave her when she spoke again.

"Oh, Connor, I was embarrassed. I'd managed to humiliate myself so completely."

He turned back. "How?"

"How? You know how."

He reached her, placed his hand on her shoulder, and trailed his fingers down to her elbow, pulling her gently toward him. This time her eyes didn't widen, but her cheeks did deepen in color.

"My aunt's idea might have worked, you know," he said. "God knows I've thought of nothing else but."

"You have?"

Her voice was tremulous, her smile fading in and out as if she cautioned herself not to show any emotion but couldn't help it.

"I've been lusting after you, Elsbeth Carew. Is that an insulting thing to say?" he asked. He honestly didn't know. Would a woman be horrified to know that she'd featured prominently in his dreams or that she was perpetually in his thoughts? Who the hell did he ask other than the woman in question?

"I can't think that anyone would be insulted by such a thing," she said.

That was too careful an answer for his peace of mind.

"Are you insulted? Does it make you want to hide even further?"

She startled him by reaching out and grabbing the lapels of his jacket. He hadn't expected that.

"Would you be insulted to know that I feel the same? I can barely get any work done, Connor Mc-Craight, for thinking of you. The cattle inspection took longer than it needed to because I kept seeing you standing on the other side of the pasture, grinning at me. You with your fancy saddle and your hat."

The word was *flummoxed*. His sister, Dorothy, had used it once, and he'd demanded to know what it meant, and then accused her of making the word up when she couldn't give him an instantaneous definition. He'd discovered the meaning later and the word was perfect for this moment. Flummoxed: to be startled, to have one's world turned upside down.

He didn't have a thing to say. Not one coherent statement occurred to him. So he did the only thing he could think of doing. He kissed her.

There wasn't a doubt in his mind that he was making a big mistake kissing Elsbeth again. But that part of his brain was instantaneously silenced by the feel of her lips.

He half expected her to pull away, act indignant, and lecture him on the impropriety of his actions. What he didn't anticipate was Elsbeth linking her arms around his neck. She stood on tiptoe, tilted her head a little, and silenced every gentlemanly instinct that might have led to his restraint.

She moaned and that was his undoing. He

wouldn't have released her if someone tried to come between them with a branding iron.

He wanted to touch her everywhere, this surprising, sensuous, beautiful woman, who smelled of pork roast and knew one end of a cow from the other.

Chapter 29

"Where is your room?" he asked. No, it wasn't just a question but a demand, uttered in a voice that sounded unlike him. "Where is your room?"

She took his hand and led him through the corridor. He didn't remember anything but the lit sconces and a vague glimpse of a crimson runner.

He entered her room, slammed the door closed with his back as he reached for her again.

The madness gripping him was something he'd never before felt. As if his mind weren't his own but belonged to some other creature, one without thought as much as need. He had to touch her, feel her skin, breathe in her scent.

He had never experienced this, never lost his sense of place. He didn't care where he was at the moment, only that Elsbeth was in his arms, that he was kissing her, then trailing his lips down her throat, hearing her catch her breath on a gasp.

He didn't understand what was happening, but then he realized that understanding wasn't important. All he needed was Elsbeth.

"Forgive me," he said a moment later, his conscience finally making itself known. He dropped his arms and forced himself to step back. He couldn't look at her, couldn't see those well-kissed lips without wanting to kiss her again.

"Forgive me," he said again.

"Forgive you?"

She did that sometimes, repeated his comments as a question. He realized she did so in an effort to give herself time to respond.

He glanced at her.

Her eyes were wide, the expression in them one he couldn't decipher. She didn't look horrified. She certainly didn't appear angry. Confused, perhaps.

Well, they were in that together, weren't they?

He should take another step away from her, back out of her sitting room entirely. He should not be here, alone with her.

He forced himself to study his surroundings rather than look at her again. It was not the sort of room he would've picked out as being Elsbeth's. Everything in it was upholstered in a dark blue fabric that struck him as masculine.

The curtains on the two windows on the far side of the room hadn't been closed, revealing their figures in a dark reflection. He stood there, braced against the door, his arms folded. Elsbeth stood in front of him, silent and still.

How did he extricate himself from this situation? Could he simply turn and walk away without a word? How did he leave, especially when he didn't wish to? When all he truly wanted to do was to take her to her bedroom and love her until the dawn sun illuminated those windows?

"Will you kiss me again?" she asked.

She wasn't smiling. Nor was she frowning. Instead, he only saw warmth in her eyes.

He shouldn't. He should escape this room before his better nature got suffocated beneath his body's wishes and wants.

Instead, he put out his hand, palm up.

She took a few steps toward him, still smiling.

"Elsbeth," he said, murmuring her name against her lips.

She was magic. The moment was magic. Perhaps that wasn't the best word, but it was the only one that made it through his physical responses to lodge in his brain.

His heart was racing; his breath was short. His body reacted to her as it had from the first, tightening, hardening, despite the company or the lack of provocation. He wanted her as he had since that first snowy night when a smile danced on her face.

"Elsbeth."

"Connor," she said, her lips curving beneath his.

She had to take this seriously. She was in great danger. He wasn't at all sure he could control himself around her, especially when she pulled back, her eyes alight with mischief and daring.

She didn't speak, merely turned and held out her hand this time.

He didn't hesitate but grabbed her fingers, letting her lead him wherever she wanted to go.

Hopefully, to her bed.

NO MAN HAD ever been in her suite. Not many people had been invited inside. She had never considered that she would lead Connor into her sitting room, turn, and face him in front of the fire.

She wasn't just being improper; she was turning propriety on its ear. She was being shocking, unlike herself. She might, if she were given to lying, claim that the duchess had given her the idea. By suggesting seduction, Rhona had broken down the barrier of Elsbeth's morality.

That was foolishness, wasn't it? She'd wanted to kiss Connor long before the duchess said a word to her.

She might never marry. Tomorrow she'd leave for Inverness to arrange for a home. Somewhere away from Bealadair, the place she'd known for most of her life.

The future would be different. The responsibility would be gone, but so would the sense of belonging. She would answer to no one but herself, and perhaps that's what she felt at this moment, the beginnings of that self-determination.

She tossed her shawl to a nearby chair, faced Connor with everything she felt showing on her face. Confusion, a little fear, excitement, enthusiasm, need, and desire. *Desire*, a word she had never considered part of her character. Not once had she thought she was a woman who might give herself to a man freely and without thought of commitment.

Her entire life, she'd been shoehorned into a role. More than once, she wondered who she might be if her parents had lived, if she'd been surrounded by people who loved her unconditionally. Who would she have been? How would she have acted? Would she have been as restrained as she felt now, living a borrowed life in a borrowed room in a borrowed house?

This, then, might be her true self. She was not acting as someone else wished her to act. If she engaged in seduction, it was for her own sake and not for the McCraights.

She took another step toward him, extending her hand. He didn't reach out to grab it. Instead, Connor stood there watching her silently. She had the sudden thought that she might truly have to seduce him. He would not be guilty of overwhelming her with passion.

She would never be able to claim that he waylaid her or kissed her into submission. Or did anything other than what she truly wanted. He was, with his silence and his immobility, forcing her to go to him.

How did she seduce him? Oh, there were a few sweethearts among the staff, and she'd seen them laughing and engaging in a kiss behind a door or in the butler's pantry.

But she and Connor weren't sweethearts, were they? Yet there was something between them, something that made the air feel as though it had sparks. The same kind of feeling she got when she walked across the carpet in the winter, and then touched a door latch.

However much she'd tried to avoid Connor this past week, she hadn't been able to stop thinking of him. Being in the same room with him changed her, made her feel foolish and young.

Yet the words to banish him would be so easy to say.

Go away, Connor. He would go; she knew that. He would turn without another word spoken, perhaps smile at her or not. But there would be a look in his eyes that she would understand. An acknowledgment, perhaps, of her inexperience.

She wasn't a duke's daughter. She wasn't a Mc-Craight. Tomorrow, she would go off to Inverness to make arrangements for a lonely future. Why should she save herself?

If she did marry—and that possibility was so remote as to be laughable—then her future husband would simply have to understand that she came to him with a past. She wouldn't be the first woman to do so.

She walked away from Connor, heading for her bedroom. Only once did she turn and look at him, wanting to bridge the distance between them. Would he know that with that look she was granting him admittance into her bed?

Would he refuse the invitation?

He followed her slowly, and she wanted to stop and watch him move. She liked everything about this man, including the way he commanded a room, even her small sitting room. She liked the way he walked as if energy was coiled inside him.

She opened the bedroom door. A screen was erected in the corner, near the bathing room. She went to it now and with shaking fingers began to unbutton her bodice.

She had never had a maid. Gavin had asked her, more than once, if she wanted one. She had always answered *no* because of her privacy. She wasn't for parading around in her unmentionables in front of another person. Yet that's exactly what she was intending to do now, wasn't it?

The screen moved and suddenly he was there, overwhelmingly male.

"Elsbeth," he said, his voice deep, a baritone that skittered along her nerve endings.

She looked up at him. Where had she gotten her courage? Where had her momentary daring come from? She wanted more of his kisses. She wanted to be held. She wanted to know what passion was like—if it was a cousin to this startling feeling she had whenever she was around Connor. She was never more alive than when he was near. As if something in her responded to him.

"This isn't wise," he said.

Of course it wasn't, but she didn't want to hear that from him. Why must he suddenly be the voice of reason?

Her bodice gaped open, revealing the lace and black ribbon adorning her shift.

She took two steps to him, placing her hands on his chest and running them slowly up to the back of his neck. She tilted her head back and looked into his eyes, wishing he was as improvident as she felt at the moment.

Yet he'd come looking for her, hadn't he?

She didn't want him to be thoughtful or rational. Slowly, once again daring herself, she pulled his head gently down.

"It may not be wise," she said softly, "but it's what I want."

And then the world changed.

The reasonable Connor disappeared, replaced by

a man who was wild, undisciplined, and thoroughly irresistible. She had the sudden thought as he backed her up to her bed, that this was seduction. When you're offered a choice and your mind tells you it's not an intelligent one, but your heart and your body overcome any resistance. She found herself smiling as he kissed her, then laughing as he nearly ripped her clothes from her body.

She didn't want to stop him, wouldn't stop him. Perhaps she shouldn't have reveled in her defilement, but it hardly seemed like that. Her fingers were talented, too, as they made swift work of unfastening his buttons. His jacket was pushed off his shoulders and thrown to the floor. Then his shirt was gone.

His chest. Oh, his chest. She had never thought that a man's chest could be so utterly beautiful with its play of muscles and thick dusting of hair. She wanted to explore all of him, slowly, with her fingers and her lips, bestow a kiss to the bandage on his shoulder.

But one sensation after another demanded attention. He was kissing her again and the world seemed to spin. He was the only constant and she clung to him gladly.

His lips trailed kisses from her jawline down her throat. How had he removed her corset without her knowing? He grabbed the hem of her shift and pulled it over her head before dropping to one knee.

He must be very practiced at undressing a woman. He unlaced her shoe and removed it. She placed a hand on his shoulder for balance as he removed one stocking, then the other shoe and stocking. All that was left were her pantaloons.

He stood slowly, bare chested, with his trousers and boots still on.

Reaching out, he traced a mark the corset had made between her breasts down to her waist. He stroked the pad of his thumb down as if to erase it.

She was trembling, but it wasn't because of the cold. The maid assigned to her room always made a point of making up the fire around this time and it was blazing brightly not far away.

No, if she trembled it was because of her own actions. She could have stopped him at any moment, but had chosen to participate in her own downfall.

"I didn't think you could be more beautiful," he said.

His hands were everywhere, tender and gentle despite their size.

She didn't even utter a sound unless it was a moan when he kissed her. She wanted more of his kisses. She wanted his touch everywhere. His calloused fingers dancing down her spine, over her hips, down her legs, everywhere.

His kisses rained down her throat, across her chest. His hands were on her breasts, his thumbs teasing her nipples.

Beneath his hands she felt beautiful, as beautiful as he'd called her, and as perfect as the first woman.

As he lifted her up to the bed, he asked, "Are you sure, Elsbeth?"

He was the one with some sense. He was the one

with more moral character. He had the ability to stop, while she wanted to continue this delightful and decadent behavior.

"Please," she said. She didn't know what she was asking for, but it seemed as if he did.

"If I don't leave now, I'm not sure I can," he said.

"I don't want you to leave," she said.

She knew the risks she took. She knew the repercussions. Yet no payment for tonight seemed too great. Let him love her and she would take the chance. Just once, let her stroke her palms and fingers over his chest, legs, all those parts that so intrigued her.

For this space of time—an hour, perhaps two—she wanted to forget her future. She wanted to pretend that he was part of it. He wouldn't be leaving Scotland, bound for Texas. He would remain with her.

Give her that pretense, for just a little while.

She'd spent the past week thinking about him. She'd prayed over him and promised God that she would be a much better person if he would just spare Connor. He'd spared Connor, and yet here she was, on the cusp of breaking her vow.

Would God understand?

"Please," she said again, and this time she wasn't certain if her entreaty was to Connor or God himself. *Understand me. Realize how weak I am. How much I want this. How much I know it's wrong and I'm wrong and how much that doesn't seem to matter.*

Blessedly, thankfully, Connor wrapped his arms around her, her breasts pressing against his bare chest.

Thank you. Thank you. Thank you.

He lifted her to the bed as he removed the rest of his clothing.

"You're taking off your boots," she said.

He stopped and glanced at her, a small smile curving his lips. "I was only jesting about that, Elsbeth."

Should she tell him it didn't matter? He could still wear his boots and his hat and she wouldn't mind. Just as long as he was with her and could kiss her and touch her and make her feel what he did.

When he joined her on the bed, his gaze was intent, almost as if he were asking the question again.

Did she want this?

How did she say yes? She did the only thing she could think of, reached up and pulled him down to her, kissing him the way he'd already taught her.

In the next moment her pantaloons were being pulled from her. Somehow Connor had untied the drawstring, loosened it, and the offending garment was thrown up in the air to land somewhere she couldn't see.

She couldn't help but laugh.

Should she feel so giddy at a moment like this? Should lovemaking be accompanied by amusement?

It seemed as if it was, because he was suddenly above her, his smile and the look in his eyes pinning her to the mattress.

She'd never thought to kiss a smile, but she did now, her hands locking at the back of his neck.

Oh, there was something marvelous and wonderful and almost otherworldly about the feel of a male body on hers. A male body that was so different from her own, and yet it seemed as if they fit together so perfectly.

How could anyone bear to wear clothes again once that discovery had been made?

He kissed her breasts, his tongue dancing on her nipples. She wanted more of that, and when she said as much, she felt him smile against her skin.

"Your arm. Your shoulder?"

"Is fine," he said, his voice deeper than normal.

He kissed her again and for a few moments she lost herself in the kiss. Was it always like that with a kiss? Did your head go spinning somewhere among the stars? Did colors always appear behind your closed lids? Or was it only kissing Connor?

His kiss seemed tied, somehow, to the very depths of her. Virgin or no, her body seemed to know what to do. She spread her legs almost instinctively, but he only moved aside, his head propped on his hand.

He seemed to be a great deal calmer than she felt. Her heart was racing; she couldn't breathe deeply. He stroked his hand from the mole next to her left breast, down and over her abdomen.

"You're so beautiful, Elsbeth."

She wanted to be, for him. She wanted him to truly think it and not to say it just to be kind.

She wished, for the first time in her life, that she was experienced, that she knew more about lovemaking. If she had been versed in the necessary skills, she might have been prepared for his hand moving down her body, exploring nooks and places she'd always been told were not proper to think about, let alone touch. But every time he did, her body responded.

"Are you sure?" he asked as he rose above her.

No, she wasn't at all sure.

"Kiss me," she said. If he kissed her, she wouldn't be able to think of anything else.

He did, his tongue touching hers, exploring. She

felt herself open to him, both his kiss and his invasion.

The sensation was shocking.

Her body was no longer hers. Somehow he commanded it, was able to harness her breath and cause her heart to beat like a shuttered bird in a tiny cage.

Even more sensations were layered atop the first. She didn't expect the pinch or the slight twinge of discomfort. She made a sound and Connor stopped moving.

"Am I hurting you?"

No. Yes. No.

She shook her head, but he didn't move, merely braced himself on his forearms.

"Elsbeth."

What a very strange time to want to weep. She wrapped her arms around him, wondering if she could explain. What she was feeling was something she hadn't anticipated, a yearning, a need to tell him how she felt.

He mustn't think that she would have done this with anyone. Only him. Only Connor.

In loving him she'd given him the only gift she had to give, her innocence. She wanted him to value it, to accept it, and in return give her something she might hold dear for the rest of her life: affection, if only for this moment.

He kissed her cheek, the corner of her mouth, the edge of her jaw, holding himself still as if to allow her to become accustomed to his size.

She was heating from inside, and she needed, wanted, must raise her hips. When she did, he raised up, kissed her lips. She met his downward stroke, her body knowing what to do without her mind's acquiescence. It felt as if she'd done this before, that she knew the rhythm and movements of this dance.

This. This is what she wanted. This feeling. This knowledge that something was going to happen and that it was going to burst from deep inside her. Not only emotion, but physical sensation. Her body's transformation from innocence to experience, from yearning to completion.

Then she lost herself, wonder stripping her of breath as she wrapped her arms around his neck and held on.

He stiffened above her, kissing her, the two of them joined in pleasure and passion.

Finally, it was over, Connor moving to lie beside her, his breath as fast as hers. She reached out, placed her hand on his good shoulder, needing to continue that connection with him.

This shattering interlude had propelled her from virginity to knowledge. It had done something else as well, something she hadn't expected. She felt as if he were wedged into her heart now, in a way that meant he would be nearly impossible to remove.

Chapter 30

Where the hell had she disappeared to now?

Douglas had informed him that Elsbeth had taken herself off to Inverness, only an hour's journey from Bealadair.

"Miss Elsbeth said she'd be back in three days, Your Grace. I'm sure she will. She never breaks her word."

"Do you know why she went to Inverness, Douglas?"

The stablemaster had looked surprised at the question.

"No, Your Grace, she didn't tell me that. Nor did I ask."

The look Douglas gave him meant Connor shouldn't have been curious, either.

He was a damn sight more than curious. He was angry.

He'd even gone to Glassey, but the solicitor had not been forthcoming with any information.

"Yes, she's in Inverness, Your Grace."

"Why?"

"I'm not at liberty to divulge that, Your Grace."

And so on and so on.

"Are you any closer to finding a buyer for Bealadair?" he finally asked.

"I've sent inquiries to a number of solicitor friends, Your Grace. Finding a suitable buyer who has the wherewithal to purchase an estate the size of Bealadair will take some time, I'm afraid."

He'd studied the man, wondering if Glassey had his own reasons for delaying the sale.

"Do what you can to hurry it along," he said. "I want to go home."

The instant he said the words, Connor felt them spring back, almost as if they were on a cord. Yes, he wanted to return home, but he would miss some things about Scotland. Not the weather, certainly, but Addy, who was a damn fine cook. Perhaps she could be persuaded to come and live in Texas. He'd gotten to know his cousin Muira a little better and thought that she might get along with his sisters well, especially Eustace.

He carefully avoided thinking about *her*, the woman who was tying his guts into knots. The same woman who just up and left Bealadair without a by your leave, or any kind of notice. The same woman who'd invited him to her bed and the very next day left as if she hadn't been a virgin and it hadn't been, well, a night he'd always remember.

What about her?

Evidently it hadn't been as important as her jaunt to Inverness.

Three days? What was she doing in Inverness that took three days? Glassey wouldn't tell him. Addy didn't know. If Muira knew, she was better at lying than anyone he'd ever met.

He found himself haunting the stable. He'd go and visit with Douglas midmorning and then again around four, just before dark. On the morning of the fourth day, he was there every hour on the hour and had given up any pretense that he was oiling his saddle or admiring the horseflesh or examining the tack room. Everybody knew—and he wasn't really concerned that they did—that he was waiting for Elsbeth.

Waiting, and not in the best of moods.

ELSBETH SAT IN the carriage on the way back to Bealadair, occupying herself with her notebook, writing down anything she could think of that needed to be done before the ball. The event to welcome Connor was to be held tomorrow. Thank heavens the weather had held. That meant that most of the people who had been invited would attend.

She needed to spare some time to endure Rhona's lecture. After all, she'd gone to Inverness without the duchess's permission. She wasn't truly a servant, although there were times she felt like one. Even though she'd made arrangements for everything to be taken care of in the three days it would take to travel to Inverness, conduct her business, and return, that wouldn't be good enough for the Duchess of Lothian.

No, Rhona would lecture her on propriety—why hadn't she taken a maid with her? If she had, she would no doubt have had to endure a lecture about taking one of the staff away from her duties. And she was certain that Rhona was going to take this opportunity to inquire about her success at seduction.

That was the topic she did not want to discuss, now or in the future.

She could tell when they were getting close to Bealadair. The great brick wall that encircled the house and its gardens ended in a magnificent wrought iron and brick gate manned by one of the footmen. Only a little farther and they would be stopped, the driver would nod and identify himself, and the bell would be rung in the gatehouse that signaled those in the house that a visitor was approaching.

Not quite a visitor, though, in this case. But perhaps she would be shortly. She had met with the solicitor Mr. Glassey had recommended, and there were several properties that matched her requirements and her budget. All she had to do was choose. She'd been able to visit two of them and although each was exactly what she had envisioned before coming to Inverness, she hadn't yet made a decision.

One thing kept occurring to her, and it was something she had never thought of until this trip. How was she to bear the loneliness?

At Bealadair, when she wished to be alone, she went to her suite and closed the door. Even the duchess gave her privacy in her own rooms. Otherwise, she was surrounded by people all the time. The staff of Bealadair were, even in the sad months following Gavin's death, of a kind and cheerful nature. There was something about them that she knew made them different from those people who worked at other great houses. Perhaps it was Gavin's insistence on educating their children or considering them part of the clan, even if they came from Inverness to work at Bealadair.

There was most definitely a feeling of family.

Did Connor know what he was going to do? Did he realize that he was disbanding a clan? Did he care about the people who would be scattered to the four winds if the new owner didn't wish to keep them on? Would the house be left unoccupied for the most part, only to be visited by an absent owner a few times a year?

What would Gavin say?

Appeal to his logic, Elsbeth. He is an intelligent man. After all, he's a McCraight.

The problem was that she could completely understand why Connor would want to sell Bealadair and return to Texas. He was born there. That was his home, his country. Although his ancestors were Scottish, he didn't feel a kinship to Scotland.

How was she to bear it when he left? That was a question she should have asked herself earlier, before she allowed herself to be fascinated by him.

She rested her head against the padded seat and closed her eyes. When he left, she'd feel an acute sense of loss. But he was an anomaly, a moment out of time in her life, an experience she had and would never have again. He was simply a stranger who'd shown up one snowy night and would disappear soon.

She wiped away her tears and counseled herself sternly. She never wept, or at least not as often as she had for the past three days. Nor had she known when it would happen, an embarrassing situation since it had occurred once when she was speaking to the solicitor and another time when they were going to see one of the properties he'd selected for her.

Something had reminded her of Connor. Some simple remark, some item recalled him to mind—and she'd acted like a schoolgirl.

It had been a very long time since she'd felt this lost and alone. She'd been eight years old and visited in the hospital by three officious gentlemen who informed her that her parents had not survived the accident, but she had, and wasn't she the most fortunate little girl?

She hadn't felt fortunate.

She had a feeling she'd feel the same way when Connor left, when he packed up his saddle and strode to his carriage without a backward glance toward Bealadair. Or her.

She'd wanted to talk to Douglas, so she'd requested that the driver take the carriage around to the stable instead of pulling into the front of Bealadair.

As if she summoned him with her thoughts, Connor was standing there when the carriage rolled to a stop. His hat was pulled low over his forehead so she couldn't see his eyes, but from his stance she could tell Connor McCraight was not in a good mood. He was leaning against a fence post, his arms folded in his leather coat, one booted foot crossed over the other.

Snow was drifting down lazily like feathers, but it didn't seem to touch him. Maybe Nature itself knew better than to bother with His Grace when he had, as Mr. Kirby had once called it, his "mad on."

Elsbeth thanked the stableboy who opened the carriage door for her.

Why was Connor waiting for her? It was quite

evident he was, especially when he pushed back the brim of his hat with one slow finger.

Oh, dear, that expression wasn't friendly at all.

Somehow, he'd acquired Gavin's frosty look when he was being all ducal and aristocratic. In Connor, it seemed to be even more intense.

She gathered her cloak around her and stepped out of the vehicle.

Connor approached her, walking slowly, almost like a large feral cat stalking a bird.

"Stop that," she said.

He stopped.

"If you think I'm going to be intimidated by that look, you're wrong. I've faced down the Duchess of Lothian all my life, so I know all about people who act all aristocratic."

"I thought she was a crosspatch, but according to Sam, she's very agreeable."

She'd never heard the Duchess of Lothian described as agreeable by anyone.

He frowned at her, which was marginally better than that glare.

"Besides, I don't act all aristocratic."

"Then stop looking at me like that."

He shook his head. "Where the hell have you been?" he asked.

"What?"

"You stop doing *that*," he said. "Repeating what I say. Just answer me."

It was her turn to frown.

"Is it any of your concern, Your Grace?"

"You were gone three days."

"I know how long I was gone," she said.

She did wish he would move back, away. He was large and rather formidable up close.

"Elsbeth."

"You stop doing *that*. You shouldn't say my name like that. It's entirely too personal."

He grinned at her, which was worse than the glare and the frown.

She grabbed her reticule and valise and tried— she really did—to get past Connor. He merely took the valise from her.

"Why did you go to Inverness?"

She turned toward the path at the back of the house. She would talk to Douglas later when she didn't have an irritated/charming/annoying duke on her hands.

"I went to see if I could buy a property," she said. "I need a place to live."

"You live here."

She sent him a sideways glance. "For now, but not for very long. You've made that abundantly clear."

He was frowning at her again.

She frowned right back.

The stableboy had disappeared, and the driver was walking the carriage into the stable. Perhaps it was better if they had their confrontation out here, where there was no one listening.

"Why didn't you tell me you were leaving?" he asked.

She hadn't expected that question. Nor had she anticipated seeing that expression on his face, almost as if she'd insulted him. Or worse, done something that had wounded him.

How ridiculous. She hadn't wounded Connor Mc-Craight.

"Well?"

"Am I to tell you my comings and goings now, Your Grace? One night in my bed does not give you that power."

"You were a virgin, Elsbeth."

She looked at him incredulously. "Thank you for informing me of that fact, Your Grace. I was well aware."

"You should've told me."

"You should have anticipated," she said, annoyed. "Or did you think I took every visitor to Bealadair to my bed?"

He pushed his hat back on his head, his mouth thinned, and he looked as if he were biting back words. He really didn't need to watch his comments around her. She was prepared for anything he might have to say.

Besides, she'd already gotten her tears out of the way on the way home.

"Why did you take me to your bed?"

"As I remember it, Your Grace, it was a mutual decision. You needn't act as if you were powerless to refuse my invitation."

"Damn close to it."

She blinked at him, startled. A warmth began to blossom in the pit of her stomach. No, she was not going to be flattered by such an admission. Nor was she going to be amused by his exasperated expression.

Good, if he was feeling the least bit confused about their relationship, it was only a small fraction of what she was feeling.

"I don't want you to leave," he said. "At least, not until the house is sold."

"You don't get a choice about when I leave, Your Grace. I have my future to consider."

He removed his hat, threaded his fingers through his hair, replaced his hat, and nodded to her.

"I know that. I'm just hoping you stick around."

"As entertainment, Your Grace? No."

"Dammit, Elsbeth, that's not what I meant and you know it."

In seconds he was there, in front of her, his arms around her. She didn't have time to protest before he bent his head to kiss her.

Anyone could have seen them, but she didn't think of that in the next moment. She didn't care that it was afternoon, that the staff would be milling about, that Addy could see them from her kitchen window. The duchess, the whole family could view them, but it wasn't something she thought about.

She couldn't think of anything when Connor was kissing her.

The world exploded in a cloud of shattering stone.

A startled yelp escaped her as Connor pushed her into a nearby bush. She lay there trying to make sense of what had just happened.

She brushed the snow off her face and began to right herself.

Connor reached her and extended his hand. She took it and stood, only then realizing that another of the statues had fallen, this time barely missing Connor.

If he hadn't moved to kiss her, he would've been crushed by the stone.

Shock kept her speechless.

Connor was looking up at the roof, his hands on his hips. Slowly he turned his head to look at her.

"Are you all right?"

She nodded.

Their gazes met.

"Damn lucky you're nearly irresistible, Elsbeth."

There was that warmth again, but it was offset by a sensation so cold that she felt frozen to her toes.

"I inspected the roof," she said, staring at the chunks of stone. This statue couldn't be repaired. It hadn't fallen in a snowdrift but had, instead, shattered on the gravel path. "The day after the first statue fell. I checked all the statues. All of them were fine. None of them were cracked. Their bases were all intact."

She didn't come out and say the words. Neither did he. She would inspect the roof again to be sure, but it looked as if the fallen statue was no accident.

Someone wanted Connor dead.

The thought chilled her through, enough that she stretched out her gloved hand and gripped his arm.

"What becomes of Bealadair if something happens to you?" she asked.

He looked down at her.

For a moment she wondered if he would answer. Should she apologize for the question? Or were they just going to pretend that someone wasn't trying to harm him?

"The ghillie hadn't been hunting," she said. "Nor had his men. Someone shot you, Connor. And, as much as I would like to think it was an accident, someone pushed that statue off the roof."

"I've made my will," he said. "My mother and my sisters will inherit everything I own, from the ranch to the property here in Scotland."

That didn't make any sense, then. Why would anyone want to kill Connor when there was no reward for it?

"You could be the target, Elsbeth."

They looked at each other.

"You were at Castle McCraight with me. Someone could have easily been shooting at you." He glanced toward the shattered statue. "That could have struck you."

She wrapped her arms around her waist in an effort to warm herself. It wasn't the weather that chilled her, but the thought that someone wanted one of them dead.

"Why? I don't own anything. I don't have any power. I can't change anyone's life."

"Don't you have a legacy?"

She nodded. "From my parents," she said. "And the bequest from Gavin."

"What happens to it in the case of your death?"

"I don't know." She hadn't made arrangements. She didn't have a will. She'd never even discussed the matter with Mr. Glassey.

Neither one of them said anything, but all too soon the moment to speak was gone, swept away by the sudden appearance of Addy and two footmen.

"Oh, by the robes of Saint Brigid, what happened, Miss Elsbeth?" Addy did a quick curtsy. "Your Grace."

"One of the statues fell," Elsbeth said, hoping that the cook wouldn't inquire any further.

She stepped away, directing the footmen to remove the remnants of the statue.

Gavin had been so careful in keeping everything that belonged to Bealadair and documenting every repair and replacement that there was one whole building dedicated to preserving historical remains. They would take the remnants of the statue there and it would be placed in a carefully labeled crate.

Suddenly, there were more people, maids and footmen, stableboys, even Douglas and Mr. Barton, every single one of them offering his opinion on how such a near tragedy could have happened.

"It's the snow, of course. And the cold. Perhaps it's cracked the stone."

"We should inspect all the statues," someone offered, not knowing that Elsbeth had done that exact thing herself.

"Perhaps they should be removed completely." This comment was from Addy, who kept looking at the shattered statue and then the two of them.

She really should move away, but she had a feeling of safety around Connor.

Yet what if he was right? What if, instead of him being the target, she was? No, she couldn't accept that, especially since he'd already been warned.

"You saw the White Lady," she said, looking up at him.

Within seconds, she heard the buzz of conversation around her and realized that someone had overheard.

"His Grace saw the White Lady."

"White Lady. The duke saw the White Lady."

"It's a warning, Your Grace," Addy said. "She

always appears to warn one of the McCraights," Addy continued. "It's been that way ever since the house was first built."

Connor surprised Elsbeth by nodding, smiling faintly at Addy, and grabbing Elsbeth's valise with one hand and her elbow with the other.

"Let's not dawdle," he said, guiding her through the throng of people to the back door of the house, making his way through the corridors with her at his side.

He didn't say another word, and from his fixed look and thinned lips, Elsbeth decided it would be wiser if she didn't speak, either.

Chapter 31

Soon enough they were at the library's double doors. He opened one and stepped aside. She went through, and then watched him close the door and lock both of them.

He held out his hands and she removed her cloak, watching as he placed it on one of the low bookcases. He did the same with his coat and hat, smoothing his hair with one palm.

She removed her hat, taking some time with one of the pins before placing it atop her cloak.

He still hadn't said anything. Nor did she break the silence.

He strode across the room to sit at Gavin's desk. He motioned her to the chair next to him, a place she'd often sat, especially when she was young and being quizzed on her governess's lessons.

The duke had not, strangely enough, ever questioned his own daughters. She had often thought that the reason he did so with her was because of the responsibility he felt he owed her father.

Even so, those times alone with Gavin had made his daughters resent her. Perhaps, if he had treated her the same as Lara, Anise, and Muira, they would have been closer growing up. Or maybe not. It was difficult to know something like that because she couldn't rewrite history.

She sat, folding her hands in her lap, just now realizing she was trembling.

"What are you doing?" she asked as he pulled out a piece of paper and began writing.

"Giving instructions to Mr. Barton to hire more footmen. I want at least two of them to accompany you during the day." He glanced over at her. "Or do you do all the hiring here, Elsbeth?"

She looked away. "I do most of it," she admitted. "However, we really don't need any extra footmen, Connor. Nor do I need an escort everywhere I go."

She wrapped her arms around herself, trying to stop shivering.

"Hell, Elsbeth, you're freezing."

She wanted to tell him that she really wasn't cold as much as frightened, but she couldn't say the words. She'd just realized that the would-be killer had to be someone she knew, either a member of the staff or one of the family. No matter how she tried, she couldn't push away that knowledge.

Connor stood, came around the desk, and scooped her up from the chair, returning to the large leather chair with her in his arms. She'd never sat on anyone's lap. Perhaps she had as a baby, but those memories were gone. She most certainly had never sat on Connor's lap.

She really should stand and go back to her chair, but the effort was simply beyond her. Just for a moment, she would lay her head down on his shoulder, her forehead against his neck. Just for a moment, she'd allow him to put his arm around her. Having Connor hold her close felt so warm and comforting that she truly didn't want to move.

The fireplace was a dozen feet away to her right. The maid had lit it in anticipation of Connor using the room. She felt a spurt of pride for the staff's industriousness.

She closed her eyes, wishing she could warm up. Wishing, too, that Connor hadn't seen the White Lady.

It was Gavin who'd told her the story about the girl who'd been abandoned by her lover. He had gone off to war or battle or some dispute with neighbors, leaving her to pine for him. When he'd never returned, she'd cried every night, her grief and anguish audible to everyone at Bealadair. Then one day she simply didn't wake up. The story went that she'd died of a broken heart.

"I think, perhaps," Gavin had said, "that she had 'willed herself no more to live.'" He'd smiled at her. "It's part of a poem I learned as a boy about the White Lady. Unfortunately, that's all I can remember of it now."

Throughout the ages, as the tale went, the White Lady visited the McCraights to warn the laird of some catastrophe, to share her anguish with them, and to prepare the family for a crisis.

Connor moved slightly, and she placed her right hand against his chest, the thudding percussion of his heart reassuring. He wasn't going to be here for the rest of her life. He wasn't going to remain at Bealadair. Neither was she. Right now she simply wanted to stop time, encase it in stone, tie down the hands of the clock so it couldn't march relentlessly onward.

Her hand reached up, her fingers brushing against his throat. He bent his head a little, his cheek against the top of her head.

She was not going to weep. Not now. But he had become, in such a short time, so dear to her. She loved the smell of his skin, the feel of his almost beard against her fingertips. His hair was thick and silky. There was not one thing about him that she would change. Not his boots or his way of walking as if he commanded the earth. Or his occasional arrogant look as he watched other people. You could not help but think that everyone failed his appraisal. He had a way of studying you with his deep brown eyes that saw through every prevarication, every shield you might erect.

He cupped his hand around her jaw and lifted her head.

Time felt as if it did stand still as they looked at each other.

Could he read what she felt for him in her eyes? Was it there for anyone to see? She should have been wise enough to hide it. Then, again, it felt too strong an emotion to be easily hidden.

Her heart felt full with either tears or longing, neither of which she should reveal.

She should leave the room, race up the stairs to her suite where she'd close and barricade the door, send word that she was recuperating from a sudden illness and would not see anyone. Only the two of them would know that he was the reason for her hermit-like state and the illness was a fever whenever she was near him.

He lowered his head slowly, giving her time to move

away. She placed her fingertips against his cheek, wishing, paradoxically, that she had the strength to deny him and that she could go on kissing him for the rest of her life.

Kissing him was like coming home, being welcomed in such a way that your heart settled and your soul expanded. She wanted to weep at the sweetness of it, the tenderness of his care for her.

She sighed against his lips, and he tightened his arms around her as if she were a sylph and he was afraid that she would escape him. What woman would ever wish herself away from Connor? Who, granted they had any sense at all, wouldn't rush into his embrace?

If she couldn't have him forever, then let her have him now. Here, on a leather chair in the middle of a winter day with the sunlight pouring in through the windows. The room was warm but not as heated as her thoughts.

He stood, lowering her to her feet. He grabbed her hand and pulled her with him to the fire.

She wanted to tell him that she wasn't as cold as she had been before, or as frightened, but words didn't seem right for this time or place.

He released her hand, pushed the two wing chairs out of the way along with the table sitting between them. The oil lamp sitting there rocked a little and she was afraid it was going to fall and shatter. He grabbed it before it fell, then grinned at her, obviously proud of himself.

He held out his hand to her and, bemused, she followed him down to the richly patterned carpet.

The door was locked. They were alone. When

he reached over and began to slowly unbutton the bodice of her dress, she didn't stop him. All she did was watch his smile, captivated by the determined look in his eyes.

She wanted to explain to him that the traveling outfit was more complicated than her normal house-keeping dress, but instead of saying anything, she merely added her hands to his, the object to divest her of all her clothes, to render her naked in the bright sun of day.

She should have been embarrassed. At the very least she should have been modest. She should have blushed or even winced inwardly at the thought of being so exposed. She did none of those things. Instead, her nature—restrained and proper until this moment—laughed aloud, gave her wordless encouragement for this shocking behavior.

It took her much longer to be undressed than it did him. Removing his clothing was so much easier that it was as if nature realized he should truly not be covered. Instead, the world should look its fill on Connor McCraight, naked.

She knelt before him, not caring that she was naked, too.

"You've taken off your boots again," she said with a smile.

He didn't smile in return. Instead, he reached out his hand and cupped her cheek, his thumb resting on the corner of her mouth.

He finally smiled, a gentle expression that was matched in his eyes. She couldn't help but smile as well, especially as he withdrew her hairpins, one by one.

From the beginning, he'd worshipped her with his words and his admiration. He'd called her beautiful in such a way that she couldn't help but believe that's what he thought. Now, with the sun creating bars of light on the floor, she felt even more cherished.

He didn't speak, and the silence in the room became oddly reverential. Here in the library, in this place of learning and wisdom, she was being educated as well.

There was such a thing as wonderment. She could feel her heart open, expanding to reach out and enfold him. She was almost brought to tears at the gentleness of his fingertip as it trailed along her jaw. He pushed her hair back, his hand trailing down her throat.

"Elsbeth."

Just that. Just her name and no more. He didn't offer her blandishments or compliments. Nor did he ask her if she was sure she wanted this to happen. Couldn't he tell by the speed with which she had removed her clothes?

He was so beautiful, if the word could be used to describe a man. *Magnificent*, perhaps, was a better term. He would have two scars on his right shoulder now. One was a badge of courage. The other a mark of someone's cowardice.

He was the one who should protect himself. He was not a man who shielded himself from danger. Instead, Connor headed directly for it.

Who would care for him on the long voyage back to Texas? Who would ensure that he was safe? If someone truly wished him dead, then the location didn't matter. They could easily waylay him some-where.

How was she going to endure losing him? How was she possibly going to live through the coming days in her new home? Especially after he'd left for Texas?

This moment, then, must suffice for all those coming nights of loneliness. She must measure and record and keep safe these memories to extract at a later time.

She would always recall reaching out and placing her hand on his left shoulder, then allowing her fingers to dance down to his chest where she placed her palm against the soft hair, feeling the steady thump of his heartbeat. She rose up on her knees and placed her arms around his neck.

"I'd like a kiss, please," she said.

"How very proper you sound."

"I was reared to be proper."

He grinned at her. "You're naked."

She grinned back at him. "So are you. That makes us both improper."

"I can't think of anyone else I'd rather be improper with, Elsbeth Carew."

He would, though. In the future he'd marry. He'd find a proper Texan woman to take back to his ranch. Would he ever think of the Scottish lass he introduced to lovemaking?

"What is it, Elsbeth? You look like you're going to cry."

She shook her head, unable to speak. She was not going to ruin the time she had with him by allowing the future to intrude. No, she was going to concentrate on now, these moments, and nothing else.

Pulling back a little, she looked into his handsome face, and the dark brown eyes that were capable of expressing so much emotion. Did he know that about himself?

She kissed him, sweetly, tenderly and then deeper, as if she wished to make him always remember this kiss on a snowy, sunny, winter day in the Highlands, in the home of his ancestors.

She lay on the carpet, extending her hand to him. He accepted her invitation and rose over her, anointing her with kisses and his touch.

The fire popped, the only sound other than her sighs.

She would never forget his hands caressing her breasts or his fingers trailing over her skin. She began to heat from within, not needing the nearby fire to feel warmed. Only Connor.

Her hands explored him as well, from his shoulders, down his arms to his chest and waist. She slid her palms over his buttocks, smiled as they clenched at her touch.

She held him between her palms, cradling his penis, marveling at how it felt. She would have liked to stroke it more, but he shook his head.

"If you continue to do that," he said, "I won't be able to pleasure you."

The words startled her, then summoned a smile.

"I most definitely want you to pleasure me," she said, wondering why she didn't feel uncomfortable saying the words. But this was Connor.

"Then shall I begin?" he said, smiling down at her.

Plunge in, pull out, her retreating, him advancing. This was a war of the sexes. A battle for love. This time, it wasn't uncomfortable in the least.

She threw her legs around his hips and held on. A moment later he startled her by reaching his hands under her bottom, then rearing back on his haunches.

Her eyes widened as she stared at him. His grin was unapologetic and almost satyr-like.

"I want to do a great many things with you, Elsbeth. Do you mind?"

She could only shake her head slowly. How could she possibly mind?

She was sitting on him, her legs extended on either side and her heels on the carpet. It was such a strange and novel position, one she had never before considered. Evidently, Connor had a great deal more experience than she'd imagined.

The thought annoyed her, which was foolish. She had no right to be jealous of his past or even his future. He would have one, just as she would. They just wouldn't have a future together.

Once again, she brought herself back to the moment. She knew she would never forget this afternoon with the two of them locked in the library, him gripping her bottom, gently raising her and then lowering her on him. These sensations were so different, so unique from the first time that her breath caught on a gasp.

"Am I hurting you?"

She shook her head. Words were beyond her.

He kissed her again.

She had never once considered that lovemaking might strip every thought from her. All her worries, all her cares, all her fears flew away. She was merely Elsbeth, whose lover was transporting her to heights she had never once considered.

Her lover.

That's what Connor was, kissing her throat, gently biting at the place where her shoulder and neck met. He held her breasts, heating them with his hands and then his lips, stroking the flames of her passion even higher.

Finally, when she made a sound in the back of her throat, he kissed her, extended his arms around her, his hands pressing against her back to bring her even closer. He raised himself and lowered himself to the carpet once again, so deep inside her she couldn't think of anything but him.

The sound that escaped her lips was a soft keen. Pleasure given voice.

Chapter 32

Elsbeth had, perhaps, spent more time in the library than in any other room at Bealadair. Yet she'd never seen it the way she did today, on her back looking up at the tin ceiling with its engraved squares.

Somewhere, perhaps down deep, so far deep that it was near her toes, she should feel shame. She was, after all, engaging in the most horrendous act. Didn't all mothers warn their daughters about the dangers of giving themselves too easily?

If so, Connor needed to come with a warning label: Here is a Texas man of strong emotions and thoughts. He will overwhelm you with one look and cause you to throw away all the rules you learned about proper behavior without a thought. Be near him at your own peril.

Yes, definitely, Connor should come with his own warning.

That's not to say that she would have been more cautious. She had a feeling that she would've been foolish around him no matter the circumstances.

She'd always considered herself a strong person, someone who was capable, for example, of standing up to the Duchess of Lothian. Granted, she didn't often have the opportunity to combat the duchess directly, but there were dozens and dozens of occasions when she had nodded in agreement at what Rhona had said, turned to leave, and decided to follow her own course.

Her strengths around the duchess, however, were not replicated around the new Duke of Lothian. She had—as had been amply demonstrated—absolutely no resolve around Connor. All he had to do was smile ever so slightly or even crook his little finger, and she was his to do with whatever he desired.

She turned her head slightly when he propped himself up on his elbow and leaned over her. See? All he had to do was look at her in that way, and she would've done anything he wanted.

"I've always thought you beautiful," he said, the words wedging their way into her heart. "But never more so than now."

She was filled with such lassitude that her hand seemed to weigh more than it should when she raised it and placed it on his shoulder. His chest was so magnificent, but so were his arms. Every part of him was muscled and tanned.

"Do you strip naked to work in Texas?" she asked.

"Just my shirt," he said. His right hand reached out and cupped her breast.

No, they couldn't start this again. She had a great many duties to perform. She would leave his hand where it was for the moment, but only a moment.

"You're not tanned anywhere," he said, smiling.

Since she was completely naked, he could certainly tell.

"A lady is supposed to avoid the sunlight," she said.

"Is that the proper thing to do?"

He tilted his head just so, as if he were considering her words.

"Indeed it is," she said.

"Your face isn't all that pale. I've seen you go out without a hat."

"One of my many flaws and failings," she said. "I'd rather not wear one. Perhaps, if I ever visit your Texas, I will become as tanned as you."

"Now that's a thought. We have a great many hills in the southern part of the ranch. There is this one that has a flat top on it. It would be the perfect spot to do what we're doing now."

His thumb was strumming across the top of her nipple. She decided that it would be wiser to remove his hand. Otherwise, she would never be about her duties.

He seemed to know the battle she was waging with herself, because when she removed his hand he just returned it to her breast.

"I really have to get up now," she said, sitting up. Where had her modesty gone? It was hiding somewhere, and in its place a curious sort of pride, especially when Connor was looking at her in that way.

She wanted to freeze the moment and keep it exactly as it was, the better to recall it years from now after he had returned to Texas and she had gone on to live somewhere else.

"What do you have to do that is so important?" he asked, his hand stroking down her spine. He really did have to stop doing that.

"I've decided to offer the position of companion to

one of the maids. That way, I'll have someone living in my house with me. It won't be so lonely. Of course, I have every intention of getting one of Daniel's puppies."

Suddenly, he stood, reaching down with his hand to help her stand.

For a moment, she stayed where she was, her gaze fixed on him, tall, commanding, and naked. What woman wouldn't look her fill?

"I suspect I'm not the only person to tell you that you have to be the most stubborn woman I've ever met."

Surprised, she placed her hand in his and allowed him to help her up.

"Stubborn?"

"There's no reason you should be in such a hurry to move away from Bealadair."

"On the contrary," she said, beginning to reach for her clothing. "It's going to happen eventually. Avoiding it won't make it easier. It's better if you just face a situation, once and for all, as quickly as possible. That way, it's done and over."

How odd that she felt more awkward about getting dressed in front of him than she had remaining naked.

Maybe it had something to do with the fact that he was frowning at her now, and that, by her comment, she had evidently made him angry. Why, though? Did he want her to wait until the very last moment, until the new owners came riding up to the broad wrought iron gates?

Could it be that he was reassessing his earlier decision?

"Are you changing your mind?" she asked. "It would be so much better for everyone if you were. I wouldn't have to worry about the children's school or the crofters and who will look after them. Not to mention a dozen other details."

"I'm not staying here, Elsbeth. I'm not remaining in Scotland. Regardless of what's happened between us, I'm not going to become a Scot."

She stared at him, her dress held up in front of her as if to cloak her—finally—in some modesty.

"You are a Scot, Connor. You may wish to renounce it, but by heritage, you are one. Legally, you are the Duke of Lothian. That's about as Scottish as you can get. It doesn't matter where you were born. Or where you've lived most of your life. You are a Scot. Wanting to be anything else or anywhere else doesn't negate that fact."

She sincerely hoped there was no such thing as ghosts—as Connor maintained—otherwise, the ghost of Gavin McCraight was no doubt standing in the corner with his nose to the wall, praying that she would hurry up and get dressed.

She turned her back on Connor and donned her clothing in record speed. No doubt she looked a little less neat than she normally did, but that couldn't be helped. Her hair was most definitely in need of attention. She was going to escape to her room, set herself to rights, and then be about her duties. Between the journey from Inverness and the accident—if that was the right word to call it—the afternoon was nearly half-gone.

She really did have myriad things to accomplish

before the ball was held. The ball to welcome the laird, the same man who wanted to renounce everything Scottish.

Finally, she turned to face Connor, unsurprised that he had dressed as quickly as she. He had that stubborn look on his face, the same one she'd seen a few times before. He was not going to speak. Words would have to be pried from between his lips. He was going to level that gaze on her until she squirmed and said the first thing that came to mind.

She might have, if she hadn't been annoyed as well. She had not made love to him in order to get him to change his mind about selling Bealadair. How dare he think such a thing.

How odd to have engaged in such delicious lovemaking, only to be so irritated at the man now. She wasn't going to talk if he wasn't going to.

She was still annoyed when she opened the library door and closed it with a great deal of force behind her. She was so intent on her thoughts about Connor that she didn't notice that there were other people in the corridor.

The one person she didn't want to see was standing a few feet away. Startled, she froze in place, her hand going to the base of her throat, her gaze on the duchess where she stood beside a pastoral landscape painting of Bealadair.

"You must be very careful of these frames. They are gilt. They must never be wiped, but only dusted and with the lightest of touches."

Beside her was a young maid, the girl's eyes wide and her lips pursed as if she were afraid to accidentally say something. Elsbeth had seen that expression more than once, especially when the duchess took one of the new girls under her wing and proceeded to give instructions on how to do her duties. As if the Duchess of Lothian had ever wielded a feather duster.

"You've been avoiding me."

Since it was true, Elsbeth didn't have anything to say. Not one witty or clever remark came to mind.

"Where have you been?"

"Inverness," Elsbeth said. "To look for a home."

"So Connor hasn't changed his mind then?"

Elsbeth shook her head.

The duchess turned and said something to the young maid, who glanced at Elsbeth with a look of thanks before disappearing down the corridor.

Once they were alone, Rhona directed her attention back to Elsbeth once more.

"I was wrong to ask you to do what I did. I hope you can forgive me. I've been told that I can be quite autocratic at times, and that was one of those times, I'm afraid."

Elsbeth was taken aback. She'd never considered that the duchess would apologize to her. Or even that the Duchess of Lothian could be made to consider her actions.

"The Welcoming of the Laird will be a success, thanks to you," Rhona added. "You've seen to everything perfectly, as you do, of course."

Elsbeth stared at the duchess, wishing she could ask one of the dozen questions now flying into her head. The only thing she did—the only thing she had the courage to do—was flee.

All the way up the stairs to her rooms she considered the duchess's words. Perfectly? Rhona thought she did things perfectly?

She'd studied hard so that she could give Gavin the correct answers when he queried her. She learned everything there was to learn about Bealadair to make him proud. Had she really tried to be perfect? Perhaps she had. She'd felt that she always had to try harder. She had to know more and do more than anyone else. If for no other reason than to justify being plucked from that hospital bed and brought to Bealadair when she was eight, given a home and a borrowed family.

Had she misjudged the duchess all this time? Had she seen Rhona as a woman steeped in propriety when all she'd tried to do was give her advice and direction like Mrs. Ferguson? Elsbeth had often expressed her thanks to Gavin for his kindness in opening his home to her. Had she once said those words to Rhona?

The feeling she was getting wasn't the least bit comfortable, like trying to wear a bodice that was suddenly too small.

CONNOR WAS CERTAIN he was losing his mind. He was acting like a person he'd never before known, someone who had evidently been hidden beneath the man he'd always thought himself to be.

Even going to war hadn't changed him as much as coming to Scotland.

It was like a giant mystery box labeled Life had been opened and he was finding things that he hadn't expected. First of all, his father being a twin. Secondly, himself.

He wasn't behaving right.

He had just seduced a proper woman on the floor of the library. And then, as if that weren't enough, he'd gotten into an argument with her when it was over.

Loving Elsbeth was like nothing he'd ever done. His body urged completion, but his mind wanted to slow the minutes, elongate them until hours had passed.

The interlude in her bedroom and this afternoon in the library would always come back to him. He would never be able to forget the feel of her, her skin soft against his fingertips. The sweet curve of her buttocks, her small waist and large breasts.

He moved to sit at the desk his uncle had used every day, thumbing through his notebook for pictures of Elsbeth that he'd drawn, seeing details he got right and things he'd gotten wrong. Her nose wasn't that upturned at the end. Her smile was broader, her jawline more sharply defined. And her hair, thick and black and glorious, tumbled over her shoulders when he'd released it.

He sat in the silence, the only sound that of the fire burning itself out. Some of Bealadair's fires were fueled by coal. The one in the library took wood and was large enough for the trunk of a good-sized tree.

How the hell did he return to himself? He needed to get home. He needed to see the back of Scotland as quick as he could.

How the hell was he ever going to forget her?

His father had turned his back on his country and all for a woman. Had he been a wise man for doing so or a foolish one? Connor had always admired his father, but in this instance he wasn't willing to emulate him.

Elsbeth was like no other woman he'd ever met. She was smart and kind, beautiful and funny. She cared deeply for people and was responsible to a fault. He loved her accent and her gorgeous gray eyes that lured him like fog and heated him like smoke.

Around her, he'd acted the idiot. He forgot that he was responsible for over two million acres, hundreds of men and their families—not to mention his own—and thousands of heads of cattle.

Instead, he'd totally and completely lost his mind.

Every time he looked at her, he saw Texas—the freedom and the vitality of it. The newness of it next to an ancient land like Scotland. Elsbeth did what she wanted. She acted independently. She was fierce and brave and stubborn.

He supposed there was something good about history and about people who came before, who knew so much and hopefully passed it down to their descendants. But there was also something good about being raw and new and young and maybe untrained.

His best lessons had come from his worst mistakes. He'd been given the freedom to fail, and he'd caused some spectacular fiascos. He hadn't been tamped down, pressed into some kind of mold, made to wear a certain kind of suit and act in a certain way. He yelled when he was happy. He shouted when he was angry. He was Texas and so was she.

She just didn't know it yet.

An idea had been niggling at him, one that would solve Elsbeth's worries and make his own situation easier. The longer he sat there, the better it sounded. He stood, tucked the notebook back into his vest pocket, and made his way from the room, sending one last glance toward the carpet in front of the fire.

Chapter 33

$\mathcal{N}$othing got better for Elsbeth as the day wore on.

The ballroom floor, unfortunately right in the middle of the dancing area, was scuffed so badly that it could not be polished to a shine. If they had had enough time, Elsbeth would have requested that this part of the flooring be replaced.

When she questioned those responsible for cleaning and waxing the floor, she got a few shamefaced expressions in return. Evidently someone had heard talk about a way to make it easier to polish the wood. The foolish individual had actually set fire to the section, four feet in diameter.

They could have ruined the inlaid floor. Even worse, they could have set Bealadair on fire.

Most people did an excellent job and were conscientious about their tasks, taking pride in the end result. She had discovered that if you berated people about not doing a good enough job that didn't necessarily mean that they tried harder. The way to inspire someone was to point out their successes, not their failures. Therefore, when the five people assigned to buff the ballroom floor received a heated lecture, it was an anomaly, not a common occurrence.

Elsbeth didn't know who felt worse when it was all over, her or the staff.

The duchess had given instructions that the serving tables were to be moved to the other end of the ballroom. She countermanded that order and made a mental note to speak to Rhona. The way the duchess had changed everything would mean that the entire kitchen staff would have to traipse through the length of the ballroom in order to replace food on the serving tables, then make their way back through the dancers and the assembled guests. It wasn't practical, and the Duchess of Lothian would be the first person to complain about the visibility of all the servants on the night of the ball.

When the seamstress appeared at the doorway, it was almost the last straw. However, the woman was only performing her own tasks. The fact that Elsbeth wasn't in the mood for a fitting wasn't her fault.

She left word where she would be and followed the woman down to one of the parlors that had been set aside for her use.

"Only one last fitting, Miss Elsbeth," the seamstress said.

She nodded, reluctantly agreeing. She hadn't needed a new ball gown. She had an entirely suitable one that she'd worn on the occasion of Lara's wedding. Very well, perhaps it wasn't all that suitable, because the wedding had been held in the summer and the gown was filled with yellow roses and quite bare on the top. The garment that she donned before standing on the riser so that the seamstress could measure the hem was entirely different.

Unlike all the dresses for the McCraight women,

this one had no swath of McCraight tartan draped from shoulder to waist. To the best of her knowledge, the Carews did not have a clan tartan. The color of the gown, however, a deep shade reminding her of old plums, was quite lovely.

The seamstress gestured to one of her assistants, who knelt on the floor and began pinning the long skirt. The train, as well as the bustle, would add substantial weight to the gown. She'd never been as comfortable with fashion as the McCraight women. She would much rather be in her plain housekeeper's dress. At least it gave her freedom to move. But she did have to admit that the dress flattered her. She wasn't displeased with her appearance in the pier glass.

Would Connor think her beautiful?

What an idiot she was being. As if his opinion mattered now. He would be leaving for Texas as soon as the ink was dry on the sales documents for Bealadair.

"Would you like me to open a window, Miss Elsbeth? You look flushed."

How did she tell the woman that her flush was the stain of embarrassment? Not only had the duchess caught her leaving the library in disarray, but she'd lost her temper with the staff.

She was most definitely not acting like herself.

"I'm fine, really," she said. "Thank you, though."

She'd been embarrassed before. A man had never been involved, however. If the circumstances were different, she had no doubt that the Duchess of Lothian would banish her for being a poor example for her daughters. But the fact remained that Rhona needed her help, at least until the ball. After that, her tenure at Bealadair might well be from day to day.

Perhaps she should make up her mind about which property she wanted to buy and send word to the solicitor.

It was, unfortunately, time for her to make a change.

Of all the people she would miss, the first was Gavin. She could almost feel his spirit follow her throughout the house, his fond smile weighing her actions, his words of wisdom in the past helping her make fair decisions.

There was Mrs. Ferguson, of course, and Addy and a host of other maids and footmen who had always made the days pass with good humor and cheer. She felt, in a way, as if she were deserting all of them.

She doubted anyone would understand her almost desperate desire to be gone. Now, before she felt any more for Connor than she did. Now, before he went back to Texas. She didn't want to be the one left behind again. First her parents had left her, and then Gavin.

This time, she would be the first to leave.

She turned when directed, stood patiently, and engaged in chatter for a half hour, most of it about the terrible accident that had almost befallen their new duke. Elsbeth didn't inform the seamstress that she was certain that it hadn't been an accident and as soon as she could she was going to investigate the roof to verify her suspicions.

When the seamstress told her she was no longer needed, she gratefully stepped down from the riser.

"We'll have the dress pressed and delivered to

your suite, Miss Elsbeth. You're the last and, if I may say so, the easiest to fit."

She smiled at the older woman. "Thank you."

"I expected Lady Muira to have some alterations. The girl certainly does love her biscuits, doesn't she? But when Lady Lara had to be refitted, that was a surprise."

"I'm glad my measurements didn't change," she said.

She made her way to the kitchen for a restorative cup of tea before going to the roof.

"Has Lara developed an affinity for biscuits?" she asked Addy.

"Biscuits? No, she's not been eating much, poor thing. She's not had an appetite at all for nearly a month now."

Elsbeth nodded. Someone might say that the uncertainty about the future had caused Lara's appetite to dwindle. Others might suggest that it was because she was with child. Three maids had come down with the same symptoms in the past year, all of them becoming mothers.

She sat stirring her tea, thinking about everything that had happened since Connor's arrival.

Someone had shot at him. Not poachers. Someone had tried to cosh him with a statue. Had the statue falling the night he arrived been an early attempt? If so, it had been poorly timed. Perhaps the accident had only given someone an idea, one that had been executed today.

But who had done it?

She didn't believe that she was the object of the attempts. No, someone had tried to harm Connor.

Felix was an obnoxious sort, always attempting to puff himself up in the eyes of his wife's family. No doubt because he owed his living to them. Nearly everything he owned was because of the McCraights.

Was Lara with child? Had learning he was about to be a father made Felix murderous?

The ball to welcome Connor to the clan was to be held tomorrow. Was Felix planning something even more hideous then?

Or was she completely wrong?

She took a sip of her cooling tea and watched Addy bustling about the kitchen, expertly directing maids and footmen like a general going into battle. Addy was the sweetest woman and, next to Mrs. Ferguson, her closest friend at Bealadair. Yet she couldn't tell either woman what she suspected. It wasn't fair to lay such a burden on them when they believed that both incidents were simply accidents.

No, the only person she could go to was the one person she should avoid: Connor.

She nodded in parting to Addy and went back to the library. It was empty. So was Connor's suite, the information brought to her by a breathless maid.

"He's not there, Miss Elsbeth. Would you like me to take him a note?"

"No, Bettany, that's not necessary. I'm sure I'll see him later. Thank you."

She dismissed the maid, grabbed her cloak from the foyer, and mounted the steps to the upper floor and the entrance to the roof.

CONNOR'S CONVERSATION HAD gone just as he'd wanted. He'd ended the meeting with a handshake and a taste of Scottish whiskey. He made a mental note to take a few crates of the stuff back to Texas before going in search for Elsbeth.

It was Nancy who told him where Elsbeth had last been seen. When he asked the girl if she would direct him, she smiled a gap-toothed smile at him, bobbed a curtsy, and nearly raced up the steps. She looked back only once, then stopped and waited for him.

"You've just been injured and here I am forgetting. And that statue, Your Grace! It's like God himself is trying to harm you."

"I doubt I'm that despicable, Nancy," he said, "that God himself wants to erase me."

Her blush deepened even further. "Oh, Your Grace, I didn't mean that. I didn't mean that He wanted you dead, Your Grace. I meant that sometimes God tries to get our attention, don't you think? At least that's what the minister says. It's us who doesn't pay attention. Not God."

He just wanted to go find Elsbeth and apologize, hopefully without a lecture about God and whether God was paying attention at the moment. He sincerely hoped that God hadn't been watching when they were in the library together. The Almighty wouldn't be happy with him.

Nancy bobbed her third curtsy and led him to a narrow door left half-open.

"Here's where I saw her last, Your Grace, but Miss Elsbeth could be in the kitchen by now."

"Where does this go?" he asked, pulling the door all the way open.

"To the roof, Your Grace. There's a terrace there

where we serve summer meals. It's too cold now, of course, but it's quite pleasant in the warmer months."

To the roof. He had an uncomfortable thought, wanted to banish it, but it reappeared. Yes, she was that foolish. Or brave.

"Is it locked?"

"Locked, Your Grace? No. Nobody would want to go up there, not in this weather. The wind is something fierce."

Nobody but Elsbeth.

He thanked Nancy and ascended the steps, wondering if he should go and get his coat first. Hopefully, he could just appear outside and see that Elsbeth was nowhere in sight before leaving.

Unfortunately, it didn't work out that way. He opened the door, peered around the edge and saw her on the far side of the roof, kneeling and examining the platform of a missing statue.

Nancy was right, the wind was something fierce and as cold as a shard of ice to his bones. At least Elsbeth was wearing her cloak.

The only good thing about the roof was that it was flat and he could make his way to her side easily.

Something caught his attention out of the corner of his eye, and he glanced in that direction to find a figure in white standing at the end of the roof. The wind made his eyes water. He blinked a few times and it was gone.

"Connor? What are you doing up here without a coat? Don't you have the sense God gave a gnat, you silly man?"

It had been a long time since he'd been upbraided, but he couldn't say anything in his defense, especially since he was standing on top of Bealadair's roof without his coat and hat.

"Did you see that?" he asked, looking back where he'd seen the figure. From what he could tell, the area was the roof over the oldest part of Bealadair.

"See what?" Her gaze followed his.

"Nothing," he said, his attention back on the pedestal she'd been examining.

"Did you see the White Lady again?"

He debated saying no, then nodded once. "I thought I did."

She looked as if she wanted to say something, but bit back the words.

The White Lady only came to warn the laird. About what? That he was going to get pneumonia if he didn't get off the roof?

He didn't believe in ghosts.

"Can you see any evidence of someone tampering with the statue?" he asked, folding his arms in front of him.

Either Elsbeth could see that he was feeling the cold, or she'd gotten the information she wanted, because she turned and headed for the stairs, leading him to follow her with a deep and profound sense of gratitude.

She stopped midpoint in the dimly lit stairwell and turned to look up at him. The stairwell was too narrow for him to move to her side, but he did stand as close as he was able.

"Someone used a chisel on the pedestal," she said.

"So it didn't fall naturally?"

She shook her head.

"Is there another way off the roof?"

She looked surprised, but nodded. "Over the old wing. It was only used by workmen when Gavin made improvements. It was supposed to have been boarded up."

"If someone used it, he wouldn't be seen, would he?"

"He?" She frowned at him. "You have someone in mind, don't you?"

"Felix," he said.

"Why would he try to harm you? It doesn't make any sense. He can't possibly think that if something happens to you everything would return to what it was like when Gavin was alive."

"Maybe he does. Or maybe he just doesn't want an American to be the Duke of Lothian."

She suddenly looked away, her expression stricken.

"Elsbeth?"

She reached behind her and held out her hand. He took it. When she squeezed his hand, then pulled free, he watched her go, his chill forgotten in his confusion.

Chapter 34

Everything was in readiness for the ball to introduce the Laird of the McCraight Clan.

Elsbeth inspected the ballroom, noting the well-polished floor, with the exception of the four-foot-square area in the middle, the sparkling chandeliers, and the bustling staff. Musicians had come from Inverness to entertain and were tuning their instruments as she approved the preparations. Dozens and dozens of china platters were arranged on the spotless linen-draped tables, all in readiness for cakes, tartlets, sandwiches, slices of beef, mutton, all manner of food and drink—the finest larder in the Highlands ready for the clan.

Those members of the staff who were not working tonight would be attending the ball. It was the annual meeting of the clan and everyone was welcome, even if your name wasn't McCraight.

Elsbeth was sure that the duchess secretly didn't approve, but it was a tradition that Gavin had begun nearly thirty years earlier. Or perhaps she was doing Rhona a disservice. She had a feeling that she'd been harsher on the duchess than Rhona had ever been on her.

Once she was certain everything was in readiness, she descended the stairs to the library, one hand on the banister, the other lifting her heavy skirts. She hadn't worn a ball gown in a while and she was finding it cumbersome.

She entered the library, opening the door slowly. Connor wasn't there. She closed the door softly, moving to Gavin's desk and sitting on the chair he'd used for years.

Despite the celebration to be held in an hour or so, she was close to tears. Tonight marked a turning point in her life, one more definite than even Connor's arrival or his announcement that he was putting Bealadair up for sale.

Her gaze went to the fireplace. Gavin's presence was still being felt. Or perhaps it was Connor's. A fire was laid in the library every day, in readiness for its occupation by the duke.

She looked up, suddenly feeling as if she weren't alone. The sensation wasn't frightening as much as strangely reassuring.

Gavin had always said that he thought she was a little fey. "You're more Scottish than most women I know," he said once. "I'm surprised you don't have the Sight."

Maybe she did. Or maybe it was simply because she wished him here so desperately.

She stood and rounded the desk, moving to the fire, sitting on one of the two chairs there. If Gavin had been there, he would have placed his hand on her shoulder as he'd done many times, in a wordless gesture of encouragement.

He might have spoken then, asked her to tell

him what was bothering her. He'd always seemed to know when something was weighing on her mind.

She spoke to him now, almost as if he'd asked: *What is it, Elsbeth?*

"I miss you. I wish you were here. Especially tonight. They're all going to hate me after tonight, you know. And this time, I won't be able to come and cry on your shoulder."

Silence answered her.

As long as she was confessing to a ghost that didn't exist, she might as well tell him the whole truth.

"I feel too much for him," she said. "For Connor. Isn't that foolish? How can that be? I've only known him a short time."

When had it begun? From the first sight of him striding toward her in the snow? Or had it been when she watched him looking at his father's portrait and feeling his sense of loss and grief? Whenever it was, it had been instantaneous—or at least without much conscious thought at all.

She put her head back on the chair and closed her eyes.

Gavin didn't answer her, but she didn't need him to tell her what she already knew. Nothing could come of her feelings. Nothing more than future heartache.

She opened her eyes, stood, and went to the door. It was time. She was about to do the unthinkable: betray the family that had taken her in.

Perhaps it was a good thing that Gavin wasn't here after all.

IT HAD BEEN drilled into Connor these past days that the ball to introduce the duke and laird to his clan was tradition, one he couldn't avoid. The ball was a function of his dukedom that he couldn't give to Glassey or anyone else. He could almost hear his father and uncle nodding and agreeing that the whole thing was an annoyance, but it was a McCraight annoyance and he'd best set his mind to doing it without complaint.

He strode into the Laird's Hall as the first strains of music floated down from the ballroom. Guests had been arriving for the past hour, but strangely not one member of the family had been on hand to greet them. He'd been told that was part of the tradition. They would all come marching in to the sound of pipers once everyone arrived. He, as the Duke of Lothian and Laird of the McCraight Clan, would lead the procession.

He couldn't imagine a more loathsome duty.

First, however, he was going to settle something.

The family was arranged on the two settees and two chairs just as they had been the night he'd arrived. The sisters were sitting together on one settee. Felix was in the chair at a right angle to it. Sam and his aunt were sitting together, and if he wasn't mistaken, Sam was actually holding the duchess's hand.

That answered a question or two.

The only person who wasn't in the Clan Hall was Elsbeth. Had someone sent her on another errand? Or was she performing another task to ensure that the family was not inconvenienced or otherwise bothered by the annoying minutiae of their lives?

That, too, was going to change.

He was tired of Elsbeth being used as a maid of all work, a term he'd heard Addy use. The women in this room, every single one of them, was a Lady, yet they didn't act particularly ladylike. A true lady— like his mother and sisters—wouldn't always send someone else to do her bidding. Nor would she talk down to others.

He wasn't impressed with the gathering of females in the room, even his aunt.

"You just don't understand her," Sam had said, just this morning. "I don't think many people do. Rhona's not like anyone I've ever met. She doesn't show her true worth to many people, Connor, but I think that's because she's been in a loveless marriage for years. She loved your uncle, but it was clear he didn't think much of her. So what was she to do but harden her heart?"

He'd been a little surprised that the older man had taken on the role of protector. His aunt hadn't struck him as needing a defender. But he had his answer now, didn't he? Sam met his eyes and damned if he didn't recognize that look. Make one derogatory comment about Rhona and Sam would come after him, tooth and nail.

Since he felt the same about Elsbeth, he couldn't fault the man.

He couldn't say the same about his relatives. He suddenly realized, standing there, why he'd felt a discordance from the beginning. He couldn't see Graham here among them. His father hadn't been perfect, but he'd been a good man, a decent man, a man who played fair and who treated others with dignity. The same couldn't be said for the group sitting in the Clan Hall.

Maybe Gavin had been more like Graham. Maybe his presence had added some honor to the people Connor faced now. Elsbeth genuinely mourned his uncle. Not only had she loved Gavin, but he had a feeling that the two of them had been outcasts at Bealadair. Two lonely people who'd banded together and created their own kind of family.

He would continue to be polite to his cousins and his aunt. Not for their sakes, but his father's. And Gavin's. And maybe even Elsbeth's. He'd been raised with manners, behavior that had nothing to do with titles or pretentious expectations.

All except one of them. He couldn't find it in his heart to be polite to someone who wanted him dead.

He took his time walking to the seating area, waiting until Felix stopped talking.

The other man was pontificating again, something about a new gun he'd purchased. Or a servant he'd upbraided. Two of Felix's favorite topics.

The door opened. He glanced over as Elsbeth entered. She illuminated the room simply by being there. She sent him a smile, making him wonder when a simple expression had acquired the power to affect his mood.

"I know it was you who shot at me," he said, his gaze fixed once more on Felix. "And tossed the statue over the side of the roof."

Sam made to stand, but he waved the older man back.

"Are you certain about this, Connor?" Sam asked.

Before he could answer, Elsbeth spoke. "No."

He turned to her. He hadn't expected her opposition, but he could understand it.

"I know how you feel about family," he said, "but Felix doesn't deserve your loyalty." He wanted to spare her the truth, but he couldn't.

She walked slowly toward him, her purple gown trailing behind her on the carpet. Her hair was arranged in a complicated twist pinned high on the back of her head. The style served to accentuate the perfection of her face.

She looked like a princess or what he'd always imagined a princess would look like, beautiful with a look of warmth in her lovely gray eyes. Every time he thought he was used to her beauty, it struck him again like a blow to his chest.

Once she was at his side, she reached out and placed her hand on his arm. If they hadn't been here, in this room, with these people, he would have embraced her. All he could do now was place his hand atop hers.

"He doesn't have my loyalty," she said, flicking a glance toward Felix. "It's just that you have the wrong person."

"I know you don't wish it to be him," he said. "But the proof is there."

"No," Elsbeth said again. "You're almost right." She turned her head slightly until she was looking directly at Lara. "It wasn't Felix, was it, Lara? He taught you to shoot. I remember all those times when I worried about you accidentally hitting one of the cattle in the east pasture." She shifted her gaze to Felix. "You never seemed to care about that, though,

Felix. You never really cared about anyone or anything if it didn't fit your purposes."

Elsbeth's hand gripped his arm tighter as she glanced back at Lara.

"You made sure the statue fell, too, didn't you? I saw the chisel marks."

"Why would I do such a thing?" Lara asked.

"For the same reason you played the White Lady."

Now that was interesting.

His cousin sat back against the sofa, her face arranged in an expression he could only consider as contemptuous. He'd met a few people with the same demeanor, but they'd been from the South, and their attitudes had changed in the face of the total destruction they'd endured.

He had a feeling, however, that Lara would retain her disdain for others regardless of her circumstances.

Some people did. They were brought up to believe that they were better than others and that opinion never changed.

"Are you daft?" Lara said. "I never pretended to be the White Lady."

"You have a white cloak. A new one with rabbit fur on the hood. It would look just like a ghostly figure when seen from a distance."

"I didn't."

Elsbeth took a deep breath. "Are you going to say that you didn't shoot at Connor? Or push the statue over?"

In his own family, if one of his sisters had done something wrong, the other four would have offered various excuses for her behavior, but none of his sisters had ever tried to kill anyone. Still, no one said a word in Lara's defense.

Anise and Muira were looking at Lara with a sort of fascinated repugnance. His aunt was watching Elsbeth, but instead of the look he expected—active dislike—her expression was neutral. That might have had something to do with Sam, who was still holding her hand.

"Why Lara?" he asked. "Why not Felix?"

"Perhaps it's because Lara's going to have a child."

Again, he couldn't help but compare the families. If that announcement had been made among his sisters—and it had been, numerous times— they would have rushed to embrace the soon-to-be mother. He had enough nieces and nephews that they would never run out of ranch hands.

In this case, however, none of the other women said a word. It was Felix's reaction that surprised him the most. Evidently, the man hadn't known that he was about to be a father. He stared at his wife wide-eyed.

"Was it you?" Connor asked his cousin.

To Lara's credit, she didn't look away. Yet she didn't rush to admit what she'd done.

"It was her," Elsbeth said. "Her child, if it's a boy, would become duke if something happened to you."

Connor didn't want to be duke, but he wasn't going to stand by and let someone try to kill him because of the title, either.

He didn't even bother asking if that was enough to make his cousin act as she had. To this group, titles were important. They might be the most important thing about a person. Not who he was or what he wanted from life, but the label circumstance or an accident of birth had slapped on him.

It was the single biggest difference between the two families, and because of it, he didn't think there could ever be any true relationship between them.

He couldn't wait to get home.

"I know you're all for sending her to the calaboose, Connor," Sam said. "I'm asking for a little mercy."

Once again, his eyes met Sam's. He wasn't going to remain in Scotland, but he already knew Sam's plans.

"What's a calaboose?" Elsbeth asked.

"I think you call it a jail," Sam said.

"Good heavens." Rhona looked at Connor, her eyes wide. "You can't send a member of the family to jail."

"One member of the family shouldn't try to kill another one, Aunt."

To his surprise, Rhona didn't answer.

"Well, what stands for the law around here?"

"The magistrate," Elsbeth said. "Shall I send word to him?"

Connor looked at his cousin, then at Sam. He wouldn't have to worry about Lara. He'd be safely back in Texas.

Did Sam really know what he was asking?

He should have expected that his cousin would start crying. Women in the family way were often tearful. Heaven knows his sisters had been. At least Felix moved from his chair to embrace his wife, pulling her into his arms and patting her back, all the while glaring at Connor.

"There won't be any more accidents," Felix said.

He was torn between ignoring the lot of them and calling the magistrate or leaving the problem to Sam. He met the older man's gaze again, considered the matter for a moment, and finally reluctantly nodded.

"I told you that I was set to sell Bealadair," he said, speaking to the whole of the family.

Every eye in the room turned to him.

"I've come to know you all and understand that it would be a major change in your lives to have to move somewhere else. Therefore, I thought long and hard about my decision."

Their smiles were tentative. He'd bet that they all thought he was going to say that he'd changed his mind, but that wasn't what he was going to say.

"I wanted the person who purchased Bealadair to continue on with the advances my uncle made, especially the school and the new farming techniques. I wanted him to be able to promise that he would revere Bealadair's history as it should be. I've received an agreement on those points. The sale of Bealadair will be final as soon as Glassey has reviewed the documents."

"You've done it, then," Elsbeth said, surprise tingeing her voice.

He looked at her. "Yes. I've done it."

"You've sold the estate?" Rhona asked.

He nodded.

"Then what's all this about being concerned about our lives changing, Connor?" she asked.

He nodded to Sam. Let him be the one who told her.

"Because I'm the new owner, darlin'," Sam said. "And I don't want any of you to move."

"You?" The duchess's eyes went wide. Her face was suddenly flushed and she was fanning herself as if it had become as hot as Texas in here. Evidently, she hadn't been aware of how wealthy Sam had been—at least before buying Bealadair.

Connor turned to Elsbeth and said, "Well, since we have to do this Welcoming of the Laird thing, will you accompany me?"

She looked at him, her eyes wide. Slowly, she nodded.

"I like your gown."

"Thank you."

"It's purple," he said.

She smiled. "It's called plum."

"I like your hair, too."

"Thank you."

Her eyes were sparkling and he was tempted to kiss her right there in front of everyone.

"You're a very surprising man, Connor McCraight."

If she was surprised now, just wait until she heard the rest of his plans.

They turned and walked out of the room, leaving the Scottish McCraights behind them.

"Have you ever heard of the Texas two-step?" he asked.

She shook her head.

"Well then, Elsbeth, I'll have to teach it to you."

He grinned at her and she smiled back.

There was only one more thing to do before he could leave for home.

Chapter 35

$\mathcal{E}$lsbeth couldn't bear this. She really couldn't.

For a week Connor had been attentive to her, seeking her out on her errands, talking with her about Texas, of all things. Texas! As if she wanted to be able to envision the place where he'd be living. He couldn't stop waxing eloquent about the place, making her feel even worse as preparations continued for Mr. Kirby to take over Bealadair and Connor to relinquish all ties to the estate.

One day they revisited the castle and she'd come close to weeping, standing on the promontory and watching as the wind whipped the waves of the firth. Soon he would be on that ocean, sailing away from Scotland, from his heritage.

From her.

Just as he was severing all ties to Bealadair, so was she. She had a long talk with Mr. Kirby, leaving him instructions on all the matters that she'd handled over the years.

"Won't you stay?" he asked in a kind voice. Almost as kind as Gavin's, which was the only reason tears peppered her eyes.

They sat in the library, a place she'd avoided assiduously for the past week, but of course she had no option when the new owner of Bealadair requested her presence.

"I think it best that I find new accommodations," she said. She'd finally decided on one of the sweet houses the attorney in Inverness had shown her. Now all she had to do was muster some enthusiasm for living there, for creating a life separate and apart from Bealadair.

At least she would be close enough that Addy could come on one of her days off. Or Muira.

"This is your home, Elsbeth."

She didn't know how to answer that. Yes, it had been a home when Gavin had been alive. He'd made it a home for her. Then Connor had filled that void for a tiny stretch of time.

Perhaps it would have been better if she'd never met Connor. If she'd left Bealadair long before he arrived.

A poem from Robbie Burns came to her then:

> *But to see her was to love her*
> *Love but her, and love for ever.*

If she'd never met Connor, she wouldn't be sitting here now, trying not to weep for the ache in her heart.

"Thank you, Mr. Kirby," she said, composing herself with some difficulty. "It's best if I leave." Before Connor did. She couldn't stand there with the rest of the staff and wave goodbye to him. That would be too much of a burden to bear.

No, she had to be gone and soon. Soon, before her heart broke.

CONNOR COULDN'T STOP smiling. Wasn't there some expression about a fool in love? Well, he was a fool in love. A fool. He was in love.

He'd never been in love before, and he didn't know what was normal or wasn't. Was the world supposed to look kind and filled with possibilities? Was he supposed to hear the birds sing even though they were probably frozen on the branches? He longed for flowers. If he had flowers, he would have taken a few bunches to Elsbeth as a floral devotional or a prelude to his stumbling words.

He had it all planned. He'd asked Addy to prepare a lunch that he could take with them to Castle McCraight. Elsbeth liked it there, despite what had happened the first time. Besides, the old castle was the place he'd first realized that what he felt for Elsbeth was something deeper then he'd expected. Something new, different, and amazing.

He consulted his pocket watch, studied himself in the mirror once more, and decided that he would do.

Should he be so nervous? He was acting unlike himself, but he supposed that was to be expected. He was about to change his life. And hers, if Elsbeth agreed.

He took the grand stairs faster than normal, grinning at the footman at the bottom. He'd had a long talk with Sam about staffing needs, and over time Sam would probably make some changes, but none of the young men who acted as footmen would be dismissed. They might be routed into other jobs or trained for something else, but he'd felt an obligation to the staff to keep everyone on, and Sam had agreed.

He nearly raced to the kitchen. He was going to follow Elsbeth on her rounds, surprise her and talk her into lunch at the castle. Then, he was going to recite the speech he'd prepared.

Elsbeth, I adore you. I love everything about you. Come home with me to Texas. Be my wife. Spend the rest of your life with me. If you will, I'll promise that you'll be the most beloved woman in Texas. Or Scotland. Or the world.

Addy was bent over the stove, retrieving some scones. He startled her by diving in and grabbing one straight from the pan.

She didn't laugh. Nor did she scold him. When she placed the pan on top of the stove and turned to him, he knew immediately that something was wrong.

"Do you have our lunch, Addy?" he asked, pushing back his instant wariness.

She nodded, but then she said, "You'll not be needing it, Your Grace."

He knew. He knew before she said another word. He didn't believe in ghosts, and he sure as hell didn't believe in the Sight, but he must have it after all because he knew.

His stomach developed a cave, a curious open space into which all his emotions flew. The happiness disappeared along with the anticipation about this day. He wasn't angry. Nor was he upset. He didn't feel anything. He was instantly the duke everyone in Scotland had wanted him to be: haughty, almost cold.

He could barely speak; his brain couldn't furnish the words.

He stared at Addy long enough that the woman

closed the door of the oven, brushed off her hands, and led him to the table. He sat on the chair she pulled out, then looked up at her.

"She's gone? Elsbeth's gone?"

She nodded again. "To Inverness, Your Grace. She's moved there, she has."

His brain abruptly began working again. One single word found its way to his lips, but he didn't voice it.

No.

She couldn't have left him. She hadn't said anything.

No.

She couldn't have. She couldn't have left him. Why had she left him?

Did she think he acted like an idiot around every woman? Did she think that he seduced every woman in a nearly public place like the library? Or that he was besotted enough to let everyone else know how he felt?

Everyone other than her, evidently.

Surely she'd figured it out. The McCraight clan certainly had. There had been a great deal of nodding and sighing at the ball a week ago every time he and Elsbeth danced.

Granted, he hadn't come out and told her how he felt. Not yet, but he hadn't wanted to say anything until everything was done and finalized.

No.

No, she couldn't have left.

But she had.

He left the kitchen after mumbling something to Addy, made it halfway up the stairs before he turned and walked back down, getting his coat and hat from the footman at the door.

She couldn't have left him. Those words were in a loop in his brain all the way to the stable. She couldn't have left him.

These past weeks, Elsbeth had been able to affect his emotions with a smile or a frown. Now she was ruining his life without a word.

No.

She couldn't have left him.

He'd never needed anyone before. Not the way he needed her. Not the way he wanted her. He'd imagined her in Texas, in his home, being friends with his mother, his sisters.

He'd thought about her carrying his child, being the mother of his children, standing with him during good times and bad.

She couldn't have left him.

This past week they'd talked about myriad subjects. He'd asked her opinion, had begun to tell her things he'd never divulged to anyone else.

When he wasn't with her, he was with Glassey or Sam, signing endless reams of papers, delegating tasks, arranging for extra wagons and carriages, making arrangements to leave Scotland.

Perhaps he should have explained everything to her. Perhaps he should have laid it out for her, bare and unadorned, but he had wanted everything finished before he did.

She'd left him.

He was just going to have to find her.

All Douglas knew was that she'd taken one of Bealadair's carriages and gone to Inverness. Where, the man didn't know. Nor did Addy. Glassey turned out to be the only person with that information and the man was stubbornly refusing to share it.

"I don't believe that Miss Carew would be pleased if I gave you her whereabouts," the solicitor said.

Connor was close to pummeling the man when Glassey looked at him with pity in his eyes.

"Do I have your word that you'll not upset her in any way? Leaving Bealadair was difficult for her."

"She didn't need to leave," Connor said, each word feeling as if it had the weight of a millstone.

"She gave word for her trunks to be sent to this address," Glassey said, scrawling something on a piece of paper. "It's a solicitor friend who's handled a few matters for us in the past."

Armed with the address, Connor returned to the stables. After speaking with Douglas and getting directions to Inverness, he made the decision to take Samson instead of a carriage.

The stallion acted as if it was a treat to be out and about on the frigid day. What was it about a Highland winter that made it colder than anything he'd ever experienced? He wasn't going to stay here long enough to figure it out.

They reached Inverness in less than an hour, the journey made faster because of the cleared macadam road.

Connor had never been to the city and didn't know his way around, but he discovered that Scots were nearly as friendly as Texans. He got good directions from one man, with a second directing him to a livery in case he wanted to stable Samson for a while.

He declined, seeing one of the Bealadair carriages in front of the solicitor's office. He told the driver that he was going to tie Samson's reins to the back of the vehicle. The man nodded and offered to help, but Connor waved him back to his seat. The rider who couldn't handle his own mount shouldn't be on a horse.

As he started up the steps, Elsbeth opened the door of the office. She saw him and hesitated, the two of them staring at each other.

She was wearing gray, a dress and coat he'd never seen before, an outfit that emphasized the color of her eyes and made her even more beautiful.

Now that he was here, now that he was standing just a few feet away, he didn't know what to say.

He shouldn't have worried. Elsbeth didn't give him a chance to talk.

"Did you buy my house?" she asked, slowly descending the steps. "Why did you buy my house?"

"What?" he asked, taken aback by her attack.

She stopped two steps above him and pointed one gloved finger in his direction.

"Why would you do such a thing? The solicitor said that the house I was going to buy was already purchased by the Duke of Lothian. You're the Duke of Lothian. Why did you buy my house?"

"I bought *a* house," he said. "But I didn't know it was *your* house. Glassey arranged the purchase."

"Why would you want to buy a house? We both know you're leaving Scotland. You and your saddle."

She certainly had a bee in her bonnet about his saddle.

"For Lara and Felix. I don't trust my cousin's acquisitive nature. I think it would be better for everyone if she and Felix lived somewhere other than Bealadair."

"Oh." She adjusted her scarf and wiggled her fingers in her gloves before focusing her attention on him again. "You should have told me," she said.

She was right; he should have told her. He should have done this whole thing differently. He was angry about his own ineptness, but more than a little annoyed at her.

"Why were you all set on buying a house in the first place? Why did you leave Bealadair? Why did you leave without telling me?"

He was getting angry, and that was evidently not a sight the inhabitants of Inverness saw often. More than one person stopped to watch them. He wanted to wave them away, but another thing he knew about the Scots: they were stubborn. If they wanted to remain where they were, nothing would budge them.

"Does it matter who leaves first? You'll not be staying in Scotland. You've made that point abundantly clear."

He'd spent the past week telling her about Texas, gradually getting her used to the idea. Evidently, he'd been too damn subtle. He should have just come out and asked her to marry him days ago.

He'd fought in a war and faced the daunting daily task of managing a two million acre ranch, but he'd never felt as lacking as he did right now, facing Elsbeth.

He took off his hat, stood there with it in his hands, and said, "You won't be needing a house in Scotland, Elsbeth."

"I have no desire to live at Bealadair any longer."

He didn't want her to live at Bealadair, either, but she seemed so determined on the point that he had to ask. "Has the fur been flying between you and the duchess again?"

She shook her head. "I'm not sure I even recognize Rhona anymore. She isn't herself. Or maybe I've always misjudged her." She looked at him with her beautiful gray eyes, almost making him lose track of what she was saying. "I don't think I've ever seen her as happy as she is now. She goes around smiling at everyone. I caught her complimenting Addy this morning. I don't think I've ever seen her in the kitchen before."

He had more important topics to discuss than Rhona and Sam's romance.

"You're right—I'm leaving, but I have a problem, Elsbeth. I don't want to leave Scotland without you."

She didn't say anything. Instead, she just looked at him with no expression at all. Her eyes seemed deeper, somehow. Almost as if tears pooled in them.

"I decided, then, that I'll just have to take you back with me," he said. "That way I get the best of both worlds. I get you and I get Texas."

She still didn't say anything.

"Besides," he said, "I've begun to think of you as a Texan."

She remained silent, her expression one he couldn't read. Didn't she realize what a great compliment he'd just given her?

"I'm not a Texan," she finally said. "I'm a Scot."

She was his Scot.

"Will you come? Back to Texas with me?"

"Do you need a housekeeper?" she asked.

"What?"

He stared up at her, wishing that his proposal wasn't being done on the steps of the solicitor's office.

"Or do you want someone to inspect your cattle?" she asked.

"I beg your pardon?"

"Why would you ask me to come back to Texas with you?"

She really didn't have any idea, did she?

"I love you, you fool woman. I want you to come back to Texas with me as my wife."

Now she was blinking at him as if she'd never seen him before. He glanced to either side of him to find that the crowd was growing.

"You can't say that," she said.

"Of course I can. I love you."

"Well, you can't call me a fool woman in the same breath."

He wasn't doing this at all well. Should he drop to one knee? Perhaps if he just told her the truth it would make a difference.

"You fascinated me from the very moment I met you," he said. "I liked everything about you. And then I found out you knew something about cattle and dogs and that you're the kindest person I know and perhaps the strongest. I know something about strong women."

She took another step downward, approaching him as carefully as if he were a hungry bobcat.

"I like the way you smile and I want to hear you laugh a lot more. I don't want you working as hard as you do, but I understand if it's something you want to do. I like how you take charge and do things before other people refuse to do them. I like how you want to learn new things and the way your mind works. I think you're the most beautiful woman I've ever met, but it's not just your appearance I like. It's your honor and your decency I admire as well."

Her dawning smile was beginning to reassure him.

"Texas is a sight warmer, Elsbeth," he said. "Right now, I'm freezing to death. Can we do more of this proposal in the carriage?"

She didn't say a word, which made him wonder if he'd misjudged her smile. He was ruining this whole thing, and it didn't help that it was being observed by dozens of well-bundled Inverness citizens.

He shook his head, reached out, and grabbed her hand, pulling her with him.

"I'LL STILL BE a duke," Connor said as he helped her into the carriage.

He gave directions to the driver to return to Bealadair, with an added caution to be aware of Samson at the rear of the vehicle.

"Does that matter to you?" he asked as he sat on the seat opposite her. "Our children will be dukes. I mean the firstborn boy will be a duke."

She could only stare at him. The idea of having his child kept her silent.

He loved her?

Well, he could certainly have told her earlier. She would have told him that if he'd given her an opportunity to speak.

"Texas is different, Elsbeth. It's bigger. It's a lot warmer. I have a house but it's not as large as

Bealadair. I haven't lived in it much. It feels too big for one man. But you might like it. If you don't like it, I'll build you another one. If you want a house as big as Bealadair, we could do that, too.

"We have something like the Highland Games twice a year. We hold a barbecue for all the men and their families and have tests of strength and a rodeo. We even have a caber toss that'll remind you of Scotland."

He was babbling and Connor never babbled. He was always decisive, always seemed to know his mind. He was the most collected person she'd ever known.

She leaned over the space between them and covered his hand with hers.

"Connor."

He cleared his throat. "Elsbeth."

"Yes."

"Yes? Yes, you'll come with me?"

She nodded. "I love you, too."

Suddenly, she was airborne, her skirt and petticoat and her unmentionables showing as he lifted her and plopped her down on his lap.

She would have protested somewhat strenuously, had he not looked her in the eyes and said, "Texas is going to love you, Elsbeth Carew, but not as much as me."

He kissed her then, and nothing else mattered.

FOR THE FIRST time in the history of Bealadair—and Castle McCraight—the Duke of Lothian was leaving Scotland. Not for a visit but, one suspected, forever.

With him was his new bride, a woman of unexpected obstinacy, given that she'd refused a massive wedding as appropriate for a McCraight daughter, but opted for a smaller ceremony held on the grounds of Castle McCraight in the middle of a snowstorm. There, overlooking Dornoch Firth and with an audience of the entire staff of Bealadair as well as the inhabitants of Ainell Village—bundled up against the weather—Elsbeth Carew became the Duchess of Lothian.

The duke had announced that it was only the first of two ceremonies. Once they returned to Texas, his mother and five sisters would insist on another wedding, one well attended by friends and ranch hands and an opportunity to have a fiesta. The new duchess had only smiled, but then she did that often.

The duke did not leave Bealadair like he arrived. In addition to losing one passenger—Sam Kirby, the current owner of Bealadair and shortly to be married to Rhona McCraight—he had assembled what had taken on the appearance of a caravan.

Connor McCraight was departing Scotland with trunks filled with McCraight whiskey, a basket containing two Scottish collie puppies—not related in case he wished to breed them in Texas—and a few members of Bealadair's senior staff.

Mrs. Ferguson, who had been promised that the Texas weather would be a great help for her arthritis, was accompanied by her sister, Belle, who was game for an adventure, and living in Texas certainly did qualify. In addition, much to the household's dismay, Addy, the cook, as well as her helper, Betty, were leaving Scotland. Plus, Douglas McCraight, the stablemaster, was all for seeing quarter horses up close. More than one footman and maid had indicated their wish to visit America, so an additional two carriages were filled with staff.

Those standing in a semicircle in front of Bealadair on this frozen winter day might well have seen something else in the duke's convoy had they been paying attention. A vague, whitish cloud adhering to the last carriage, almost like a vapor or the filmy garments of an otherworld creature.

In the annals of McCraight history, those journals painstakingly compiled by the 13th Duke of Lothian and kept in the library at Bealadair, long and detailed sections had been written about the various legends and lore surrounding the family and clan. According to this history, the White Lady took her protective duty very seriously. Her task to warn the McCraight Laird—and subsequent duke—of any danger meant that where he went, the ghost was sure to follow.

Even to Texas if need be.

Author's Notes

XIV Ranch was modeled after the XIT Ranch in Texas, which consisted of three million acres and was a result of a transfer of land to pay for the building of the Texas State Capitol in Austin. The transfer, authorized by the 17th Texas Legislature, was actually performed in 1882. I've used a little literary license to make it earlier by a few decades.

The ranch was located primarily in the Texas Panhandle. I've moved it farther south in *The Texan Duke*. Also, the XIT Ranch averaged handling 150,000 head of cattle within its 1500 miles of fencing, statistics I used in the book.

Bealadair is based on a compilation of Highland castles and great houses.

The information about Texas Longhorns is as true as I can make it, thanks to my research and friends who raise Longhorns. (Being a Texan has its advantages.) Although most Longhorns will never attack, they use their massive horns to move and manipulate objects and to scratch. Anyone who isn't careful around them can get hurt.

My sources tell me that dogs can and are used to control herds of Longhorns—except during calving season. Longhorns are very protective of their calves and will attack dogs. I'm not sure if this is a universal practice, however.

Trapshooting dates back to the eighteenth century in England, where live birds were used as targets. Glass balls became popularized in the 1860s. Clay disks weren't used until the 1880s.

In a very broad sense, a Scotch collie is an old breed name for a spectrum of dogs. A wonderful website to learn more about Scotch collies is: http://www.oldtimefarmshepherd.org.

The first Stetson hat, the "Boss of the Plains" was manufactured in Philadelphia, PA, a few years after the end of the Civil War. I like to think that Sam, in his travels, found the hats and brought them back to Texas just in time for Connor to wear his to Scotland.

The poem by Robert Burns that Elsbeth remembers is called "Ae Fond Kiss."

KAREN RANNEY

In Your Wildest Scottish Dreams

978-0-06-233747-4

Seven years have passed since Glynis MacIain made the foolish mistake of declaring her love to shipbuilder Lennox Cameron, only to have him stare at her dumbfounded. Though Lennox can still unravel her with just one glance, Glynis is no longer the naïve girl Lennox knew and vows to resist him.

Scotsman of My Dreams

978-0-06-233750-4

Once the ton's most notorious rake, Dalton MacIain has returned from his expedition to America wounded and a changed man. But Dalton's newfound peace is disturbed when Minerva Todd insists he help search for her missing brother Neville. Though Dalton is tempted by the bewitching beauty, he has no interest in finding Neville, whom he blames for his injury.

An American in Scotland

978-0-06-233752-8

Desperate and at her wits' end, Rose MacIain crafts a fake identity for herself, one that Duncan MacIain will be unable to resist. But she doesn't realize that posing as the widow of the handsome Scotsman's cousin is more dangerous than she knew. And when a simmering attraction rises up between them, she begins to regret the whole charade.

RAN2 1117

SIZZLING ROMANCE FROM
USA TODAY BESTSELLING AUTHOR
KAREN RANNEY

The Devil of Clan Sinclair

978-0-06-224244-0

Widowed and penniless unless she produces an heir, Virginia Traylor, Countess of Barrett, embarks on a fateful journey that brings her to the doorstep of the only man she's ever loved. Macrath Sinclair, known as The Devil, was once rejected by Virginia. He knows he should turn her away, but she needs him, and now he wants her more than ever.

The Witch of Clan Sinclair

978-0-06-224246-4

Logan Harrison, the Lord Provost of Edinburgh, needs a conventional and diplomatic wife to help further his political ambitions. He most certainly does not need Mairi Sinclair, the fiery, passionate, fiercely beautiful woman who tries to thwart him at every turn. But if she's so wrong for him, why can't the bewitched lord stop kissing her?

The Virgin of Clan Sinclair

978-0-06-224249-5

Beneath Ellice Traylor's innocent exterior beats a passionate heart, and she has been pouring all of her frustrated virginal fantasies into a scandalous manuscript. When a compromising position forces her to wed the Earl of Gadsden, he discovers Ellie's secret book and can't stop thinking about the fantasies the disarming virgin can dream up.

RAN1 1117

At Avon Books, we know your passion for romance—once you finish one of our novels, you find yourself wanting more.

May we tempt you with . . .

- **Excerpts** from our upcoming releases.

- Entertaining **extras**, including authors' personal photo albums and book lists.

- Behind-the-scenes **scoop** on your favorite characters and series.

- **Sweepstakes** for the chance to win free books, romantic getaways, and other fun prizes.

- Writing **tips** from our authors and editors.

- **Blog** with our authors and find out why they love to write romance.

- **Exclusive content** that's not contained within the pages of our novels.

Join us at
www.avonbooks.com

An Imprint of HarperCollins*Publishers*
www.avonromance.com